THE
ROAD
WE
TOOK

THE ROAD WE TOOK

Four Days In Germany 1933

CATHY A. LEWIS

AUTHOR DISCLAIMER

The Road We Took—Four Days in Germany 1933 is a work of fiction based on elements of a true-life story. Many of the incidents and dialogue, and characters, except for some well-known historical figures, are products of the author's imagination and are not to be construed as accurate. Where real-life historical figures appear, the situations, incidents, and dialogues concerning those persons are entirely fictional. They are not intended to depict actual events or to change the entirely fictional nature of the work. Any resemblance to actual persons, living or dead, occurrences, or locales is entirely coincidental in all other respects.

Printed by Ingram Spark
Editorial Team: Ann Creel, Amy L. Berk, Nancy Nichols, Emily Colin
Cover Design: BookCoverExpress.com
Interior Design: BeAPurplePenguin.com
ISBN: 978-1-7370267-0-9

Library of Congress Cataloging -Registration Number- TXu 2-256-640
Lewis, Cathy A.
The Road We Took / Cathy A. Lewis
1. American Boy Scouts-Rochester-New York- 4th
World Jamboree-Godollo-Hungary-August 1933
2. Jews-Baranovichi-Poland-Munich-Germany
3. Hitler-Nazis-Munich-Dachau Concentration Camp-Bremen

www.cathyalewis.com

In loving memory of all the survivors.

We must never forget.

"From the end of the earth will I cry unto thee when my heart is overwhelmed: lead me to the rock *that* is higher than I."
Psalm 61:1-2

For my brother, Jeffrey Raymond Lewis

Acknowledgements

SPECIAL THANKS AND gratitude to beta readers, Nancy Peterson-Hearn, Becky Sohr, Amy L. Berk, Marian Collins, Sharon Fusco, Rich Harris, Ellen Fanning, Rick Horne, Melissa L. Bell, Ashley Judd, and Tania Silverstone Wolochwianski.

My appreciation to Cousin Tania Silverstone Wolochwianski, who first inspired me to write, insisting this story must be told.

Many thanks to all of my family and friends who encouraged me on this journey, especially Tina Pavlis, Melissa L. Bell, Dr. Sharon Piper, Lana Suiter, Lynne Teckman, Bonnie Heim, Amy L. Berk, Dr. Xiao Zhao, Nancy Nichols, Brock M. Bell, Benjamin L. Bell, Richard A. Bell, Jennifer K. Bell, Cathy DeSimone-Piciulo, Dr. Damian Nesser, Tania Silverstone Wolochwianski, Tom Black, and Revi Ferrer.

Sincere appreciation and thanks to Editors Ann Creel, Amy L. Berk, Nancy Nichols, and Emily Colin.

My thanks and gratitude to the team at Books Forward and Books Fluent.

Author's Note

IN 1933, BEFORE World War II and the Holocaust, the world was unaware of Hitler's plans to exterminate millions of innocent people, not only in Germany, but in all of Europe. By virtue of being set in this time period, *The Road We Took* provides an illuminating vantage point from which to view the coming storm.

While many, many, novels have been written about the Holocaust itself, this book is set apart by the fact that my writing is based partially on a true story. During the summer of 1933, my father and his American Boy Scout troop took a six-week trek through Europe on their way to the 4th World Jamboree held in Godollo, Hungary. My father kept a daily journal, documenting the troop's daily activities along with his thoughts and impressions.

At the conclusion of the Jamboree, my father's troop traveled for four days through Germany, while on their way to the port of Bremen to take a ship back to the United States.

My father wrote at length about the sights and sounds of the Nazi movement he witnessed spreading through Germany, while constantly aware of the ubiquitous presence of Nazis and Hitler Youth.

Ten years after his European trek, my father married my mother, a Jewish immigrant raised in South America whose extended family was murdered by Nazis in the small border town of Baranovichi, Poland, now called Belarus.

My father kept his journal and treasured artifacts from his trip in a small leather suitcase. I rediscovered the suitcase after he died in 1995 but failed to fully examine the contents. My life at that time did not allow for a thorough investigation, as I'd just moved south to Nashville, Tennessee to open my restaurant.

In 2018, while undergoing a lengthy recovery from ankle surgery, I had the perfect opportunity to explore my father's journal. As I read, his voice spoke to me through the pages, bringing to mind and to life stories he shared with me during my youth.

After reading the journal, I felt compelled to write about my father's travels. It became my priority to explore the vast history of that time in the world, leading me to complete copious amounts of research on the years between 1925 and 1933 in Germany. For the sake of authenticity, I felt it was important for this novel to portray the social mores and language of the time, even though they are not the terms or attitudes expressed in the present day.

Many of my characters come from my imagination, though they communicate my own personal stories and experiences. I find the element of human suffering to be continuous and timeless.

I write often about faith, because of my personal faith and strong belief. My characters speak of faith because it sustained them through the cruel punishment inflicted upon them. The Nazis stripped the Jews of everything—however, the one thing they couldn't strip away was the faith inside them.

Through my research, I understood that from day one of the ruthless Nazi regime, starting on January 30, 1933, the endgame was always the same—exterminate all Jews, and everyone that didn't fit their Aryan ideals. History has taught us a painful lesson and extended a fervent admonition: how instantaneously hatred can rise up to destroy this fragile world, and the people in it.

Thank you for reading.

Cathy A. Lewis
Nashville, Tennessee, August 2021

CHAPTER ONE

Buster and Wolfie

AUGUST 1933, MUNICH, GERMANY

OUR BUS IS a chartered German vehicle called Büssing, slate gray with tires that appear a size too big. Inside, the bus is stuffed with stiff seats that don't do a thing to cushion our ride. Wolfie Wolferman is pointing and directing the hired bus driver where to stop. Our bus slows down as it rolls over a few bumps, rocking us all back and forth. Wolfie laughs as our bodies slide around on the seats, jolted by the movement of the bus over the knobby road. The bus pulls up in front of a small, simple affair with a rust-colored roof made of tin. The house sits upright and straight on a flat piece of land. The roof looks even, except for the left corner that dips down a few inches. The sight of it gives the appearance of tired wood, doing its best to keep an angled edge.

The yard has lost hope, as the hot Munich sun has deprived it of even the palest shade of green. It's dotted with a few sporadic, stoic flowers that look as if they wish for rain.

There is a gravel driveway shared between two houses, Wolfie's being the first house, and two hundred feet past it, another one conspicuously like the Wolfermans'. I wish my German brother could spend the day and night with us, but he promised his aunt and uncle he would come directly home. His father will be expecting him.

Wolfie is standing at the front of the bus, viewing his new American friends, his eyes taking in the twelve of us Boy Scouts he now considers his brothers. The warmth of his smile, congenial and joyful, conveys the love he feels for his friends.

Wolfie came into our world thanks to the Boy Scouts, at a time when we were already eleven days into our European journey towards our destination, the 4th World Jamboree in Godollo, Hungary. The scent of campfire still lingers on us all, permeating the clothes we wear, our hair and skin. The fragrance is a reminder of our last night at camp, under a brilliant star-filled sky in the Royal Forest.

Our troop of twelve bonded as brothers over many nights of campfires. As the logs incinerated, we forged friendships, sealed with a promise of what we hoped would last a lifetime. But truthfully, Wolfie and I were closer than any of the other boys. We understood each other, and sometimes found ourselves about to say the same thing or ask a question at an identical moment. Wolfie has no brothers or sisters and neither do I, but we have more in common than just the obvious. We both lost our mothers at an early age. We suffer a grief that doesn't depart but lingers in the deep webs of the mind. Only someone who has encountered a similar blow can truly relate to the sharp ache that hollows your bones every time someone asks about 'Mom.' We sense the presence of it within each other without a word being spoken. Eyes hold the image of grief that the soul toils over and carries.

We don't speak of it much, but if we need to, we know we can, and that offers some small comfort. I think of my German friend as my little brother, as I'm a good two months older than him, even though Wolfie towers over me by four inches.

As I glance out the window toward his home, I wonder what the inside of his house is like, curious as to who takes care of him and his father. Does someone come and cook and clean? We have yet to speak about those domestic aspects of life made difficult without a mother.

I'll have to ask him in a letter. We plan to write each other with regularity.

Wolfie is saying the last of his goodbyes. I said mine first to him, a kind of 'see you later' sort, and now I watch the others bid him well. Wolfie told me, "I don't believe in goodbyes anymore. Not since my mother died ten years ago." The way he put it caused me to consider how I view goodbyes. I said my final goodbye to my mother when I was ten. I've taken a few moments at various times to consider his philosophy, like before I fall asleep at night, when the world around me is quiet except for the chirping of crickets and katydids. I often find that I agree with it.

Surrounded by the other Scouts, each one ribbing him or giving a fond farewell hug, Wolfie doesn't notice the long, black automobile parked along the side of his house, partially blocked by a large, old spruce tree. The broad branches and full boughs distract the eye from the vehicle.

But I see it.

I don't give it much thought.

At first.

I wish Wolfie didn't have to leave us. Instead, I'd have him travel back to America with us, as he's part of our family now. Wolfie would fit in simply fine, and there's plenty of room at our house.

Wolfie's English is near perfect, his accent distinct. He could receive his schooling and play soccer. He could join our Scout troop. He knows us all—it would be a perfect fit.

In four days, my troop will leave on a large, seaworthy vessel, sailing for America, home. By the time we arrive in the New York City port, six weeks will have passed since we began our European trek. While I'm overjoyed that our trek brought us Wolfie, leaving him behind makes me feel deeply glum, and melancholy.

I continue with my 'what if' daydreaming while Wolfie raises both of his hands, grinning broadly and commanding all of our attention. The amiable Wolfie stands at six feet, tall for a sixteen-year-old. His skin, like all of ours, is tanned by the sun thanks to the outdoor activities of marching, soccer matches, hiking, and camping. His blond hair is almost white.

Wolfie's baby face belies his body. His frame is thin but strong and fit from years of playing soccer. His father, Frederick, started kicking a ball around the yard with Wolfie when he first learned to walk, and he learned to run by chasing after the black-and-white leather ball.

"This is it, my brothers," Wolfie says. "So long, for now. Please write, and I pray we can be together sometime soon. Don't forget, the Summer Olympics will be here in 1936. So, try out for your national team and maybe we will be paired to play each other!"

Wolfie is an elite soccer player, the best I've ever seen. He's fast as lightning, blessed with agile footwork and skill. He has what talented players would call 'killer instinct with a nose for the net.' He'd never admit he was the best player at the Jamboree, better than even the boys from Spain. But he was, by a long shot.

"My brothers, I almost forgot and absconded with this! Here are the borrowed uniforms, in this bag."

I tell him in a loud voice, speaking over the other boys, "Keep everything as a souvenir and a reminder of our time together at camp."

I call out to my brother Scouts, "All agreed, say Aye."

The twelve of us shout, "Aye!"

After more hugs and back slaps are given, Wolfie thanks Leader Lewis, saluting him, shaking the hands of my father and the two other chaperones. Wolfie takes one last glance, giving a final wave to us all before leaving the bus, running down the four steps.

That's when all hell breaks loose.

Three men dressed in black, each with a bat in their hand, get out of the long, black automobile. The faces of the men appear threatening and ominous. They head straight for Wolfie. He doesn't see them until he turns around, when one of the goons calls out his name.

Before he has time to react, he's met with a gang of clubs, bringing crushing blows with every swing. Leader Lewis sees them, letting out a horrified gasp and a loud, high-pitched, "Oh my God!" The boys on the left side of the bus crowd the right side, kneeling on the seats, watching in horror to see the gruesome sight below.

We watch, as if time is suspended. The sight paralyzes each one of us, our faces and hands pressed against the windows of the bus. I cannot breathe; the oxygen has all but vanished. No one moves, no one goes to help him. My mind feels numb, shocked into stasis by the violence my innocent eyes take in. The men who descend on Wolfie like vultures after prey lift their bats high for blow after blow, bringing the bat down with a force so powerful, I can see blood squirting out from Wolfie's body. He is utterly defenseless against the attack.

I'm frozen in place, paralyzed, wanting to move, but my body not responding to the impulse and directive, my knees somehow stuck to the bus seat as if glued.

This moment is like in a dream where you want to run, but your legs are leaden, and they weigh a thousand pounds.

I hear Wolfie's screams and his pleas, "Stop, stop!" His body, not able to withstand the blows, drops to the ground. The men are still beating him with bats. One blood-spattered man turns and walks to the bus door, shouting at the driver in German, "You better leave now, or you can expect the same treatment!" Our troop leader translates the message.

The driver does not need to be told twice. He takes off with the bus engine roaring as he gives it the gas, flooring the pedal, throwing us all back in our seats, the force of it like a slap across the face, waking us from our trance-like state. The bus barely travels a few hundred yards when our troop leader, Jim Lewis, bolts from his seat. He's standing next to the driver, yelling at him, "Pull over!"

As commanded, the driver pulls the bus over to the side of the road, stopping the forward motion, the brakes grabbing the tires. The inertia jolts my body, as the engine idles while the driver shifts the bus to park. The driver seems nervous. He keeps glancing back to see if the black car follows after the bus.

Leader Lewis's face is crimson. He's spitting out words, yelling, "What the hell just happened back there? Who were those men?"

The driver shakes his head, his eyes now glued to the road before him, afraid and fear-filled, too scared to speak the truth. He must know the answer; otherwise, why would he seem so afraid? But Leader Lewis won't let him off the hook, waiting for the driver to give an excuse or explain what happened to Wolfie.

I find strength to move, and I do, to the front of the bus, taking the empty seat vacated by Lewis. I don't want to miss a single word. I'm so close to the driver I can see beads of sweat trickle down from the side of his temples.

I feel like I want to cry, my emotions are ready to burst, but I stop myself. What happened, what happened to my friend? Who were those goons?

Lewis continues his interrogation, "I know you understand and speak English, so don't play dumb with me. Who were those men?"

The driver takes a deep breath, exhales, and slowly turns to view Lewis, without making eye contact. He says one word. "Gestapo."

Returning his focus to the road ahead, the driver moves his foot to give the engine gas. He shifts the stick to drive and pulls the bus back onto the road.

We all jiggle in our seats as the bus shakes, going over the curb. We sit numbed by the violence we witnessed, a beating so brutal, I've never seen anything like it before. The thought wounds my tender conscience.

Troop Leader Lewis, not satisfied with the one-word answer, steadies himself as he continues to question the driver, speaking in his ear. I can't hear what he is saying over the roar of the bus engine. The driver is still flooring the pedal.

A minute passes, it could have been ten. Then Lewis nods at me as if to say, "Move over," and he takes his seat. After a moment, he moves back three seats, next to my dad and the two chaperones. I sit alone, in isolation, and feel a fiery fury building within every inch of my body, like I'm going to pop, or explode.

I wonder, *what is the Gestapo?* I've never heard the word before. A thought dawns on me, and I realize that the driver, while aware of what the Gestapo is, did nothing to warn us or tell us how we could help our brother. Did he know in advance? How could he?

Would it have made a difference if he did? It's possible he never saw the car or the men until it was too late. He appears just as shocked as we are.

I've read when terrible things happen, the first thing humans do is seek someone to blame. I want to blame this driver for not warning us. I want to punch a wall. I don't know what to do with these feelings. How can a person survive such a beating? Did they kill Wolfie, is he dead? I try to make eye contact with my dad—he can tell me what to do, how I should feel. I'm confused by all this emotion. But my dad doesn't see me straining to get his attention.

Father and Leader Lewis confer, their heads close, speaking privately. Then our leader rises, straddling the center aisle, holding onto the back of a seat for balance, and he addresses us:

"Boys, we are all shocked by what we saw. What we witnessed is something brutal and reprehensible, and it's not okay with any of us. We will seek information about who this 'Gestapo' is and see what we can find out about Wolfie after we check in to the hotel."

We all nod in agreement. I wonder—is that it? Can't we go back to the scene of the crime? Did they beat him and just leave him there? Did they take him somewhere else?

I walk back three rows to my father and ask him, "Why can't we turn around and go back? What if he's just lying there in a pool of blood with no one to help him?"

My dad tells me, "According to the bus driver who knows about this Gestapo, we cannot get involved. Wolfie is a German citizen and we cannot interfere."

I search my father's face, which is as blank as his poker face. "Are you kidding me? Since when do we not go and rescue one of our own? That is a horrible answer and I'm not buying it." Bitterly I ask, "Are we all cowards?"

We walk back to the front of the bus. I sit, he slides in next to me, and with his arm around my shoulder, he tells me, "Listen, we are all upset and worried about Wolfie. But we do not know the reason this happened. Things have taken place that we don't know or understand. We are guests in this country, and we cannot involve ourselves in how the government and authorities treat their citizens. This man Hitler sets the rule of law. It's obviously different from how we do things in the U.S., but there is only so much we can do. I promise we'll check into this and do our best to find out where Wolfie is and the state of his condition."

I can't help but notice my dad seems fidgety, nervous. I ask him, "Wouldn't it seem the best place to check first would be a local hospital, that is, if he's still alive?"

"Son, we will do our best."

I feel no more consoled than when I first approached my father for answers.

As I search the faces of my Scouting brothers, everyone appears pale despite their tans. All have a similar blank stare, and I can almost hear everyone breathing.

But in my mind and heart, there is a deafening roar of anger and confusion. I sit, steaming, trying to make sense of what happened. But I can't. All I see is Wolfie, blood squirting, his screams echoing inside my head, and the bats hitting him.

The driver waves his hand to get Leader Lewis's attention to come forward. He does, and I hear the driver tell him in English, and in no uncertain terms, "Leave Germany and don't try and find the boy. You do not want to get involved or have any trouble with the Gestapo."

We cannot follow that order. We will not follow that order.

The driver points to the roadblocks closing off the road from all but two directions, north and south. I hear the driver say something to Leader Lewis about a small parade today at 1:00 p.m. and because of it, he will deliver us to a back entrance of the hotel. The driver tells Leader Lewis that he must leave quickly to return the bus back to the depot.

Silently we grab our duffel bags, march out of the bus single file, and follow our leader into the hotel, down a long hallway to the lobby. Anyone observing us would think we were part of a funeral procession. Just an hour ago, we were experiencing the afterglow of two wonderful weeks of camping, laughing, teasing each other, having simple fun. It strikes me how life can turn in a split second from wonderful to woeful.

Our accommodations are in the Hotel Bayerischer Hofname. It is a historic property in the center of Munich. As the story goes, King Ludwig I of Germany expressed his desire for a first-class hotel to a friend, Joseph Anton von Maffei, who commissioned his favorite architect to design it. From the back view, it resembles a huge castle. I wonder if Wolfie is familiar with this hotel. *Wolfie. What's happened to my friend?* I can't stop thinking about him. I hear his pleas in my head.

We Scouts drop our bags on the floor and stand around the lobby while the adults go about the business of being adults. They take care of checking us in and getting our room keys. My fellow Scouts wear a similar expression, like each one of us is carrying an unseen wound.

The fear feels like a sucker punch in the gut, and the ache does not subside. Even more harrowing to consider is what happened to Wolfie after we left. Did they go on beating him? Did someone view the event and come to stop it? Did they kill him? What could he have done to call for a beating like that? Did he kill someone, and this is retribution?

There are no answers.

I flood my brain with guilt. Why didn't I do anything to help him? Why didn't any of us go to his aid and rescue him?

Leader Lewis gathers us around him and, after handing out room assignments, he instructs us: "We will go about our business like normal, go to our rooms, drop our bags, wash up, and reconvene at eleven fifteen for lunch in the dining room."

Nothing feels normal.

Silently, my fellow Scouts and I walk down a hallway in search of our rooms, four boys to each. Once inside the confines of our quarters, I unpack and take out a clean Scout uniform shirt.

A recollection floods my mind.

Just two days ago, with Wolfie by my side, we washed a few uniform shirts, hanging them on a makeshift clothesline, leaving them to dry in the hot Hungarian sunshine.

I picture Wolfie and his shirts, the ones given to him by Ollie and me. The memory causes my chest to tighten. I smile at the image of Wolfie, always wanting to make his friends smile and laugh.

He charmed a troop of nervous-looking Scouts from India. He did handstands, then walked up to each Scout, shaking their hands as he introduced himself and then me. Then he took out his yoyo and showed the boys how to do cat's-cradle and walk-the-dog. The boys relaxed, and after a few minutes we were all laughing at Wolfie's antics.

I miss my friend. I hope he's still alive.

I search the faces of my roommates, Bobby, Jack, and Ollie, as they sit in the middle of the beds with hands folded. Their expressions are as pained as mine. I speak first.

"Okay boys, now what? Any ideas or suggestions?"

Silence.

Bobby says, "Buster, your ears are red."

I have no doubt that steam is about to pour out of them any minute.

I add, "I feel helpless."

It's agreed upon, we all feel helpless.

Bobby tries his best to be optimistic. "Don't give up hope yet. Perhaps there is an explanation."

"Bobby, I don't know how anyone could explain a beating like that. Who knows how badly he's hurt?"

I know Bobby feels bad too.

We all feel lost.

We don't know what to do other than follow the orders of our troop leader.

Bobby, Ollie, Jack, and I gather at the entrance of the hotel dining room, nodding to the other Scouts as they enter, everyone standing around with their hands jammed in the pockets of their uniform shorts. No one is talking, which is unusual for a bunch of loquacious Boy Scouts.

While waiting for our chaperones and leader, I see my father coming down the hallway next to the lobby. I walk to meet him. I want to know the plan and how I can help.

Dad says in a whisper, "Listen, son, I'm working on a plan, keep the faith. I'm going to make a few phone calls and will fill you in once my plan is in place. We must be careful to not speak about it now. After what happened with Wolfie, I don't trust anyone in this damn country. Don't break with the boys, stay in a group, keep your eyes and ears open, and be careful. And keep your chin up."

"Dad, are we going to find Wolfie?"

"I can't answer that right now."

"Do you really have a plan?"

While he nods, he will not reveal any other details, but I want answers now.

No one feels much like eating. I push the veal schnitzel and noodles around my plate, smashing the accompanying green peas, using my fork to stab them, taking vengeance on them. I hate green peas.

But not as much as the Gestapo.

No one talks much, as everyone is preoccupied with their own thoughts.

After lunch, Leader Lewis gathers me and my troop.

"Boys, keep your wits about you and remember, we are Boy Scouts. Be prepared, be ready to offer help to anyone in need. Let's stick together."

As a group, we leave the hotel through the front doors, out into the blinding sunshine. I wish the sun wouldn't be so darn happy, shining so bright like all is well in the world.

After today, our trip itinerary has our troop staying less than forty-eight hours in Munich, then traveling by bus to the port city of Bremen where we will spend a day and night, and then boarding our ship to take us back to America, to the port of New York City.

There isn't much time to find Wolfie. Where is he? Is he even alive?

All I can do is hope and pray.

CHAPTER TWO

Nazis

AUGUST 1933

OUR ROUTE FROM Godollo, Hungary through Austria to Munich, Germany was perfect—or so we thought, because we could bring Wolfie right back home from the World Jamboree.

The one persistent thought that runs through my mind is, *What happened to Wolfie?* He should be home by now. I pray he's not lying in a pool of blood, dead. My mind is full of images of Wolfie—his bloodied face, his body, beaten and torn, his clothing, soaked with deep red blood. My heart feels heavy, like it did when my mom died seven years ago.

I do everything I can in my mind to vanquish that pain from my thoughts before it takes over, but I can't. It comes like a slow moving shadow that starts blocking out the light as it creeps closer and closer to me. I'm immersed in darkness, with no beacon of light peeking through to lead me away.

But I can't ignore what's taking place around me, distracting me from my thoughts of Wolfie like a mosquito buzzing in my ear.

Before us is the Konigsplatz, the Square in Munich, which is now overflowing with people, young, old, large, small, and everything in between. The sun is beating down; the temperature must be high. I see sweat forming on the brows of my brother Scouts around me and feel the sweat runs from my forehead and trickles to the middle of my back. As it does, a sick feeling in my stomach makes itself known to the rest of my body. I swallow, but it's difficult. There is no presence of saliva to help dispel my dry throat and nausea.

I'd never heard the term 'swastika,' 'Nazi,' or the name 'Hitler' until yesterday. I don't know much about Hitler, only what my troop leader told me after I asked him about all these new terms. I try and remember the words he spoke. "Hitler rose to power in January of this year and is now leading a new party in government, the National Socialist Party, called Nazi for short."

I state the obvious to Bobby, who is standing next to me. "So, this is the 'small parade' the driver referred to. What a bald-faced lie."

Bobby nods, agreeing with me. "I'm beginning to form opinions about Germans even before I've spent two hours in this blasted country."

As our eyes take in the sight before us, Bobby continues, "I'll tell you what, there are a lot of people here. My guess is there are ten thousand people in attendance."

Trying his best to distract me from my worries, he points. "Turn your gaze over there, and you'll see pretty girls dressed in charming attire. Have you ever seen so many blonde-headed girls in all your life?"

I nod weakly. I can't stop thinking about Wolfie—even pretty girls can't muddle my thoughts.

Then I notice something you might see at a college football game—and I bring it to Bobby's attention. "From what I can see, most of the people here are wearing a Nazi armband or waving a small Nazi flag that's attached to a stick. And look over there, almost every sizeable building has a Nazi banner or flag."

Bobby strains to see the buildings. I continue pointing until he nods his head in confirmation.

The flags wave, moved by the most subtle of breezes. I wish the breeze that moves the flags would come down from the higher atmospheres and cool us. It's blazing hot, and all these people are sucking up every last ounce of air, making it worse. The buildings all have the giant flags which I pointed out to Bobby. I count ten giant flags, and those are only the ones I can see.

"Don't you find it odd how a country or city that doesn't have enough money to help their people has money for these huge flags, which are everywhere? And money for uniforms, trucks, tanks, and parades? Wolfie says the new chancellor and government are rotten to the core."

Bobby nods and, as if reading my mind, asks, "Shouldn't we go back to Wolfie's house? Shouldn't we at least follow up there? Could a neighbor be a witness to something they saw? Leader Lewis acts odd, don't you think? He seems like he's worried, but he's not doing one thing to try and find out what's happened to Wolfie. I can't figure it out. Does it seem odd to you?"

"Yes, my sentiments exactly, chum. As soon as the bus driver told him not to search for Wolfie, Lewis accepted that and moved on, like, 'Oh, well. It's not part of our schedule.' Like Wolfie didn't matter to him in the least. Odd is right."

Bobby sizes me up, and, knowing me well, says, "I wouldn't get any bright ideas, like taking off. Not everyone here speaks English. The idea of us losing our way doesn't thrill me. Who would help us find our way back?"

Giving my friend a sidelong glance, I say, "I guess you're right."

The noise around us is loud, and I try to tune it out with no success. I try and think of a popular song to hum in my head, but the encompassing noise wins that battle. It's so stinking loud, and now there is a band playing. People start waving the small flags, raising their arms with a straightened hand, which I assume is a salute. Everyone around me seems to know the song the band is playing; it must be a German national song.

Bobby reminds me, "In Austria, there were many swastika flags as well, fastened to a number of buildings. People go batty over this symbol. I wonder why people are so wildly enthusiastic about the swastika flag. We love our stars and stripes and celebrate it, but this is something else, don't you think?"

I tell Bobby, "My father said something about a book Hitler wrote a few years back, which outlines the fundamentals of what he believes to be true. Father tells me socialism is only one step away from communism and is the enemy of capitalism. With socialism, the government controls everything, including the people they govern. He calls this Hitler character a fascist loony."

Bobby shakes his head, agreeing, "I can't say that I understand much about him, but one thing is for sure, the people surrounding us with their noise and exuberance appear to be in love with this Nazi thing."

Another word I never heard until recently: Hitlerjugend. Hitler demands that every German boy is supposed to join the Hitler Youth group, withdrawing from all other organizations, like church groups, sporting clubs, even Boy Scouts. A boy in Germany and Austria can only belong to Hitlerjugend. Nothing else exists.

Wolfie doesn't like that. He said, "We're not sheep."

I don't think Wolfie has joined the German Hitler Youth group. He's been in Vienna with his aunt and uncle since the end of the school year.

That's where we all first met Wilhelm "Wolfie" Wolferman, a little over three weeks ago. Our troop traveled through

Vienna on the way to the Jamboree in Hungary, stopping for a day and night there. We were on our way to a hike along the Danube River when he approached us, asking us who we were and where we were going.

After some persistent begging, Scout Leader Lewis said he'd allow Wolfie to join our group, "seeing he is a Boy Scout already." Chances are he knew we'd pester him without ceasing and thought it wise to just give in rather than have the twelve of us buzzing around his ears like gnats. Our troop leader has little patience for such things.

So, the lot of us, bus and all, went to his aunt and uncle's house, who readily gave permission for Wolfie to attend the Jamboree with us. My dad supplied the extra cash for Wolfie to attend and pitched in a few uniform shirts. Ollie, the tallest one of us, provided shorts, and in true Boy Scout fashion, everyone contributed something to outfit Wolfie to the nines. Wolfie, not shy about his looks, thought he made the American Scout uniform look even better. He's such a ham, he struck a pose and makes us all laugh. What a character.

At the time, Wolfie wasn't in Germany, so it seemed like an excellent idea for him to come with us, with no repercussions. His heart was set on attending. The way he viewed it, our meeting was more than serendipity.

Suddenly, a loud, booming noise, like a cannon fired, snaps me out of my thoughts, and I'm back among the crowd of sheep. The sun is beating down and I'm parched. I gaze at the expressions of the people around me in the Square, their eyes full of anticipation. Beaming smiles cover the faces of each person. Small children sit aloft a parent's or friend's shoulders, clutching a small swastika flag, a similar expression of excitement on their cherubic faces. I hear some chatter and recognize a few of the German words. Hitler must be close to making his entrance.

Bobby and I stand a few feet away from the rest of the boys. We are within the gaze of Troop Leader Lewis.

I nudge Bobby. "Hey Bobby, remember the movie we saw at the Saturday picture show, *The Testament of Dr. Mabuse?* The people here seem as if they are under a spell, like in a trance, one in which they surrender all power. Remember how Dr. Mabuse hypnotizes people in the asylum to commit crimes for him? The people here in Munich have a similar appearance to Mabuse's victims."

Bobby laughs at my comparison, agreeing with me. "You can say that again, a trance is right!"

I wonder what this man Hitler has done or what he has said to cause this kind of reaction in the people of Germany.

While contemplating that thought, we hear another loud noise, like stomping, but in unison. The sound is very clear and precise, like marching, shoes striking the surface of the road, sounding like a thunderclap before lightning. And then I see them, coming from the left, down the street that leads to the center of town. It must be the boots they wear and the way they walk that makes the unique sound.

Bobby and I strain to peer over the people in front of us, so as to view their uniforms. We move to the left, passing a few people to get closer. I squeeze by a couple of older women who seem intent on not allowing me to get closer than I already am. Someone makes an attempt to hit at my hat and slaps my head, causing my ear to sting, but I remember my manners. I'm a Scout and a gentleman, so I smile at them and remove my tall hat, which must have blocked their view. They didn't have to hit me.

What we couldn't see before, we see now: the marching men are not men, but boys, my age and maybe younger, clothed in matching uniforms with swastika armbands. They seem soldier-like, in perfect formation, as if they're marching off to war.

We've positioned ourselves in the front row and can see them up close.

The boys are mostly blond with funny haircuts, shaved on the sides, longer on top, and combed straight back or to the side and slicked into place with some type of hair tonic. Bobby and I exchange glances, and he comments, "That seems strange. Not one boy is smiling."

I agree with Bobby. It does seem strange.

If you ever see Boy Scouts marching, there are smiles plastered on every face. The joy is palpable and contagious. We have so much fun when we march and if you're lucky enough, you get to carry the colors, our flags. These boys seem like regimented soldiers, stern and serious.

After seeing such a display of perfection, however, Bobby and I agree that our troops could undoubtedly improve our marching form and technique.

Upon further examination, we notice something strange about the way they step, which I realize is the source of the striking, thundering sound. It's a marching step they do, where they each swing a leg straight out and off the ground while keeping their other leg rigid with knees locked in place.

The step they make allows their boots to strike the surface of the ground with force, as hundreds and hundreds of boot heels hit the ground in syncopation. It is something to hear and behold, and I admit to being slightly fascinated by the display. I tell Bobby to try and count the many rows of boys, but it's impossible. I feel dizzy attempting to count the rows, which move so quickly, and I cannot keep up.

I give up completely and resort to saying the obvious: "There are hundreds of boys marching."

For as long as I live, I will never forget the sound of their boots striking the pavement.

I break my gaze, searching for my brother Scouts and Troop Leader Lewis. I see them, gathered together about ten or twelve people away from us.

Troop Leader Lewis sees me and Bobby, and he beckons, waving his hand for us to come closer to the rest of our group. We stick out like a sore thumb in our Boy Scouts of America uniforms with our United States flag patches on our left sleeves near the shoulder. We're all wearing our felt 'Lemon Squeezer' Scout hats, so we're easy to spot. We make our way through the crowd once again, this time with more difficulty. Undoubtedly, Hitler must be coming down the parade route and the crush of the crowd is intense. No one is paying any attention to us as we work our way through the crowd like fish swimming upstream against the current.

We're causing a disturbance for them—a distraction from the focus on the parade and what's coming next. A few of the people grow irritated and give Bobby and me a push to help accelerate our movements. These Germans are not observant of manners as applied to strangers. Some even curse at us for impeding their view.

Once we've rejoined the troop, Lewis leads us out of the throng of people, which is not an easy feat. It takes fifteen minutes to reassemble in front of the Hotel Bayerischer. Inside the lobby, Lewis motions us to come closer to him, as if to speak as privately as possible. He raises his arms, signaling to us to huddle.

We oblige and do that, locking arms around each other's shoulders. Lewis crouches down in the middle of our huddle, speaking in a whisper. I strain to hear above the roar of the crowd, just outside the double doors of the hotel.

"Boys, I had no idea that we'd end up in the middle of a Nazi rally. I'm confounded as to why our driver did not mention it. Small parade, my back! If there is no news about our friend, then we will have to pray and hope for the best. There is nothing we can do. He's a German citizen, and we cannot interfere with the authorities here. Our plans to explore Munich were shot down for obvious reasons." He continues, "I suggest we stay close to base here."

With his eyes fixed on me, he adds, "There will be no wandering off by any of you, that's an order. If we choose, we can go back and watch the rally as a group, or we can stay put, but whatever the decision, it must be unanimous. So, what will it be?"

My mind wanders, and I barely hear the rest of the words Leader Lewis speaks.

I want to go back to Wolfie's house. Wolfie said his father was working, I wonder when he's done with work and what time he gets home. *What have they done with Wolfie, where have they taken my friend?*

I must find him before we leave Munich.

CHAPTER THREE

Maddie

AUGUST 1933

MADDIE HAS SPENT the last day hiding in the shadows of Munich. With all the commotion from the Nazi rally and parade, she's relaxed for a rare moment, finding shelter inside the Hotel Bayerischer Hofname. She's outmaneuvered her pursuers once again.

Casually walking across the lobby, she waves at the man at the front desk, who is busy with a phone call. Pretending she is a guest, Maddie saunters down the hallway to the left. Further down the hall, she spies four boys in uniforms exiting their room and walking toward her. Maddie smiles and nods, not making eye contact, walking past them. The four boys notice her; how could they not? She is a beautiful and petite young lady with dark hair and alabaster skin. They smile at her, but she doesn't pay them a bit of attention. She has more critical issues at hand to contend with.

Taking a deep breath, she tries to calm herself, but to no avail. Maddie is food- and sleep-deprived. She takes note of the room number where the boys are: 125. Walking past the room to the end of the corridor, she sees there's a door to the outside of the building. But when she tries the handle, it's locked. Waiting at the door for a moment, she contemplates her next move while trying to decide if she should take a risk. Reasoning with herself, she wonders if they could be going to dinner. Not having a quick exit route if she needs one concerns her. *I'll have to go through the lobby again to escape.*

She walks back to the door the boys emerged from and, glancing both ways cautiously, she listens to hear if there is anyone still in the room.

Maddie stands before room 125 and tries the doorknob.

Unlocked.

If you're going to do this, now is the time, go!

She darts inside the room, closing the door silently. The shades are partially drawn, the room semi-dark and cool. *What a relief.*

A quick survey of the room confirms the telltale signs of the young male occupants: shoes lying around, clothing on the floor, some clothes hanging out of a halfway-opened duffel bag, two double beds, not unmade but rumpled. Maddie bends down to look under the bed, the one closest to the door.

Good, there's enough space for me to fit under here. If I can just sleep for a little while and regain some strength, I can figure out my next step, where to go, what to do. God, help me.

Maddie kneels on the floor and slides her body under the bed, adjusting her skirt, which creeps up to her thin thighs while she moves to the center. She exhales a long breath. She is lying face down; she turns her head to the side, using her arm for a pillow. *There. Finally. Now I can sleep.*

But she can't sleep.

Her mind begins to spin, like a top on a flat surface, creating a disturbance in her head. The turmoil floods the silence of the room with noise, visions, and scenes of where the trouble started, after attending a concert with her violin instructor, Professor Stanislaw Birnbaum, two nights ago at the Munich Philharmoniker. Her dear friend and former teacher Elenena

Laurent had bought her a silk skirt with a beautiful blouse to wear for her first attendance at the symphony. Elenena tells Maddie that she's taking an adventure, and the symphony experience is the 'maiden voyage.'

With painstaking precision, Maddie recalls every moment of the night, not missing one detail. She remembers the smell of sweet jasmine in the air while walking with her professor from his apartment to the event. He offered words of encouragement and advice.

"Maddie, tonight I want you to put your playing and performance mindset on hold. Tonight is a night for pure enjoyment. You will listen to the music with three things—your ears, your mind, and your soul. Let the music reach down and fill you. As musicians, we must learn how to listen when others play. I know you understand that music has healing powers; it can soothe you in ways nothing else can. It can touch brokenness and repair those places. You have experienced this yourself. Tonight, you must listen without distraction."

And of course, her professor was right. She felt the music touch her soul, experiencing the curative restoration as the notes seeped into her broken and wounded places.

Maddie remembers gazing at the bell tower fixed atop the highest church steeple in Munich. It chimes a full note at every hour, a full note at half past the hour, and a short half-note at the quarter-hour. The bell chimed at seven forty-five, alerting the crowds of people walking towards the symphony hall that the eight o'clock hour was approaching. The setting sun, with its pink and purple hues, blanketed the sky.

The sunset offered Maddie a hopeful sign. She has a habit of watching sunsets, hoping to find messages as if her unknown parents or family, if there are any, can speak to her through them.

She anticipated the performance. The thought of it made her giddy, like she was walking on air. The night felt exquisite and promising, full of possibility.

Maddie and Stanislaw made their way up the smooth gray stone steps leading to the hall, like the steps of a Roman monument.

Once inside, Maddie marveled at the beautiful, marbled floors, the gilded walls, the ceiling with its carved, gold-toned woodwork and moldings. She'd never seen anything so grand. Her eyes beheld people dressed in finery, women in flowing, beaded, and sequined gowns, with hair swept up in the latest fashion, held in place by jeweled crowns and tiaras, men in crisply starched tuxedos with cummerbunds and tails. Maddie's head spun, her senses overwhelmed with all the glorious beauty and elegance. This crowd was a completely different class of people than she was familiar with. She had only read in books and magazines about nobility, and the stunning apparel they wore.

So much silk, lace, and intricate beadwork, what grandeur!

Her professor took her hand, leading her through the throngs of people that all funneled to the doorways leading into the symphony hall. An usher with a flashlight helped them find their seats.

Maddie turned to face her professor, her demeanor demonstrating a perceptible sense of gratitude. Doubtless sensing the emotion percolating in her, he patted her hand. No words were necessary—Maddie's blissful elation was in her expression.

After much applause, the conductor took his place behind the podium. With baton in hand, he signaled his orchestra, and the music began. Maddie, conscious of what her professor had told her, followed his instructions to close out her mind to thoughts, to the people around her, to the voice in her head.

Ludwig van Beethoven's Symphony No. 3 in E flat major, Op. 55, the *Eroica*, four movements, was on the program for that night. The music performed was sweeping and textured, capturing Maddie's body, moving her with each harmonic tension. Extraordinarily complex with differences in each movement, the music communicated a brilliant struggle, as if a fight was taking place, with the two sides surrendering before forging a path together.

Feelings of restoration flowed through her, and like the swell of an ocean wave, the music lifted her up to a dizzying height.

She felt as if she could fly and find a new freedom, on another shore, in another country or world. Captivated by the music, she was taken by it on a flight she'd never expected.

From the moment of the first note, the symphony continued at a rapid pace, minutes clicking off like seconds. Maddie felt like she could live happily in this place, if only the music could go on forever. But the conclusion brought her flight back to earth, wings clipped. Maddie was back in reality, with conflicting feelings of disappointment and giddiness from her soar through the heavens, guided by the music performed.

Her professor comforted her. "The sign of a great conductor, program, and orchestral performance is that they leave you wanting more. This is only your first concert in a line of many!"

Maddie's effervescence and pleasure from what she experienced that night were abundantly clear. Her professor told her, "It brings me immense joy to see you so happy and moved by the performance. This is the way people will react when it is your turn on the big stage. People will be captivated by you, your talent, and they too will never want the night to end!"

Maddie blushed at the praise. She hesitated for a moment before taking a deep breath and fearlessly stating, "My hope is to perform someday at a level worthy of a great symphony orchestra like this one."

Stanislaw's eyes watered, brimming with hope and desire for his pupil. "My dear, you reach for the moon, and I promise, it will reach back!"

"Oh, professor, that would be a dream come true for me."

As the patrons and ticket holders began to file out of the hall, the line slowed to a snail's pace. People ahead of Maddie strained their necks to see what was slowing the line. Like a whispered secret making its way around the hall, they learned that all attendees must show identification cards or papers before exiting.

The lobby was full of hundreds of people, waiting around while a Brownshirt questioned concert attendees and checked identification. From what Maddie could see, there were three long desks forming a line end to end, which stretched out before two of the exit doors.

Each desk had a Brownshirt standing before the tables, and three SS officers sitting behind it with a large bolt of paper, writing down information and comparing it against something that must have been similar to a census list. Maddie overheard the women in front of her say, "I don't know what else they could use to verify the addresses of the people."

While waiting in line, Maddie appraised the crowd. Never having seen or experienced anything like this, she questioned her professor as to whether or not they were in fact nobility. He told her in a whisper, careful that no one was close enough to hear him, "They are the socialist elite, officers, wives, and mistresses, all members of the Nazi party. I always see them attending concerts and symphonies, sitting in the best seats. This class of people always come dressed in their finery-living a life high above the rest of us plebeians."

Maddie nodded but was still not sure what 'socialist elite' meant. The line was moving at a quickened pace. She asked Professor Stanislaw, while peering toward the front of the line as they inched closer, "What is the reason that the men at the desk do this, take information?"

"Up until tonight, I have only read about this practice of the SS, they are the enforcement branch, the police of the Nazis and it is taking place before our eyes. If a person's last name sounds Jewish, if they are in fact Jewish, then the address of the person in question will be recorded. Hitler commanded that all Jews in Germany be accounted for, while his henchmen the Brownshirts and SS Gestapo carry out the orders."

Seventeen-year-old Maddie had no identification. She was not a German citizen, and even if she was, showing identification was not a requirement until a person turned eighteen. When it was their turn in line, Stanislaw explained to the Brownshirt, "Maddie is visiting from Poland and has no identification."

The Brownshirt still demanded some form of identification where none existed. Stanislaw repeated, "She's not a German citizen!"

Unsatisfied with the answer, the Brownshirt gazed at Maddie with suspicion, as if curious as to why a Polish girl would be in Munich with no papers of identification. He asked her directly, "Why are you here from Poland, are you Jewish, are you a communist or some kind of agitator?"

Her clear deep blue eyes focused on the man asking the questions, Maddie said, "I am not a communist." She refused to confirm that she—like her professor—was Jewish.

The Brownshirt continued questioning Maddie with punctilious detail, dripping with accusation. "Do you belong to any organization that is in opposition to the Third Reich?"

Nervous and fearful, Stanislaw tried to circumvent the rising suspicion, stepping in front of Maddie, physically protecting her, blocking the view of the Brownshirt, so that the man would question him, not Maddie. He was a good foot and a half taller than she was, and she could easily stand behind him.

Nervous and twitching, Stanislaw began to tell the man again, pleading with him, trying to reason. "She is young, only seventeen, she is my music student, she's done nothing wrong."

But it was for naught. The man's pointed questions continued; this time directed at Stanislaw.

"Are you in political opposition to the Reich? Do you agree with the government and its leader, or do you feel hostility and believe it's in your best interests to resist?"

Stanislaw fell right into the trap. His nerves got the best of him, and without thinking, he spoke his mind, forgetting that to Nazis, even the smallest expression of dissent was a crime.

"I pay no attention; I go about my business and obey the laws."

An expression of disapproval and animosity crossed the face of the Brownshirt. He shifted his weight from one foot to the other, leaning in and inspecting Stanislaw like he was a bacterium on a petri dish under a microscope. His tone changed. "What do you mean, you pay no attention? Answer me yes or no, are you in support of the Reich?"

Stanislaw's pride got the better of him. With umbrage, sticking his chin out, he told his questioner, "I'm neither for it nor against it."

The Brownshirt had heard enough. He motioned, waving to the SS officers standing at two of the four exit doors.

That was when Stanislaw turned, whispering to Maddie, "Make a run for it!"

Their eyes met. Then he pushed her away, in the direction of the doors.

Survival instinct took over her mind. She had done this before, was familiar with the aspect of running for one's life. She ducked down out of the Brownshirt's view, maneuvering quickly through the crowd. Then she spotted an exit door, unattended by any form of police, and hurried to it, walking out into the night air along with other attendees.

Terrified, Maddie forced herself to blend in with other attendees, not knowing if Brownshirts also mixed into the crowd. Her anxiety created adrenaline; all she could think about was survival. She tried to calm down, walking quickly, just short of running down the steps of the concert hall.

Her feet finally hit pavement, where she picked up her pace and began to run. Her head was spinning, her breath came in short gasps. She fought back tears, but to no avail. She had no idea where she was going. Panic took root in her stomach, grinding away. There was nothing she could do to quell all the feelings and thoughts shooting through her mind, then her body, like bullets fired from a gun.

She caught up to a large group of people and slowed to a walk, trying her best to mix in so as not to be spotted alone.

The Brownshirt takes Stanislaw into custody. Stani listens as they speak about Maddie, the Brownshirt tells the SS officers, "Clearly, she's a communist, why else would she run? Don't worry about her. She must belong to one of the groups of agitators in Munich. We will apprehend her." The Brownshirt tells the SS officers while pointing at Stani, "Just take care of him."

The SS was determined to get more information out of Stanislaw about the supposed affiliation to a "communist group." They had well-developed techniques of torture, used to extract information from political opposition and entities, or anyone with an opinion of the Reich that was not favorable. If the prisoner was not willing to talk, severe beatings would follow, as would a stay in Dachau Concentration Camp for even more horrific treatment. Ruthless and irrational, they operated in the realm of complete lawlessness when it came to Jewish people. Their hatred was unequivocal.

An SS officer took Stanislaw by the arm, half-dragging him to the exit doors, and took him into custody. Stanislaw couldn't believe nor understand why he was being treated like a criminal.

He asked the officer, "What are you doing, why am I being arrested? What have I done?"

No answer.

Pulling handcuffs from his belt, the SS policeman secured them around Stanislaw's wrists so tightly they cut into his skin. He then dragged Stanislaw from the Hall down the front steps. Stanislaw tripped and almost took the officer down with him. Gathering himself, he asked again.

"What have I done wrong? You must tell me. You cannot just arrest a law-abiding citizen, this is insanity. What did I do, you must tell me!"

No answer.

An ominous-looking, long, black car, unmarked with darkened windows, awaited in front of the Philharmoniker Hall. The back door opened, and Stanislaw saw two more men in the back seat, both gagged.

The officer pushed Stanislaw into the back and told him, "Shut up, you Jewish communist, or I'll be forced to silence you. You know what you've done."

But he did not.

CHAPTER FOUR

Frederick

FIFTEEN DAYS BEFORE WOLFIE'S
ATTACK BY THE GESTAPO

AFTER A LONG day at work, weary Frederick Wolferman walks home in his well-worn boots with his metal lunch pail in hand. He's walked this road back and forth to work at Dieter Faulkner's Garage for eleven years, always walking to work despite occasional offers of rides from passersby during inclement weather.

He goes over his mental checklist, revisiting the repairs made on automobiles and trucks. As he nears home, he wonders about his son, Wolfie, who will be home in two weeks from Vienna. Frederick surmises that because he has not had a letter from Wolfie in some time, he must be having fun with Rolf, Frederick's older brother, and his wife Cecile.

He walks up the gravel driveway, the cracked sidewalk, and up the three steps to the screen door. To the right of the door is a mailbox attached to the house. Reaching in, he pulls out a letter, an official government envelope from a Reichsjugendführer Baldur von Schirach. *What could this be about?*

Once inside, he kicks off his boots as he walks into the kitchen, takes the metal coffeepot, and puts it on the stove to rewarm the leftover coffee from the morning. He pours a cup and sits at the worn and wobbly wooden kitchen table, opening the letter with his pocketknife. He slurps his coffee, wiping his mouth with the back of his hand.

He pulls the letter out of the envelope and begins to read.

The letter demands that Wolfie join the Hitlerjugend at once, with a deadline set for next week. It includes an address and phone number. Frederick convinces himself that it would be better to appear in person before the Reichsjugendführer. If he did so—rather than having a faceless phone conversation—surely the authorities would view the situation with genuine understanding.

This is all I need right now. I will have to take off a day from work for this.

The last time Frederick took a day off was to bury his precious wife, Elise, the victim of a ghastly and quickly-spreading cancer. She died at age twenty-seven. He has never gotten over missing her. Frederick recalls the last words she spoke before slipping into a sleep from which she would never awaken: *Be patient with our son, and be good to yourself, my love.*

Frederick picks up the phone to call Rolf and talk to Wolfie directly, informing him he must come home as soon as possible to follow the imposed demands.

"Hello, Rolf, I hope I'm not interrupting your dinner, may I speak with Wolfie?

"He's where? What? In Hungary with the Boy Scouts of America? How did this happen and when did this happen, why wasn't I asked or told about this?

"You forgot?

"Yes, Rolf, I'm hot under the collar because first, that's my son—I should be consulted. Secondly, I'm holding a letter from the Reichsjugendführer demanding he join Hitlerjugend by August 16. You're damn right I'm mad. No not mad, I'm angry!

"I don't want to hear excuses. I know he wanted to go, but we cannot always have what we want! This is bad. Both of us will be in trouble—Wolfie and me. I have no idea what they will do, but you know how this regime works. Extreme everything.

"So, when is he supposed to arrive home? On the eighteenth? Oh, no. That is no good, he only has until the sixteenth to comply.

"Oh, for the love of God, why didn't you call and ask me first? No, I had no way of knowing about the letter. But still, I am his father.

"Okay, okay. I'm planning to go in person anyway. Yes, I know. Okay, I will. Goodbye."

Frederick calls his boss, interrupting his dinner, explaining the predicament with Wolfie and the Hitlerjugend. His employer allows him the next day off from work, after Frederick agrees to work an extra day the following week to make up for the time he'll miss.

Once morning comes, Frederick dresses in his only suit, a black pinstripe, with a tie his wife bought him for Christmas the year before she died. He shines his shoes, buffing them to a high sheen. Now clean-shaven, hair combed, with tonic, he stares at his reflection in the mirror. He frowns, noticing his suit hangs on him, not fitting as well as when first bought due to the weight he's lost. Death of your beloved can do that to you. He speaks to his reflection, "Well, it is ten years old, what did you expect?"

He leaves the house, walking down the front steps, and sees his neighbor, the widow Mrs. Ingrid Stuterberg. He waves to her. She sees him and waves back.

Frederick makes his way to the address on the letterhead, walking at a brisk pace.

Talking as he walks, he tells himself, *Stay calm, Frederick. Do not let your temper get the best of you.*

Frederick enters a typical government building, nondescript except for the giant Nazi banner hung from the top of the building, both four stories high. Viewing it, he shakes his head.

He approaches a large, sweeping staircase leading up to what he believes to be a reception area and offices. Taking the steps two by two, Frederick passes through large glass-and-steel doors, while seeking a directory to guide him.

Two Brownshirts round a corner, walking straight toward him. Frederick pauses, stopping to ask the men, in a polite tone, if they know where he might find the office of the Reichsjugendführer. They shake their heads and keep walking past him.

Thanks a lot. Helpful as usual, bastards.

Walking down the first hallway on the left, he finds a number on the door, 317, which matches the one listed in the letter.

He tries the handle; it turns. He opens the door, deciding not to knock first.

The room is quite small, occupied by a young man with a pencil-thin mustache and short clipped black hair, sitting behind an old desk that's seen better days. He's dressed in a Nazi uniform, typing fervently, ignoring Frederick.

Frederick stands in front of the desk, invisible. He clears his throat.

In a clipped and impatient tone, the typist asks, in German, "Can I help you?"

Frederick snaps back into the moment.

"Yes, I'm trying to find the Reichsjugendführer. You see, I received a letter about my son's joining the Hitlerjugend. There has been a small delay."

Before Frederick can finish the rest of the story, the man stands and says, "This way."

Frederick follows behind the thin, tall Nazi, who is a vertical version of his mustache.

They walk to the end of the hallway, where there are two

doors on either side. They pass through the one on the left. The man says to the woman sitting behind a desk, "Hitlerjugend."

The woman behind the desk nods and stands. She is a short, stout woman in a dress one size too small, with severely bleached hair, pockmarked skin, and plenty of thick black eyeliner.

Her voice, raspy from too many cigarettes, croaks: "This way."

She raps on the door in front of them, and a voice inside says, "Enter."

Frederick walks into the office and approaches a desk, behind which sits a man bedecked in a snappy SS uniform. Frederick extends his hand and begins to introduce himself.

The man holds up his hand.

"Don't speak, let me see your letter."

Silently, Frederick hands the man the letter.

He looks around the room. It is plain, with no personality. The desk has a lamp; there are three filing cabinets, and no windows. The only decorations are four pictures of Führer Hitler lined up with precision. The exact distance between each image is the same. The pictures are of Hitler speaking at rallies. The photos are shot at an angle that makes him appear tall.

Frederick laughs to himself. *Anyone seeing him in person knows he is on the shorter side, with no resemblance at all to the Aryan he pictures as the perfect specimen. The Nordic warrior is the replica that Hitler waxes on and on about, portrayed as healthy, muscularly built, with rugged good looks, golden hair, and blue eyes. In fact, Hitler looks nothing like that; he is the exact opposite of that image. Someone should hand him a mirror.*

The overwhelming, concentrated aroma of cigarette smoke in the office causes Frederick's eyes to water. *It stinks in here!*

While the man is reading the letter, Frederick cautiously watches him. He's dressed in a jet-black uniform with red

Nazi swastika armbands and "SS" patches at his collar. There are two medals on his right breast pocket, and his shirt is black, as is his tie with a swastika. The uniform makes an immediate impression.

The man studies a list on his desk, comparing it to the letter. He glances up at Frederick, looking him up and down twice. Then he shifts in his chair and asks, "Why hasn't Wilhelm joined the mandatory Hitlerjugend? Isn't he a member of the Boy Scouts?"

Upon hearing the accusation, Frederick begins to feel anxious. He clears his throat, feeling the constricting onset of tension. He strains to speak, and when he does, his voice comes out softly. "We were not aware it was mandatory, sir," he lies. "And, yes, yes sir, he was a Boy Scout—but no longer. Wilhelm is presently in Vienna spending the summer with his aunt and uncle. He will be home soon, on the eighteenth, and will join Hitlerjugend at once." Frederick hopes this will appease the man.

The officer sits back in his chair, pursing his thin, colorless lips. His facial expression reveals dissatisfaction with Frederick's answer. He takes off his glasses and ceremoniously cleans them with a handkerchief from his back pocket. He notices a piece of lint on his tie and flicks it away.

The officer peruses Frederick up and down again, allowing a few moments to pass, which adds to Frederick's growing anxiety. With his elbows on the desk, the man matches up his hands and fingers, opening and closing his hands several times before finally addressing Frederick.

"So, you're saying Wilhelm is no longer a Boy Scout, is that right? And why August 18?" Without a doubt, the officer is aware of the beginning and ending dates of the World Jamboree. It would not take a lot of research to find the exact date the Jamboree ends or the route back to Munich.

Frederick clears his throat again, answering, "It's just a date we picked, no reason. And, yes, he quit the Boy Scouts."

Frederick feels a weight bearing down on him, knowing he's just lied to a Nazi officer. Tension is increasing and spreading through his body by the second.

"So, since Wilhelm is no longer a Boy Scout, then certainly he can be back by the date listed on the letter and join. Or is there a problem with that, Mr. Wolferman?"

Before Frederick has a chance to answer, the officer says, "I'd like the name and address of where the boy is staying, if you don't mind, and I'd like to speak to him, if he's available. Do these people have a telephone?"

Frederick is in a full-blown sweat, the back of his neck wet with perspiration emanating from the top of his head, running down his forehead, and dripping into his eyes, making him blink and flinch. He's keenly aware the officer is watching every sweat bead running down his face. The fear carries a scent that stings Frederick's nostrils.

In Nazi Germany, lying to an officer of any stature is a treasonous offense, punishable by serving an unspecified length of time in jail, or even in a concentration camp.

"Yes, sir, they have a phone, I have the number somewhere in my wallet." He reaches into his back pocket and fumbles nervously with his wallet. As his fingers sort through the scraps of papers, he is painfully aware, as he drops the last note his wife wrote him—which he always carries—and watches as it slides under the desk, that it is irretrievable. *Damn it!*

"Ah, yes, here it is. The number is..."

The officer interrupts him mid-sentence.

"Hand me the paper, and I'll write it down. What are the names of this aunt and uncle?"

"Cecile and Rolf Wolferman. Rolf is my brother."

The officer stares at Frederick, making him even more jittery. He tries not to meet the officer's eyes, fearing he will give himself away, but it is too late.

The officer dials Rolf and Cecile's number.

Frederick pleads a silent request. *Please do not answer, please do not answer, please do not answer.*

The officer waits for a few minutes, letting the phone ring and ring.

Finally, he hangs up. Perturbed, the officer says the obvious, "No answer."

He hands the phone number back to Frederick.

Then he asks him, "Mr. Wolferman, would you wait outside?"

Relieved, Frederick says, "Yes, sir. Thank you."

"But don't go anywhere."

CHAPTER FIVE

Maddie

AUGUST 1933

MADDIE IS AWARE of her breathing now, as she remains tucked under the bed in room 125, hiding in yet another small space. Maddie cannot sleep, although she is exhausted after running and hiding for the past thirty-six hours. She thinks if she recalls the audition with her professor two years prior, she might drift off into something resembling sleep.

She pictures her professor's personable face, the kindness in his eyes, and thinks of the patient way he taught her technicalities. Her latest performance was reflective of his instruction.

Professor is such a gift to me, Maddie thinks, recalling her first meeting with Professor Birnbaum.

"Miss Turetzky?"

Maddie snapped to attention. "Yes, sir, I am she."

"Well then, please do come in. How do you do. I am Professor Stanislaw Birnbaum; I am pleased to meet you. Mrs. Laurent tells me to expect greatness from you."

Maddie felt inordinately anxious. *Nothing like the highest of expectations before I perform.*

She shook the professor's outstretched hand. "Thank you, sir, for this opportunity to audition for you."

Maddie walked behind the man who would help to determine her future as a concert violinist. He led her into a room. Maddie took notice of the walls and ceiling, wondering about the acoustics.

The professor took his seat in a chair directly placed four feet in front of her.

Maddie had never performed or auditioned before, and at close range, under such scrutiny, her stomach was roiling with nerves. *Can the professor hear my stomach?* But after two years of tutelage by Mrs. Laurent, she was ready to take the next step in her quest, her journey to become a renowned artist, a first chair in a symphony orchestra.

She took her violin case and placed it on a chair. As she removed her violin and bow, she dropped her bow, which rattled upon hitting the floor. She willed herself to avoid making eye contact with the professor. Her hands were sweaty, and she felt close to hyperventilating.

She adjusted the stand, straightened it to her liking, and placed her sheet music on it.

Feeling a combination of butterflies and performance anxiety, Maddie focused on one thought: *Calm down, remember your breathing.*

Mrs. Laurent had told Maddie last week, in anticipation of the audition, "Whatever happens is meant to happen. You must trust and go in confidence, believing in your talent, your gift and yourself." Maddie wondered at the sudden empty feeling, like her musical gift had suddenly evaporated and left her. She panicked as she thought, *I cannot remember the sequence of notes at the beginning. Remember to read the notes, the music will come to me.* She wiped her sweaty hands on the lacy silk skirt Mrs. Laurent had bought her for the recital. *Breathe, Maddie, breathe!*

Maddie secured a stray lock of her dark hair behind her ear and took her violin and bow in hand. She heard her teacher's voice, *Confidence, Maddie.*

Briefly checking her bow and strings, tuning her instrument, she straightened herself. She stood erect, aware of her posture, and assumed her performance stance.

Taking a deep breath, she was ready to perform. Another wave of nerves washed up on her mind. *Why is he sitting so close to me?*

Professor Birnbaum asked Maddie about the selection she would perform and the reasoning behind her choice.

Maddie said sweetly and respectfully, "Thank you for allowing me this time and opportunity to perform for you. I've chosen Bach's Chaccone Partita No.2 in D Minor. This piece has a spiritual connection to me. The notes make me feel like I'm on cascading waves. I feel as though I have no fear. The rolling and swelling of the waves take me higher and higher, up to the heavens, bringing me to a place I've never seen, never experienced. It feels ethereal, otherworldly."

Birnbaum nodded.

Maddie told herself, *Be aware of your breathing. Relax. God, please be with me.*

Raising her violin to her chin, adjusting her head, she grasped her bow as her eyes made contact with the professor's. He smiled at her and said, "Please begin."

Maddie began to play with a stern and commanding presence. Her fingers were nimble, assertive. She interpreted the complexity of various themes within the piece. She struck the strings with her bow as the music issued forth from the instrument in a moving, evocative manner. The piece called for changes in emotional intensity, and, plucking the strings, she felt her confidence begin to swell with the music. As the notes came to her, she felt in command and played with abandon, losing all sense of herself within the music, becoming one with it.

The weight and influence of the piece extended beyond the partita itself through Maddie, melding her to the music.

The composition was captivating. Maddie injected the intensity of her emotions into each note. As for the arrangement itself, it was awe-inspiring, proving Bach to be a musical architectural genius. Maddie had chosen an ambitious and intricate choice for an audition. The finale, a flourish of urgent short notes, restated the theme at the end with new and powerful harmonies.

Maddie glided through each note, to the very last, with finality.

After completing the piece, she took the violin from her chin and held it in her right hand with the bow. Her left hand holding her skirt out from her body, she curtsied with her head bowed.

Enthusiastically, Professor Birnbaum jumped up from his seat. "Well done, Miss Turetzky, well done! Please, sit down here and let's talk." Professor Birnbaum pulled another chair close to his, motioning for Maddie to sit.

Maddie's head was swimming. She was feeling the adrenaline rush of performance and completion of a challenging piece, knowing she'd played it with precision, with all her heart and soul.

She could feel her face was flushed with color while her heart pounded at a fast rate as it pumped blood through her veins. *You did it, Maddie, you did it!*

He began his critique, searching her eyes, her face as he started. Maddie felt anxious, hoping the critique would be honest and kind.

"Almost perfect. If the performance were perfect, you'd not need me. However, there are some technical issues which, I assure you, we can address. I would not consider you a worthy pupil if you did not have the potential, the skills it takes to be a master. You own the proper balance of passion and intensity along with the technical ability to interpret a piece. That is a gift! You chose such a complicated piece to play, surprising even me! Do you know Johannes Brahms said of Bach's Partita in D minor, 'On one stave, for a small instrument, the man writes an entire universe of the deepest thoughts and most powerful feelings'? It's indeed a magnificent piece. Tell me, what did you think of your performance?"

Feeling self-conscious, Maddie summoned confidence from within, saying with a smile and twinkling eyes, "It's the best I've ever played this piece!"

"Excellent, my girl. Self-confidence is necessary for a performer, along with a sense of fearlessness. You must be courageous! You communicate that quite well. I'm without doubt those traits are strong within you. How did you become so fearless?"

"Years of training, sir." *He had no idea how much training.*

As Maddie recalls the audition, she begins to cry, her chest heaving with emotion despite the close quarters. Whimpering, she whispers, *He has been so good to me, I must help him, somehow. Where do I start, where do I go? Will I find him, is he at home, or did the Nazis take him away?* She wipes her nose on her arm and feels like she could cry more, but she stops breathing when she hears a sound.

The sound of the hotel room's door opening and closing.

Then, footsteps. Coming right toward her.

CHAPTER SIX

Frederick

AUGUST 1933

THE THIRTEEN BARRACKS at Dachau Concentration Camp in the town of Dachau, ten miles from Munich, are nothing more than converted empty space in dilapidated buildings formerly housing a munitions factory.

The entrance to the camp has a large iron gate with words in iron above the gate that say, "Arbeit macht frei." Translated, it means, "Work will make you free."

The prisoners do nothing but work. And there is no freedom, no matter what the sign says. Since the prison opened, each prisoner that passes through the gates wonders the same thing, *How will work make a person free?*

The answer is ambiguous.

Inside the barracks is a type of bunk bed, made from wooden flats, ten sets stacked three high, with two men to a flat, sixty to each of the barracks. There are rudimentary tables and benches, and a concrete floor. The crude and decrepit buildings have cracks in the walls. There is rotting wood around the windows that allows for blasts of air and rain to seep inside. During the brutal, frigid winter, those blasts will be icy and piercing. It would be an understatement to say the accommodations leave a lot to be desired. The barracks for Jewish prisoners is worse. They are sequestered from the other prisoners.

There is rampant brutality, torture, and murder of the prisoners at the hands of the SS guards. Tree hanging, standing at attention for hour upon hour, and floggings are regular occurrences. The Jewish prisoners sustain the worst of the savage treatment.

Frederick Wolferman has spent the last thirteen days at this camp. After the interrogation by the office of the Reichsjugendführer, Frederick is officially charged with lying to an officer of the Reich. He is charged over a minor detail, with no legal basis for arrest or imprisonment. The office of the Reichsjugendführer decided to make an example out of him.

Frederick feels the pain and bitter anguish of the consequence in his soul. He cries from his heart, *where is my son, what happened to him, and why didn't I pay attention to the signs posted all over Munich? This is all my fault.*

His distress will drive him through his daily work at Dachau. Affliction and suffering can be positive motivators when it comes to work.

This is what "work will make you free" means. You can forget your problems for a while and lose yourself. The harder you work, the more distant the troubles seem. Until you go to bed, when the lucent apparitions of fear and doubt make their entrance. They haunt your sleep, swirl around your subconscious, poke at you, and cause you to question. Your mind becomes restless as your soul aches for answers that do not come. They are frequent visitors and have no favorites. It is possible that work does make you free, but it does so only temporarily, until the darkness begins to waft around your senses.

All prisoners are sleep and food deprived. Regardless, they must be on their toes and watch out for the guards and the kapos.

So far, Frederick has only had one serious run-in with a kapo. The kapos are prison functionaries, assigned by the SS, the Schutzstaffel, the Protection Squadron stationed at the camp as guards.

There are a few good, fair kapos and many devilish, devious kapos. Frederick's run-in was with one from the second category.

The first day at the camp, not yet familiar with the routines, Frederick made the mistake of asking when they would eat.

In German, the kapo asked Frederick, "Is your stomach growling, would you like something to eat now?"

Frederick thought the man was serious and answered affirmatively. The kapo laughed and took the steel pipe he carried and hit Frederick directly in the kneecaps. Frederick dropped down to the ground, and as he did, the kapo put his large foot on the side of Frederick's head, grinding his face into the dirt. "You eat when we tell you to eat. Understand?"

Frederick hasn't spoken an unnecessary word or posed a question to any kapo or guard since.

That same kapo reported three Jewish men to a guard, saying, "I found them trying to escape, through a tunnel they dug in the soft earth." There is no evidence of a tunnel, anywhere. And the earth at Dachau is anything but soft.

The men had no opportunity to defend themselves.

The guard, named Dukolf, took the three men, lined them up outside of the repair garage where Frederick works, made them kneel as they faced the wall, and systematically shot each man in the back of his head at close range.

Then the guard directed Frederick to move the bodies and dump them in "the pit." Frederick then had to wash down the wall, which was splattered with blood, brains, and skull fragments.

"The pit" is the open grave where the bodies of Jewish men and others considered political adversaries, homosexuals, gypsies, or criminals are placed after they're murdered. Some are beaten and kicked to death, some are shot, while others are pushed into the electric fence and electrocuted. The means by which their life ends are interminably gruesome.

Frederick hopes they go to a better place, supposing such a place exists. He wonders at times if it does.

Clearly, he has yet to find evidence of such a place. An inner curiosity and desire to find out are always present within his deeper thoughts, like the specter of a premonition that hovers around his other cognitions.

Anything must be better than Dachau. Hitler issued an edict saying that Dachau and all other concentration camps were not subject to German law as it applies to German citizens. SS Headmasters, the commandants of the camp, have free rein to run the camp and hand out punishments as they see fit. In other words, it's a barbarous, bloodthirsty, chaotic situation. It takes a certain kind of man to administer brutality daily. The kind of man that is soulless.

Because of Frederick's aptitude and technical knowledge of car and truck engines, he secures one of the highly-esteemed positions in the camp as chief auto mechanic. He replaces a man who recently died from tuberculosis, one of fifteen men who died from an outbreak.

Frederick's charge includes maintenance of the Reich vehicles, including any number of automobiles in the Führer's pool of cars. He services the staff cars, military motorcycles, and the biggest challenge, the Leichttraktor, an armored tank. Even some of the guards bring in their personal vehicles for Frederick to service or repair. In return, he gets an extra ration of bread or a sausage. Frederick never keeps the extra food for himself—he saves it and gives it to a prisoner who is sick and needs extra strength.

Last week, the kapo in charge of the garage told Frederick he'd get a helper soon, someone who would empty the oil bins, full of dirty engine oil, and change tires on cars and trucks so Frederick could focus on the engine repairs and the like.

"The Führer expects all serviceable vehicles to be repaired and ready to deploy into service as soon as possible. You must work faster."

Frederick nodded and thanked the man, but as soon as he left earshot, Frederick had a few choice words for the man, spoken under his breath.

Frederick wonders if there will really be a helper or if the man is just toying with him. *I'll believe it when I see it.*

Every few days, any number of buses pull up, discharging passengers to walk the red brick road to the camp under supervision of machine gun-toting SS guards.

One of the prisoners brought into camp recently is younger than most of the men. He keeps to himself, averting his eyes from the other prisoners.

Upon entrance into the camp, procedures begin. First, the prisoners' information is recorded into a large book, with their name, age, and city of origin. The prisoners then take a number as identification, as if their name no longer exists.

Next, the men strip off their clothing. They're hosed down, deloused, and escorted to a building, stark naked, before receiving their prison clothing. It doesn't matter if it's the middle of summer or the dead of winter. Naked they go.

One of the prisoners tries to make conversation with the young man. He's curious as to how the young man ended up in Dachau. He whispers, asking him, "What happened?"

The young man hesitates to answer. He says nothing.

One eye bears the mark of a severe beating. It's completely closed, swollen, and dark. Covering much of his body are large bruises and open sores still oozing blood.

The fingers of terror wrap tightly around the young man's throat, so much so that he can't speak.

He trusts no one.

CHAPTER SEVEN

Stanislaw and Elenena

AUGUST 1933

PROFESSOR STANISLAW BIRNBAUM continues his pilgrimage back and forth to the wall, where he deposits the contents of two large metal pails. In twelve hours, he's made twenty-eight trips, dumping fifty pounds of rocks, gravel, and dirt each trip, bloodying his hands daily. The bleeding blisters on his hands are a result of the pail handles. Stanislaw wraps rags around the metal handles to keep the blisters from becoming increasingly worse. The rags absorb the blood and add a degree of cushioning.

Spying Stanislaw using rags, Dukolf approaches him from behind and hits him in the back of the head with his club. Stanislaw crumples to the ground while Dukolf rips the rags from a bleeding Stanislaw.

One of the guards' questions Dukolf, asking him, "What's the big deal if he uses rags on the pail handles?"

Dukolf responds with his usual crassness, "It makes for comfort, and no commie Jewish vermin is going to have any form of comfort at Dachau!"

Stanislaw came straight from the Munich Philharmoniker to Dachau Concentration Camp as a prisoner without a trial, based on suspicion of being a communist agitator. As a result, he had had his clothes and shoes stripped from him the day he entered, never receiving anything to wear. He remained barefooted.

Not all Jewish prisoners receive this extreme treatment, but many do. Stanislaw is a communist, according to the Nazi SS Police. The guard Dukolf hates communists as much as he hates Jews. To him, Stanislaw is doubly offensive.

Stanislaw's active imagination carries him through the first days at Dachau. He imagines himself to be a bird—an eagle—soaring high above the camp, transporting his troubles, gripped by sharp talons. Then comes the momentous letting go, depositing them over the bank of a steep ravine. The troubles tumble and crash, despairing that they no longer inhabit human form.

A verse from the Prophet Isaiah keeps Stanislaw's weary spirit lifted.

But they that wait upon the LORD shall renew their strength, they shall mount up with wings as eagles, they shall run, and not be weary, they shall walk, and not faint.

Stanislaw's faith, scriptures, and thoughts of the two women he loves motivate him throughout his days and nights at camp. It is his thoughts of Maddie that propel him through his day, giving him a reason to live. *I must find out what happened to Maddie.*

And my Elenena.

Stanislaw meets another Jewish prisoner, Stephan. He is bitter and filled with hatred towards the camp guards. It is the motivation of hatred that keeps him going through each day of slave labor and drudgery. Stephan believes he has only two options: Either escape or end up eventually in the pit. Stanislaw, on the other hand, has no doubt that he'll be released back to his pleasant life as a violin instructor.

Stanislaw's life was peripatetic, traveling from Berlin to Munich weekly to tutor students in both cities. The closest the bachelor came to marriage was to his student, Elenena Laurent. She stole his heart.

Their first meeting had been in Munich, in 1925. The day marked the last week of July, an ideal time for a summer stroll through a Munich park. That day, Stanislaw felt especially alive as he strolled with pleasure through one of his favorite parks. His eyes beheld the verdant green of the sprawling park and the lush floral blossoms, and his senses absorbed the sweet, chamomile-scented air. The sun, warm and inviting, penetrated his skin.

Stanislaw had an inkling of intuition that the day would have a unique quality. He felt an intangible hope, a quiet, growing happiness and contentment within him. Over the years, he had learned to recognize the signs of hope and blessing.

Conscious anticipation grew with every step, as he sensed the day held possibilities.

He heard music while meandering through the park. He was drawn by the transcendent sound of a piece by Bach, played on a fine instrument by a gifted violinist.

Stanislaw didn't need to see the instrument or the musician to affirm the talent. He only needed to listen. His ears led him to the source of the music. He found himself struck not only by the finesse of the performance, but the sublime beauty of the musician. Elenena Laurent apprehended his heart in one fell swoop; he was smitten at first sight. Later, he confessed to her, "Your music first captured my ears, but your beauty captured my heart."

Elenena told him she'd dreamt of having more formal instruction, like she had when she lived in Poland, but never thought it possible at this age. She thought she was too old to be a student. Who would want to instruct a woman of twenty-four? She had a desire to teach violin, to learn as much as she could about the craft and then teach it to young, hopeful musicians. This was where her gift and desire lay:

communicating and mentoring young people, teaching them the proper mechanics of the violin, encouraging them to play with confidence and abandon.

Stanislaw jumped at the chance to take her as a student. He taught her for four years until she could progress no more. Then he spoke the words she hoped for, "You're ready for students of your own!"

Despite the disparity of twenty years in age between them, it didn't make a difference to either one. They thoroughly enjoyed each other's company. Their lively and spirited discussions about music, books, art, philosophy, and God could cause hours to pass without their knowledge.

But the relationship would not progress the way Stanislaw had hoped.

Elenena couldn't make Stanislaw understand that she had no desire for marriage.

"I'm not the marrying kind," is what she told him. "I know it wounds you to hear me speak these words, but I've always known in my heart that I was born to be single. I don't know how else to explain it, but I've known this for as long as I can remember. Why should you get the remnants? Stani, you're worthy of someone far superior to me. You deserve a woman who will be completely devoted to you in every aspect. I just give you crumbs."

Occasionally, Stani tested the waters to see if her opinions and feelings about marriage had changed. One day Elenena gauged his reaction to something that might become a reality: "Perhaps if I were to move away, it would be easier for you?"

Despite his pride, Stanislaw took the crumbs. His intense love for her kept him faithful, with no desire for anyone else. "Elenena, be my friend, be my companion. I will take what you give, even if it's less than nothing."

With no pressure, their friendship was solid. They enjoyed their talks, walks in the park, attending concerts, and reading poetry.

But if he were honest, he'd have to admit he longed for so much more.

The last conversation they'd had was two days before the Munich concert, which Elenena was not able to attend. She was in Baranovichi, completing the details and legal aspects of her sister's estate.

Stanislaw discussed the concert's details and the program with Elenena. He told her, "The more beautiful everything is, the more it will hurt not having you there. But alas, I know it will thrill Maddie, and we will go. But I will miss you."

"Go and have a magnificent time, my dearest."

Stanislaw's daydreaming comes to an abrupt end when a guard calls out to him, "Hey, Jew, get to work before I beat you."

Stanislaw finds himself daydreaming, awakening to the stark reality of his existence: his nakedness, the pails, the rocks, the bloody blisters, and beatings. The kapo will beat him for inactivity. "Yes, sir. I'm sorry, sir."

"You will be more than sorry when I get done with you!"

That night, after fourteen hours of labor, Stanislaw, along with his barracks-mates, is required to stand at attention for three hours before being excused. This cruel demand is another example of the manner in which the guard's exact punishment and torture on the Jewish prisoners. Several men drop to the ground from sheer exhaustion.

Stephan, who has been imprisoned at Dachau since a week after it opened, stands alongside Stanislaw and whispers, "What I wouldn't give to put a bullet from the German 9mm Luger in his holster right between Dukolf's beady Nazi eyes. Me and some of the other men, we talk about overtaking these bastards. There's more of us, we outnumber the dirty scoundrels thirty to one. These men are not your usual type of police guards. This lot is nothing more than ignorant beasts, uneducated morons. They have no training. Are you in?"

After two days of inhumane treatment, Stanislaw is sunburned, hungry, and has bleeding hands. He answers unequivocally, "Yes."

Stephan continues telling Stanislaw his intentions. "I have a plan; I've hidden some officer uniforms. If we can get enough men on our side once we know what numbers we're working with, we can formulate a way to take over this hellhole. We will not be here as prisoners forever, that I can promise you."

Stanislaw sees no point in raising concerns or being contentious. He's biding his time. He will be agreeable for the sake of it.

Having a good relationship with fellow prisoners has its advantages. There is a Ukrainian Jewish dissident who has some healing salve he lifted from the infirmary where he works, washing the floors and removing patients' waste. He tends to the wounds on Stanislaw's back. There's Jakob, a Polish Jewish man accused of making disparaging remarks against the Reich, who works in the depot, where he accepts delivery of foodstuffs for the guards and helps himself to rationed sausages, bread, and cheese. He shares these rations with many men, especially the ones denied food whenever Dukolf feels like it.

Despite the most horrendous of conditions, there is a spirit of camaraderie among the Jewish men. They cover for each other. And many of them pray together.

Stanislaw whispers to Stephan, "You're still a young man. Perhaps you will be released and can start over, take your life back. Don't you hope for that?"

"No, I don't. There's no chance of that happening. I don't know what hope is, it's an anomaly to me. I go for the tangible, like hatred. Something that is real, I can sink my teeth into and bite, giving me strength."

"I say this to you as your elder—don't let your hatred consume you. It will swallow you alive if you let it. Don't give it that much control and sway in your life. You're in control, until you're not."

Two days later, Stephan disappears. It is the prisoner Jakob who overhears Dukolf telling another guard what happened to Stephan, eavesdropping on their conversation while he stands laundering and ironing the uniforms in the guards' compound.

Dukolf sits close by with another guard at a table where they drink, smoke, and exchange stories. While slurping his third beer, the pugnacious Dukolf brags, "I used that commie Jew troublemaker for target practice. Shot him full of lead when I caught him trying to escape. Another troublemaker gone, one less mouth to feed. I'd kill them all if the commandant would allow it. But that wouldn't work—who would do the labor?"

CHAPTER EIGHT

Elenena

While traveling by train to Bremen, Elenena recounts the story of her early days in 1925 Munich to her American valet, Charles Whitecliff. He accompanies her, as she prepares to take the voyage to the United States.

SUMMER 1925

IN THE SUMMER of 1925, twenty-four-year-old Elenena Laurent moves from the comfortable home of her Aunt Noelle in Baranovichi, Poland to the big city of Munich, Germany, leaving her older sister Marcella behind. After arriving in the Munich train station, she buys a local paper and searches for a section that advertises rooms for rent. She finds what she seeks, and after making an inquiry of a young man for directions, she walks the three blocks to Ludwig Strasse, armed with only a suitcase and her violin.

Standing before a large brownstone row house on the quiet neighborhood sidewalk, she spots the "room for rent" sign in the window. Gazing upward, past the building into the sky, she encourages herself, *you've made it this far, Elenena, keep going. You can do this.*

Alone and without much money except for the modest amount her aunt gave her, Elenena hustles up the front steps, knocking on the solid wooden door. The house owner and landlord, the unmarried thirty-year-old Annie Heinrich, answers the door, her expression conveying immediate suspicion toward the bright and cheerful face of the beautiful young woman standing before her.

"What are you selling?"

Finding courage to speak while the woman gives her an awkward once-over, Elenena points to the sign in the window and says, "I'm here to inquire about the room for rent. How much do you charge?"

The woman stares Elenena down for an uncomfortable ten seconds before answering, "Come in and we will discuss it. My name is Annie." Annie turns and holds the door open, telling Elenena, "Well, don't stand there all day, come in!"

Elenena does as commanded and enters the house. Walking a few steps behind the woman, she keeps her eyes on the floor and follows her into the kitchen.

Annie points to a chair and tells her guest, "Sit," while she fills a teakettle with water and sets it on the stove. She goes about retrieving two teacups and saucers from a modest, simple cabinet. Elenena looks around the small room, and with nervous chatter she begins to tell the woman that her kitchen reminds her of the small kitchen in the Paris flat where she grew up.

Not waiting for a response, Elenena continues on breathlessly, launching into her plan.

"I don't know what you charge by the week or month, but I can do anything, clean your house, cook, wash windows, anything at all in exchange for rent. At some point, I would like to teach violin and help young budding artists hone their musical gifts and talents."

The teakettle whistles abruptly, and Annie goes about pouring the boiling water over the leaves in the teapot. She brings the pot to the table along with the cups, setting before

Elenena a teaspoon and a dainty linen napkin along with a milk pitcher and sugar bowl.

"Now tell me what you're babbling about, work for rent."

Elenena feels her courage dissipate, drain right out of her. She peers into the teacup before her, catching a glimpse of her reflection. She tells herself, *you'd better speak now before you lose all your nerve!*

"While I don't have money now for rent, I can cook, clean, run errands, do anything you need in exchange for rent."

"What's that instrument, a violin? You could sell that for money for rent."

Horrified at the thought, Elenena rebukes the very idea. "Oh, no! I could never do that; I hope to teach one day!"

"You hope for a lot of things, Miss... What is your name?"

"Elenena Laurent."

"What kind of name is that? Is it French?"

"Yes, ma'am. It is, I was born in Paris."

"And why are you here?"

The question perplexes Elenena, and her answer doesn't seem worthy.

"I needed a change, to, to explore a world different from the one I lived in."

Annie slurps her tea and asks, "And what world was that?"

"Poland. Baranovichi, Poland."

"Poland? I thought you said you were from France?"

"Well, I was. My parents died, and my sister and I were raised by my Aunt Noelle, my mother's sister, who lives in Baranovichi."

Unsatisfied with the answer, Annie continues her probing.

"But why Munich. Why Germany?"

Nervous and fearful to reveal too much, Elenena says carefully, "The 1918 Weimar Republic of Germany paved the way for creative expression in the arts, along with free thinkers developing new theories, like Albert Einstein, already renowned for his many discoveries. The atmosphere throughout Germany is ripe with freedom and that is what I will pursue."

This statement causes no small reaction in Annie.

She glares at Elenena and spits out the words, "The ideal you seek no longer exists here, nor does that soul-rotting gibberish about freedom of expression and the arts. Music is gone, swept away by a greater force. The force is of such magnitude and power, it reclaims the historical legacy that is Germany. Soon enough the world will know that Adolf Hitler is the leader of not only Germany, but all of Europe, and eventually, the world."

As if someone slapped her across the face, Elenena sits numbly, with a blank expression, contemplating the words the woman spoke to her. *The ideal no longer exists. Swept away? Soul-rotting gibberish?*

Annie notices the vacant stare of her guest and goes on prodding.

"Well, what do you have to say for yourself now? Are you a communist?"

Elenena snaps back into the present moment.

"Excuse me, what did you call me, a communist? I am not a communist, I don't even know what that means!" Clearly, this is the time to make her exit. "Thank you for the tea, but I must be going to continue my search."

She gets up from the table—but Annie grabs her by her wrist.

"Wait. Not so fast. We didn't discuss your room and responsibilities."

Elenena pulls her wrist away from Annie, confused. "What do you mean, are you saying I can rent the room?"

"Yes, that is what I'm saying. We will discuss your political views later. For now, your responsibilities will include cooking during the week. I will supply the groceries and tell you what to make. You will keep the front room, dining room, and kitchen clean, dusted and mopped. What you do on weekends is your business. If you play your violin, it must be during the hours that I prescribe. Do we have an agreement?"

Annie sticks her hand out to Elenena, gesturing for her to shake to cement the deal.

Elenena pauses for a moment, confused by the strange behavior of her host.

Annie grows impatient. "Well, do we, or don't we?"

Elenena, feeling bullied into the expected response, shakes her hand and agrees, "Yes, we have a deal."

The creaking stairs off the kitchen lead to her small room two flights up. The walls are as drab as the furniture in the room, but the room is adequate for her needs. There is a window that faces the east from which the sun rises in the morning. The undersized, sparse room is enough for Elenena. On sunny mornings, the light streams through the large window, greeting her as she throws open the window and welcomes the golden rays.

Elenena buys a music stand at a nearby secondhand store, the owner of which sells it to her at a price she can afford, with the little money which was given to her by her aunt.

While her collection of sheet music rests on the stand, she uses the one chair in the room to station her precious violin.

The house is situated in a neighborhood where there are interesting shops and peddlers. Three blocks away is a beautiful, lush, and sprawling park. Munich has several parks, each beautiful, fertile, and well-kept. Germans love their parks, appreciating any opportunity to spend time in them.

Elenena has a spring in her step, grateful and alive within every inch of her being. Her newfound independence and freedom suit her well.

When the weekend arrives, Elenena takes a job working in a small bakery, Schweitzer's, three doors down from the brick rowhouse.

It is on the weekends that the Schweitzers make their famous rye and pumpernickel loaves.

The bakery has large glass windows and a storefront with a counter where a cash register sits. Behind the counter are wooden racks, built and secured at an angle. As soon as the loaves come out of the oven from the production room in back, rye on the right, pumpernickel on the left, they are placed on the wooden racks to cool. Under the racks are cubbyholes for bags in which to put the bread, once purchased. Often the older customers are fussy about which loaf they want. While the loaves are all the same weight and size, some are a smidgen browner than others, depending on the location in the brick-floored ovens where they bake.

The constant aroma of freshly baked bread is intoxicating, the savory smell finding its way out the door, luring passersby inside the storefront.

Elenena takes pride in her duties, working as if the shop is her own. She wipes down the front door, along with the counter where customers receive their goods, and when eight o'clock rolls around, she turns the front sign to "Open."

Waiting on customers is her priority. Her duties are simple, her boss tells her. "Smile and be gracious, thank each customer before they leave." Neither owner minds having a bright and attractive young woman as their representative at the helm of the shop. At times, a stray customer arrives too late, grumbling that the bread is sold out. "Your hours say eight to four, it's

3:00 p.m. now and you're out of bread!" On these occasions, Elenena nods, sympathetically telling the customer, "Please come back again, earlier in the day would be best."

The bakers and owners of the shop, Fritz and Greta Schweitzer, unapologetically believe it is better to run out of bread than to have it left over. Fritz says with regularity, "Leave them begging for more!"

Elenena feels at home in the bakery, surrounded by such luscious aromas, and when the daily breads are baked, the combination of yeast, flour, malt syrup, and salted water tantalizes her nose, bringing back fond memories of the rectangular cramped kitchen in the Laurent Paris flat. She can still envision her mother kneading the dough on the small wooden kitchen table, rolling out baguettes, braiding the rich egg dough into challah.

Bread always arouses the memories of her childhood, some of which are good memories, but more often than not, her mind becomes stuck, like a tire in mud, on the most painful recollections. There is one memory in particular that Elenena cannot seem to resolve—what happened after Elenena and Marcella Laurent lost their father, Giles.

Giles Laurent, a brave Frenchman, died in battle fighting in a garrison of French soldiers in the Ouaddai War in 1910. Mabelle, the girls' mother, never got over the loss, dying a few years later from a heart crushed and broken, overflowing with wasted dreams of what could never be. She took her own life one night, jumping from a tall bridge into a ravine two hundred feet below. Mabelle picked the location so that her daughters would never have to view her dead body, a vision that would be impossible to erase from their memory. They were old enough to survive, and young enough to grow past the loss. Regardless, the girls always held their heartbreak inside.

Their mother kept a family secret. Her first child, a daughter, born before the birth of Marcella and Elenena, was given away at birth to Giles's childless aunt and uncle.

The only other person aware of this secret is Mabelle's sister, Noelle.

Weeks after the fateful event, Elenena, ashen and grief-stricken, told her sister, "Mama did what she thought was best."

Marcella, two years her senior, couldn't agree with such thinking.

"How can you say that? We are the ones left behind. We have no parents—how will we live, how will we go on, how can we ever be happy?"

"We will find a way."

After Mabelle died, because the girls were minors, French authorities sent them to live with their next of kin, Mabelle's sister Noelle, in Poland.

The girls were sent by train to Baranovichi, a small Polish border town in the eastern part of the country, with Russia to the east.

It was there that Elenena found the violin to be her instrument of choice. She basked in the peace discovered by submerging her entire being into her playing. Her aunt scheduled musical instruction and lessons for each of the girls—Marcella piano, Elenena violin. The two would put on concerts for members and friends at the small synagogue they attended. This supplied some semblance of structure for the girls.

Elenena's older sister Marcella was bossy and stubborn. Aunt Noelle explained to Elenena why her sister behaved the way she did: "When we suffer great loss, or a broken relationship where no healing has occurred, we feel the need to try and control everything and everyone around us, and your sister is an example of this."

Elenena countered, "But I do not feel that need, is this true for everyone who suffers loss? We suffer all kinds of loss at one time or another in life. No one seems exempt from such things."

Noelle agreed, telling her, "I believe your tender heart leads you along, as you see truth beneath the very surface of reality. There are many who do not draw such conclusions until they are old and gray-headed!"

Hugging her aunt, Elenena found solace in the words she heard: "Keep your dreams until you find a space big enough to release them, and let them fly, let them carry you to fulfill what you desire. All things are possible to those who believe."

Elenena snaps out of her trip backward in time, realizing it's time to turn the sign at the bakery and close the front of the shop. After performing her duties, the Schweitzers pay Elenena a frugal wage, along with a loaf of the prized bread from the first batch of the day for her to take home on Sunday afternoons when the bakery closes.

Along the journey home, she carries her treasured loaf as if it is a baby, cradled in her arms. The fresh bread is one of the highlights of her week. She arrives home ready to share the bounty of a loaf with her landlord, when they sit down to Sunday supper.

Elenena doesn't think it odd nor give much thought to the fact that she's the only tenant out of five allowed to partake in a meal with the landlord. She believes it's solely due to the cooking and cleaning she does for Annie.

One night, over the simple evening meal of vegetable soup and fresh baked bread, Annie suggests to Elenena, "Why don't you try your hand at baking bread? The oven is true, I've had it calibrated, you can make whatever kind you like. I'll provide the ingredients, as usual."

Elenena, loving a challenge, responds, "It would be a pleasure and I would love to make my mother's challah."

"What is challah?"

"It's a dough enriched with eggs that is braided and baked in a hot oven. The eggs help the dough to rise and create light, airy bread, vastly different from heavy German rye bread."

"Eggs are expensive, but I have a friend who raises chickens. Perhaps I can barter for the eggs. If you make an extra loaf of this challah in return, I'm sure Martin will be willing to exchange eggs for bread."

Annie changes the conversation and asks Elenena about her political convictions.

Not sure how to answer, Elenena decides to play it safe and tells her, "I'm still formulating mine. I've not engaged in such discussions; my music takes up my spare time. I'm not familiar with the issues, perhaps you can fill me in?"

Annie appears pleased. She speaks with passion about the political group she belongs to that has lofty goals and dreams for a different Germany.

Annie espouses the views of the group, telling Elenena, "There is a local affiliated group that meets on Saturday mornings." Annie asks Elenena to attend, but due to her work in the bakery, she cannot. She tells Elenena about a book she's reading Mein Kampf by Adolf Hitler, the leader of the Nazi party. Elenena recognizes the title from seeing it on a table in the small sitting room at the front of the house, next to the chair where Annie sits to read.

"You should read the book when I'm finished," Annie says, "although I may just read it two or three times."

Elenena has yet to share with her landlord that she's Jewish, trusting her gut instinct because anti-Semitism is present in Munich. The animus stems from the successes Jews have in the banking industry, stock market, and medicine, as well as other professions. Elenena knows the history of her people, that good things occur for those who are willing to work hard and do what it takes to achieve aspirations and goals. She also knows of persecution, centuries of poverty, imprisonment, and slavery. Elenena is aware that the Germans erroneously blame their tactical failures and the economic collapse of the Great War on the Jewish people of Europe.

After Sunday supper, with dishes washed and chores completed, Elenena takes out her violin to practice and play. Knowing Annie will be pleased, she prepares to play a composition by Ludwig van Beethoven after a few minutes of tuning.

"I will play something special for you, a sonata from one of your countrymen!"

With haste, Annie turns off the brighter lights in the sitting room, and lights the candelabra, two simple brass stands holding three candles each.

The candlelight illuminates Elenena's features, while supplying light for her to read the sheet music on the stand. Feeling self-conscious, she avoids making eye contact with Annie, who studies her face, her body, with scrutiny. She can feel Annie's eyes on her, glancing up and down while she performs.

As she completes the piece, Annie responds with clapping. Elenena offers: "Next time, I can play for the other residents in your house as well!"

Annie quashes the notion at once.

"No, I don't think so, I enjoy the privacy. I like having my own private concert."

Feeling awkward, Elenena uses the moment to escape the uncomfortable atmosphere caused by the unwelcome attention Annie creates. She bids her landlord goodnight before another word is said.

There is something about Annie and the way she gazes at Elenena that causes her to feel ill at ease, but she doesn't give it much thought, attributing the attention to loneliness. Elenena is the only tenant in the house that has direct and regular contact with Annie. She is also the only tenant that uses the kitchen to cook.

Elenena runs up the wooden stairs, two flights to her room, and flings open the door. Once inside, she takes a small towel out of the violin case and dusts off her violin, removing any fingerprints. Then she lightly kisses the scroll, places the violin back in its case, and bids her instrument goodnight, resting it on the chair. "Goodnight sweet friend, until tomorrow."

On Sunday evenings her routine includes writing her sister and her aunt.

I must write a positive letter, speak of all the good things happening in my world. But her mind will not allow her to let go of something that's troubled her since first arriving in Munich. She has yet to speak of it, but the thoughts swirl around, nagging at her conscience. *The reason I chose Munich originally was because of the Weimar Republic and all the freedom of artistic expression. Annie says the ideal no longer exists, calling it soul-rotting gibberish. And what is this powerful force that will take over Germany, Europe, and the world? Should I ask the Schweitzers first? Is it true what Annie says?*

Would Aunt Noelle know about this Hitler and his Nazi party? *Should I ask her, or should I share with her the things Annie told me? No, no. It will only cause her distress and give Marcella opportunity to gloat, that there is a problem already. I won't mention it for now.*

She sits down on her bed, the springs creaking with each movement. "Quiet, bed."

Taking out a piece of paper and her favorite fountain pen, she writes, practicing her best penmanship.

Dear Marcella and Aunt Noelle,

I hope this letter finds you both doing fine.

Life in Munich is lovely, there is much to enjoy. Just this past week I strolled through one of the parks, the one closest to the house, three blocks away from where I live. I brought my violin, prepared to play in the outdoors, which suits me. I adore filling the air with beautiful music. While playing, a kind man approached me, a Jewish man named Stanislaw Birnbaum. I am told by my landlord that Professor Birnbaum is an excellent violin instructor, teaching in both Berlin and Munich. He believes he can be of help to me and aid me in my quest to instruct.

Professor Birnbaum has a pedigree, having studied in Vienna. We had a marvelous conversation and I found him to be like-minded, having a love of music, art, and literature. I will see him again; he will come to the house next week to give me my first lesson Sunday evening.

I'm working on weekends at a bakery. The aroma of baking bread takes me back to our Paris home, with memories of watching Momma make bread. I'm going to try my hand at baking; my landlord has encouraged me to do so. Would Aunt Noelle have Momma's challah recipe? I want to make that first. I would be happy with any recipes she has for bread-making or cooking. Would you think about coming to visit me? I miss you.

Please write. My love to you, Elenena

CHAPTER NINE

Buster and Maddie

AUGUST 1933

IWALK DIRECTLY TO my room, as the sunshine and the exuberant noise of the parade have become overbearing for me, causing me to feel ill. Combine that with my worry over Wolfie and you have a recipe for malaise. Troop Leader Lewis hesitated to let me go, but I persuaded him—not before he told me one more time not to wander off anywhere. I decide to go to my room to rest. I wonder about the calls my dad spoke of—who is he calling?

Once back in my room, I lie down on one of the beds, thinking if I sleep, I might feel better, but sleep seems impossible. Surveying the colorless walls, the shoddy furniture, and the drab color of the bedspread, I consider my room. Is it really this lifeless, or is it how I feel? My mind races, and I go over the distressing event in my mind, which refuses to slow down regardless of my efforts to control my thinking. I'm nauseated with worry. Could Wolfie's father be home from work? I have the address, could it be possible to return to the scene of the crime?

Troop Leader Lewis already told me no, we would not go back, and for the life of me I cannot understand why. Wolfie could be inside the house, or in a hospital recovering. Perhaps his father, home from work, knows something. I begged, but he gave me his answer with no hesitation, a flat, "No, we will not return, we have a schedule to follow."

I'm lying on the bed, trying to conjure an alternative way to get to Wolfie's house, when I hear someone cough. That's strange—the sound seems like it came from this room, but I'm the only one here.

Standing up, I go to the door, thinking someone must be in the hallway outside. I open it to find no one.

As I return to my bed, I notice a piece of material, feminine like lace, and I walk over to see what it is, bending down to pick it up. When I do, I find it's attached to something.

I get down on my hands and knees, lifting the bedspread to peer under the bed. What I thought was some stray piece of material is not. It's attached to a skirt worn by a girl under my bed!

Our eyes meet. She squints at me, and we stare at each other for a few moments before I come out of shock, and ask the girl, "Who are you?"

After more moments of staring, it occurs to me the girl may not speak English, so I ask her, "Do you speak English?"

"Yes."

While surprised at my findings, I feel no fear. I'm not afraid of her, and it seems, nor she of me. "Please, I won't hurt you, please come out from there. My name is Buster."

She speaks, "What is the uniform you wear, are you a Hitler Youth?"

"No, I'm a Boy Scout from the United States."

Suddenly, there's a knock on the door outside, and the young woman puts her finger to her lips, giving me the sign for, "Shhh, be quiet." I tell her, "It's okay, stay where you are for now."

I answer the door and feel relieved to find it's my dad.

"Son, Leader Lewis said you were ill, how are you feeling?"

My dad is an imposing figure at six-foot-two. At forty-one, he's slender and fit. The signs of aging and gravity that affect most men with a telltale middle spare tire or a drooping middle have not befallen my dad. His hair has yet to show any gray. He is what most women would call dashing. Women always smile at him, their eyes traveling from the top of his head down to his shoes. If he notices this, he pays little attention.

"Yeah, I'm okay. It was just so hot outside and with all the noise, made me feel sick."

"And Wolfie?"

"Yes, and Wolfie. Where have you been?"

"Making phone calls. But with no luck yet."

Dad says he made a phone call to the U.S. Consulate in Berlin, to his friend, Ambassador William Dodd, whom he works with in the United States State Department. My dad is a lawyer, employed as the State Department's legal counsel, reviewing and giving his opinion on policies and agreements with other countries. Dad is fluent in three languages, making him a valuable legal resource. He speaks French and German, along with English.

"Ambassador Todd said because Wolfie is a German citizen, he cannot interfere unless Wolfie's life is in danger, and he needs advocacy since he's a minor."

"It seems pretty obvious to me that his life is in danger, wouldn't you say?"

"Yes, of course, and I told the ambassador what happened. Wolfie's next of kin is his legal guardian, who would be his father. He is the only one who can advocate for Wolfie."

Distress must envelop my face, as I see my dad's eyes fill with compassion for me. He tells me, "Let's not give up just yet, okay? I went back to the crime scene only to find no one home. I asked the woman who lives next door to the Wolfermans if she saw what took place, or if she knows when Mr. Wolferman comes home from work."

I sit expectantly, feeling a glimmer of hope rise within me, expecting my dad to say something encouraging. I'm waiting for a good word, something positive to tumble forth, but instead, he grimaces, as if what he has to tell will crush me.

"The neighbor told me he left in a suit and tie well over ten days, maybe two weeks ago and has not returned since."

My nausea returns full force. If I had more food in my stomach, I would surely vomit right there on the dull and scuffed wooden floor.

Discouraged and weak, my energy sapped, I ask, barely audible, "What now?"

"Well, there is some hope. The ambassador made a call to a camp outside of Munich called Dachau. He's waiting for a return call. It's a labor camp—he called it a *concentration camp*—where the government and police, authorities, and such take criminals—"

I interrupt with an objection. "Wolfie's not a criminal!"

"I know, son, settle down and let me finish. Petty criminals, those that break any laws, no matter how minor, are taken there. There's a good chance Wolfie may be there for transgressing some law. There is a mandatory enlistment in the Hitler Youth—"

I interrupt again, "Yes, yes, Dad, that's right, Wolfie told me about it. Would the police beat him to a pulp over such a small offense?"

"The ambassador thinks they might, telling me this SS group is big into making examples out of their citizens, even for the smallest offense. Brutality and intimidation are the tools they use, and with abandon, the damn fascists."

A female voice enters the conversation, "Yes, that's true."

The strange and hidden voice surprises Dad, who asks, "Who said that?" He glances at me and I shrug while I point under the bed. With the deftness of a cat, he's on his hands and knees in a split second, lifting up the bed ruffle off the floor, exposing the commentator. Dad's voice bellows, "Come out from there! Who are you and what are you doing?"

Immediately, he turns his eyes back to me, piercing through me, asking with suspicion, "Did you have anything to do with this, this girl, why is she under your bed?"

I feel impaled by his tone and the expression on his face. It's rare for my dad to use such a sharp and severe tone with me.

"You'll have to ask her that, I'm as puzzled as you are!"

The girl crawls out from under the bed, standing quickly, her hands straightening her rumpled silk skirt and blouse, smoothing her hair into place. She stands before us, inspecting us as we do her, all of us feeling collectively awkward. She must feel some amount of fear, now that's she's been found out, like a stowaway on a ship. She has a scowl on her face, and I try to make eye contact with her, to smile, and let her know we won't hurt her or cause trouble.

I forget my manners, but Dad does not, pulling a chair over from the wall. "Please, Miss, please sit." Dad assesses and sums up the situation quickly, "Are you in trouble of some sort, is that why you're hiding?"

As though a dam is breaking from the pressure of too much water behind it, the force causes the water to cascade over the walls. The tears flow readily in great supply from Maddie's eyes. As if embarrassed by her outpouring of emotion, she covers her face with her hands as she weeps. She stands there, like a beautiful statue, crying, not moving, still as a stone.

Taking out his handkerchief from his pocket, Dad hands it to her and puts his hand on her shoulder. He makes his best attempt to comfort her while I squirm in my chair, thoroughly unaccustomed to seeing such an intense display of emotions and feelings, especially by a young woman. I've only witnessed my mom crying.

My dad makes his best effort to alleviate this stranger's grief. "Now, now, it can't be all that bad, would you like to talk about it?"

"It is all that bad!"

"Why don't you tell us what's wrong, perhaps we can help?"

Dad's display of compassion brings thoughts of my mom to the surface of my mind. I recall how he would hold her when she cried as she received one gloomy medical diagnosis after another. I haven't seen this depth of compassion in my dad since then. My assessment leads me to believe that it's only present and visible with women in distress. I hope I have some of that in me, as I consider it an honorable attribute. But for now, I'd rather run out of the room. I feel like an intruder and altogether uncomfortable.

"Let me introduce us first. I'm Raymond Wellington, and this is my son, Buster. How do you do Miss—"

"Turetzky, Maddie Turetzky." She extends her hand to meet Dad's and they shake. Then she reaches for mine, and I wonder if she feels how clammy my hand is as we make polite gestures.

"That's a start, Miss Turetzky. Tell me, now, what happened, why the tears, why you're hiding. Tell me everything if you wish. Perhaps we can help?"

"I don't think you can."

"Ah, you don't trust us, do you?"

With a cautionary tone and downcast eyes, she says, "No, I don't know you. How do I know you're not working with the Gestapo?"

I almost jump out of my skin, close to falling off my chair. I state the obvious. "Dad, she knows about this Gestapo!"

Maddie has a confused expression on her face as I turn to tell her, "We're trying to find my best friend. We saw these

Gestapo people beat the living daylights out of him this morning. We don't know where he is, or if he's even alive."

A tender look of compassion traverses Maddie's china-blue eyes, and she reaches out to pat my hand. "Oh, my, what a woeful, horrible event to witness, I'm so sorry for you and your friend."

Her touch, her hand on mine, sets off an electrical charge inside of me. It is at that precise moment I feel my heart swoon, *she is so beautiful.* I almost choke on my saliva, nodding at her as if to say, "Thank you," but no words come out. *I'm utterly taken with her. Captured is more like it. Water. I need water.*

Tentatively and with trepidation, Maddie begins to tell us her story. She speaks of the concert, where the trouble began. She tells of the Brownshirts who chased her.

"I've been on the run from them for two days, going on three now. I don't know what's happened to my professor, my dear friend Stanislaw Birnbaum. I'm afraid the SS took him away, somewhere."

Pondering Maddie's words, Raymond adds, "Perhaps this SS took your friend to the same place where Wolfie may be held. And, come to think of it, those Brownshirts are always nosing around in the lobby. Could they suspect you're here, in the hotel?"

"I would expect them to come searching for me. Along with the Gestapo, they don't like appearing foolish, and they have nothing better to do than cause trouble. The hotel would be as good a place as any to hide. I can't go back to my professor's home, as the SS more than likely has his address. I'd walk into a trap there."

I must ask. "Maddie, I don't fully understand. Why are these people after you, what have you done that would make them come after you?"

"They singled me out at the concert for a reason. They think I'm a communist from Poland, an instigator of some kind, because I'm here living in Germany. I'm under the tutelage of my professor. At the end of the concert, a public event, each attendee had to show identification including their address, as a result of a new law put into place by the Gestapo to single out a certain group of people. Because I'm not eighteen, I'm not required to have identification. We told them this. But they didn't believe me. They were ready to take me into custody when I made a run for it. My running away must have convinced them that I have to be a communist. The Germans hate the communists. They blame them for the Reichstag fire in March. Since the fire, the Gestapo and the Nazis have unleashed a widespread campaign of violence against the Communist Party. But I am not a part or member of that party."

I pose the question, "But you're a young girl, how could they think such a thing?"

Maddie pauses, with Dad and I on the edge of our seats as we listen to this incredible story, waiting to hear what she'll say next, never having heard of such crazy behavior by the so-called police.

Her voice changes, and she speaks in a whisper, as if by speaking louder it will give validity to what's she's about to say. "There's something else, you see, the plan of this man Hitler, the Chancellor of Germany. He embraces an ideology he's made known since the first day he took office. He has these ideas about racial purity and has a diabolical plan to address what he calls 'issues in need of solutions.'

"His goal is to rid Germany of anyone who doesn't fit the profile of an 'Aryan' by tracking them. That's the reason behind asking for identification, including the collection of names and addresses. His plan is to murder, annihilate a group of people he carries a deep-seated hatred for, even more than he has for the communists. And when I say kill a group, I'm not speaking of a few, or one hundred, I'm talking about millions of people. I fit into that category, this classification of people."

Both Dad and I must appear perplexed, because before we can respond with questions as to why, her answer comes forth. Maddie stammers for a moment. Her words are cautious, laced with anxiety and tension, her eyes flash with fear.

"Hitler hates Jews. He wants to kill every Jew. And I am Jewish."

CHAPTER TEN

Wolfie and Frederick

AUGUST 1933, WOLFIE

I AWAKEN IN WHAT I imagine to be a transport truck, basing this conclusion upon the proximity of other people in the vehicle, who are sitting so close together that only a breath exists between me and the person seated to my right or left. Even if I cannot see them, I feel them.

We sit on a bench that lines both sides of the vehicle. No one speaks. There are windows in the back of the vehicle that supply light, albeit a small amount. I see the feet of those sitting next to me and on the other side of the truck. Some have shoes, some don't. There is a pungent smell in the air, yet I can't say what's causing it, nor can I name its source. I hear the engine of the vehicle wheeze and grind as the gears shift.

Our destination is not known to me as I dare not ask a question, afraid of the answer.

I cannot recall the turn of events that came after boarding a bus with my American friends. That is my last clear memory. *Have days passed since then?* I do not know. Touching my face brings a strange feeling to my fingertips, along with painful tenderness.

The oozy substance I feel is my blood, which is confirmed by examining my fingers with my other hand.

My body has many areas of shooting spasms. I reach to touch a few of the places where the pain emanates, feeling more blood. I lift my head, which would under normal circumstances be a mindless endeavor, but now causes searing pain.

I cannot see straight, and it takes me more than a moment to comprehend that my left eye cannot open—the mere touch of my probing fingers causes distress.

Holding my head up is ache-inducing, so I let my head drop back to the former position. *Ah, yes, that's better.*

The momentary relief lasts only until the vehicle rolls over a bumpy road, causing me to bounce in my seat, and my agony to reach a crescendo. I cannot recall a time in my life when I hurt and ached as much as I do now.

The vehicle begins to slow down. As it does, I hear a man shouting. His voice sounds shaky.

A hand grabs my arm and drags me to my feet. I stand but not for long, as I crumble under my weight, my legs refusing to support my body. The voice grows louder now, as it is in close proximity to me, but what's said is indiscernible. Now two hands grab me, one on each side, and I feel a scorching ache in both my arms. The hands drag me off the vehicle, and the bright light, which must be daylight, blinds me. I feel myself collapse.

I awaken to someone yelling at me, close to my face, but I cannot respond.

I'm lying down on what feels like a flat surface, but I cannot tell if it's wood or concrete. Without notice, I'm drenched in cold liquid, *water?* Perhaps. I feel it cover me when I notice I'm without clothing. Everything feels like one woozy experience to the next, and I'm not sure if I'm dreaming or if these events are actually taking place.

On both sides of me, I feel people, perhaps two, maneuver me to sit on what feels like a bench. These people work on clothing me.

The hands lift my limbs, pulling pants up to the top of my thighs, while pulling something like a shirt over my head.

I feel shoes go on my feet. I feel sharp smarting everywhere. A hand touches the back of my head while someone puts a cup to my lips, and a voice tells me to drink. It must be water.

The voice tells me to eat, and something akin to bread is placed in my mouth. I begin to chew, but not without more throbbing aches alerting me that my teeth hurt.

Then something stabs my arm, like a needle. Next time I awake, I feel slightly more alert but still feel some confusion. I'm on a flat surface and gingerly, I sit up. I bump my head, realizing I must bend my neck to avoid banging my head again.

There is not a single familiar sight. I'm in some sort of housing; there are bunk-type platforms around me. Everything appears gray.

A voice breaks into my internal conversation and says, "Good, you're awake, can you stand?"

"I don't think so, but let me try."

My mind feels as though the fog has lifted. My body still aches, with a pulsing, thud-like torment that keeps rhythm with my heartbeat.

When asked my name and where I live, I must take a moment to think, concentrating on standing first. My feet planted on the ground, I lift my body, holding onto the post of the bunk platform. I stand up and take a laborious, deep breath. When asked how I feel, I tell the questioner, "I ache all over."

The man asking the questions suggests to another man, "Perhaps another shot of Eukodal is in order."

"Let's wait and see if he can answer questions. Commandant expects us to record his information first."

The man asks me my name, once more.

"My name is Wolfie."

"Can you tell me your full name, and where you live?"

"Very strange, I can't remember."

"How old are you and what is your date of birth?"

"I don't know. Can you tell me what day it is, and the time?"

"Yes, it's August 18, 1933, and the time is 4:00 p.m."

"I cannot remember how I got here, what happened, do you know?"

"No, I do not have that information."

"Can you tell me where I am, at least?"

"Yes, you're in Dachau."

"What is Dachau?"

"It's a concentration camp."

FREDERICK

It's a late summer day, the sun waning in the August sky, but the heat and humidity coalesce inside the garage, like a low-hanging ceiling of cloud cover. The camp's garage is one of the newer buildings in Dachau. A kapo tells Frederick the Nazis will use the prisoners to build an even larger garage in the future. Frederick knows today is August 18, the day Wolfie comes home from the Jamboree. *What will he do? He won't have any idea where I am. He'll call Rolf—Rolf will help him.*

There are four bays in the garage, into which you can drive a car or a truck, steering it over a hydraulic lift. The doors to each bay, which can be rolled up or down, are suspended on a rail.

While the garage has its benefits in cold and inclement weather, there is a downside as well. Due to its low ceilings, the building holds the heat and moisture even with all four bay doors open.

Frederick finishes the oil change on Camp Commandant Eicke's vehicle: a Mercedes-Benz SSK sports car, a two-door roadster with darkened windows, an engine powered by a supercharged SOCH 16, four-speed, non-synchro, manual. The vehicle is a showpiece, and fast. The torque ratio gives the valves higher engine-power output.

Wiping the sweat from his brow and the grease from his hands on a raggedy cloth, Frederick stands back from the car, snapping down the hood of the vehicle. He awaits Commandant Eicke's arrival. Eicke shows up moments later.

Theodor Eicke, the second commandant of Dachau, took an immediate liking to Frederick. He comes to the garage himself instead of sending an aide to pick up the car. Eicke is fascinated with the Führer's many autos, making a beeline for the garage whenever given notification on the arrival of one from the stable of vehicles sent to Dachau for repair. Eicke knows Frederick is quickly gaining a mechanic's reputation of the highest order. Even Berlin knows they have an excellent mechanic in Frederick. The commandant takes credit for any compliment thrown his way from Berlin, even when they're not meant for him personally.

Eicke is fond of trying to impress Frederick with his knowledge of his vehicle's sublime engine function. The other prisoners in the vicinity of the garage, laboring with the rocks, notice the commandant's trips to the garage. They take note that Frederick has become a 'favorite' of Eicke's. They assume it's mostly because he's German.

The commandant can be very personable with German prisoners whom he deems worthy of his attention. But with regard to the Jews, Eicke is hateful and his behavior completely different than with his countrymen. He is viciously brutal, encouraging beatings, with no conscience regarding prisoner abuse.

Eicke lovingly pats the side panel of the auto, smiling lovingly at the car. He says, chuckling, "In fourth gear, with raised torque, the engine snaps to attention in overdrive, and your head jerks back at the thrust of power!"

Frederick smiles, pretending to be impressed. He laughs along with the overweight officer of the Reich and watches as Eicke tugs uncomfortably at his collar. *Too much strudel and beer. How does he fit behind the wheel?*

"Herr Commandant, I will tell you, the fuel line has a tiny crack, and it's leaking a minimal amount of fuel, just a drop here and there, nothing to worry about. I've ordered the part, it will come from Berlin next week. This part takes longer than usual because it is a specific piece that must come directly from Mercedes, a substitute will not do. When the part arrives, I'll notify your aide your car is ready for repair and replace the part."

Frederick silently wishes the leak would cause an explosion while the commandant is driving.

Eicke considers the mechanic's words. Holding the keys Frederick placed in his hand just moments earlier, Eicke dangles them in front of Frederick's face. He offers them to Frederick as a parent would to an infant. Eicke seems to be under the impression he's tempting Frederick, that he'll jump at the chance to drive his car, a Mercedes! He nods at the automobile, "Take her for a spin around the camp if you wish!"

Not knowing if the offer is a trap or a test, Frederick refuses, but with gratitude.

"Thank you, Herr Commandant, but I should get back to work. I have several vehicles to attend to, but I am grateful for your offer."

Eicke sizes up his prisoner, further baiting him. "Well, once we get you a helper, perhaps you'll have more time, and

THE ROAD WE TOOK

can drive with me as the passenger. I'll show you just how powerful this engine is—seeing is believing!"

"Yes, Herr Commandant. I will enjoy that very much, thank you."

Eicke becomes serious, wrinkling his brow, raising a foot to rest on the bumper of the car, posing what he must think to be a profound question. "Tell me, do you enjoy driving as much as you do tinkering with auto engines?"

Frederick thinks about Eicke's statement, indicating that the commandant knows he's promised a helper. *Could one come after all? Tinkering? Is that what he thinks I'm doing? Tinkering? What a moron.*

"Yes, Herr Commandant, I do enjoy driving very much. I love to drive fast. I would be a race car driver in another life. But I'd also leave time to tinker with auto engines." *Asshole.*

Eicke informs Frederick, "Mercedes competes in The Grand Prix Motor Racing with the Silver Arrows. They are the best racing team in the world! Too bad you're a prisoner here. The Team could use someone like you." Staring with a far-off gleam in his eye, Eicke tells Frederick, "I'll have to mention it to the powers that be. Perhaps one day you could be a part of that team!"

Frederick knows not to get his hopes up, giving a perfunctory, "Yes, sir. Thank you."

"Good. Right. Well. Back to work!"

Eicke turns on the heels of his spit-polished jackboots and climbs into the auto, driving it out of the garage. Frederick watches as the exhaust from the muffler pummels the air in its path, leaving a gray trail of noxious fumes.

The kapo in charge of the garage, Henrik Merkel, disturbs his train of thought.

"Frederick, I've been told your helper will be here shortly. Put him to work as soon as possible. The Reich will deliver twelve trucks and two automobiles, one of which will be the Führer's Mercedes, while the other belongs to Göring," he says, referencing Hitler's henchman. "All of the vehicles will need servicing, engine tuning, along with tire and oil changes. Once serviced, they need to be ready to go the next day, leaving enough time for traveling to Nuremberg for the big rally, which starts at the end of the week. You may need to work all night to finish—whatever it takes."

"Yes, sir."

Merkel pivots and leaves the garage. Frederick mulls over his orders. *Easy for you to say, 'whatever it takes.'*

Moments later, Frederick sees Merkel taking a prisoner into custody from another kapo, pointing to the garage.

Frederick decides to take a break and have a cigarette. As he does, he watches the prisoner Merkel spoke with moments before. Lighting a cigarette, he takes a long drag and puts the pack back into the pocket of his greasy camp uniform along with his matches. As he watches, he stands up straight, not believing his eyes.

The prisoner is his son.

What is my son doing here in this evil place? Thank God, at least he's here with me, I can protect him.

And in that moment Frederick considers, *could there really be a God?*

He talks to himself. *Be calm, Frederick, whatever you do, do not arouse any suspicion, and take it slow. Don't run up to him, let him walk to the garage.*

As Wolfie comes closer to the garage, Frederick can see something is visibly wrong with his son. Wolfie is limping, and his face appears horribly bruised, with one eye closed.

Frederick watches as Wolfie glances up at him as he approaches the garage. Frederick appraises the area around them, spying other prisoners milling about along with an occasional kapo. Gazing directly at his son, he brings his index finger to his lips as if to say, "Shhh."

Just as Wolfie walks closer to the garage, the prisoner who carries the rocks to the wall, naked and shoeless, walks past him. He stops and puts the pail down, turning to face Wolfie.

Wolfie would rather run into his father's waiting arms, but from the signal he gave, that might not be the best thing to do. Besides, he couldn't run if his life depended on it.

Wolfie doesn't want to waste time talking, since his father was standing and waiting for him, but out of respect and shock, he can't ignore the poor naked man. His mother would expect him to stop and talk, show respect, and be polite.

Good manners meant something to her. "They show we are civilized and care about the person before us."

He can still hear her words; no matter how faint they sound.

The naked man addresses Wolfie.

"Oh, my, what happened to you? Don't tell me, I know—those bastards. My name is Stanislaw. Tell me your name."

"My name is Wolfie, sir."

"Wolfie, I'm pleased to meet you, but I'm perplexed. You're young; why are you here?"

"I'm not sure."

"Did those animals hit you in the head?"

"They must have. My head hurts, and I ache all over."

"From the sight of you, it's no wonder. God bless you. I must get back to my duties. We can speak more at another time. Goodbye, Wolfie."

Frederick has tears running down his face, which he wipes with his arm. He longs to embrace his son. There is so much he wants to say. *Will he forgive me for failing to sign him up for Hitlerjugend and putting us both in this horrible situation?* Feeling racked with guilt, Frederick maneuvers to get his feelings in check. The last thing he wants is for anyone to know Wolfie is his son.

Wolfie hobbles to reach Frederick. Both stand there in awkward silence, each one desiring to unburden their heart and mind and ask for forgiveness, but not exactly sure where to begin.

"Wipe your tears, son, we are together, notwithstanding in this hellhole."

Frederick tries his best to suppress his emotions. Then the guilt within takes hold, overcoming him. He cannot withhold his own tears. The words pour out of his mouth, rolling quickly, like a fast-moving current of water.

"My God, Wolfie. I'm so sorry. I've brought this trouble upon our heads. Will you ever forgive me? I'm so sorry, son. I don't know what to say. I can thank God we're together despite our present surroundings. Do you forgive me, can you forgive me? Can you believe we are together? It's a miracle. Here we are. Please, son, please forgive me."

"Yes, Poppa, of course, I do. But this is my fault we're here. We should have asked you first if I could attend the Jamboree with my new American friends, but Uncle Rolf and Aunt Cecile saw the opportunity and thought, why not? What would be the harm? Little did we know. A world of trouble for one small choice. It's just as much my fault. I'm learning, for every choice, there is a consequence, for good or for bad."

Frederick has nothing but compassion for his only son. "How I wish I could hug you right now. There is much to say, but we must be careful and not let on. Do they know your full name, the guards or the kapos?"

"No. When they brought me in I was woozy and couldn't answer any of the questions. I only told them 'Wolfie,' no last name or address."

"Okay, that's good, because some kapos won't like it, and I can guarantee other prisoners will be equally angry. They'll think it's favoritism, and they frown upon that, they'll mistreat you as a result. We don't need more cruel treatment. We will find time to catch up, but we have to be extremely careful, okay?"

Wolfie readily nods in agreement.

"First things first, do you know your barracks number?"

Wolfie shakes his head no.

"No matter, mine is ten."

Frederick grimaces, checking around, seeing if anyone is close by who could eavesdrop on the conversation.

"Okay. We don't have a lot of time now, but we will talk. I'm afraid the kapo will come back and question why we haven't begun working. I don't want to give him any reason at all to separate us. At least, this way, working together, I can watch out for you and keep you safe. First off, don't question a kapo. Agree with everything they do or say even if you don't. Keep to yourself. Tell me, what did the naked man say to you?"

"Is he always naked? I didn't know what to think. He introduced himself to me; he wondered what I'm doing here. His name is Stani-something."

"Yes, he arrived two or three days ago. The guards bully and beat him; he's undoubtedly Jewish. The guards terrorize the Jewish prisoners, encouraged to do so by Camp Commandant Eicke. He will do his part to eliminate as many Jews as he can. His hatred of Jews is renowned here. Try and keep your distance from the Jewish prisoners; you don't want the guards beating on you for no reason. Now follow me, and I'll show you how our system works here."

Looking at his son, Frederick wonders, *could this be a miracle? I think this may qualify. Now, how do I get us out of here?*

CHAPTER ELEVEN

Raymond, Buster, and Maddie

AUGUST 1933

RAYMOND WELLINGTON NEVER told his son Buster about his long-standing reservations about Troop Leader Lewis. Raymond already had suspicions about Lewis being anti-Semitic. Six months ago, at a monthly Boy Scouts meeting, Lewis offered Raymond a copy of Henry Ford's book, *The International Jew*. He refused it.

Raymond knew about the book and such writings by Ford, pledging never to buy his book or motor cars. The thought occurs to Raymond, *who was Wolfie telling that his mother was Jewish?*

He tells himself, *One battle at a time, Raymond.*

Finding Wellington alone, Lewis confronts him about Wolfie.

"This kid is not our problem, and anyway, I heard him say something yesterday about his mother being Jewish, which makes him a Jew. Who cares what happens to him? He's just another piece of shit. Like all of them, he's a useless, worthless Jew. They're all going to die anyway."

Raymond's indignation and fury rises at the words. Feeling his blood boil, he tightens his fists, putting them up in front of his face just below his chin, telling Lewis, "Say another word, and I'll knock your block off."

"What's the matter, Wellington, are you a Jew-lover?"

"Yes. As a matter of fact, I am. And you are a coward."

Raymond takes a threatening step closer, narrowing his

eyes, ready to punch his adversary's face into another shape. Stepping backward, Lewis tells Raymond, "Remember, I'm in charge here, so don't try anything."

Taking a more relaxed pose and a deep breath, Raymond questions Lewis, "Now let me get this straight—all the concern on the bus, was that for show only? You don't have to answer, I already know what you're going to say. Aren't you the duplicitous bastard?!"

Lewis stands firm, though nervous, and again tries to assert his authority. "We leave here as scheduled for Bremen; our travel visa runs out the day we sail from Bremen. If you plan to come back to the U.S., you and your son had better be on that ship."

Raymond laughs at the threat. "Or what? You'll throw a fit? You are a ridiculous man. It's a good thing you have no children of your own, you'd ruin them! And, while we're having such an intimate conversation, you need to know that I'm aware of your penchant for parlaying crises into power. You'll use this experience of a defenseless boy, beaten to death, to climb your way up the Boy Scouts' corporate ladder. I can hear it now from the headlines in Scouting News, 'Troop leader valiantly shepherds Scouts to safety after an attack by extremist troublemakers.' Your intentions and motivations are obvious, clear to all except you."

Lewis gets defensive. "I don't give a damn about you or what you think or do. Just avoid me, and there will be no problems."

With that, Lewis starts to back up before turning to walk away. His pace is quick, though he glances over his shoulder twice in fear.

Pulling out a pen and pad from his breast pocket, he makes a few notations. *Extend visas if necessary.* Can't forget about that.

Raymond walks with haste to the front of the lobby of the hotel. He spots the three Brownshirts hovering about and is reminded of Maddie. *Poor kid.*

Lewis cannot find out about Maddie. He'll report her, the spiteful bastard.

Raymond approaches the front desk and asks the clerk for a phone to make a call to the U.S. ambassador's residence in Berlin.

The clerk puts the call through. When there is an answer, he hands the phone back to Raymond. "Your call, sir."

"Hello, Bill? Yes, I realize it's a day's journey. The names are Frederick and Wolfie Wolferman of Munich, and Stanislaw Birnbaum, also of Munich. Right. We will expect you tomorrow. I'll explain more when I see you. Thank you. Goodbye."

Hanging up the phone, he hands it back to the clerk and gives him some Deutschmarks for the call.

Back at the room, he explains his plan to get Maddie out of the hotel. "Maddie, we have to sneak you out of here. I've planned it around the time the troop leaves for Bremen. There will be enough confusion, which will buffer us and serve as a distraction. Then, the ambassador will pick us up."

Earnestly Buster asks, "Will we search for Wolfie?"

"That's the plan." Raymond adds as his eyes meet Maddie's, "And Miss Turetzky's friend as well."

Contemplating first Buster's face, then Raymond's, Maddie begins to speak. "Mr. Wellington, you are under no obligation to help me, and honestly, I have no idea why you would."

With the innocence emanating from his sheltered life, Buster asks, "What would you do if we hadn't come along? You couldn't go on hiding. You have no money, no food, nowhere to go, your host is abducted, what would you do?"

With tears in her eyes, Maddie sees the reality for what it is, as Buster drives home the truth. "I would have to surrender to the SS."

"Miss Turetzky, as a representative of the United States State Department, you are now in my custody. I must protect you and ensure your safe passage from here to a point yet to be determined. Any questions? For the time being, we're all staying put in this room. Buster, you gather up the other boys' belongings, I'll plan for them to stay in another room. Meanwhile, don't answer the door, and if perchance one of the boys uses a key, keep the chain lock in place until Maddie can hide. With dinner and the evening activity over, the troop will head back soon for bed check and sleep. Under no circumstances does anyone find out about Maddie, understand? When the boys come back to the room, tell them you're sick with a bug and quarantined, and I'm arranging for another room for them. I'm also going to arrange for dinner. Lock the door behind me, and please, use the chain lock."

Unfortunately, Buster doesn't follow his father's instructions. The door opens, and his roommates Ollie, Bobby, and Jack are standing there, their eyes fixed on Maddie.

At the front desk, Raymond pays for an extra room for Buster's three roommates, telling the clerk his son is sick and doesn't want the other boys to get sick. The clerk nods and receives the money from Raymond. He gives him a room key.

Raymond's next destination is the dining room, where he plans for three dinners, wheeled on a cart to room 125.

On his way through the foyer, Raymond spots Lewis talking with the other two chaperones, Williams and O'Mara, the latter a crony of Lewis's.

As Raymond approaches the men, their voices go silent.

The two chaperones squirm awkwardly, their eyes pointed at the floor.

Raymond barely slows his pace and displays a wicked grin. Walking by, he says, "Buster has come down with a bug. For the safety and health of the other boys, I've quarantined him and made arrangements for the other boys to have a separate room. Sorry I didn't consult you first, boss."

Under his breath, Raymond says, *Go to hell, you bastard.*

Giving Lewis a two-finger salute at the temple, Raymond continues on his way to the room.

He knocks lightly at the door and whispers, "Buster."

Raymond senses trouble the second he sees his son's face. The door opens, and there in the room stand Ollie, Bobby, Jack, and Maddie.

Feeling the fire of anger beginning to rage from within, he swallows, trying to calm his building frustration. *Why didn't he follow instructions? It's obvious he didn't use the chain lock on the door. It's no matter now.*

"Okay, so boys, Miss Turetzky is helping us find Wolfie. She's a friend I found while out searching, who lives near Wolfie."

Taking over where Raymond leaves off, Maddie adds, "That's right, we're school chums. I guess I should be going now, it's getting late and my parents will wonder where I am."

She hesitates, slow to leave, and acts as though she's searching for a coat or a purse.

Raymond says the obvious, even if it is a lie. "Boys, Buster is not feeling well, so I've taken the liberty to arrange for another room for you three. I wouldn't want you to get sick."

Spotting their duffel bags by the door, Raymond points to them and thanks the boys for understanding. He puts the room key in Jack's hand, telling him, "Through the lobby on the other side of the hallway. Rest well, good night!"

Raymond herds the boys out into the hallway with duffel bags in hand. He closes the door and leans on it. Choosing to forego the chiding which under normal circumstances would take place as a consequence of Buster not obeying a direct order, he speaks in a muffled voice, barely above a whisper. "Whew. Well played, Maddie. Now tell me what happened and what you told the boys?"

"I told them she's a friend of Wolfie's. I was stalling for time by asking the boys questions about the rest of the day that I missed, what they did, where they went, when you came in in the nick of time."

"You're sure that's all, right, nothing else was said or talked about?"

"Yes, Dad."

Maddie nods in agreement.

A knock on the door interrupts Raymond. "Ah, dinner is served."

Cautiously, Raymond opens the door partially and thanks the waiter, telling him, "I'll take it from here, thank you."

Once the waiter is sufficiently far down the hallway, Raymond wheels the cart into the room. He takes the stainless steel covers off each plate, and the aroma of cooked food whets the appetite of the three. Pulling up chairs to the table, Raymond motions for Maddie to sit down first. "You're our guest of honor!"

The three sit down at the table to enjoy their meal. For the first time in days, Maddie has food. The first bite of dinner causes her to swallow hard, pushing down the flood of emotions that come tumbling forth.

Her last meal, lunch, was with Stanislaw, two days ago.

She thinks about him, where he is and what's happened to him. *How can I sit here and enjoy a meal when I have no idea what has happened to my friend?*

Her eyes moist with tears, Maddie attempts to focus on her meal.

She takes another bite of her dinner, which is baked chicken with carrots and potatoes.

Maddie pauses. Her feelings of guilt won't allow her to enjoy the food.

"Mr. Wellington, I'm embarrassed. I'm never this emotional. So much has happened in the last two days—I haven't slept, how can I ever—"

Raymond stops her midstream, putting his hand up. "There will be no more of that. If it were my son in your circumstances, I'd pray to God that some kind person would help him. It's what we as Scouts are supposed to do, we pledge to help people."

Ruefully, Raymond considers Troop Leader Jim Lewis. *There is an exception to every rule.*

Maddie still is not convinced, and persists, "Is that all, I mean, is that fully the reason you want to help me?"

Raymond answers quickly, "What, do we have an ulterior motive or the like?"

"That's not exactly what I meant. I mean people do things for certain reasons. I was wondering what would motivate you to display such goodness and kindness to a total stranger."

Taking a deep sigh, Raymond puts his fork and knife down. Meanwhile, Buster is happily plowing into his meal, listening without adding to the conversation. He remains silent while focusing on consuming the delicious food before him.

Maddie also puts down her utensils, keenly aware that she struck a chord in Raymond, based upon the sorrow on his face. Hesitant to speak of such melancholy matters, Raymond determines, *My son is old enough to know the truth.*

It's not that I ever intended to be secretive. It's something we've never discussed, and time has a way of burying the unspoken.

Meeting Maddie has changed that for Raymond. Knowing the persecution she's received because she's Jewish brings even the most obscured and buried memory to the surface for him.

Raymond rubs his eyes. He folds his hands, resting them on the table. Maddie appears to be waiting, as though in anticipation of a great mystery not yet revealed.

Buster puts down his utensils, feeling anxiety at the thought of profound revelations. He squirms in his seat, his eyes downcast.

He asks, "Why do people always have to talk about feelings?"

Raymond smiles at his son's honest reflection, scratching his forehead and running his hand through his hair, as if to jar his memory.

"Son, it's more than feelings. It's more like words spoken, or actions occurring that trigger painful memories. There is a difference."

Buster nods, still full of questions.

Raymond recognizes the fortuity of the moment. With no small effort, over time he's released this painful part of life, while letting go of the memories. Their shadows still remain.

Must he call them back and revisit them?

Passions unexamined and unexplained are often opportunities lost.

CHAPTER TWELVE

Elenena and Annie

SUMMER 1925

D ID YOU SEE the extra eggs on the counter? They're for your special bread. I'm curious, is that a Jewish bread you make, this challah?"

Elenena takes her time walking over to the sink to wash her hands, giving herself a moment to construct an answer. She's not sure if the question Annie asks is a trap.

She ignores the question, commenting instead on the lovely weather.

"Don't you just love summer days like today? The air smells so fresh, the sunshine feels delicious on my face, like a harbinger of good things to come! I feel hopeful with weather like this. Does it do the same for you, Annie?"

Annie gives her boarder a once-over. Tilting her head, she says, "You didn't answer my question."

Elenena decides to go on the offensive and put the question back on Annie. "Why do you ask, and who told you that?"

Not expecting a question in return, Annie continues, "When I asked my friend Martin about the extra eggs, he asked me what they were for, and I told him for your challah. He said, 'It's the bread Jews make.'"

"Oh, that's interesting, I've never heard that before. In Paris, where I grew up, my mother made all kinds of bread. She loved to bake bread, many varieties, it was her specialty."

Somewhat satisfied with the answer, Annie changes the subject.

Elenena feels sickened that she lied about the challah, the bread of her people, but reminds herself, *Self-preservation is as vital as breathing.*

Annie seizes the moment and uses it as an opportunity to proselytize Elenena. "You need to come to a meeting. We're having a special one, Thursday evening, at the Bier Cellar. Adolf Hitler, the leader of the party, will give a speech about Bolshevism. He is a magnificent orator; I think you'll enjoy hearing him speak. He's so passionate and captivating. I could just sit and listen to him for hours on end. He inspires so much hope and courage. He cares about the people of Germany and wants us to experience a better life."

Elenena observes the change in Annie, noting that the color in her cheeks rises to a full blush when she speaks about Hitler. She is curious if Annie feels something resembling romantic passion for this man. *He must be very handsome. She almost swooned when speaking of him.* Elenena thinks about questions to ask Annie about Hitler, but instead allows the moment to pass, deciding to withhold her inquiry. *No sense in stirring the pot, no good would come from it.*

Elenena still has no evidence or idea, any information whatsoever about the party. So, she agrees to attend the meeting for the sake of keeping the peace with her landlady. "Okay, I'll go with you. Tell me again, what is the name of the party?" *I know she told me before, I hope she doesn't rage because I've already forgotten the name.*

"It's the National Socialist German Workers' Party, Nazi Party for short."

Elenena repeats the word.

"Nazi, oh, yes, that's right. I've heard that name before,

one of the customers in the bakery on Saturday was handing out small armbands, calling it 'a gift from the Nazi Party to all members and potential members.' The armband has a black hooked cross on a white disc with a red background."

Beaming with pride, Annie smiles brightly, energized by the conversation. Her voice bubbles with excitement. "Yes, that's called a swastika. That's the symbol of the Nazi Party. The color schemes are the colors of the Imperial flag of Germany, black, white, and red. In ancient Eurasia, several distinct cultures used the swastika, but it was Herr Hitler who developed the emblem used by our party. The meaning of the swastika is to signify 'good fortune.'"

There is an awkward moment of silence between the two women. Annie waits for Elenena to speak, but she doesn't.

Filling up the void of silence, Annie confirms, "Then it's settled, you'll come to the meeting on Thursday." She does not await an answer, promptly leaving the kitchen before Elenena has a chance to change her mind.

The next day, a letter from Marcella arrives for Elenena, along with her mother's challah recipe. She walks into the kitchen to read the letter, sitting down at the small table with two chairs. The kitchen is clean and smells of ammonia, as Elenena washed the windows earlier that day. The sunshine streams in through the windows, making the room warm. The stark walls are softened by the copious sunlight.

Elenena recognizes her aunt's perfect penmanship, so different from the left-handed handwriting of her mother. Penalized as a child for being left-handed, as an adult, her mother wrote with her left hand out of spite. At school, the teachers would chide, "It's the hand of the devil" and force her to use her right hand. Elenena hears her mother's voice as she reads the recipe.

"When preparing to bake bread or cook, always read the recipe two times first, then assemble all your ingredients, then your tools, everything you need before you begin to bake or cook. The French chefs call this preparation your 'mise en place.'"

Oh Momma, how I miss the sound of your voice. You left us too soon. I'll always miss you.

Elenena and Marcella had a complicated relationship with their mother, even from an early age. As small children, the girls, like others their age, would live in their fantasies, creating plays and pretending, as children do. But their mother didn't like make-believe: "Too much fantasy disturbs a child's learning."

"Elenena, are you alright?" Annie interrupts Elenena's walk back through time, entering the kitchen without her noticing.

"What? I'm sorry. Did you say something?"

"Yes, I did. Will the bread be ready for Thursday? Martin will attend the meeting. I will give him his bread then."

"Oh, yes, I'm sorry. Yes, it will be ready in time."

Annie continues to stare at Elenena, boring holes through her as she stares, making Elenena squirm under the scrutiny. After a prolonged moment, Annie gets back to the tasks at hand.

"I've left some carrots and turnips there on the counter, can you turn them into a soup?"

Elenena nods, saying, "I will do my best."

"I have some errands to run, I'll be back later. Dust the front room and wash the foyer floor, and the hallway."

"Yes, of course, I will, and after that, I need to practice."

Elenena practices her violin for two hours every day.

"Your practice time does not concern me. Just finish the chores and make the soup."

Sunday after work will be Elenena's first lesson with Professor Birnbaum. Thoughts of music lift her spirits; she hums a melody as she prepares the ingredients for the soup. *If I put some potatoes in with the carrots and turnips, they'll make for a nice consistency, making it thicker too.*

While the soup cooks, Elenena goes about her task of dusting the front room. The afternoon sunlight, golden and warm, streams through the floor-to-ceiling windows, and with the drapes drawn back, the dust is illuminated by the light, making the chore at hand seem more pressing. Elenena sighs to herself as she concentrates on her tasks.

While dusting the coffee table next to Annie's chair, she spots the book, *Mein Kampf*. Annie told Elenena it is Hitler's autobiography.

The thought occurs to her, *Since I'll be attending this meeting, I should see what this Nazi Party and this man Hitler is all about.* Hesitantly, she peers around the room and out the windows just in case Annie should make a surprise entrance. Slowly, she picks up the book and begins to thumb through the pages. It's written in German, and she does not read German all that well.

But she can make out some of the words. *Who are the international poisoners, the racially inferior? What is this word, Untermensch?* She continues to thumb through the book, finding increasingly disturbing words and sentences, especially concerning the "Juden Problematik."

Feeling unsettled by the book, the notion crosses her mind, *I should have asked someone about this man Hitler and this political party before agreeing to go. But who could I ask? Now it's too late.* She considers, *What if I don't like what I hear, how do I tell Annie? Will she be angry with me, will she expect me to join and become a member?*

Elenena feels troubled by the thoughts about the meeting, wondering what's in store for her if she attends. *I'll bet the professor knows.*

But she won't see the professor until Sunday, days after the meeting. She doesn't have permission to use Annie's phone, so she cannot call him.

Elenena focuses on carrying out her work, deciding she'll go to the bakery before it closes at four and ask the Schweitzers about this man Hitler and the Nazis. She returns to the kitchen to check on the soup, watching its steady simmer, as the slow-moving bubbles of the potage break the surface ever so gently. Taking a whiff, she confirms it to be tasty based on the aroma and turns off the flame.

Elenena washes the floor in the front room and hallway, then completes the dusting. She checks the soup one more time, tasting it, and decides to adjust the flavor with a little salt and pepper. She puts the lid on the pot, then sets the table in the kitchen for two. Hurrying to leave before the bakery closes, it occurs to Elenena that she cannot lock the door to Annie's house; she doesn't have a key. She grabs her purse and her sweater, pulling it on as she trots down the front steps and has taken four steps to the left when she hears a stern flat voice, "Where are you going?"

Elenena stops dead in her tracks, feeling a slight chill, and slowly turns around, knowing it is Annie who poses the question. A curious look on her face, her head cocked, eyes narrowed into a squint, Annie stands stiffly on the sidewalk in front of her house.

Thinking fast on her feet, she tells Annie, "I was going to stop by the bakery to see if there are any leftover loaves or rolls that might not have sold. A little bread, or a roll, will go nicely with the soup, don't you think?"

Annie continues to give Elenena an unsettling expression of doubt, but adds, "Good idea, I'll go with you."

Her plan momentarily thwarted, Elenena agrees, "Perfect, that's great!"

They walk the three hundred feet to the front of the bakery in silence. Just before opening the door Elenena tells Annie, "Oh, I forgot, I didn't lock the front door of your house, and I'm sorry, I don't have a key. Is it okay that the door is unlocked?"

Pausing before taking another step, Annie considers the question. "Ah, yes, not locked. Alright, I'll meet you back at the house." She turns to walk away but not before warning Elenena, "Don't let that happen again."

Relieved, Elenena enters the bakery, the familiar smell greeting her nostrils. It's just minutes before four, when Greta or Fritz will come to lock the door and turn the sign around to "closed." In a loud voice, which Elenena intentionally drops a few octaves, she smiles and says, "Hello, are you still open?"

Greta shouts from the back of the bakery, "No, we are out of bread, sorry."

Elenena plays along, disguising her voice, and pretends to be a disgruntled customer, "What, closed? Out of bread? It's not even four, and your hours on the door state you're open until four. What is the meaning of this?"

Both Fritz and Greta come to the front of the store ready to fight when they see it's Elenena.

Fritz's gentle laugh warms Elenena, as he says, "You had us for a minute there! How are you today?"

Elenena nods hello to Greta, who smiles broadly at her. "I'm sorry, I didn't mean to startle you. I hope you've had a good day."

Greta, usually upbeat, nods. "How about you, to what do we owe this visit?"

Elenena glances around and out the windows before asking if it's okay to turn the sign and lock the front door. Fritz says, "Of course," while gazing curiously at their part-time helper.

Elenena gets right to the point: "I don't want to take up your time just as you're closing for the day, but I wanted to ask you a question. As you know, I'm new here in Munich, not having made many acquaintances yet. I have some questions and didn't know who to ask, so I came to you. You may not be aware, as I've told no one here in Munich, that I'm Jewish, and I know you are as well. I've seen the small Star of David by the back of the counter in the kitchen."

Fritz and Greta understand her situation. Greta says, "The teakettle is still hot. Let's go in back. We'll have a cup of tea, and you can ask us anything you like."

Feeling immediately relieved, she follows the Schweitzers to the back of the building and sits on the chair in front of the desk where Greta writes checks and orders supplies for the bakery. Greta nods to Fritz, who goes back to work, brushing out the charred crumbs and bits of bread from the large, two-shelf, brick-deck oven, part of his daily duties while closing shop for the day. He grumbles to himself, prompting Greta to ask, "What now?"

"It's the burner, must be the gas line from outside the building causing the flame to burn unevenly. That's why the bread is burning on the left side toward the back of the oven. Something about air in the line, or the flow isn't steady, consistent. This is a real problem; I'm not grumbling for the sake of grumbling." He lifts one of the cooled stone pieces, turning up the gas, and shows his wife. She sees the problem.

"Okay, you're right, I see it. I will call the city and ask them if they will check the gas line. Problem solved?"

Fritz mumbles again, "Well, not quite, but it couldn't hurt. The problem may be more than what I've told you, but I cannot be sure. First things first, have the city check that and go from there."

Greta ignores her husband and pours a cup of tea, handing it to Elenena. "Tell me, what's on your mind?"

Feeling comfortable enough to inquire, Elenena asks Greta, "My landlady asked me to attend a meeting of a group called Nazis, to hear Adolf Hitler speak. I know nothing about this group or Hitler. What do you know about him, or the Nazi Party?"

Fritz stops brushing out the oven, holding the large broom in his hand, gazing at his wife. They exchange a silent word spoken with their eyes, and Greta shakes her head at him as if to say, "No."

Greta begins, "Elenena, we understand your apprehension. What is keeping you from attending, did you hear or read something?"

Fritz walks over and stands behind his wife, his face full of kindness, which Elenena sees. She perceives it to be compassion.

"Well, my landlady has a book, *Mein Kampf,* and she reads it with real enthusiasm. The book is on her table in the front sitting room. While she was out today, I peeked at it, trying to read some of the words, yet not understanding it all. It's written in German, and I'm limited in the language, but I understood enough to feel uneasy. My feelings may be unfounded, but my instincts tell me to be wary. Should I be worried?"

Fritz leans forward, his eyes earnest, meeting Elenena's, and with a cautionary tone he whispers, "Yes. You should be worried indeed. There is plenty to worry about."

CHAPTER THIRTEEN

Wolfie, Frederick, and Stanislaw

AUGUST 1933, WOLFIE

WHILE STANDING FOR Appell, or roll call, I feel my strength leaking out of me. I'm weak, from the lingering effects of the concussion suffered that morning. I feel faint. I whisper to a prisoner next to me, "How long do we stand here?"

"Until they damn well please. We do this twice a day, get used to it."

Having only the swill that is referred to as soup, bread that tastes horrible, and a small potato, I am not replenished. My strength is sapped from the physical labor of the work in the garage with my father, lasting for four hours before roll call. Dragging the oil container and dumping the oil in the metal bin was more challenging than I initially thought. I spilled a great deal of it, then slipped in the slick it created, falling in it, and getting drenched in dirty motor oil. The oil seeped through my flimsy camp clothing, into my cuts and wounds, stinging sharply. A kapo saw my mishap and hit me at the knees with his baton, then tasked me to shovel dirt over the oil to cover the mess.

"The commandant doesn't like messy or sloppy work. Better not happen again, or you'll pay."

My father told me to be careful. It's not that I wasn't careful, I wasn't paying attention. My view of the naked man making his trips back and forth to the wall with two full buckets of rocks distracted me. Naked, sunburned, bleeding, bruised, but not broken.

The man always has a smile on his face. I'm fascinated and confounded all at once. How does he do it? I must find out his secret. Here he is in this godforsaken place, and he's smiling like he hasn't a care in the world. My father told me to steer clear, but I must speak with him. If he tells me his secret, if he shares it with me, is there a way I can survive this place smiling?

The group of us, fourteen men, stand waiting to be counted. I ask the prisoner next to me, "What is our barracks number, and where are the Jewish barracks?"

A voice in the group says, "Shut up, kid—you're going to get us in trouble."

Then the voice says, "Twelve."

I whisper, "Thank you."

Then the same voice tells me, "The Jewish barracks is the last building straight ahead. There are four you have to walk by to get to it."

The voice of a guard rings out, "Werden Seien Sie ruhig, schmutzigen Bastarde!" *Be quiet, you dirty bastards!*

"See?"

I whisper, "Yes, sorry."

I heed the warning, and we stand in silence for what feels like an eternity. My legs are about to give way when the guard finally calls my number. I step out and say, "Here." I can barely remember my number. Am I trapped in a dreadful nightmare, or is this reality? I could cry but won't give in to tears, no matter how horrible I feel.

The kapo who hit me in the knees comes into the barracks and hands me a clean uniform, consisting of a striped work shirt and striped pants. "I'll turn the water on for three minutes. Have one of the men help you wash that oil out of your wounds. The sores will fester if you don't."

I stand there, dumbfounded—an act of kindness. I'm shocked by the words.

"Well, don't just stand there, go wash now before I lose patience!"

I strip off my oil-soaked clothing, and the kapo motions one of the men to come help me, then leaves to turn on the water. I'm told by another prisoner that water rationing is like everything else here, in limited supply. It's only turned on for brief periods, part of the psychological warfare waged against prisoners by guards and kapos.

The man who's helping me calls another man over. "Get some of that salve that the Jewish doctor gave Victor. Let's get you cleaned up, young man."

Very gently, the man directs the water over my body and throws some powdered soap on my wet skin. He starts to make a lather, washing me as I stand helpless. The water is ice-cold. The water pressure hurts, causes me to wince in pain, but, at the same time, numbs my wounds. And with no warning, the water is gone.

The man helping me says with irony, "Sorry, there are no fluffy warm towels for you to dry yourself!"

I find myself laughing for the first time since I was with my brothers on the bus. And then, without a hint of a warning, the tears begin to flow. As one of the men rubs salve on my wounds, the other man who washed me holds me, and I collapse in his arms, crying, my sobs filled with anguish.

"Why did this happen to me?"

"Son, we all ask ourselves the same question every day at least once."

"I'm busting out of this place as soon as possible!"

"We all say that as well. But we're all still here."

I put on the clothing, thanking the men for their help. One of them, named Franc, asks me why I'm here.

"I think it's because I failed to join the Hitlerjugend."

Franc, who speaks perfect English, shakes his head at the alleged reason, telling me, "You're a young boy, so what if you didn't join their damn club. These Nazis are insane. They're going to destroy the world unless someone or something stops them. I've read Hitler's book, and he thinks he's going to take over the world. Someone must kill that sick bastard."

An idea enters my mind.

Father says we work on Hitler's cars. How could we rig one to blow up with him in it? I must ask my father.

And that's the last thought I have before drifting off to an uncomfortable but much-needed sleep.

FREDERICK

Frederick sits on the floor next to his bunk, wondering about Wolfie. *Did anyone help him? Did the kapo bring him the clean clothes that I begged for and water to clean out his wounds?*

The kapo seemed curious as to why I would have such an interest in another prisoner, but I told him, "If I'm going to get the work done that's demanded of me, I better have a healthy helper."

That made sense to the kapo, so he agreed.

My heart feels broken for my son. My silent prayer begins, concealed within my heart and mind to a source, God, whom I'm not even sure exists.

The only proof I have so far is that I'm united with my son. I guess that's a pretty big sign and confirmation enough. Elise used to tell me, "Now, faith is the substance of things hoped for, the evidence of things not seen."

I must get us out of this place, but how, how can we get out? The trucks come in two days. Twelve trucks, two official automobiles, one being the Führer's auto... Hmmmmm, the Führer's automobile.

What can we do, can we kill two guards, strip their uniforms? The prisoners spoke about how we outnumber the guards. Wolfie and I can wear their uniforms and take one of the trucks and escape.

Frederick, wake up, man, are you crazy? They'll figure it out in one second flat. Or will they? I feel mad enough to do something like this. To risk it all to get Wolfie out of here. He's sixteen years old, this is all wrong. God, if you're there, please help us, how can we escape this hell? Give me an idea, a plan, some hope, anything, I'm begging you. Can we hide in the back of one of the trucks?

It's usually just one driver and another soldier when they drop off the Reich's autos and trucks. After Appell in the morning? What can I do to make this work, how can I get us out of here? I know all the roads; I know how to get us back to our district. But then what? Indeed, they'll come for us. Where could we hide? I need a plan. Munich is only ten miles away, could we go on foot? No, the dogs would find us.

Climbing onto the flat wooden bunk, Frederick considers the smaller of the dwellers that share the barracks. *Tonight, I won't sleep on the floor with the rats. Rats run free while we're held as prisoners. I see one scurry by, and I whisper to it,* "Run little rat, run free while you can.

STANISLAW

"Jakob," Stanislaw says to his friend, his tone worried, "you were late after Appell. What happened?"

"Dukolf."

"That bastard, I'm so sorry. Are you okay?"

"I'm okay." He hesitates. "While viciously beating me and kicking me in the genitals, he tells me, 'Dogs are more worthy of life than you, you useless Jew.' As if that wasn't bad enough, he finishes the abuse by urinating on me."

There is a moment of silence between the men. Then Jakob begins to speak again. His voice cracks, filled with emotion. "Stani, I've lost my hope."

Stani reaches out and takes his friend by the hand.

"No. I won't allow it. We cannot lose hope. If we have no hope, we have nothing but the hellish reality we come face-to-face with every minute of every day."

Desperate to encourage his friend, Stani continues, "We can pray together, and may I encourage you to pray throughout the day? Keep the pathway open to God, with praise and thanksgiving. I know it seems implausible to find anything to be thankful for, but we can be thankful for each other, and our Jewish brothers. Together we are the silver lining to this dark cloud."

Not convinced, Jakob goes on, "Stani, I'm not like you. We are beaten, hungry, confined in this barracks with no comfort, not even a pillow or a blanket. I have nothing to hope for, my family is dead, I have no one outside the walls of this dreadful place, no hope of a reunion with anyone. I've lost the little bit of belief in a future I once held. There is nothing for me. Hope has all but evaporated, the shadow of it lost in the distance. Like the setting sun, I see it no more. But you know, when you arrived here, from the first minute I saw you, I knew we would become friends, and we have—like we've known each other our whole lives.

"Carrying rocks with someone for sixteen hours a day gives you a lot of time to get to know a person. Good thing you love to talk! Your stories, your friendship, your life before Dachau was sweet. Mine was not. I escape through your stories—they lift my spirit. Especially while we carry rocks. Tell me again about your young friend Maddie. Speak to me about music, anything to distract me from this hell. Tell me one of your good long stories. I will lose myself in your stories."

The two men lie next to each other in the Jewish barracks, on the wooden bunk, in the dark, on a moonless night. As they whisper back and forth, Stani tries his best to fortify his downtrodden friend. Stani starts by telling the story of Maddie.

"Maddie, ah, what an amazing young lady. Her path has not been an easy one. She has faced many a hardship in her young life—she's only seventeen.

"My dearest friend Elenena introduced us four years ago. I knew Maddie had a gift from the moment I heard her play the violin. She auditioned for me after receiving four years of tutoring by Elenena, who was my student for two years in Munich before becoming a teacher.

"Maddie came into the life of Elenena's aunt and sister in the most interesting of ways. You might call it serendipity.

"While Elenena was still under my tutelage in Munich, she received a letter from her sister, Marcella, who lived with their Aunt Noelle in a small eastern village in Poland, near the annexation. The letter was about a small girl she met one night.

"One dreary, rainy, cold February evening while walking home from synagogue, Noelle and Marcella spotted someone whom they assumed was seeking shelter on the small porch of Noelle's home. Elenena's aunt has a lovely home. I know this because I have visited for Passover. The train ride from Munich to Baranovichi is quite lengthy; it was on that train ride I learned all about Maddie. And then I met Maddie for the first time on that visit.

"So, getting back to the story, as the two women approached home, a small waif-like girl ran away from the house, into the rain and down the road. Noelle called after her, but the girl continued to run.

"After changing into dry clothes, the women had a small supper. Marcella built a fire in the fireplace in the front room of the house, and Noelle brought tea for the two to enjoy. Before sitting down, Noelle brought a small tray and a plate of dried fruits, some bread with jam, and a cup of tea, along with a blanket, leaving it on the front porch.

"'Just in case she comes back.' Noelle had what you'd call instincts for such things. Some might call it an intuition. After twenty minutes, while Marcella was playing the beautiful piano in the parlor, Noelle sat poised by the window. She spotted the girl, who came back slowly to the porch.

"Noelle watched her approach, noting how she did so with caution, looking all around. It was still raining, mind you. Observing her, Noelle commented to Marcella, 'She can't be more than ten years old!'

"Noelle continued to watch inconspicuously, as the girl wrapped herself in the blanket and, leaning with her back against the house, appeared to fall asleep.

"After a while, Marcella and Noelle prepared for sleep. Noelle opened the front door to peek at the girl, who was still there. She appeared to be sleeping, but her teeth were chattering as if she was freezing. Noelle motioned to Marcella, who came to the door. The two women decided to lift the girl and bring her inside the house.

"They placed her in front of the fire to warm her up. While putting her down, the girl awakened, terrified, like she'd seen a ghost. Noelle told her, "Don't be afraid—we will help you."

"Marcella went to the guest room to make a fire to warm

the room. Noelle went upstairs to find pajamas for their guest.

"When they returned to the room, all they saw was the blanket. The girl had left. The women searched up and down the road, but it was so dark and rainy, they couldn't see a thing.

"They decided to go to bed and returned the blanket to the porch in case their mystery visitor came back.

"A little bit past midnight, about an hour or two after going to bed, Marcella and Noelle awakened to the sound of firetrucks clanging their bells. In this small village, everyone knew when there was a fire.

"The fire was at the Polish orphanage a few blocks away from Noelle's house. Noelle told Marcella, 'There will be many displaced children if the fire is bad. I'm curious if we will have more visitors.'

"Later in the day, Noelle spoke to a neighbor who knew everything about everyone, what you'd call a 'busybody.'

"She told Noelle, 'All the children are at the fire department, there are thirty children, not one left behind or injured by the fire, a real miracle.' So, Marcella and Noelle walked to the fire department shelter. Armed with money in her purse, Noelle was prepared to hand over the cash if it meant allowing the girl to come stay at her home. They arrived, and after checking on the children, they determined that their little visitor was not among the displaced orphans. Stumped, they walked back home, feeling discouraged. But lo and behold, their visitor was sitting on their front step with the blanket wrapped around her. She waved at the two women as they approached the house. She stood and said, 'Thank you for the blanket and food. I came back to say thank you.'

"Sensing the girl had nowhere to go, Noelle asked if she'd like to come inside and have dinner with them. The girl cautiously agreed. Noelle asked her if she knew anything about the fire, testing her to see if she was an orphan. She shook her head, no. 'Do you have any family or parents?' Again, she shook her head, no.

"Noelle explained, 'I have a room that needs someone to live in it, would you like to live in the room for a night?' She shook her head, no. Noelle decided she'd asked enough questions, for now, didn't even ask the girl her name. So, the women and the girl ate their dinner, with the girl listening to every word the women spoke. They talked about Elenena and random chitchat. The girl was still silent.

"After dinner, while Noelle and Marcella cleaned up the dishes, the girl wandered into the guest room and lay down on the bed. Marcella went to find her—she was sleeping.

"Marcella tended to the fire in the guest room and left.

"Noelle sat by the fire in the front room knitting, while Marcella read a book. After a few hours, the girl appeared from the room. Quietly, she walked up to Noelle and stood before her, then climbed into her lap. Plain as day she said, 'I'd like to live in that room forever, if it's okay. I like the bed.'

"She said this with a broad smile that won over Noelle's heart. 'Is that so? Well, I'm delighted to hear that. Since you will stay in that room, you can tell me your name. Mine is Noelle Silberstein, and that is Marcella Laurent, my niece.'

"'And I am Maddie Turetzky.'

"It turns out it was Maddie who burned down the orphanage. The truth came out much later. While examining the children the state physician discovered that many of the orphans showed all the signs of physical abuse. Most had bruises; one child had a broken arm, not set. All the children were thin and malnourished.

"Maddie spoke of a room with no light, locked for sometimes two or three days, with a child inside. You can imagine how that treatment damaged those little angels. The headmaster of the orphanage went to jail for child maltreatment and mismanagement of state funds.

"Maddie did not tell Noelle the truth about the fire until three years later. She woke the other children before the fire spread, and then knocked on the door of the orphanage's headmaster. To this day, the fire department has never discovered who started the fire. It was determined to be arson. I've never asked Maddie about it; it wouldn't be right to ask just to settle my curiosity. No, some things in life don't need to see light unless the person is willing. And the rest, they say, is history!"

By this time, Jakob is ready to fall asleep, grateful for the distraction the story provided.

"Stani, you are a good friend to me. God bless you; I am grateful for you."

These are the last words Jakob speaks.

He doesn't awaken the next day. The early morning light finds a way to stream inside the cracked and dirty windows, into the squalor of the living quarters, revealing the creaky, splintered wooden bunks where the prisoners sleep. The fractured light shines enough to reveal a large, fresh bruise on the side of Jakob's temple, stretching to his swollen forehead. The obvious trademark of Dukolf.

Stani hovers over his friend's body, lamenting him, while tears of grief and loss fall softly.

"Oh, Jakob, Jakob, poor soul. You deserved so much better than your life ending like this."

Stani prays over his friend. "Most High God, receive Jakob, hold him in Abraham's bosom in paradise until the time comes to bring him home for all eternity. May his journey be swift."

There are rules to follow when a Jewish prisoner dies in the barracks. If another prisoner finds him, they must report the death to a kapo at once. The kapo tells one of the camp guards who, in turn, notifies the commandant. They record the name along with the cause of death.

They keep the records ready for review should an officer of the State make an inquiry.

But the records are full of lies, never exposing the truth, that the guards kill the Jewish prisoners in a variety of ways and methods.

Stanislaw notifies the kapo, who in turn tells another kapo, one of the bad ones. He comes into the barracks and approaches Jakob's body. The kapo pokes Jakob's lifeless body with his baton. He probes various body parts, lifting Jakob's limp forearm, dropping it back on his body, before giving the dead body one last whack, which causes Stanislaw to wince. He says nothing.

By now, he knows better.

Stanislaw assumes the kapo will follow protocol, asking about the cause of death, and Stani will supply him with a prepared answer to incriminate Dukolf. But the kapo doesn't ask.

Instead, he tells Stanislaw in a brusque tone, "You found him. Now carry him to the pit and drop him in."

Then the kapo announces to the other Jews in the barracks, "You should all be so lucky. Now get to work!"

After Appell, Stani goes back to the barracks and sits with his deceased friend. He recalls the orders, knowing that at any minute a kapo or guard could come in and give him the same treatment, beating him to death. He doesn't care. "Jakob, I cannot do this to you."

Stanislaw knows he does not have the lack of conscience, heart, or stomach necessary to complete the cold-blooded act of carrying him to the pit and just dropping him in like he's garbage. He closes Jakob's eyes and prays over his friend again, as tears of loss and sadness continue to fall. *Am I crying for myself or for you, my friend?* He looks around the grim, dilapidated barracks, as if seeing them for the first time. *I didn't notice the condition of this place with Jakob around.* Stani feels sure that even though their friendship on earth was ever so brief, in eternity it will last forever.

"You are home now, Jakob. You are in the presence of HaShem. Your spirit can run free, the air is sweet, and now you can feel loved for all of eternity. No more pain, no more suffering will plague you now. Those things have passed away. Rest in peace, dear friend, I will see you again."

After praying, Stani faces the reality of not being able to complete an order that was given to him.

I won't do it. I can't do that to my friend. God, please send someone to help me.

CHAPTER FOURTEEN

Raymond, Buster, and Maddie

AUGUST 1933

D ESPITE THE AWKWARD sleeping arrangements, Maddie in one bed, Raymond, and Buster in the other, the three manage to put together a few hours of sound sleep. Raymond awakes, disturbed by the urgent knocking at the door.

He bolts out of bed, disoriented for a moment. His clothing is rumpled, his thick hair and appearance disheveled. The drawn drapes cut out the light and for all he knows it could be the middle of the night. He checks his watch; it's a quarter to 7:00 a.m. He groans, lamenting under his breath about the extra thirty minutes of sleep he won't get.

The knock comes again with a louder banging. "Wellington!"

Raymond opens the door, finding the two chaperones, Williams and O'Mara, standing before him, both appearing bedraggled and exceedingly pale. Raymond sidesteps the men, closing the door behind him.

The three men stand awkwardly in the hallway, the dim glow from the hall light casting a yellowish tint on them and their day's growth of beard. The corridor is cold, causing still half-asleep Raymond to shiver.

There is a moment of silence before Raymond asks, "What's wrong?"

Williams peeks at O'Mara, who nods towards Raymond, silently encouraging Williams to speak.

"Well, you see, we, um, I don't know how to say this, we…"

O'Mara loses patience quickly, saying, "Out with it!"

"Jim Lewis is dead."

The declaration hits Raymond like a slap in the face. He shakes his head, wondering if he's dreaming or hearing things. He blinks a few times and repeats the words to himself, before asking, "What, what do you mean Lewis is dead?"

O'Mara takes over the conversation, as Williams runs out of words.

"We went to his room at quarter past six; his call time was 6:00 a.m."

Williams finds his voice and states with authority, "Jim never oversleeps!"

O'Mara seems perturbed by Williams, inserting himself and interrupting.

"We couldn't hear any noise or activity when we knocked on the door. We checked the hall bath; no one was there. We went back to the door. After a few minutes of knocking, I realized something must be wrong."

Williams finds his voice and words again. "I went to the front desk and asked the clerk to open his room. He opened the door, and there was Lewis, in his bed, his eyes open and dead as could be."

Neither man had ever viewed a dead body before. Each was put off by the sight, now indelibly stamped in their minds.

Raymond shudders at the words and asks, "What is the cause of death? I mean, what happened?"

Both men shake their heads. O'Mara adds, "The clerk called for the doctor and coroner to come and confirm. There is a protocol the hotel follows should a guest die on property."

"Yes, yes, of course, there is. But what happened? Is it plausible he had a heart attack, dying in his sleep? I can't believe it."

After a moment of pause, O'Mara ponders, "But why would his eyes be open if he died in his sleep?"

This thought provokes Raymond. "I wonder how thorough an autopsy will be, or if there will be one." He adds, "Well, gentlemen, we must join forces and do what's best for the troop. Did the clerk mention what is to be done with the body?"

Williams shakes his head and replies, "He told us we need to contact the U.S. Consulate, to speak to the ambassador regarding arrangements for getting the body back to the United States. The transport requires the body to first be embalmed, and then shipped in a pine box, I mean, casket."

Raymond asks, "Do either of you know if Lewis has next of kin whom we should contact? And who will break the news to the troop?"

An uncomfortable silence falls among the men. Then Williams says, "We were thinking it might be best if you did. Being a lawyer and such, we think you'll have a better way of explaining the situation."

"Of course, alright, I will. But what about next of kin, do either of you know?"

Both men shake their heads.

"Right, well, I'll dress and meet you in the lobby in twenty minutes. We have breakfast scheduled for 7:30; we're not too far off-schedule. Assemble the troop in the lobby. I'll take it from there. Okay?"

Both men nod.

Before Williams and O'Mara leave, O'Mara pauses. "Hey, um, I forgot to mention, I noticed something strange."

Raymond and Williams fix their gaze on O'Mara, waiting for a revelation.

"Well, I forgot to mention it before, but I noticed some dried blood in one ear. It's nothing, maybe he scratched it,

137

but there were also a few drops of blood on the pillowcase as well, I guess. You didn't see it?"

Williams shakes his head.

O'Mara adds, "The coroner and doctor will have an explanation, no doubt."

The three stand there for a moment in jarring stillness.

Raymond concludes, "Right. Let's get to it, gentlemen."

Back inside the room, Buster is sitting up in the bed. Maddie is still sleeping, her breathing regular and low.

"Dad, what's going on, who was at the door?"

Raymond peeks around the corner and motions for Buster to get out of the bed and come to the entrance of the room.

Expecting an immediate answer, Buster asks again, "What's going on?"

Raymond tries to deliver the jolting blow gently, in degrees.

"I have some shocking news to report. I'm sorry to tell you this, but Troop Leader Lewis passed away during the night, seemingly from a heart attack. We cannot know for sure, but for now, that appears to be the most obvious cause."

Buster is silent, but the shock registers on his face, as his usual rosy, tanned cheeks become pale.

"I detest giving you shocking news. I know you liked him."

"Whoa. Wow. That is a shock. Wow. Do the other boys know?"

"Not that I'm aware. I'll speak to the troop before breakfast. I'm sorry, son. I'm sure you'll miss him."

Hesitantly, softly, Buster adds, "Yes, kind of, but not as much as you think."

"Why? Did you have a falling out with him, something I don't know about?"

"No, no nothing like that, and meaning no disrespect, but I, I always thought he was kind of creepy. But this is shocking news, I don't know what to say."

Confused by this new description of his adversary, Raymond asks, "Creepy in what way?"

While Buster searches for the right words, Maddie calls out, "Buster, is that you?"

"Yes, I'm here with my dad."

"Is everything all right? I heard some knocking at the door but wasn't sure if I dreamed it or not."

Maddie, having slept in her clothes, crawls out from under the covers and stands up, assessing the condition of her apparel.

She asks, "What is our plan for today?"

Out of respect for Maddie's privacy, Raymond remains at the entrance of the room.

Buster whispers, "Good morning, Maddie. Sorry about the disturbance. How are you this morning, how did you sleep?"

Yawning and stretching, she says, "Thank you—quite well. I hope you both did too."

After a moment of hesitation, Raymond changes the subject, telling Buster directly, "I'm going to my room for a quick wash-up, shave, and change of clothes. For Maddie, I think the best we can do is to outfit her in a Scout uniform. She can tuck her hair under the broad Lemon Squeezer hat. We'll use this disguise to move her out of the hotel. I have no doubt the Brownshirts are still residing in the lobby. Buster, can you produce a uniform for Maddie? Then like before, keep watch while Maddie uses the facilities to wash up. Are we in agreement?"

"What about shoes for Maddie, Dad?"

"Shoes, hmm. That could be problematic. I'll buy some if necessary. First things first. Wash, then put on your uniform, and by then I'll find shoes. I'll get breakfast brought back to the room for you two after I make a call to the ambassador. Let's get to it."

Raymond pauses, and before leaving asks Maddie, "By the way, what is your shoe size?"

"I wear a size thirty-nine."

"Wow, you must have huge feet!" Buster begins to laugh at the thought of feet that big. He hadn't noticed her feet before.

Raymond scowls at his son for his blunt comment. "Buster, that's about a size seven in American shoe sizes. Okay you two, get busy."

Raymond washes, shaves, and changes clothes hastily before heading to the front desk in the hotel lobby. The sunlight is plentiful, but he doesn't take time to reckon with it or appreciate it. Something about Lewis's sudden death troubles him. His gut tells him the man hadn't died from natural causes. *But what else could it be?*

The desk clerk approaches, directing his focus on Raymond after first nodding to the two ubiquitous Brownshirts.

"Can I help, sir?"

"Yes, I'd like to place a call to the U.S. ambassador's office in Berlin."

"But it's only 7:15 a.m., sir, do you think they'll answer?"

Raymond has no time for silliness. He says curtly, "Place the call now."

"Yes, sir, of course, with pleasure."

While the clerk places the call, Raymond turns his gaze on the Brownshirts, who are speaking in hushed tones while staring back at Raymond.

Raymond stares them down in turn, which must make the men uncomfortable. They step away from the desk and stand at the entrance of the hotel.

"Sir, your call is connected, you can speak."

Raymond takes the receiver but waits for the clerk to remove himself first. "Do you mind?"

"Certainly, sir, of course."

"Hello. This is Raymond Wellington with the U.S. State Department. I need to get a message to Ambassador Dodd. Yes, I am aware he's on his way to Munich. Please tell him this verbatim. We have some odd circumstances here which will require your attention. Our troop leader Jim Lewis passed away during the night from an apparent heart attack. I know there is a protocol to follow. I'm told a doctor and coroner will come to examine the body. Yes, his name is James Lewis. Fine, will do. Thank you."

Raymond calls out to the clerk, "How much for the call?"

"There will be no charge, the hotel covers that expense when there is a deceased guest on property, it's billed under the arrangements."

"Right, thank you."

Raymond is suspicious, thinking any call made would have another set of ears listening in. *Dirty bastards.*

Making his way to the dining room, Raymond orders room service once again, but this time for just two. No sense in giving them any ideas that there's an extra person in the room.

He signs the bill, giving the waiter cash for breakfast, and tells him, "I'll wait here for it and take it myself. And put a full pot of coffee on there, please." *Buster and Maddie can eat. Just coffee for me.*

The waiter brings the breakfast on a wheeled cart. "I've included a full pot of coffee for you, sir."

"Good thing, thank you. We'll leave the cart in the hallway when we're finished, is that satisfactory?"

"Yes, sir, that will be fine, thank you."

Raymond checks over the contents of the cart, making a mental inventory: coffee, check, two servings of sausage, eggs, and toast. The waiter had added a small pitcher of water with two glasses, a coffee cup and saucer, silverware, and napkins.

He wheels the cart, which squeaks, through the lobby and down the hallway. Then he spots Williams and O'Mara shepherding the troop of boys in his direction, toward the lobby.

O'Mara picks up his pace and jogs to meet Raymond. His large feet pound the carpet, which muffles the weight of his steps. He nods, as a form of hello. "We've got the boys together. No one knows anything yet."

"Let me get this down the hallway to Buster. He's still sick. I'm hoping he'll be able to eat something. Can't have him sapped of strength and emotions. I'll be right back to address the boys."

Raymond knocks at the door, pleasantly surprised to find that Buster remembered the chain lock on the door. Good boy.

"Who goes there and what's the password?"

Raymond chuckles, despite the circumstances. He honestly could burst out laughing as a way to let off steam, releasing the pressure that's building in his brain.

As inappropriate as laughter seems, he knows it would help if he could just let go. So much to think about: Lewis, the coroner, the troop, departure, the ambassador, the transport, Buster, Maddie, Wolfie, Dachau, Maddie's friend, keeping Maddie hidden. Good grief!

"Let me in, or else."

Buster helps wheel the cart into the room.

Raymond observes his son, concerned for any grief he might feel in addition to being reminded of his mother's death.

"How are you doing with the news? Is there anything I can say, or do, to help you? Would you like to talk about it?"

"I'm okay, Dad, but thanks for asking. I'm worried about Wolfie and Maddie's friend. Yes, I guess I'll miss Leader

Lewis, but in a way I won't. It's strange, but I'm almost relieved he's gone."

Raymond wants more answers. Looking directly into his son's face, he places both hands on Buster's shoulders. "As much as I'd like to have a deeper discussion about what you're saying, I don't have time right now, but I promise to make time after I speak with the troops. For now, I must wash up and change clothes. I can't say I'm not disturbed by your words, I am. I'm concerned. Should I worry, son? Something you haven't told me?"

CHAPTER FIFTEEN

Elenena and Annie

SUMMER 1925

ELENENA PREPARES TWO loaves of challah, following her mother's instructions explicitly.

Her mother's voice, seared into her memory from a copious number of baking lessons, guides her through each intricate step of the process.

Annie recently hired a man to calibrate the oven. A calibrated oven can almost guarantee the bread baking evenly. The desired results are also achieved by applying egg wash twice to the raised loaves before putting them in the oven to bake.

It takes every ounce of Elenena's willpower not to tear into the perfectly-braided challah loaves. She longs for a taste of the warm bread; her mouth salivates at the thought of it. The memory of her mother's words reminds her. 'No greater pleasure can compare with the likes of fresh bread, still warm from the oven, at the height of deliciousness, a slice spread with butter, watching it melt on the surface of that slice. Then comes that triumphant first taste of heaven, the best taste of the whole loaf being the first one.'

Elenena wants desperately to enjoy the flavor and warmth of the bread, knowing it would rekindle memories and visions of her mother. But that will not happen. Annie made it clear they would only enjoy the bread after the meeting was over.

Elenena wishes she could express the joy of the warm bread to Annie. She would never understand. She has no appreciation of small pleasures unless they have to do with Nazis or Hitler.

How sad that her view only includes all things Nazi. If their Nazi group collapsed, what would she have left?

She wraps the extra loaf of challah for Annie's friend Martin in a clean dish towel, tying it with some twine, putting the bread on the table for Annie to take.

Annie disrupts her quiet moment.

"Ready to go?" Annie's face is highly animated, reflecting the excitement in her voice. "Oh, you are in for such a treat! We will leave early to get a good seat. If we can get close enough, you will be able to see and feel the sheer passion and power, the charisma that comes forth from Herr Hitler. I can barely stand it, I'm so excited, aren't you?"

"Oh, yes, we should go now and get a good seat."

The trap having been set, Elenena tries to sound mildly enthusiastic, worried that too much exuberance will force a commitment she is not willing to give.

The Schweitzers made it clear to Elenena that the Nazis and Hitler are the hostile enemies of the Jewish people. She needs to be careful and cautious. Fritz's words: 'Be prudent, dear. Be incredibly careful not to get too close.'

The words sent a chill down her spine, which is recreated as she recalls them.

Putting on her stylish red linen coat, Elenena twirls once, modeling it for Annie. "My Aunt Noelle gave me this coat, it's from Paris. How do I look?"

Annie puts up her hands. "Oh, no. You cannot wear a bright red coat to a meeting, no."

Confused, Elenena asks the obvious. "Why not? I love this coat; my aunt gave it to me."

Annie hisses at her, "I don't care who gave it to you. Communists wear red coats. You cannot wear that coat ever again. I'll be right back."

Surely this prognostication about red coats is not true: no one would think anything of it. Red is a beautiful color on Elenena, especially against her porcelain skin.

Reaching inside the small closet off of the kitchen, Annie retrieves a dull black coat that smells like mothballs. "Here, wear this. Now let's hurry, we're wasting time!"

Annie points to the package on the table. "Is this the bread for Martin?" She doesn't wait for a response and grabs the loaf off the table.

Dumbfounded and offended, Elenena keeps her feelings to herself. *The fresh air will drive the stink of mothballs away, I hope! At least no one will bother me because of the smell. How ironic. A Nazi carrying a loaf of challah made by a Jew, bringing it into a meeting of Nazis, for a Nazi. Oh, will Aunt Noelle and the Schweitzers roar with laughter over that! I hope I live to tell them!*

Annie prattles on continuously while the women walk the six blocks to the meeting. She speaks about the Nazis and Hitler's plan for Lebensraum.

Elenena asks, "I've never heard that term before, what does it mean?"

Annie begins a tutorial on the definition of the word. "Well, you see, if the German people are going to grow and flourish as a country, we need room to expand. Lebensraum literally means living space. If the strongest are to be able to survive, our society needs specific geographic considerations that they do not have at the present time."

Elenena thinks about the words Annie spoke. The plans to spread out don't make sense. How would Germany acquire more land? So, she boldly asks, "But don't sovereign nations have borders? How does such an expansion occur?"

Annie flinches, reluctant to answer such a pointed question.

With irritation in her voice, she huffs, "Well, I'm sure Herr Hitler will explain the plans in detail as time goes on."

According to Fritz Schweitzer, Hitler embraces the romantic notion of Lebensraum as manifest destiny, selling this idea to the German people, beginning first with the Nazi Party and then the German youth. The German geographer Frederich Ratzel appraises eastern Europe as the clear source of the German expansion. Due to social and economic pressures of overpopulation in German states, many thinkers of the time believe that land and valuable resources are wasted on lesser people. People considered racially inferior, like the Jews and the Slavs, are included in this category.

The idea of Lebensraum is not a new or original philosophy.

Annie and Elenena arrive at the Bier Cellar with ample time to find choice seating.

Annie greets a man who stands watch at the side door. The place is called "The Bier Cellar," as delineated by the sign above the doorway. Annie whispers to Elenena, "His job is keeping out any rabble-rousers."

Hmmm. Like red-coat-wearing Jewish girls, perhaps?

"Heinz, I'd like to introduce Elenena Laurent, who I think might become a regular after hearing our leader speak!" The glee in Annie's voice and glint in her eyes is something Elenena has not heard nor witnessed before this moment.

Elenena gives a weak smile as he nods to her. After appraising Heinz, she assumes his thug-like appearance is intentional. From what Elenena can see, and smell, he needs a shave. And a shower.

Annie whispers confidently to Elenena, "He will stand watch until the Brownshirts show up for crowd control."

Elenena ponders the thought. *Crowd control? Are they expecting a riot, or thousands of people to attend?*

The women descend the grimy stairwell, and Elenena realizes, *It really is a cellar!*

At the bottom of the stairs is an opening to the right, through which the women enter into the main room. The room is dimly lit, full of people with Nazi armbands over their coat-sleeves scurrying about, arranging chairs, and setting up a podium. The smell of stale beer and cigarette smoke stifles Elenena's senses, causing her to feel dizzy. She can see a gray haze of smoke hovering over the low ceilings, with no escape route in sight.

Leaning against a post, trying to adjust to the oxygen-stealing atmosphere, she asks, "How many will attend this meeting?"

Grinning ear to ear, Annie says, "As many as they can pack in here!"

Elenena finds humor in Annie's response while at the same time being distressed by her landlord's enthusiasm and expression over all things Nazi and Hitler. She is without question obsessed. She appears drunk with excitement, but that elation evaporates when a man in a Nazi uniform approaches the two women and offers armbands to each of them. "Here you are, ladies, your armbands."

Annie accepts the two sets, grabbing them quickly. Her face is now full-on crimson. Her angry expression makes Elenena think Annie's head might explode from the building pressure. She acts embarrassed and ashamed, as if by leaving the house without her armbands, she's violated a rule amounting to a cardinal sin. She scolds herself after the man leaves. "How could I be so stupid to leave without my armbands on! It must have been your coat that distracted me! Oh, well. Here, put yours on."

Elenena cannot hide her shock at Annie's unnerving request.

Does she expect me to become a member without having a say in the matter?

Elenena hesitates, frozen, unable to move a muscle.

Annie's tone grows terse. Her anger becomes visible, starting as a slow surge across her face. Her eyes narrow to beady bullets, frightening Elenena. *Is she going to kill me right here, right now, in front of all these witnesses?*

Annie growls, "Here, take them. What's the matter? Herr Hitler will expect all his members to wear the armbands." She holds the armbands out, shaking them ever so slightly, as she repeats herself, her voice raised. "Here! Must I put these on you myself?" She's taken two threatening steps closer to Elenena when a tall, handsome man approaches, greeting her loudly.

"Annie!"

This must be Martin, Elenena thinks.

"And who might this lovely creature be?" Without notice or warning, he takes Elenena's hand in his, kissing it gently.

Irritated by her friend's grandiose and presumptuous behavior, Annie interrupts. There is obvious displeasure in her tone. "She's the girl I told you about—the boarder, the bread-maker."

"Ah, yes, pleased to meet you, boarder and bread-maker. My name is Martin Metz. I raise chickens, and I'm a farmer as well. I had no idea you would be gracing us with your presence this afternoon." And then directly to Annie, "You never mentioned your boarder was beautiful!"

Annie grunts and tells Martin, "Here, take your challah." She pushes the loaf of challah into his chest. He ignores her, unable to take his eyes off Elenena.

Before either woman can answer, Annie grabs Elenena's arm and leads her to the front of the cellar, snapping at Martin, "We need to get to our seats. See you later!"

In a harsh whisper she chides her guest, "If I knew you would draw this much attention, I'd have never brought you!"

Elenena breathes a quiet sigh of relief. *She'll think twice about bringing me again, and this will not become a regular event. Thank God!*

While holding Annie's attention, Elenena says, rolling her eyes for effect, "Oh, you know how men are, they can't get ahold of themselves. They act ridiculous, like schoolboys."

Elenena hopes this will diffuse the negative energy Annie hurls at her. Instead, Annie rebuffs, "No, I do not know how men are, they've never paid attention to me, not as they do with you." The two sit there in awkward silence while the men around them buzz like busy bees in a hive.

Moments later, a man dressed in a military uniform appears at the front of the room. He's wearing the armbands, an iron cross, golden eagle insignias at his collar, and a large hat with a high arching top, with another eagle across the brow of the military headgear.

There is no mistaking this man. He reeks of official importance. While he straightens the podium and speaks to other official men in uniforms, they begin to scurry about. One man announces, "It's time," as he tells the crowd to take their seats and quiet down. There is still a significant buzz of noise from people conversing. The air is thin and stale.

Elenena casts her gaze around the room, taking in all the sights and sounds. *What a pitiful gathering place—ramshackle is what my aunt would call it. The chairs don't match, and this place needs a good cleaning.* To distract herself from the lack of cleanliness, she asks Annie a question.

"Annie, tell me what the eagle on the uniforms and hats signifies?"

With a fraction of irritation, Annie curtly tells Elenena, "You're very observant, and you ask a lot of questions."

Elenena can't tell if the comment is a criticism or a compliment.

Annie takes a deep breath and inspects Elenena's face, searching for cynicism or mockery. Finding none, she continues, "It's called the Parteiadler, the emblem of the Nazi Party. Its roots are in Roman history. You can read about it in the library if you wish."

Annie refers to the small library in her house that holds five hundred books, many of them on Darwin, Nordic tribes, the Roman Empire, eugenics, the occult, and German military.

The first time Elenena spied the library, perusing the books, she pondered at Annie's unique and curious assortment of reading materials. She decided the collection must belong to Annie's father. The totality of books had a decidedly masculine theme.

Someone flicks the lights, and everyone finds a seat. Annie sits up straight in her chair, her face full of excitement, as she tells Elenena, "Oh, this means he's about to come to the podium."

Annie grabs Elenena's hand in a rare act of contact between them. As she does so, she's almost panting. Slowly, Elenena releases her hand from Annie's tight grip, timed perfectly as the crowd begins to applaud. The man Annie is so passionate about is nothing like she imagined.

In her mind, from how Annie spoke about Hitler, Elenena conjured up the image of a tall, strong, ruggedly handsome man with a full shock of blond hair and beautiful blue eyes— Aryan, like he'd described in his book as the desired attributes.

Striding to the podium is a short man with dark greasy hair brushed to one side, one unruly lock choosing to occupy part of his forehead. The man wears an odd mustache that resembles a thick paint-stroke. He is starkly pale, an unhealthy shade of pasty white. There is nothing outwardly attractive about the man. The clothes he wears do him no favors. The leader of the Nazi Party wears a beige-brown war surplus military shirt with a black tie, and the traditional leather strap called a Sam Browne belt featured prominently across the front of his shirt. He has Nazi armbands on each arm.

Elenena strains to see the rest of his attire, and finds he's in jodhpurs and black jackboots. She watches his facial expressions as he takes in the crowd's obvious admiration and obsession. He breathes in the adulation, his eyes closing often. His chest heaves as he absorbs the electricity in the room, basking in the scene and outpouring of devotion.

Herr Hitler surrounds himself with pistol wielding Brownshirts flanking him on either side. They stand behind him, invoking a strange, unspoken but threatening message of power, a sentry of violence.

But these people in attendance are his supporters—why do the guards stand with him, ready to fight?

Nervously, the man with all the power forges a smile, one which appears phony, and lacks confidence and warmth. His dark eyes flash, sensing the magnitude of the moment. He must be fully aware he causes this reaction, like a lit match to a fuse, as he stands before his rabid supporters.

He has a certain brand of charisma that connects to the people before him, his faithful. Elenena likens it to people who have been deprived of liquids: when he appears, there's suddenly an increase in their parched condition as they thirst for his words, and he quenches them with an impassioned speech. They drink it up. Or so she imagines.

As if on cue, the majority of the crowd jumps to their feet and raises their right arms at a forty-five-degree angle, their hands straight as arrows, fingers pressed together in a salute, saying all at once, "Heil Hitler." They're animated, captivated, like in a trance, and downright gleeful just at the mere presence of this man.

He hasn't said one word, yet this is their reaction.

Above the roar of the crowd, Elenena observes Annie, who is reeling, intoxicated by the moment, her cheeks ablaze with color, her dark eyes glazed over, like someone in a drug-induced state of being. Annie turns to Elenena and shouts over the buzz of the crowd, her words dripping with devotion, "Didn't I tell you he is special?!"

CHAPTER SIXTEEN

Wolfie, Frederick, Stanislaw

AUGUST 1933, WOLFIE

AFTER APPELL, I check out the location of the guards and kapos, slowly walking towards the Jewish barracks. I walk at a moderate, steady pace; my injuries will not allow my usual long-legged, fast gait. It's better this way, as to not draw any attention. The air bristles against my skin and I shiver. My uniform is thin, and the breeze almost passes through the material.

If the sun was out, I wouldn't feel so cold.

Lack of sleep causes me to feel every little internal and external thing, from my sores and bruises to the ache in my gut.

I'm hungry, I'm constantly hungry. My stomach growls and grumbles in protest, as the hunger does not leave.

I try and forget about it for now, along with the thoughts of Scout brothers.

Let's see, he said over here, past the four buildings.

I approach the building said to be the Jewish barracks. Opening the door to the rickety, ramshackle building, I'm amazed that it opens and closes. The hinges appear worn out, like they'll fall off any minute. Out of the shadows of the room, I hear a voice calling out-—faint, but real. The acrid smell of human excrement and urine embedded in the splintered walls of this decrepit building assaults my every sense. I wonder how this devilish place qualifies as barracks.

As my eyes adjust to the dim environment, I see where the voice originates from.

"Young man, can you help me?"

And there he is, the naked man.

I hurry to his side. There's a lifeless man lying on the lowest wooden bunk. There are many bunks in the one room, all close to each other, but no one in them. It's just the three of us. The sounds outside the barracks seem muffled as I focus on what I see before me, a man who is dying or dead. Something I've never seen before, and I have a feeling this won't be the last time. I feel sick to my stomach from a lack of food, the emotion, or both.

The naked man speaks. "I'm so sorry I'm crying. You see, this man was my friend. I am quickly learning friendships here must be appreciated right now—there is no guarantee of tomorrow."

I ask, "What happened to your friend?"

"That miserable excuse for a human Dukolf beat him, hit him in the head, here."

Stani points to the bruise on the dead man's forehead. Because of the lack of light, I can barely see it, not that I want to. I try not to see the naked man.

He speaks again. "Do you remember me? I'm Stanislaw, Stani for short, we met—"

"Yes, of course I do."

How could I forget the sight of you?

Through his tears and sorrow, he says, "And you are Wolfie!"

Softly, I answer him, "Yes, sir, that's right."

The sudden urge to vomit begins to overtake me—there is little I can do. I burp and try my best to hold back the gagging reflex. It takes every ounce of strength and mind control I have not to vomit. Sweat breaks out on my forehead, under my arms. In a moment, I'm soaked with it.

"Stani, tell me, what happened to your friend? I'm sickened by the idea that someone would beat this poor, emaciated skin-and-bones man to death."

What threat did he pose? He can't weigh more than ninety pounds.

"He's Jewish. Because he's Jewish he's abused, like all the Jews in the camp. We Jews can only sit and wait before it's our turn to be murdered. There's nothing more to tell, really."

"Oh, no. Why do they do this? And is it only Jews that receive this treatment?"

"No. They also hate the weak-minded, the gypsies, indigents, the homosexuals, the political dissidents, opponents of the Reich, anyone who is not German, Aryan. But they especially hate us Jews."

I feel self-conscious because while I am German, I am also Jewish.

Through tears, Stani tells me, "My friend here, Jakob, I'm ordered to dump him in the pit. I cannot do that."

I can't even imagine what that means. I ask, "The pit?"

"Yes, the pit. The pit was dug by the first prisoners here."

Stani tells me the pit is where the dead Jewish prisoners are dumped over the edge, on top of the other dead bodies. "There are other bodies in there as well, those groups I spoke of, but the majority are Jewish."

My mind races with thoughts: *This must be the single most horrific thing I've ever heard in my life. Why, just last week, I was with my brothers at the Jamboree, laughing, telling tales around a campfire, and now this, I'm here? How did this happen? How did my life become a nightmare overnight?*

Appraising the situation at hand, I tell Stani, "I don't think you are strong enough to carry your friend, so I will do the task for you."

Stani wipes his tears, but more fall. "I'm stronger than most think. No, I cannot have you do that. If Dukolf sees you helping me, he will beat you, too."

"I'm not scared of him."

"You should be, he's as evil as they get. But it's the kapo that told me to do the deed."

"I'm not afraid of him either."

"Okay, we should do this now, get it over with."

I bend down to lift the man. Even though my body feels weak, the anger surging through me gives me Herculean strength. I lift the man as though he's lighter than a feather.

We walk outside into the overcast day and suddenly I'm grateful it's not raining or worse.

It's bad enough to have to perform this task. And the thought occurs to me, *Jakob's interminable suffering has ended. Surely there is something good awaiting him on the other side. Or is there?*

Stani directs me to the pit, but frankly, the smell is enough to lead me to its edge. While I carry the body, Stani tells me about another prisoner, Stephan. He says that I remind him of Stephan.

I ask, "How so?"

"He wasn't afraid of the guards or kapos either. He said his hatred kept him strong. It gave him courage to face another day here."

I can relate to that; I feel an ample supply of strength surging through me.

I tell Stani, "I'm going to break out of here. I don't plan on staying here for any length of time."

Stani shakes his head. "Ironic you should say that. You sound just like Stephan. I pray you don't meet your end like he did. You don't have to worry anyway—you're not Jewish."

Now is not the time for that conversation. Even my father doesn't know I know.

As we perambulate toward our destination, my senses awake to the unmistakable stench of death and suddenly, it conquers me. I drop Jakob's body and retch, dry heaving, nothing coming out. I hold my sides, which hurt as I heave. My bruised ribs ache and I sweat profusely.

After a few moments, I regain what's left of my fortitude and continue the bizarre and macabre funeral march with Stani and the dead man, Jakob. I try desperately not to think. Or see. Or breathe.

We don't speak until we reach the pit. I bend to lay Jakob's body at the edge. As I stand up, the view is beyond vile and repulsive, my eyes taking in a sight that even turpentine could not remove. Many bodies, some clothed, some naked in various stages of decomposition, lie in a true pit, over an area that stretches fifty yards long, and about ten yards wide. *Don't look, don't take it in, don't remember, keep your eyes closed.*

It's not a very deep pit. I sit on the edge and somehow, I find the wherewithal to step down two feet into the pit without stepping on a body. I worry my foot might sink inside the stomach and guts of a once-living soul. I maneuver my feet between a few corpses. I try with all my might not to stare or see any more of the horror before me.

My senses have become used to the smell. While it sickens me, there is no more vomit to come out of me; my guts feel wrung dry. I gag a few more times while I drag Jakob's corpse into my arms. With my eyes closed, I kiss his bruised, beaten, cold forehead and lower his bony corpse into the grave.

Is this real? Am I putting a dead man on top of other dead men that lie on top of other dead men?

"Goodbye, Jakob. I'm sorry I never knew you."

Stani gives me his hand and helps me out of the grave.

I can do nothing to assuage the images or the reality I find myself in. I cannot take the time to think about what I just saw or what I just did. If I do, my conscience will break me down; I will crumble, fall apart. I cannot allow that. I cannot survive if I do.

Stani pats me on the back. "I knew you were a fine fellow the moment I saw you."

I tell Stani, "I've lost sight of the kapos and guards. Is the coast clear? Do you see any kapos or guards nearby?"

"No. Not yet, let's hurry back to my barracks."

While we do, the thought occurs to me. *This man is stark naked. What else will become familiar to my increasingly-numbed senses?* More thoughts of horror creep into my subconscious; I push them away.

Back inside the barracks, after our task is carried out, Stani reveals valuable information. He whispers, "Stephan was in the stages of planning a breakout when Dukolf shot him to death. He stashed officers' uniforms from the storeroom in a hiding place. I had only been here a day or two when he asked me if I agreed with a breakout. I answered 'yes.' He told me of a plan, do you want to hear it?"

No need to ask twice. I answer, "Yes, I do, please tell me."

Suddenly the barracks door bursts open, the hinges barely holding on, and in walks the corrupt and depraved guard Dukolf.

His eyes zero in on me. He wastes no time marching over to us, to interrogate us.

We remain seated.

His gaze bears down on me. While he reaches for his bat, he asks, "What are you doing in the Jewish barracks?"

I stand. My six-foot frame towers over the pudgy and short, sinister bully.

Without an ounce of fear, I state, "I'm new here, I lost my way."

"Are you being smart with me? If you are, you'll regret it, I promise you!"

With authoritative defiance in my tone, I tell the miserable piece of flesh before me, "I work in the garage, by order of the commandant. I must leave and get to work. Stanislaw is a helper in the garage as well. Are you ready to go now?"

Stani follows my lead. "Yes, yes, of course."

I stride by Dukolf, with Stani in tow, leaving Dukolf to wonder what just happened.

Once out the door, we pick up our pace, giggling like little kids at our audacity and fearlessness. We make our way inside the confines of the garage, finding my father standing before the assignment work detail board, chewing on the end of a pencil, pondering the day and the amount of work before him.

I tell my father all that's taken place this morning and introduce him to Stani. My father, not one to hide his obvious anger, stands stiff and tense. By his tone, I know he's not pleased.

"Yes, Wolfie, I know all about the pit. In fact, the experience of it was thrust upon me during my first days here, and like you, also in a horrible, brutal way. You have my sympathies."

His stare could melt wax. I feel the heat of it. The smell of grease and oil causes me to feel queasy once again.

"When you weren't at breakfast, I became worried that something happened to you. Here, take this."

My father reaches in his pocket and hands me a sausage and a small piece of bread. I give it to Stani, displeasing my father again.

My father's expression is stern, reminding me he warned me to keep my distance from the Jewish prisoners.

When my father is angry his jaw line is tense, the bones in his face standing firm, angular, like a sharp edge of metal. My father's anger alarms me, but I continue talking, eager to share news of a possible escape plan.

"Poppa, Stani has some ideas about escaping. We all need to talk."

With peaking irritation, my father replies, "Now is not the time. We have more work than we can handle, and that's not my concern now. I'm told the Führer's car will need to take top priority over the other vehicles. I have no idea how it's humanly possible to get this work done in the time allotted. We might have to work straight through the night. Now, let's get to work." It's impossible to mistake my father's annoyance for anything else.

Stani agrees, "Yes, now is not the time. I will see you later."

And with that, Stani heads to the wall to begin his job of carrying rocks. As if my courage to stand up to Dukolf made him feel less fearful, he leaves our presence whistling a song.

My father wastes no time telling me, "Let's get to work, enough standing around."

"Poppa, you seem angry with me."

I don't fully engage with my own anger. I have enough sense to know now is not the right time. But there are so many questions. Like why he never told me my momma was Jewish. I can keep my anger tucked away, for now. He doesn't know that Uncle Rolf and Aunt Cecile told me all about my mother.

In a hushed tone he states, "I told you to stay clear of the Jewish men. You willfully disobeyed me."

"You're right, I did. But I think I met Stani for a reason. He can help us."

My father is incredulous that I am stalling his attempt to return to work. "Son, have you lost your mind? How is a naked Jewish man going to help us?"

"What if we used Stani to dump oil and change tires? We could get more work done, I could assist you more with repairs, and do oil changes myself while you gap engines and repair fuel lines, radiators, and the more complicated servicing."

This thought makes my father stop and consider for a moment. "He will have to have a uniform. He can't be in the garage stark naked."

"I'm sure that's not by choice. But he seems strong. If he can carry rocks, he can carry the oil bin and tires. And, while we work he can tell us of the plan Stephan designed and engineered to escape from here. It's a good plan, almost watertight."

"Yes, well, you cannot be talking openly about escaping, do you understand? Aside from that, I think you've got a point there. Okay, I'll talk to Merkel, the garage kapo, and see what he says."

And for a lightning-quick moment, I feel a faint, flashing glimmer of hope.

CHAPTER SEVENTEEN

Buster, Raymond, and Maddie

AUGUST 1933

WILLIAMS AND O'MARA have the troop assembled in the hotel lobby. The boys are wondering why their troop leader is not present.

Ever present are the two Brownshirts, but not the third. The morning sun rays warm the dusty lobby, while the boys, some still sleepy-eyed, huddle together, chatting quietly amongst themselves.

Raymond approaches prepared as best he can for the task at hand. Bobby runs up to him, inquiring about Buster. Hopeful, he asks, "Mr. Wellington, how is Buster feeling, is he better?"

"Kind of you to ask. He's doing better, but still a bit sick. I'll tell him you asked about him."

O'Mara quiets the troop, raising his hands and shushing them, before nodding, "Mr. Wellington?"

Speaking in a modulated, hushed tone, Raymond delivers the troublesome news to the boys.

"Boys, good morning. I have some difficult news to share with you all."

He pauses. The air is heavy. All eyes are on him. He takes a courtroom pose, standing with his weight to the left, his hands folded before him, at his waistline. Taking a deep breath, he continues.

"During the night, Troop Leader Lewis suffered a medical event, which we now believe to be a heart attack. Having no earlier knowledge of any health conditions, we can only assume this to be the case. A local doctor and medical examiner will be here to make the determination.

"I'm sorry to have to share this news, but Leader Lewis has passed away. I know it's painful and shocking. I know you all cared about him very much and enjoyed him as your Leader. I'm so sorry, boys. Life is like this sometimes, the unexpected happens. This is one of those times. But we will soldier on, in true Boy Scout form and fashion. Leader Lewis would expect no less. Mr. Williams, Mr. O'Mara, and I are here if any of you need to talk about this or have any questions. Don't hesitate to ask anything at all, any question you have; we want to help you through this time. I know this is a shock; it is to us adults as well. We will help each other; we will go through this together like good Scouts, okay?"

Eleven-year-old Walter Johnson's hand shoots up. Raymond cringes internally, feeling his body stiffen, anticipating it's a question about death.

"Yes, Walter, you have a question?"

Walter's eyes are brimming with tears, his face red. He stands slouched, as if he's preparing for a whipping. He asks timidly, "Is Leader Lewis dead?"

Grimacing, Raymond's eyes meet Walter's. The sadness in them penetrates Raymond, as though Walter is peering into his soul. "Yes, Walter, he has passed."

Raymond wonders why Walter's tears stop at the news of Lewis's death. *Is that a smile on Walter's face? Is he happy about this?*

Some of the younger boys begin sobbing, not knowing what to do with the news, while a few of the older ones put an arm around the shoulders of the boys who are expressing grief. O'Mara gathers the boys into the dining room for breakfast. "Let's stay on schedule, boys. We're Scouts, Leader Lewis would expect as much from us. We can talk more about this after breakfast. For now, let's keep with the program."

Raymond would prefer to allow the boys time to talk, but keeping to a schedule is for the best. He ruminates about this decision while Williams makes his way over to him.

Williams commends Raymond, and sheepishly adds, "Well done—you handled that with perfect aplomb, couldn't have said it any better. Now what do we do? What's next?"

"You and O'Mara will take over. I recommend contacting the bus company, then heading for Bremen as planned. The relevant information is in our itinerary. I've got a matter to attend to on behalf of the State Department. I'm meeting with the U.S. ambassador, who is on his way here. He'll help with the legal arrangements to get Lewis back to the U.S. I can stay behind and attend to these matters. Do you feel well enough staffed with O'Mara to handle the troop for the rest of the trip to the ship?"

With a grin, Williams says, "Oh, yes, of course, the boys are no trouble. The biggest troublemaker will stay behind with you—Buster."

As the implied jest falls flat, Raymond stares clear through the back of Williams's balding head.

"I'm joking with you, Wellington, trying to lighten a dire situation."

"Yes, right. I find it hard to laugh about anything right now, so forgive me. I sure wish we knew if Lewis had next of kin, or extended family to contact. Do you know of anyone at all?"

"O'Mara said something about a family member in Hungary. Budapest, I think, although he wasn't sure what the connection is, mother or father's side."

"Right, well, I'll let you get to it. I've got to check on Buster; he still has a slight fever."

"How is he taking the news? Wish him our best, would you?"

"Like everyone, he's shocked, but I will extend your wishes, thank you."

How could Williams make jokes at a time like this? *And now, I must face the other matter. The truth about Buster and his mother. How did Maddie know something was amiss, how did she instinctually know I was hiding a secret?*

Time to get it out in the open. No more hiding, no more lies.

Raymond knocks on the door, whispering, "Buster, it's Dad, let me in."

Raymond enters the room and says, "Well, I see you're both cleaned up. Maddie, you bring that uniform to life, better than expected!"

Maddie shrugs. "I guess, so, but the hat feels a bit ridiculous; I've never had anything this big on my head before! I just need shoes."

"Right. Buster, Ollie is the smallest of your gang—how many pairs of shoes would he have brought? Two?"

"No telling. He's from a big family; he's lucky to have one pair. But Walter is small, and he's an only child. I bet he has two pairs at least."

"Okay, good. The troop is eating breakfast and I've told the chaperones that we might as well get them out of here and on the road to Bremen. That will help us a great deal. The ambassador will be here later today, and I'll have to go with him, fill him in on details and such. I need you two to stay put here. I'm going to find a bookstore to get you a book or two to read, or a magazine or paper. You've got to be bored stiff by now, locked up in here."

Buster smiles at Maddie, with a knowing glance of something shared only between them.

With confidence, speaking for both of them, Buster says, "We're not bored, we have plenty to talk about."

Maddie blushes, avoiding direct eye contact with her friend. After a moment, she raises her eyes to meet Buster's gaze. He breaks the brief, intimate connection, addressing his father.

"Will you tell me what you were going to speak about last night? You never began, but I want to know if it's something to do with me. That is, if you have time. I realize you're juggling a dozen eggs right now."

Stalling for a moment to gather his thoughts, Raymond glances at his watch.

"The ambassador won't be here for a few more hours, and who knows when the doctor and coroner will show up. Is there any more coffee in that pot?"

Maddie jumps to attention, pouring Raymond a cup. After serving him, she says, "Is this something you'd rather talk about without me here? I don't want it to be awkward for you because of my presence. I don't know where I'd go, but you could go somewhere more private." She says this while nodding towards Buster.

While seating himself in a chair, Buster says, "If it's okay with you, I don't mind Maddie being here, do you?"

"No, of course not, son. It's Maddie's plight that brought this up to begin with."

Raymond sits on the edge of the bed. Never short of words, he finds himself grasping for a cogent place to begin. "Let's see where to start."

Raymond is apprehensive, but full of compassion, knowing this story could wound his son.

"Let me preface this by saying that the reason I've not spoken of this yet is because I wanted to protect you from hurt, keep you from suffering over something you can do nothing about. But everyone deserves the right to grieve and grieve we must: it is the pathway to healing. Now you are old enough to know the truth of your genesis."

The heft of Raymond's words causes Buster to sit back in his chair.

"Whoa. What do you mean, the truth of my genesis? What are you talking about?"

Without missing a beat, Raymond continues, "The identity of your birth mother."

Incredulous, Buster shouts, "My birth mother? He spits out the words, frothing with anger.

"Son, I tried to protect you, keep you from experiencing more pain than you could handle, you were so very young the second time. I just couldn't bear to tell you about the first."

Buster fumes, "If Maddie never came along, you wouldn't have told me, would you? Maddie is the catalyst for the truth!"

Raymond hesitates, waiting to see if his son will continue. "No, I would have told you anyway. The circumstances seem right, and there is no time like the present. Know that it's not my intention to cause you pain."

"But does this mean you've lied to me up until now, withholding something that directly impacts my life? How could you, Dad? How could you be so cruel?" Buster crosses his arms, feeling bitterness rise within him as he glares at his father. "Well, out with it, let's hear it."

Struck by his son's harsh attitude, Raymond tells him, "Hey, hold on a minute, I won't tolerate insolence no matter what the situation." The tension in the room rises, causing the oxygen to all but evaporate.

Maddie raises her hand, wanting to add to the conversation. "May I speak for a moment?"

Raymond wastes no time telling her, "Maddie, while I know your desire is to help, I don't think it's your place to get involved in this discussion."

"With all due respect, I think I can be an objective mediator."

Buster takes the lead. "Be my guest, you have the floor."

Raymond winces, as though he is preparing to be slapped.

Addressing Buster, Maddie begins, "We've spent quite a bit of intense time together here. We've talked a lot and bared our souls over some things. I feel like to a certain extent I know you, enough to say this and speak to your heart. Give your father a chance to explain himself before you pass judgment. Believe him when he tells you it's not his intention to hurt you. From what you've shared with me, your father is a remarkably good man. Measure your life in its entirety and examine all the good he's done for you. Gauge it against this one revelation. In other words, judge him for the overall good, not this one incident."

Buster speaks to Maddie as if his father isn't even in the room. "Yes, but now, who knows what else he's lied to me about; how can I ever trust him again, or believe anything he says?"

"You can stay stuck here in your anger, or you can give him a chance and hear what he has to say."

Buster toys with a pencil, as if unconvinced.

Raymond's eyes drop to the floor. He stays silent.

Buster continues, "The pain I feel is too great to be tamped down by a few words. The newness of this wound has yet to sink in. The size of it is far too great to comprehend right now."

Maddie doesn't give up, bringing up the most pivotal point of all. "Do you know your father loves you?"

"Yes, of course."

"Then give him the benefit of the doubt. Wouldn't you want him, expect him, to do the same with you?"

Softening, Buster glances at his father and then Maddie. He struggles to find the right words. "I guess you're right." He turns to his father. "I'm sorry. But I'm angry and I don't know what to do with these feelings. This news combined with the sadness I feel about Wolfie is just too much to grapple with. Add Leader Lewis to the mix, and this is more than I can handle. I'm confused by it all, all these feelings, I'm overwhelmed, and it will take more than a moment to completely understand."

Gently, Raymond adds, "That is totally understandable. Your mother helped me to express myself, to talk about my feelings rather than hide behind them or push them away. Expressing feelings is not what most men do. But I will tell you, there is no greater peace you will have, once you discover that you can resolve your feelings."

"I have no inkling what that means, 'resolve my feelings.' I'm only sixteen, remember?

And I don't like to talk about things I don't understand."

The air is heavy and fraught with tension. They sit in silence, the three of them, each contemplating what to say next. It is Buster who speaks first.

"I know I can come to you and talk about these things, my feelings, and that lifts some of the heaviness."

Raymond crosses the small space between them that moments before seemed like an abyss and hugs his son.

Buster asks his father, "Will you continue with the story? I want to hear more."

"Okay, on the condition that you're sincere, I will."

Buster nods.

Taking a deep breath, Raymond begins, "While attending

the University of Rochester, I fell in love with a young woman named Rachael. We both sang for the glee club and became friends in choir during our freshman year. Rachael was Jewish. I wanted more than a friendship with her, but that wasn't possible at the time. She had a boyfriend—a Jewish boy. He did not treat her well. I caught him yelling at her and being brutish with her on several occasions. He was a bully. One of the times I saw him mistreating her, I stood against him to protect her honor, fighting him. Eventually, Rachael broke up with him and started to date me.

"But all was not well; her family did not care for me because I was not Jewish. Even after explaining the treatment by her former boyfriend, her parents still thought she needed to marry the Jewish boy. Their families were friends, they attended the same synagogue, they long ago planned their children would marry.

"This revelation astounded me—how Rachael's parents would think an abuser was better for their daughter than I was. It made no sense, at least, not to me.

"Upon graduation, against her parents' wishes, we were married at City Hall by a justice of the peace. My mother and father, your grandparents, welcomed Rachael, knowing I was in love with her. They made the decision to love her too, but my sisters did not, and made life unpleasant for her. They had animosity for her because she was Jewish, and I never found out the real reason they had such ill feelings towards Jews. No one ever harmed them, they had no dealings with Jews. They hated for the sake of hating. My sisters were quite evil towards Rachael. I know they were jealous of her beauty and the fact that she captured me, had all my attention. They wrote poison pen letters to her, sent anonymously, but I knew who wrote them."

Buster puts a hand up, stopping his father, asking, "Are you serious? How did you know, and what would the letters say?"

"My sisters tried to cover their tracks, by saying the letters must have been from Rachael's 'former classmates.' The letters were full of venom, and terribly mean-spirited. You see, in their eyes, I was the golden boy of our family, the eldest. They thought Rachael was unworthy. Can you imagine? Now you know why I have little to do with my sisters. Rachael's parents all but disowned her. But at the time, we thought it didn't matter.

"We were so in love, we felt we could scale any mountain, overcome any challenge. If we were together, nothing seemed impossible. This is the emotional and predictable response of youth, young love. We hoped her parents would soften over time and accept our marriage.

"After receiving my law degree and passing the bar exam, I worked for my father's law firm. His firm specialized in litigation of policy for the U.S. government, much like the work I do now for the State Department. We worked at the state, and eventually at the federal level. After three years on the job, I began to travel often to Washington, presenting briefs to federal attorneys and the like.

"In January of 1916, your mother became pregnant with you, and reached out to her parents to share the good news. The idea of a grandchild thrilled them, especially since Rachael was their only child. They came around a bit, made overtures to reconcile, which made us happy. They bought a bassinet and a highchair; things first-time parents would need."

Raymond wipes his eyes, not expecting an avalanche of emotion to overcome him while recounting the story. He takes a deep breath before going on, and to calm him, he lights a cigarette, and takes a long drag, hoping smoking will settle his nerves.

"I haven't spoken about this for many, many years. I've kept it hidden. I never thought this would be so painful to speak of, to share."

Maddie and Buster listen, engrossed in the story.

Reaching for a glass of water on the tray, Raymond gulps it down, wiping his mouth with the back of his hand. "This is the tough part." Pacing the floor in the small room, he continues smoking his cigarette, stubbing it out before finishing it. Rubbing his eyes, he begins to tell the pain-filled part of the story.

"You see, your mother became ill before she gave birth to you. She developed bacteria in her bloodstream, sepsis, and, and it took her life after giving birth to you."

Buster shakes his head, not sure he's heard correctly. His disbelief gathers like a dripping faucet filling a pot. "What did you say? Did you say it killed her?"

Slowly, Raymond nods, whispering, "Yes."

Buster wastes no time throwing himself into his father's arms. He weeps, not sure if he's weeping for his mother or himself, or both.

"I don't even know what to miss, but it hurts all the same."

While holding his son in warmth and love, Raymond encourages Buster, "It's okay to cry, son, it's a very sad story."

CHAPTER EIGHTEEN

Elenena and Annie

SUMMER 1925

AFTER WHAT SEEMS like an eternity to Elenena, Hitler finally begins the process of wrapping up his speech. His discourse is filled with ranting and a full display of the impassioned maniacal ideology he's known for, endearing his followers to him in full-blown commitment. Sweat is dripping off his face and perspiration stains his shirt.

"The consequences of this campaign are extraordinary. Apart from modest correction of its frontiers, our interest is in safeguarding peace in our region of the world, and building our economic strength, procuring the production of goods needed for us to grow in might and power. This means jobs, and income for all!" Clutching at his chest, he exclaims, "My heart is bursting with joy. Join with me in our national revolution and together we will garner worldwide esteem, respect and admiration! We will be a force to be reckoned with! We will be the envy of the modern world! And we will usher in a thousand-year Reich for our motherland, Germania!"

At the end of a two-hour harangue, the crowd, jubilant with emotion, applauds and cheers at ear-splitting levels.

Twice, Elenena has to jolt herself awake as Hitler drones on and on. Not only is she bored, but her back bothers her from sitting in one position for two hours. While Annie still cheers boisterously until Hitler leaves the makeshift platform and podium, Elenena plots her responses to the countless litany of questions she imagines Annie will ask once the clamor subsides.

Annie's friend Martin wastes no time coming back to visit the creature of his fascination, despite his friend's obvious discomfort. He smiles at Elenena, appraising her with an auspicious expression, like she's a meal for him to consume.

"Annie, I forgot to give you this before, here are more names for the list. I know I don't have to do your work, but I thought you might appreciate the help and as a reward, invite me over for tea with Miss Laurent." He says this while nodding expectantly at Elenena, hoping for a positive reaction from her, but there is none.

Snatching the paper from his hand, Annie rolls her eyes at Martin. "Not tonight, I'm sorry. We have things to do."

Elenena wonders what is so urgent.

Even though Martin is as crazy as the rest of these Hitler supporters, it might be nice to have company.

"Oh, why not, Annie, what have we to do?" she says impulsively. "It will be fun to have company!"

Annie's cheeks redden, and she huffs like she's about to burst with anger and throw a fit. "Well, there's supper, for one, and there are tasks I'd like you to take care of tonight. And don't you have to practice your violin?"

Annie's tone, flat as ever, enunciates each word as a way to convey her frustration.

Elenena dismisses Annie's excuses. "I do, but I can always do that later, after supper, when my chores are done."

Martin jumps at the opportunity. "Then it's a date?" Barely able to contain his joy, he beams broadly at Elenena and for a moment she appraises him, taking into account his masculine appearance, the thick and wavy dark blond hair that frames his face, his even white teeth, and his casual, but neat attire. For a farmer, that's saying something. Only his muddy boots give him away.

Feeling obliged and outnumbered, Annie gives in, scrunching her face in disapproval.

"Oh, for God's sake, all right, but our supper will be meager divided by three."

Martin considers her words, tilts his head, and flashes his best charming smile, saying, "But at least we'll have plenty of bread!" He holds up his prized loaf, while putting his arm around a surprised Annie, giving her shoulders a hug, and catching her off guard. Visibly flustered by the attention, she blushes. Then her ornery temperament takes over again, and she shouts a commanding, "Well, then let's go!"

Martin is tall, well over six feet, with a muscular build. He leads the way, making room for the two women behind him. Elenena is in the middle only because Martin turned to grab Annie's hand. She recoiled at the gesture, pushing Elenena between them.

He turns around protectively, watching his charge, making sure no one stops them or holds them up from advancing towards the exit. Men speak to Elenena as she passes by, as she, in turn, forces a smile.

Martin takes the steps two by two and the three make their way out of the Bier Cellar and into the evening air, which feels exhilarating and fresh-smelling to Elenena after hours spent in the dank, dim space. The gentle breezes of the evening will clear out the disharmonic thoughts racing through her mind. She feels squashed by the weight of a two-hour long barrage of negativity.

Martin is happy to make conversation. "So, is Elenena a French name? I notice your last name is, so you must be French."

Martin asks so casually, Elenena is unsure how to answer. She decides it's better to keep her guard up and stay with the same story she told Annie. "I was born in Paris and grew up there. How about you?"

"The Motherland is home to me. Munich is where I was born and where I will die. I love living here. I'm a generational farmer, I farm the same land as my great-grandparents. My chickens are twenty years young." With a coy smile he adds, "They love Munich too!"

Annie pushes past Martin and Elenena, sighing loudly as Martin openly flirts. She walks briskly past while telling them both, "Don't dawdle, let's get home!"

Neither Martin nor Elenena respond to Annie's command.

Martin whispers something that Elenena already knows. "She likes to be in charge."

Elenena acknowledges his comment in the affirmative, nodding.

"So, you play violin, how enchanting. Are you any good?"

"I wouldn't say I'm good or bad but will improve. I start lessons with a new teacher Sunday; I'm extremely excited to start. Annie tells me he's a highly-respected professor."

Annie stops dead in her tracks and turns around to face Elenena. Her eyes narrowed, she barks, "I never said he was highly respected."

Having learned from past tempestuous conversations with Annie, Elenena decides it's as good a time as any to change the subject. She glances up at the sky, pointing to the moon, shining brilliantly like a beacon, a few days from completing its cycle.

"It's a lovely moon, a hint from full. If we were outside the city, we'd see the stars too. The sky is chock-full of them tonight."

Not missing a beat, Martin takes the opportunity to invite Elenena to his farm. "My farm is on the outskirts of the city, a mile and a half from here, where the sky seems larger. You can view a full complement of stars on a clear night. I love gazing at the heavens. Another thing we have in common."

He winks at Elenena, but she pretends not to notice.

The trio arrive at Annie's brownstone. Annie stomps up the front steps, unlocks the door, and flings it open. She wastes no time laying down the rules.

"Now Martin, you can't stay long. Have your supper and leave."

Despite the inhospitable nature of his host, Martin takes no offense, asking, "How can I be of help and service?" Once inside and in the front room, he points to the empty fireplace. "The night air is cool; would you like me to make a fire? I can make one in no time!"

Softening momentarily, Annie agrees, "Okay, that would be nice, thank you. There are kindling and cut logs outside behind the kitchen, on a rack. Make sure you replace the tarp over the wood when you're finished."

Ready to give more orders, Annie marches into the kitchen and summons Elenena. "Light the stove and heat up that soup you made yesterday. There is the roast chicken, we can have that with the bread. Slice up his loaf but save ours."

Taking off the mothball-scented coat, Elenena hands it to Annie. "Thank you for allowing me to wear your coat."

"Go hang it up yourself if you're really grateful."

"Yes, Annie, of course."

Before leaving to hang up Annie's coat, Elenena points to the kitchen table. "Is there a third chair we can use for the three of us, to sit here in the kitchen?"

Annie responds with prickly irritation. "No, we won't all fit in here with Martin's big feet. We will eat in the dining room. I only hope he has the good sense to shake some of that mud off his boots first, or you'll be washing that floor after dinner!"

"I will mention that to him when I go to set the table."

"Good, you do that."

Annie leaves the kitchen and heads straight into her bedroom. She shuts the door just short of slamming it.

Elenena goes about her kitchen duties, heating up the soup after lighting the stove. Then Martin meanders into the kitchen. He watches with pleasure as Elenena handles a knife with skill to debone the chicken and slice it. Lastly, she arranges the cold chicken on one of Annie's porcelain platters.

"Say, you're pretty good at that, and I should know, seeing I raise such birds and am very familiar with every part of their anatomy."

Elenena pays him no attention.

With blatant passion, Martin announces, "I'd like to become more familiar with your anatomy to be honest," as he reaches for a sample of the roasted bird. His sheepish grin and unabashed boldness cause a smile to crack the surface of Elenena's serious demeanor.

Wasting no time shutting down any thought of such an adventure, she tells him firmly but sweetly, "Nice segue, but that will not happen."

"What won't happen?"

Annie, standing in the doorway behind Martin, is eavesdropping on the conversation.

Elenena stiffens and Martin brushes off the question, asking Annie, "What's next, boss, set the table? Where do you hide your precious silverware? Show me and I'll make three place-settings. Don't seem so surprised, Annie. I'm housebroken. There's more to me than my handsome appearance!"

"Fine, but what about your dirty boots?"

"I'll shake them off outside!"

While leaving the kitchen, Martin catches Elenena watching him. He winks at her.

She whispers under her breath, "Brazen flirt."

Annie's dining room, like most of the house, lacks warmth. No pictures or photographs depicting a happy or pleasant history lend personality to the room. There is an old hutch taking up one wall, holding worn porcelain china with a faint pattern of roses that is still recognizable. Crystal glasses and goblets take up the other shelf. The credenza has crocheted doilies to hide the scratches on the surface made by a former resident, a surly twenty-pound tomcat named Brummbär. The yellowed, faded wallpaper shows its age. The room itself is clean, making up for its shortcomings.

Annie opens the drawer to the credenza, taking out three place-settings of silverware and napkins, handing them to Martin. She takes three bowls and three plates from the hutch, also handing them to Martin. Together they set the table in silence.

Suddenly self-conscious, Annie makes excuses for the room. "I don't eat in here often. You know, when you don't use a room, it can seem cold. I can't remember the last time I had company over."

Martin smiles warmly at his host, saying jovially, "We'll have to make this a regular event so your room will not be lonely."

Annie can't tell if Martin is making fun of her or if he's sincere. With her usual crustiness, she tells him, "I'll go check on Elenena. Sit down."

Once in the kitchen, Annie questions, "Are you ready, is the soup hot?"

"Yes, Annie, it's in the tureen. I'll follow with the bread and chicken."

The women enter the dining room.

Elenena serves the soup. Then Martin jumps up to hold her chair.

"Annie, would you mind if I say a blessing over the food?" he asks. "In my house growing up we hold hands and say a blessing. Okay with you both?"

Annie nods, giving Martin a curious glance. "I never thought a farmer would be so religious."

He says nothing, instead he holds out a hand to each woman. The three hold hands while Martin blesses the food. "We thank thee O Lord for the blessings we are about to receive. Bless the hands that prepared the food and the pockets of those who provided it. Amen."

Annie provides Martin with another inquisitive stare and mumbles, "Thank you."

Martin makes conversation about a topic he knows will bring his host to life, the meeting and their leader, Adolf Hitler. "So, kamerad, what did you think of tonight? It was a good turnout. The speech was long—longer than usual."

Annie slurps her soup and contemplates her answer, perturbed Martin would criticize Hitler before a non-party member.

"Oh, I don't know. I could listen to him speak forever, for hours on end. I am fascinated by his depth of knowledge, his familiarity with history. He has so many facts at his fingertips, and he speaks with passion and authority."

"Yes, I would agree. He certainly does. Quite an orator, certainly gifted. Tell me, how many names do you have on the list?"

Elenena is quiet, listening to the two, while forming opinions. She breaks her silence and asks, "I'm curious, what is the list?"

Matter-of-factly, Annie tells her, "The list is the list of names of Jews living in Munich. We gather names and addresses in every German city where there is a Nazi Party presence. We all have a job to do!"

As if reading Elenena's mind, Martin answers the question before she asks it. "We turn in the lists to the officers in the party. We keep track of the Jews all over Germany. Someday soon, the list will include the countries of Austria, Hungary, Poland, and Lithuania, as well as Northern Europe, like Latvia, and hopefully even more."

Elenena feels the sudden onset of nausea. Her stomach churning, she reaches for the platter of challah and passes it to Annie and then Martin before taking a slice for herself.

Annie takes a bite, and then another and another, barely stopping to savor the bread while Martin takes his time, first smelling the slice and then delicately taking a small bite. His eyes roll back as he exclaims, "This is the most delicious bread I've ever tasted."

Not a second elapses before Elenena thinks, *Jewish bread made by Jewish hands, just for you Nazis. Please choke on it.*

Annie praises the bread as well. "I'm curious, what is the sweetness in the bread?"

While gazing at Elenena, Martin adds, "The hands that made it, no doubt."

Mildly embarrassed by the praise, Elenena shyly tells the two, "Just a touch of honey. And the quality of the eggs makes a difference, as well. Baking in an exact oven also helps greatly."

But Elenena has questions, the bulk of them exploding between her ears.

Annie returns to the conversation about the lists, speaking in a tone fraught with both hostility and pride, like she's letting out a secret. "Your violin instructor is on a list, and so are the owners of the bakery where you work—in case you didn't know, they are Jews."

Elenena tries to maintain a calm demeanor while escalating fear churns in her gut. She keeps her head down, consuming a spoonful of soup, demurely asking the question, "But why Jews? Why would you need to keep track of them?"

Martin's earlier warmth and irresistible attraction to Elenena evaporate on the spot. The air becomes charged with electricity as his demeanor makes a one hundred eighty-degree shift.

Incredulous, he shouts while pounding his fist on the table, rattling the china, silverware, and the nerves of the two women, "What does it matter? Are you kidding me? What does it matter?" His tone is icy, voice raised. Even Annie seems surprised by his sudden change in personality.

Martin continues his rant, waving his hands while spitting out contemptuous words. "All the problems we Germans face are due to the Jews. Don't you know, because of them we lost the Great War, because of them our country is in economic ruin due to the thieving Jewish bankers and money movers? Going back centuries, the Black Plague, along with other various illnesses and poisonings that befell our nation, were due to those dirty and evil miscreants. We have suffered at their hands for generations and it's time for it to stop."

For emphasis, in chilling fashion Martin takes his index finger and drags it along his throat, making a slashing motion.

"We intend to rid our country of them in the time to come. Herr Hitler's plan is to rid the world of them if it is possible."

Regaining his composure, he tucks his hair behind his ears, calming himself.

Breathing deeply, as if there is a sudden shortage of oxygen, he continues, "Herr Hitler intends to proceed one step at a time. While keeping faithful to his vision, his commitment to the people of Germany and our heritage, we will reclaim all of that and more once the dirty vermin are gone."

His tone becomes relaxed again as his face lights with an idea. He reaches out and places one of his large, rough hands atop Elenena's.

"We can fight this fight together, side by side, and do our part to help Germany." With excitement in his voice he says, "I can visualize it now. Tell me you will?"

Elenena blushes under such pressure, while both Annie and Martin glue their eyes on her, waiting for her reaction and answer. As diplomatically as possible, Elenena says, "Like you said, one step at a time. Now, I'm ready for tea—may I prepare some for you both? I'll turn on the kettle."

Extracting her hand from Martin's, she rises to clear the plates from the table. He jumps up, offering, "Let me help you."

"No, you are a guest, please stay." She smiles brightly at him, saying as calmly and cheerfully as possible, "I'll only be a minute."

Elenena carries the armload of dishes into the kitchen, trying to gently place them in the deep sink, but without much luck—the silverware clatters loudly against the porcelain surface. Her body stiffens with fear, her head throbs with tension. She gasps for air, turning on the water. It comes out ice-cold. She places her hands, which have become suddenly hot, under the faucet as she trembles. Her mind is spinning in every direction. The water causes her to feel cold all over. Turning it off, she grips the countertop with both hands, feeling faint with fear. A desperate sensation saturates her with a panic she has not felt since childhood.

Elenena recognizes the sinking, drowning feeling at once. It's how she felt after receiving the news her mother jumped off the bridge.

How did I become trapped in such a position with these two? Dear God, I've got to get away from these people! They're lunatics! They'll kill me right now if they find out I'm Jewish!

CHAPTER NINETEEN

Wolfie, Frederick, and Stanislaw

AUGUST 1933

AS PROMISED, TWELVE trucks and two motorcars, one being the Führer's Mercedes, are on the grounds of the camp for service.

The weather is pleasant. A southerly breeze blows through the garage's open doors, cooling the space. Frederick smokes a cigarette, watching as the garage kapo approaches.

Merkel reminds Frederick while winding his watch, "Don't delay on the Führer's auto. Get that done first. The Führer expects every piece of equipment to be ready. I don't care if it takes all night, you do whatever it takes as long as you complete the work, is that clear?"

Merkel passes the clipboard with the work orders to Frederick. After pouring over the papers Frederick nods, and then poses a question to the kapo.

"Considering the amount of work that needs to be done, may I use another prisoner who is strong enough to help? Perhaps he could assist us, dumping oil and helping with the tire changes on the trucks. Do I have your permission?"

Merkel sizes up Frederick. "Okay. But I promise you, if you do not complete the work there will be hell to pay."

"Yes, sir. I would expect nothing less. I'll need a garage

uniform to identify him, that is, with your approval."

Merkel takes the clipboard and scribbles an order, signing the paper. "There. Now get to work." Merkel leaves the garage to attend to other matters.

Frederick makes eye contact with his son, nodding to him.

While Wolfie finds Stani, Frederick marches to the storeroom to hand in the uniform requisition. The uniforms Wolfie and Frederick wear are different than those worn by the other prisoners. Frederick and Wolfie must move the service trucks and vehicles, driving them in and out of the garage and parking them in a lot next to the pit. The uniforms identify them as garage workers.

Merkel informs the commandant's personal guard that the work has begun. The guard then tells Eicke, who makes it a priority to get to the garage.

Eicke is in the garage, munching on a piece of strudel and dropping crumbs that rest on his extended belly, when Frederick comes back from the storeroom with a uniform for Stani. While going through the work orders on the board, Frederick enters the garage. Eicke greets him, "Frederick, so you have your work cut out for you!" He stares curiously at the uniform in Frederick's hands. "What have you there?"

"Good morning, Herr Commandant. This is a uniform for another prisoner who will help with the oil and tire changes. In order to complete the work orders as quickly as possible, I'll need some extra help."

The commandant reflects upon Frederick's words. "Yes, yes, of course. You know we have very few prisoners to spare—all are working on the construction of new barracks, new buildings. More prisoners will be arriving, putting our camp totals at four thousand. Big plans. Our camp will be the model for every other camp in the system."

While offering Eicke a cigarette and holding a match for him, Frederick inquires, "Forgive me, sir. More camps?"

"Yes, we will build many subcamps, supplementing Dachau, along with other camps in and around Germany. There is much work to do; we need all available hands, as many as we can find to do the labor."

Frederick finds the commandant's words disturbing. He returns his focus to Eicke, who says, "Frederick, as soon as you finish the work on the Führer's auto, make sure I'm notified. I'd like to take it for a spin before it's transported to Nuremberg." He winks at the mechanic. "That will be our little secret!"

"Yes, sir. Will be sure to, at once."

Eicke leaves the garage, whistling while he walks at a fast pace.

Wolfie and Stanislaw hide around a corner of the garage until the commandant is out of sight. Frederick spies them, waving to signal the coast is clear, then hands the uniform to Stani.

"Here's your uniform. Now, follow me and I'll explain our system to you."

Stanislaw stops to don the uniform. With gratitude, he turns to Frederick.

"Thank you. This is the first clothing I've had since I've been here. No one will recognize me!"

Wolfie muffles a laugh, but Frederick is serious as ever. He shows Stanislaw the work orders, how to follow them, and how to check off the boxes once he finishes the job.

"This workspace is better than I thought—very organized!"

Frederick ignores the compliment, launching into an explanation of the system of work orders. "Wolfie and I will drive the vehicles in and out of the garage. Make sure you match the vehicle plate number to the work order and the box you check. It's easy to lose track, so make sure you do that as soon as you're done. Any questions? If not, then let's get to work."

Frederick goes about installing a double-plated windshield on Hitler's parade car, a standard-issue Mercedes 770. The Reich has a deal with the Mercedes Benz company. They supply the Reich with vehicles and trucks. Many of the Reich's high-ranking officers drive the 770.

The Roots-type supercharger engine housed in the auto has exceptional features, with an inline eight cylinder made of extremely wear-resistant, chrome-nickeled, alloyed gray cast-iron. The Mercedes is the most technically advanced automobile Frederick has ever worked on. Luckily for him, he has the technical manual from the manufacturer in his possession.

He reviews the work order, finding a note on the second page, 'There is a vibration in the engine.' Frederick starts the vehicle, listening carefully as he revs the motor, wondering if it's the engine damper causing the problem.

Meanwhile, Stanislaw works under the first truck with Wolfie, accessing the oil pan, connecting a hose to drain the dirty engine oil into one of the oil bins. In a quiet voice, Wolfie asks his partner, "Stani, if Germany is so poor, where do all these vehicles come from?"

Stani cranks the tire wrench to tighten the lug nuts on a flatbed truck, completing a tire change. Wiping his brow, he tells Wolfie, "Allegedly, the Germans and Russians have a clandestine operation in Russia, and there is some form of agreement between Stalin and Hitler to fund the rearmament of Germany. This is in violation of the Treaty of Versailles, but the Allies don't know. It's been going on for almost two years."

Surprised by what sounds like inside information, Wolfie asks, "Where did you learn this, is this public knowledge?"

"No, it is not public knowledge. Jakob told me Stephan told him. Stephan, the prisoner I spoke of, had a brother-in-law, a scientist who worked for Nazis. The Nazis murdered him for selling secrets to Soviet spies."

For the most part, there is very little chatter among the men. They've each been going about their tasks for ten hours straight when the kapo Merkel appears to check on their progress.

"I would have checked sooner, but there were barracks inspections all day, with high-ranking officers checking out the camp. They'll be here in the garage tomorrow and might ask questions. I hope they won't be too much of a distraction."

Merkel frowns when he sees the Mercedes 770, assuming it would be in the lot with the other vehicles, repaired and ready to go.

Perturbed, he asks, "Why isn't the Führer's auto finished? The instructions were to repair it first. Why wasn't this order followed?"

"Sir, there was a problem with the overhead cam shaft. As you know, the engine on this auto is technically advanced and requires a lot of time to disassemble. There is also an issue with the engine damper—it vibrates, causing a severe rattle. The damper seems to have a faulty part installed, which I removed. I had to order a new one from Berlin. The other kapo, Henrich, signed the requisition. The new part will hopefully arrive by tomorrow afternoon."

The kapo chews on his lower lip while inspecting the garage. "Hmm. How many breaks have you taken today?"

"Not one, sir."

"Not even to smoke a cigarette?"

"No, sir. Not once."

Merkel inspects Wolfie and Stani, who stop what they are doing to stand at attention in the presence of the kapo.

Nodding towards them, Merkel asks, "How about those two—how many trucks have they completed, and how many breaks have they taken today?"

"Five trucks, and none, sir. No one has taken a break."

"Well, if you're going to work through the night, you'd better take one now. And get some food. I will requisition you extra rations. Eat, have a smoke, and back at it. No delays, understand?"

"Do I have your permission to bring the food back to the garage, to eat in here?"

"Why would you want to do that?"

"So as not to waste a moment's time, walking back and forth, sir." Frederick nods at Stani and Wolfie. "Those two can keep working while I get the food."

"I see your point. Okay. Here."

Merkel signs a slip of paper with the extra rations provision and the instructions for Frederick to leave with the food.

Once Merkel is out of view, Frederick gathers Wolfie and Stani around him.

"I will get our food. Keep working and do not stop until I return. Then we will talk. I have a plan."

Wolfie asks, "Why did you tell him we only have five trucks completed? We have eight finished."

Frederick bestows a rare smile on the two, and says, "You'll see."

With his father gone and within the quietness and solitude of the garage, Wolfie takes the opportunity to ask Stani something that has puzzled him since he first saw him, smiling, while carrying the rocks.

Stani still has a smile on his face even now, as they work, without a break, and hums quietly to himself. Wolfie asks, "You know from the first time I saw you, I've been perplexed by how, in the worst of times, you still manage to smile and have a cheerful disposition. I do not understand it. Can you explain to me how you keep such a good attitude?"

Stanislaw stops what he is doing to look at the young man before him. He puts the wrench in his hand down on the long table behind him that holds various wrenches and tools.

"My boy, we have to find an antidote for the emptiness and despair that is part of the human experience. Hurt and heartbreak are all a part of the continuum of life, just like love and joy are.

"For me, thoughts of my two loves keep me going. Thinking about them, their presence in my life, is part of my antidote. The other part lies in trust—trust in what we cannot see. This comes from faith, which is my strong anchor during the most tempestuous storms of life. It's taken time and life experience to understand that faith is the substance of things hoped for, the evidence of things unseen."

Wolfie's feelings about his mother well up in him, until he cannot hold back the pain. Tears escape his eyes, and embarrassment clouds his thinking. "I'm just a baby. I cry—men shouldn't do that."

"Who told you that lie? We are only human—we all have emotions, some emotions stronger than others. It is good to cry, to let go of the pain, release the pressure of disappointment, or frustration. No one in this world has it easy. Everyone experiences loss, hardships, trials, sometimes fiery ones. Not one person is exempt from the painful experiences that life presents. It is our job to find the balance, find the sweet moments that balance out the bitter.

"And hope, we must never let go of hope for better days, a grander life than the one we have now. Does this make sense to you, or speak to you in any way?"

Wolfie stops working, taking a moment to consider the words his friend has spoken. "Now that I think of it, every time I pause and consider what a wonderful time I was having just a short while ago at the Jamboree, I smile, but then I want to cry because of where I am right now. It is like the present moment steals that joy from me."

"Yes, yes, it does. Now we must reverse the order in which you think about those moments. Instead of thinking about them as gone or over, think about them as unending, and how you will continue the friendships in the future, with more joys to share. Think also about what you will do when you see your friends again, how you will camp and enjoy all of those elements once again."

Wolfie's mood grows grim as he feels the clutches of despair grab firm hold of him. "With no disrespect meant, how can that be nothing more than a fantasy, a dream? What if I never get out of this hellhole; what if I spend my life here, or worse, they kill me like Jakob, or Stephan?"

"My dear boy, we need to have faith, something to believe in. And we must believe with every ounce of our being that God works all things together for good, despite the circumstances, regardless of how dire things seem and appear now."

Bewildered by Stani's words, Wolfie confesses, "I have no idea what that even means!"

"Have you ever read the Scriptures—do you know anything about God?"

Wolfie thinks back to the words his Aunt Cecile would share with him, especially after his mother died. "I remember something my Aunt Cecile told me, 'The Lord is my shepherd,' but I don't understand it. Do you know what that means?"

At that moment Frederick returns to the garage with one plate of food for the three of them.

Stani nods to Wolfie, "We will continue this at another time, okay?"

Wolfie agrees, "Yes. Of course, we will, but for now, let's

eat! Would you look at that, wow, a veritable feast for us, and something more than the watery sludge they call soup."

Making the most of the situation, Stani says, "We'll have a picnic!"

Wolfie laughs heartily at such a ludicrous thought. "Prisoners having a picnic in a concentration camp garage while surrounded by Nazi trucks!"

Stani chuckles at Wolfie's description. "I call that making the best of adverse circumstances."

"Poppa, Stani and I were just talking about finding ways to live above our circumstances. Do you think we can do that?"

Frederick can't keep from grinning ear to ear. "I think we can do even more than that."

"Pop, you're smiling a lot lately, something you rarely do. What's going on?"

Frederick sets the plate down, and the three of them sit while he hands out two sausages apiece, two boiled potatoes each, and from the deep pocket of his garage uniform, three pieces of dark bread.

"Please forgive my meager presentation—at least the food is on something other than a metal bowl. We have an actual plate, imagine that! Let's eat."

Stani bows his head, silently giving a prayer of thanks. Wolfie watches his every move.

Aware that Wolfie is watching him, Stanislaw finishes giving thanks and winks at Wolfie, saying softly, "Attitude of gratitude."

Frederick scopes out the garage, then gets up and walks outside, surveying the perimeter, making sure there is no one within hearing distance.

"Okay, here's my plan." While they eat, he speaks in a hushed tone about a proposal to escape from Dachau.

"Stani, how can we get those uniforms you spoke of, the hidden ones? Do you think you could get your hands on them?"

Before Stani has a chance to answer, he's interrupted by a visitor.

"Oh, you're having your dinner."

Out of thin air, Commandant Eicke appears at the entrance of the garage. All three men scramble to their feet, standing erect before the camp commandant.

"Relax, relax, no need to be formal now—you're eating your dinner, I interrupted!"

Suddenly, Eicke's eyes narrow as he spots Stanislaw. His jovial voice turns menacing as he asks, "What are you doing here?"

Frederick steps forward to speak. "Herr Commandant, he's helping us with the work detail. He's a fast, strong worker and can change the tires. In fact, he's finished with seven trucks already."

Eicke reflects upon these words, then changes the subject. "Tell me about the Führer's auto, why is the repair not finished?" He rubs his hands together. "I had hoped to drive it tonight before it's transported to Nuremberg."

"Yes, sir. There were multiple transmission issues, along with a rattle or vibration in the engine, which I believe to have discovered the cause of."

"Oh, what's the cause?"

"It's the engine damper, Herr Commandant."

"Do you have what you need to repair it? How long will that take? I don't mind staying here waiting if it's a quick repair."

"I'm waiting for the part to come from Berlin tomorrow afternoon. After that, it should be an easy fix, about two hours from start to finish. It's a complicated piece to get to—the engine has to be disassembled to access the damper."

"Hmm. I see. Unfortunately, I think time will be the

enemy—we won't have enough of it to get a spin in. I'm leaving for Nuremberg this evening. Well, next time it comes for service, we will take a ride, how does that sound?"

"Thank you, Herr Commandant. Very good, sir."

"Good. Now go back to your dinner!"

Eicke is all smiles until his eyes rest upon Stanislaw.

He asks Stani an uncomfortable yet obvious question.

"Are you a Jew?"

Proudly, Stani tells him with a smile plastered across his face, "Yes, sir, I absolutely am."

Eicke glares at Stani, then directs Frederick, "You make sure he keeps up the pace. Most Jews are lazy creatures, they need constant supervision. If he fails in any respect, there will be punishment, understand?"

"Yes, Herr Commandant, I do understand."

Eicke leaves, and the three sigh with relief. Frederick shakes his head as he tells Stani, "I'm troubled by Eicke's display of hatred toward you. What have you done wrong, except exist? The prejudice that Jewish people continually suffer is a persecution I've never had to face. And I'm sorry you're treated with such disregard and hatred."

Stani steps forward and shakes Frederick's hand as a show of solidarity. "Thank you for saying that. I ignore those Neanderthals and you should too."

Frederick quickly walks the perimeter of the garage once again before he continues, "Okay, coast is clear. Stani, can you get access to the uniforms, and how many are there?"

"Yes, I can—they're stashed not far from where the trucks are parked near the pit. There are three or four uniforms."

"And these are officer uniforms?"

Stani confirms, "Yes, officer uniforms."

"Good. When you're finished with the last of the trucks,

go with Wolfie when he drives them to the lot. Grab the uniforms, then get back to the truck. Avoid the towers and the searchlight, wait for them to pass before you walk out in the accessible area. I don't think they reach the pit, but the dogs are close by. Try not to make them bark.

"Once you get the uniforms in the truck, keep them stored there for the time being. I'll retrieve them when the time is right."

Next, Frederick directs Wolfie, "Don't transport the second-to-last truck once it's serviced. Leave it here, down from the lift and parked. When you bring the last truck back for service, the one that only needs new tires, let Stani change them. I want you to take as many rags as you can find, stash them under the front seat in the parked truck I spoke of, and start tying them together, end to end. You're going to do this by periodically sitting inside the parked truck for a few minutes at a time. And just in case a kapo walks by, I want us to be visible as much as possible so as to not look suspicious. Tie the rags end to end as neatly as you can, and wind them like you wind a rope so we can let them out, unwind them when the time comes. And Stani, those four full oil bins— don't dump them."

Stanislaw and Wolfie stare at Frederick. While each assume the gist of what he has planned, they are not fully aware of exactly how he plans to execute the job, not to mention where they will be while the garage burns.

But Frederick has plans to do more than just burn the down the garage.

CHAPTER TWENTY

Ambassador Dodd

AUGUST 1933

U.S. AMBASSADOR TO GERMANY William Dodd has only assumed his post in the last four months. President Roosevelt had a challenging time filling the position. Dodd's work as an ambassador is a new development. He worked for the State Department in Washington during the last two years, after serving in the intelligence community for ten years.

The president felt Dodd could be a real asset as ambassador, considering the fragile relations between the United States and Germany. His job is to keep the official diplomatic relations with Germany cordial, while "unofficially" doing what he can to protest the Nazi treatment of German Jews. Using his intelligence background, he can keep a watchful eye on known spies and their counterparts.

President Roosevelt assigns three special staff who are at the ambassador's disposal, to use as he sees fit. One of their goals is to decide if foreign agents are working with American Nazi groups, while keeping a watchful eye on German American espionage.

Dodd is aware he's stepping into the hornets' nest of a power-drunk fascist.

While driving from Berlin to Munich, a torrent of rain impedes his progress. Sitting in the back seat of the State

Department vehicle, a Mercedes 770, Dodd chatters away to his aide and driver, Phillip Winslow, whose focus is on the road.

"It will be good to see Wellington. A friendly face, a good man. He's a fair-minded individual. He might offer some helpful counsel on how to delicately handle the problems we face in Berlin. The president sees the problem of Nazi harassment towards the Jews through the lens of a political more than a humanitarian issue."

"Not sure I follow you, sir."

"President Roosevelt is concerned with the Jewish vote in the States. There's been an outcry from the German Jews to their relatives across the great ocean, and they're putting pressure on the president to do something about the increasing animosity and harassment by Hitler and the Nazis. I honestly don't know what to do—how to quell this rising anti-Semitism."

Dodd lights a cigar and rolls down the window a crack, blowing out a large plume of smoke. "Perhaps Wellington will have some ideas. He's a strong communicator."

Dodd smokes his cigar and continues his mostly one-sided chat.

"I'm sure beyond a shadow of doubt that the news I have will shock him."

"What news is that, sir?"

"You know, about the fellow with the Boy Scouts, James Lewis?"

"Ah, yes. That news."

"You know it was the Department of the Treasury that first had a lead on him. Did I mention he was a Hungarian national?"

"No, I don't recall that fact, sir. Did he use an alias?"

"Yes, as a matter of fact he did. His birth name is János

Lajos. He changed it to James Lewis when he obtained his U.S. citizenship some twenty years ago. Possessing dual citizenship, he had been involved with the Nazis for some time. He was hand-picked by them to help with a scheme because they knew he had contact with higher-ranking officials in Hungary, outside of the monarchy. Lajos was a notorious Nazi sympathizer, involved with several felonious groups in the states with deep ties to the Nazis.

"Yes, Lajos was a crafty fellow. He flew under the radar for quite some time. Federal intelligence, the Cipher Bureau, became suspicious and began gathering information on him.

The Bureau flagged my office after learning about the advent of the Boy Scout trek through Europe and into Hungary, then through Germany for their return to the States."

"What was the man's mission, or is that under wraps?"

Puffing on his cigar, Dodd clenches his teeth while chewing on the cigar stub. He says one word. "Counterfeiting."

"How so, sir?"

"Considering the frailty of the German economy, this group of criminals thinks by producing British notes and American dollars, perhaps in the future they can destabilize their markets. This scheme is in the earliest of stages, but our intelligence picked up a conversation between a German national and Lajos. Lajos would pass intelligence from the Hungarians to the Nazis, who would in turn provide the Hungarians with valuable information—espionage secrets and the like. Lajos was an engraver, and somehow convinced the Nazis he could help them in their pursuits of carrying out their goal of printing foreign currencies. Hungary seems to be in on this, seeing that they're in the middle of a fiscal crisis.

"Italy is also in dire financial straits, as are Hungary and Germany. Hitler hopes to form a closer alliance with Mussolini by engaging him in the counterfeiting plan. You know, Mussolini hails Hitler's ascension as a victory for his own fascist ideology. Truth be known, our sources tell us neither leader trusts the other. Yes, it's a dirty world these groups run in. The Nazis have no problem snuffing out anyone they lose trust in, which leads me to believe something went wrong with Lajos. I doubt it was a heart attack that killed him."

CHAPTER 21

Raymond, Maddie, Buster

AUGUST 1933

WHILE IN PURSUIT of shoes for Maddie, Raymond ends up in Walter Johnson's room and reaches a deal with him, trading ten dollars for a pair of hiking boots.

A windfall for Walter is but a pittance for Raymond.

"I won't be needing these anymore, seeing our camping is over and I sure could use the ten dollars to buy a present for my mother, stepfather, and my aunt and uncle!"

"Glad to be of assistance, Walter."

"Mr. Wellington, why would Buster need my hiking boots? I don't think we'd even wear close to the same size—he's much bigger than me."

"But he has small feet, like his mother. Okay, well, thanks so much, Walter."

"Please tell Buster I asked about him, and I pray he's better soon. He needs to be, because we'll be taking the ship home, and he gets so seasick."

Tousling Walter's full head of red hair, Raymond feels the impact of another lie. Even the smallest of lies troubles his conscience.

God, forgive me.

"Yes, quite right, son. I'll tell him you asked about him. On another note, how are you doing—how are you feeling about Leader Lewis?"

Walter stares down at the floor. He tells Raymond in a soft voice, avoiding eye contact, "I'm glad he won't be the leader anymore."

Confused by this statement, Raymond asks Walter, "Why is that, son? I saw you crying when I broke the news to the troops."

"It's nothing, I'm just happy we will have a new leader, that's all."

"Are you sure you wouldn't like to talk about it some more?"

Walter shakes his head. "No, sir."

"Okay son, but if you change your mind, you can always talk to me."

"Yes, Mr. Wellington, I know that."

After leaving Walter's room, Raymond finds O'Mara, whose room is a few doors down. He knocks gently on the door, and O'Mara shouts, "Enter!"

Raymond walks in to find Williams and O'Mara busy making plans for the rest of the trip. Papers and maps take over one of the beds.

Williams calls out to Raymond, "Oh, hey, Wellington. Come in, we're going over the itinerary. What are your plans, will we meet up with you and Buster in Bremen?"

Raymond observes the general messy condition of the room—clothes on the floor, the unmade beds. The room smells sour, reminiscent of a wet dog. *Nice example you're setting for the boys.*

Raymond hedges.

"Yes, well, I'll have to see first about the arrangements for Jim, after I meet with the ambassador. Plus, we're going to make another trip to Wolfie's house. My hope is we can find more information."

O'Mara seems surprised. "But I thought that was a dead end. Why would you waste any more time on that kid?"

"I'm doing this for Buster's sake—you know how close he and Wolfie became. Perhaps the neighbor might have current information. Quite frankly, what does it matter to you what I do?" *Great, another anti-Semite like Lewis. No wonder they were friends.*

O'Mara snaps at Raymond, "I don't give a damn what you do; I'm just asking a simple question."

After the terse exchange, the three men stand in awkward silence, no one wanting to broach the subject of the dead James Lewis. O'Mara lights a smoke and goes back to examining the papers with the plans.

Williams breaks the silence in his usual approval-seeking manner. "Well, what a trip. Jim was a fine fellow. I can't believe he's gone. The boys are a bit shaken up, so we have some plans to try and cheer them. We're taking them for ice cream after lunch, before we leave on the bus. We're going over camp songs, and putting together a plan for games to play, to help pass the time, keep their minds occupied. It's a long drive to Bremen; I hope at some point the boys will sleep. At least, that's the plan."

O'Mara adds, "Yes, let's hope so."

Raymond listens, and thoughtfully adds, "It might serve the boys well to allow them to talk about it rather than avoid the subject completely."

O'Mara doesn't like the sound of that and with a lampooning tone says, "The sensitive side of Raymond Wellington emerges. Boys don't need to talk about feelings, that's for sissies. Let them move on and forget about it. They'll get over it. And what do you know anyway about counseling boys regarding grief? Let me guess—you have a degree in psychiatry?"

Raymond will have none of O'Mara's wisecracks.

"I've lost two wives. I know how important to the human psyche it is to discuss these things."

O'Mara smirks, "Two wives? Wow. That's some accomplishment!"

Raymond declines to take the bait and turns to leave the room, sarcastically adding, "I've got more pressing matters to attend to. I'll be sure to keep you good gents updated with my every move and breath I take."

Meanwhile, in room 125, Buster's just poured his heart out to Maddie about Wolfie and the grief he feels. Desperate for a change of subject, he says, "Maddie, tell me about life in Poland, at the orphanage. What was it like?"

Buster watches as Maddie's body language changes; she stiffens her back and clenches her hands. Concerned he's upset her, he asks, "Is this too painful for you? If it is, you don't have to talk about it. I don't want to force you."

Maddie reaches out and pats Buster's arm. "No, it's okay. I can speak about it. The headmaster was an evil man—the things he did to us children were criminal. He forced us to do things, dirty things. And if he wasn't beating us, he starved us. If he wasn't doing that, you can be sure he was up to no good. We were helpless against him. I decided I had to destroy the place and rescue my friends from his clutches. I knew it was a risk. My hero is Esther in the Old Testament, and I finally decided— like she said, 'If I perish, I perish,' but first I'll make sure the other children get to safety and away from that horrible man."

Buster's eyes are wide with disbelief.

"How old were you when this happened?"

"All of ten years old."

Buster's respect for Maddie skyrockets. "Wow, Maddie. You are fearless!"

While gazing at the lovely girl before him, Buster tells Maddie, "You are the first girl I've spoken to for any length of time—sharing stories and talking openly about life in a purely simple honest way. It feels novel and wonderful." Speaking with a soft tone, Buster continues, "I've not had many friends in my life—girls, I mean, that were my friends. My mom, not my birth mother, but the woman who raised me, before she passed away, she taught me valuable lessons, considering how short a period we had together. She'd tell me to cherish my wife when I marry: 'A happy marriage brings a joy and fulfillment that nothing else can.' I've always wondered how much more she would have taught me if she had been here up until now. I feel slow, or behind the other boys in several things."

Buster piques Maddie's curiosity. She turns to focus on his handsome features, noticing how green his eyes are, framed by his thick eyebrows.

She admires his wavy, almost curly brown hair, that does not lay flat on either side of his head as though it has a mind of its own. She pays special attention to his perfectly-formed lips as he speaks. She decides he is very handsome—a little immature, but most boys are, in her opinion. She waits for him to reveal more, but when he doesn't, she asks him, "Really? What are you behind in compared to the other boys? Like what?"

Blushing, he says nervously, keeping his eyes averted while occupying his hands with a piece of loose thread from the bedspread, "Well, for one, I've never even kissed a girl before."

He watches her as she gets up from the edge of the bed and sits down next to him. He turns to face her, and she plants a soft and sweet kiss on his lips.

"There. Now you have that under your belt. You've kissed a girl."

With a restless smile and sweaty palms, Buster says tentatively, "Well, that's almost true!"

Feeling emboldened by her kiss, he faces Maddie again and this time, kisses her back, just as softly and tenderly.

Trying his best not to stammer or stutter, still blushing, Buster says to Maddie, "You've eased my worry about my friend. Thank you."

The sudden and firm knock on the door makes them both jump. Buster anxiously stands and moves to the door, all the while keeping his eyes locked on Maddie.

He releases the chain lock and opens the door a crack. Raymond pushes the door open, at once noticing the color in his son's cheeks. "Buster, do you feel all right? Your cheeks are red, I hope you don't have a fever."

With a bashful smile, Buster gives Maddie a knowing wink, while telling his father, "I'm fine, Dad."

Turning to Maddie, Raymond holds out the boots. "Courtesy of Walter Johnson. And Buster, he sends you his best wishes."

Another loud and rapid series of knocks on the door startles the three.

Standing in the doorway before Raymond is a balding, overweight fellow in a crumpled and creased suit, with small spectacles perched ever so gingerly on the end of his nose. He speaks with a thick German accent.

"Mr. Wellington, I presume? I'm Dr. Bernard Gunder. The front desk clerk and one of your compatriots told me you'd go with me to examine the body of your troop leader, James Lewis. There must be a witness present. Does this sound correct? The police inspector and the coroner will arrive shortly. I'll communicate all my findings to them for the paperwork involved, and I'll tell you, there is a lot of paperwork!

"Since the deceased is an American citizen, there is a protocol—the body cannot be moved, and you will attest to that. And I'm told you're connected to the U.S. State Department? How convenient!"

Raymond doesn't know if the man is being serious or sardonic.

"Yes, that's correct on all fronts."

Raymond eyes his son, while Maddie attempts to hide behind him.

As Raymond walks out the door, pulling it all but closed, he tells his son, "Buster, stay put. I'll be back."

The doctor carries a traditional physician's black satchel, which he swings while he waddles at a fast clip. "I'm told the room is right down the hallway, second room on the end, is that correct?" He doesn't wait for an answer. "So, Mr. Wellington, regarding the deceased, are you aware of any health issues? Previous problems with his heart, his overall condition?"

Raymond hesitates to answer; he knows nothing of the man's health.

"To be honest, I don't know much about the man outside of our Scouting interactions."

Dissatisfied with Raymond's answers, the doctor continues to probe. "When your troop hiked, and I'm assuming you hike, you're Boy Scouts; did the deceased ever seem to have trouble breathing, seem excessively tired? Have you observed him checking his pulse, or placing a hand over his heart? How about excessive perspiration, or heavy alcohol consumption, cigarette smoking, unhealthy dietary habits?"

The doctor succeeds in raising Raymond's ire with such questions. "No, Doctor. I've told you that I don't know much about the man, and furthermore, I can't really say that I've noticed or paid attention to the condition of Mr. Lewis. I'm usually too busy doing my duty, which amounts to focusing on the boys in my charge."

The doctor stops and gazes at Raymond with curiosity. "From my observation and your answers, I gather you don't care much for the deceased, am I right?"

"Sir, you're generalizing and making assumptions based on questions that have nothing to do with a relationship with the deceased. I'm merely supplying information and answers to your questions."

The two walk the rest of the way to Lewis's room in silence. The doctor takes the key given to him by the desk clerk and turns the handle, opening the door. The stench of death greets them, overwhelming Raymond. Trying his best not to retch, he yelps, "Oh, my God!"

The doctor states plainly, "Yes, that's normal. The body begins decomposing almost at once."

Weakly, Raymond asks, "If it's all right with you, can I stand back here? You do what you have to do. I can be a witness right here, from this position."

The doctor grunts in response while tossing his bag on the bed, directly on the body of the deceased. He pulls out a few tools from the satchel—a stethoscope, small flashlight, and reflex hammer. The disrespect the doctor shows for the deceased troubles Raymond, who notices more than just the obvious odor of death. He feels the presence of James, as if his spirit hadn't vacated the hotel room yet.

The room itself is clean and orderly, nothing like O'Mara's pigsty. A sadness comes over Raymond as he notices the simple worn and battered suitcase, the clothes folded neatly over the chair with the shoes lined up underneath. *I never even liked the guy. He's my age, early forties, and his life is over.*

With no warning. It's different when a lengthy illness takes a soul, but like a candle snuffed out before it burns down, the ending came quickly for James Lewis.

"I feel like I'm invading the privacy of the deceased while being here during this examination."

"That's normal. Turn off the lights for a moment, please." The doctor uses the small flashlight to examine the eyes, the pupils. "Turn on the lights, please."

With his stethoscope, he listens near the heart and then the front of the forehead. He tests the limp arm, the wrist, tapping it with his reflex hammer.

From this examination, the doctor determines that the man has been deceased for at least ten hours. With heightened curiosity, he asks, "What's this?"

On the pillowcase, just as O'Mara had said, there is a small amount of blood, and a small amount in his ear. "That's odd." The doctor fumbles through his satchel, removing another tool like a mini-telescope, which he uses with the small flashlight.

He begins to peer into Lewis's ear canal. "Turn off the lights, if you will."

Raymond switches the lights off, now curious himself.

"Aha! All right, switch the lights on."

Raymond hears men speaking behind him while he hovers in the doorway, turning around to find two Nazi auxiliary policemen coming down the hall.

"In here, officers."

They nod at Raymond.

"Doctor, am I needed here, or are we done?"

The doctor greets the policemen in German, not aware that Raymond speaks German.

Quietly, in hushed tones, the doctor tells the officers, "This man has been murdered. Come, see here at his ear, I would assess someone drove a spike or thick needle through his ear canal, into the temporal lobe, killing him instantly."

The news staggers Raymond. He steps back from the doorway as though he'll somehow be contaminated by the heinous crime committed. The doctor's words reverberate through his mind. *Murdered, murdered, murdered.*

The doctor sees Raymond and acknowledges him. "Yes, Mr. Wellington, you're free to leave. Thank you. I've been told you've contacted the American ambassador, and he's on his way here?"

Numbly, Raymond answers, "Yes, that's correct—Ambassador William Dodd."

"Fine. As soon as the coroner arrives, and after the investigator and coroner examine the body, they will fill out the forms for the ambassador."

Eyeing Raymond, the policemen ask the doctor, in German, "Who is this American?"

The doctor tells them, "Another one of the people involved with the Boy Scouts."

One of the officers asks the doctor, "Who is responsible for the body?"

"The American ambassador from Berlin. If there is an investigation, here is my number if you need to contact me."

Raymond hesitates, but before he leaves, he feels like he should say a prayer or recite some scripture over the body of James Lewis. *This is a murder.*

Let that sink in—this is a murder. The realization is disarming, and he's not sure what to do. Taking one last view of Lewis's body, he feels remorse for their last words, and the way they spoke to each other. But a corpse can't offer words of absolution, nor make peace with the living.

The time for that has passed, and like a wave rolling out to sea, it carries with it everything left behind on the sand.

CHAPTER TWENTY-TWO

Elenena and Annie

SUMMER 1925

ANNIE WALKS INTO the kitchen, unnoticed. "Elenena, are you all right? I thought you were going to put the kettle on."

With no small showing of her usual aggressive behavior, Annie grabs the teakettle and all but pushes Elenena out of the way to access the sink. She clunks the kettle loudly on the stove burner, then lights a match while turning the dial to jack the gas up, causing the flames to lick the side of the kettle. Then she shifts her focus back to Elenena, asking, "What's wrong with you?"

"I'm not feeling well, Annie—my head is pounding, I must lie down. I'll come back down and do the dishes, but I must lie down now. Please give my regards to Martin."

Elenena turns and walks slowly up the back stairs to her room, taking each step deliberately, knowing Annie is watching her.

Once inside her room, she closes and locks the door from the inside, using the small deadbolt. Panicky, and close to hyperventilating, Elenena racks her brain.

What am I going to do? I've got to get out of this place, find a new place to live. Oh, my goodness, these people are evil. How could that man say such wicked things about Jews, where does this hatred come from? I've never known such contempt and malevolence. God, you must help me. And how do I get those lists from Annie, what can I do? I cannot let this name-gathering continue; it imperils my people, the professor, the Schweitzers, and all the Jews in Germany.

Oh, why did I have to come here and live in this house? I need a plan. I need to get away from here and take those lists with me. Emotionally and physically exhausted, she falls asleep on her bed while praying for help.

Elenena sleeps until the morning, arising early. Washing her face, she peers at her reflection in the mirror. Worry wears on her face, confronting her with the truth she already knows, that she must make a decision. *Oh, why couldn't this work out, why did this have to happen?* She thinks about her mother. *Momma, you would tell me to make a change, to leave, not to suffer like you did. You felt like there were no choices, you only had one way out. You would want me to leave, while I have a choice to leave, I can feel it. Elenena, you must do something. Today.*

Resolved, but feeling interminably shaky, Elenena washes and dresses before making her way downstairs to the kitchen, prepared to clean up from the evening before.

Her feet hit the kitchen floor and not a moment later, Annie's voice croaks, "The dishes are done."

Annie is sitting at the small kitchen table, drinking tea. If her mood had a substance, it would be like thick vapor. Annie's grumpy morning attitude is the same as it is every morning. Her coloring is as gray as the dreary, overcast skies.

"Martin offered and did the dishes, so he could hang around hoping you'd come back downstairs, but I told him you would not, and of course I was right." Annie looks at the tea in her cup, then turns her focus on Elenena. With a tone that borders between contempt and resentment, she says, "He's quite taken with you."

Elenena stands to the side of Annie, waiting to hear what she'll say next, feeling the temperature in the room drop, much like an uncomfortable frostiness.

"I have a pressing matter at hand, and it must be discussed with you now. Stop standing there and sit down."

Elenena sees Annie has papers and a pen to her left.

Cautiously, Elenena pulls out the other kitchen chair, wondering what Annie's going to try and talk her into next. She sits down, eyes downcast, praying—for what, she doesn't know.

"I need to know now if you're ready to make a commitment pledge to join the Party. I have the form right here—all you have to do is fill it out and sign it, and I'll take care of the rest. Here are the rules. My rules. Number one, if you are to see more of Martin you must join, and number two, if you are to continue living here, you must join. Understand, you must join. Now."

Annie pauses, accusations ready to fly. "Unless there is something you're not telling me that would keep you from joining." Annie stares at Elenena like a beast inspects its prey, ready to pounce at the slightest of movements. Then she tries a softer approach. "Don't you want to be part of something, something bigger than yourself, to belong to an ever-growing population of like-minded individuals?"

Elenena pauses, searching her mind frantically for something to say, hoping to deflect the trajectory of the conversation. *What can I say, what can I do?*

"Let me get a cup of tea, please. I'm barely awake and would like a minute before we begin such conversations."

Those words ignite a fuse within Annie, and like dynamite, with one breath she explodes.

"Well, haven't you become Miss High and Mighty, telling me what you'll do in my house!" Annie's pitch becomes high, squeaking like a wheel in need of grease. The sound of her voice rises along with her anger. "You don't give the orders around here, in case you've somehow forgotten. It is me who is doing you the favor, allowing you to live here for almost nothing. I would expect you to show some gratitude and appreciation!" The temperature of the room continues to climb simultaneously with the angry tone of Annie's voice. Icy just a moment ago, now burning with rage.

Annie points her finger towards Elenena's face, only inches away from her nose.

"You either do as I say, or you can get out right now. You know, I've had my suspicions about you all along, there is something amiss here. You are lying about something, and I can spot liars."

Elenena begins to cower, as if she's been slapped, never having been spoken to like this before in her life. Annie's voice becomes increasingly loud and shrill, scaring the life out of Elenena, who is afraid she will hit her or worse. Annie's temper flares—if sparks could fly off of her, they would.

"Have you nothing to say? What are you, a statue? An ice queen, frozen with no emotions? I've done a lot for you; this is what I get in return? You really think you are something, don't you? You think you can use your beauty to get anything you would like in life. I'll tell you; life isn't like that, it doesn't work that way. I have seen women like you—aloof, stoic, untouchable, thinking they're better than everyone else. Turning up your nose at an opportunity most women would jump at. I'm sick of you. You disgust me. Pack your things and get out. Get out now before I throw you out!"

Elenena jumps out of the chair and backs away from the table when Annie stands, menacing, and comes towards her. Elenena walks backward until the wall stops her, entrapping her.

Fiendishly, Annie says the obvious. "Oh, yes, nowhere to run now, is there? Just who do you think you are, the Queen of Sheba? You get what you want by batting your pretty little eyes. Well, let me tell you, there will be no more of that, not here, not now, never!"

Suddenly, with no warning, Annie grabs Elenena's wrists, raises them above her head, pins her to the wall, and presses her body into hers with her full weight.

She's much larger and taller than Elenena, who cannot fight back from this position. Annie knows she has her little mouse trapped.

"What will you do now, ice princess? Nowhere to run, is there?"

With that said, Annie zeros in on Elenena's lips and forcibly kisses her, jamming her tongue into Elenena's mouth, while pushing hard against her.

Elenena closes her eyes and begins to cry. She cannot turn away, as Annie is much stronger. Finally, she breaks the lock-hold on her wrists and pushes Annie away. "Stop, stop, what are you doing? Leave me alone!"

Annie backs up and takes a few steps away from Elenena, as if shocked by her own desperate behavior.

Elenena waits for a moment, then turns quickly, running up the stairs.

Like a cat after a mouse, it doesn't take long for Annie to follow.

Elenena reaches the top of the stairs, running into her room, locking the door, pressing against the back of the door with all her might.

Moments later, Annie starts pounding on the door, screaming, "Let me in, you bitch. This is my house—how dare you lock the door!"

Elenena will not suffer any more bullying. Frantic and panicky, she considers jumping out the window, her only way out. But the drop is two stories. Inevitably, she would break something.

She cries out, "Stop it, Annie, stop it!"

But her pleas do nothing to quell Annie's anger. She pounds even harder on the door.

Elenena backs away from the door, and with a hard shove, Annie pushes the door open, snapping the small lock.

Her tirade doesn't end there.

"Just who do you think you are? Locking me out of my own house? I knew you were trouble, and I should have never had mercy on you, but I did, and this is how you repay my kindness?"

The anger is seeping out of Annie, her face contorted by her emotions, as she walks towards Elenena, who picks up her violin to use as a shield.

"You think that's going to protect you?"

Elenena summons up the courage to speak, but she's frightened by Annie's overtly aggressive actions, her words, her tone. She's worried Annie might try to kill her. The anger coming from Annie is palpable, like a gale wind, blowing with such force and fury.

"Annie, I don't understand why you're so angry with me. What have I done to upset you? Is it because of Martin? Because he paid attention to me, and that caused you to be jealous? Because he likes me and that feels threatening to you? Why? Because you like me that way?"

Elenena strikes directly at the epicenter of Annie's hostility, hitting the bullseye. Elenena continues: "Why would you attack me; I've done nothing to you! I've followed every rule and regulation you've set forth. I work hard and do as you ask. This is ridiculous, and I don't understand your behavior."

Annie, losing traction, starts to mumble, sputtering with embarrassment over her behavior. She blurts out, "I don't know what came over me," sounding almost solemn in comparison to her earlier bellowing.

She shakes her head, her skin tone returning to a normal hue from the full flush of red she had just moments before. She turns to leave and runs down the stairs. Elenena hears the door slam, signaling Annie has retreated to her room.

"*Leave now*" reverberates repeatedly through Elenena's head, with all the momentum of a locomotive steam engine at top speed. She begins to gather her belongings, bustling around her room like a small whirling dervish. *How will I escape her grip, how can I get away, where will I hide? Where will I go? Will she hunt me down, follow me, try to destroy me?*

But something slows her momentum, gnawing away ever so gently at her conscience. Her fear begins to dissipate but does not slow her forward progress. *What is it, why do I take this treatment, what is it that has allowed me to stay even this long? She's obviously a bully.*

Then the realization hits her.

I feel sorry for her.

CHAPTER TWENTY-THREE

Wolfie, Frederick, and Stanislaw

AUGUST 1933

T HREE DAYS PRIOR, a munitions truck came into the Dachau garage for servicing. The truck brought a small number of explosives at the request of Commandant Eicke, the purpose being to help with the excavation of a plot of land. The digging will begin and soon the guards will have a swimming pool.

Armed with only shovels, the prisoners could not break through the dry, crusted, and compacted earth compressed by years of erosion. Two kapos assigned to oversee the labor detail inquired of the commandant about the possibility of using explosives to start the excavation. Eicke approved the request, and three days later, dynamite is on the grounds of Dachau Concentration Camp.

It's a breezy morning with warm temperatures. Frederick feels the sun on his face, which warms him briefly before strong wind follows, taking the heat away. *At least I can be thankful for better weather—the garage won't be so hot.* While walking from his barracks to the garage, Frederick stops by the plot of land, roped off for the future pool, and speaks with one of the friendlier kapos, Ferdinand Faulkner.

Ferdinand makes pleasant conversation with Frederick after the mechanic offers him a cigarette. Taking a deep drag, he exhales, rolling his eyes. "A swimming pool for the guards, can you believe it? At least the weather will be good tonight or tomorrow for the work to begin. We're waiting for the wind to die down, so we won't get much dirt blowback from the dynamite."

Dynamite? This catches Frederick's attention.

"Dynamite, where'd that come from?"

"From that truck you're going to service this morning, which came from Berlin. Eicke ordered it after we requested help with this cement-like dirt. I'm a general contractor by trade, that's why I'm overseeing the job."

He says this while kicking at the dirt with the toe of his shoe. Frederick nods, agreeing with the assessment of the dirt.

"How much will you need to do the job?"

"As I see it, only a few sticks to get the work done, a few extra for good measure."

Frederick offers encouragement. "It's good to have the tools you need, right? When do you plan to detonate it? I want to be out of the area, my ears are sensitive, you know—the Great War all but ruined my hearing."

"If I could predict what the wind is going to do, I could tell you when we'll begin. Eicke wants this completed in a month's time."

Frederick contemplates being bold and asking a blunt question, but without expecting an answer.

He gets one.

"Where are you holding the dynamite for the time being?"

Ferdinand snuffs out his cigarette under the heel of his shoe.

"It's in a crate in the truck parked in the garage. I'll be by to pick it up after you're done servicing it."

Frederick can't believe his luck. *Are the Nazis really that stupid? That careless, leaving dynamite in the back of the truck?*

"I'll keep a watch for you. I best get to it."

Once inside the garage, Frederick reviews the work orders for the day. He approaches the truck from behind. Breathing heavily, peering around, craning his neck to make sure no one can see him, he gingerly opens the drop-down tailgate of the truck, and at once spies the crate.

A gigantic smile comes across his face. Only seeing his son Wolfie brought a bigger smile.

Hello, beautiful.

And just like that, a plan for escape begins to percolate in Frederick's mind.

Around 3:30 a.m., when the camp is quiet with only two guards on duty, Wolfie and Stanislaw pile into the last of the completed serviced trucks. Wolfie drives to the parking area where the other trucks are kept, already serviced and ready to go to Nuremberg for the big rally. Wolfie observes, "It's a perfect night for our mission. How did we get so lucky?"

Stani, sitting inside the dimly-lit cab of the truck, smiles at Wolfie, and points upward.

"If God be for us, who can be against us?"

"Okay, Stani, you have your shovel. Keep an eye out for the searchlight and watch for the dogs. Be incredibly quiet!"

Stani jumps down from the truck, not closing the door all the way but enough to dim the cab light, leaving it ever so slightly ajar. The truck's engine idles, Wolfie deciding to leave it running. While Stani retrieves the uniforms, Wolfie finishes tying the last of the rags, fifty-seven in number.

Stooped down like a cat on the prowl, Stani makes his way past the searchlight and the dogs to the place where Stephan hid the officers' uniforms. The wretched smell coming from the pit leads him. Behind a group of shrubs and tall grass, Stani begins to move the earth that is on top of a crate that holds the uniforms, the shrubs giving him cover.

Stephan, being one of the original prisoners, was part of the crew that dug the death pit for the Jewish prisoners, and eventually, his own grave.

During one of his first work details after arriving at the camp, Stephan stashed a shovel in the tall grass and shrubs, saving it for future use. The camp is understaffed by guards, men who are lacking in intelligence, and lazy by nature. There were many occasions and opportunities to steal from the officers' storeroom, mostly things like cigarettes, food, canned goods, and prized officers' uniforms. Stephan thoroughly understood the importance of not arousing any suspicion. The barracks are searched daily, so he couldn't hide anything there. Carrying out a bag of uniforms or food to take to his special storage area would be too obvious, so he devised simple means of transporting the goods. Because the guard Dukolf hated him, he chose Stephan to be the body transporter, in charge of transporting the dead Jewish prisoners to the pit. Stephan clearly saw the opportunity this responsibility provided.

Dukolf asked him one day, "Who will carry your dead carcass when I decide to kill you?" Stephan's hatred of Dukolf was a motivator beyond measure, causing Stephan to design all kinds of plans for stealing goods, right under Dukolf's fat, bulbous nose.

After a heavy rain when the earth was soft, he dug a hole at different points during the day and night, within the tall grass behind the shrubs, until he had a space large enough to bury the wooden vegetable crate he planned to steal from the storeroom. The next time a prisoner died, and he had to transport him, Stephan made haste, breaking down the crate in no time, taking the pieces of it, putting them in the arms and legs of the uniform of a dead prisoner before removing the body to the pit. At night, he reassembled the crate and buried it in the hole he dug. This is where he hid his stash of uniforms and food. His method of transporting officers' uniforms took a similar route.

When assigned to remove dead bodies to the pit, he'd dress the dead in a German officer's uniform he stole from the storeroom. He would then transfer it to the body of the deceased, replacing the dead man's prison clothes with the uniform, and transport the body to the pit. Stephan had a stash of rags, and using the officers' bottled water, he'd wash the remnants of blood off the body, so as not to stain the uniforms. Dead bodies don't bleed. During the darkest part of the night, Stephan would creep out of his barracks to remove the uniform from the dead body, storing it in the crate.

Stephan used the dead bodies to transport food as well, stuffed in the pockets of the camp uniforms. He had a few close calls with kapos but was convincing enough to get away with his deception. The kapos and guards rarely checked up on him; they wanted nothing to do with dead bodies or the pit.

He managed to complete this operation three times. Dukolf shot him in the head before he could complete another mission.

On Stanislaw's second day in Dachau, Stephan explained his plan during Appell. He spoke to Stani in Yiddish.

"Stani, I've got a plan. I have officers' uniforms stashed—three for now and will try for a fourth soon. We outnumber the guards—we have to find a way to overtake the camp and break out of this hellhole. What do you say?"

Stephan's plan was to wear the uniforms right out of camp, leaving in a hijacked Reich truck or motor vehicle.

Stani recalls the conversation while quietly and cautiously digging. The dogs are quiet. Stani makes no sounds to disturb their slumber.

Within a few moments, he feels his shovel hit the top of the crate. He gets down on his hands and knees, digging the rest of the way with his hands, enough to pry the crate's lid open. Reaching in, he pulls out the laundry bag Stephan used to store the uniforms. In the bottom of the bag are some canned goods that weigh the bag down.

You thought of everything, Stephan. Thank you—we do this in your honor. We couldn't do this without you. God bless your soul.

Stani closes the crate and returns the soil over the top of it, and with all the stealth of a spy, avoiding the one searchlight, he returns to the truck undetected, with bag and shovel in tow, and climbs into the truck. Joyfully, he tells Wolfie in a whisper, "Mission accomplished!" Both are giddy with excitement. Stani warns Wolfie, whispering, "We need to temper our celebrations and save it for when we escape for good!"

Wolfie puts the shift in reverse, and the word "Halt" suddenly rings out, piercing the darkness and the cool night air.

Within a second, a camp guard is at Wolfie's door, shining a flashlight in his face. The guard questions him, "What are you doing?"

Wolfie freezes. His voice catches before he collects his composure. It comes to him speedily. "This truck is the last of the twelve. It is about to be serviced for the rally for the leaders in Nuremberg."

The guard shines the light in Stani's face, asking Wolfie, "Why is a Jew in the truck and in a garage uniform?"

"Because he works in the garage on the orders of the commandant. He is a valuable worker, with mechanical abilities. We are on a tight schedule. The commandant will be angry if there is a delay for any reason. Three SS officers from Berlin are in the garage waiting for the work to finish on the Führer's automobile. We must hurry and finish the work!"

The guard considers Wolfie's words, then shouts, "Go!"

Wolfie steers the truck into the garage over the lift, and both get out, nodding to Frederick. The three snap into action, executing the beginning steps of their escape plan while working together seamlessly, with precision.

Frederick goes about closing the doors to the garage bays, leaving one open.

With Stani's help, Wolfie lines up the oil bins, two on each side of the truck. Then, taking the rags, he submerges one end into an oil bin, soaking them completely with oil. He dunks the next section of the bundle in the second bin while Stani takes the other end, feeding it under the truck to the other side.

Repeating the same procedure, Stani ensures that the end submerges in the oil bin and its twin, then gives Wolfie and Frederick the 'thumbs up' sign.

Meanwhile, Frederick takes the laundry bag from the truck, reaches into the bag, and pulls out three officer's coats and three pairs of pants. He puts a uniform on the back seat, and one on the passenger seat. He slides into the car on the driver's side, gliding across the smooth black leather seat, and fires up the engine of Hitler's Mercedes. Quickly, he puts the uniform over his garage clothes, while Stani gets in the back seat and does the same. Wolfie then dresses in the front seat.

Frederick gets out of the car and ignites the small matchbook, lighting a handmade torch, applying the fire to the middle point of the oil-soaked rags. The rag fuse begins to burn, burning all the way to the oil bins, which catch fire. Small, then large billows of smoke start to form, filling the garage with thick black smoke. Earlier, Frederick placed two dynamite sticks in the truck, propped up with a wrench to allow the fuses to burn freely. He lights a cigarette, then ignites the fuses. Because the dynamite is construction-grade, the sticks have long fuses. They will take at least four minutes to burn down before they explode.

Frederick jumps back into the driver's seat as the smoke from the burning oil becomes increasingly dense. He gives his partners in crime a once-over and, with a snicker, says, "Don't we all look fancy?" Then with complete seriousness, "Time to go!"

Frederick maneuvers the big, sleek, and powerful Mercedes out of the smoking garage, through the dusty camp, and down the road, gaining speed, past the barracks to the exit gate of the Dachau Concentration Camp. The guard recognizes the Führer's automobile and opens the gate even before the car passes by their station. He salutes with a "Heil" sign, assuming the work is completed and the three SS officers from Berlin are on their way.

Once through the entrance, Frederick flicks the last of his cigarette out the window, making a gesture, a ceremonial statement. "So long, you bastards!"

In the rearview mirror, Frederick sees the small flicker of light coming from the garage. "Turn around, boys, and say goodbye to the gar—"

Before he can finish his sentence, a gigantic, booming explosion occurs, caused by the dynamite and the truck and auto with full tanks of petrol. The garage is blown to kingdom come. It goes up in a flaming fury, the oil in the barrels doing their necessary job of burning, creating an inferno of smoke and flames. The three German officer imposters cheer from inside the comfortable confines of the Führer's auto. Soon, the whole camp will fill with thick, impenetrable black smoke.

Triumphant, Frederick says while laughing, "Eicke informed me of their plans to build a new garage, so we did them a favor, the hole is already dug!"

Wolfie and Stani cheer, slapping hands. Momentary relief washes over the escapees.

The flickering glow of an intense conflagration fades into the background of the moonless night. The Mercedes forges a course, propelled like a bullet on a steady trajectory towards its mark, gliding with ease down the road that connects the camp to the civilized world, and the three prisoners to freedom.

Maddie, Buster, and Raymond

AUGUST 1933

IN ROOM 125 of the Hotel Bayerischer Hofname in Munich, Maddie tells Buster she has a dream of going to America. "I have no family. The professor is the closest thing I have to family here in Germany, but I cannot live with him forever. I cannot go back to Poland. I am afraid to live there alone, almost as much as I fear living in Germany.

"Do I stay here and do what, run from Nazis? I feel like I've been running most of my life, escaping danger, abuse, now people who want to imprison me. Shouldn't I have more in my life than running and fear? You know, I imagine what big cities in America are like. I see them in my mind's eye—how there is so much activity. People of all nationalities, moving about, going places, working—so much energy happening all at one time."

Buster listens intently, his eyes on Maddie.

She goes on, revealing more of her plans and dreams.

"I want to live a vibrant life, forge a new path for myself, learn more, perfect my craft, play with a symphony orchestra, become famous. I want to see America, and travel the country, learn about the people, their customs.

"To me, America sounds like the most wonderful place in the world, I dream about it often. All I know is that life is not like a work of art, and that the moments cannot last, but I want to be able to experience as many of them as I can while I have breath in my lungs."

Buster stands listening with his hands jammed in the pockets of his khaki shorts. His facial expression is a cross between pain and fascination.

There is momentary silence between them. Maddie observes Buster. She senses his discomfort, as he contemplates her dreams and wishes.

"What about you, Buster, what do you dream about, or hope for? If you could be anything you wanted to be or go anywhere you wanted, what would you be, where would you go?"

Perplexed, Buster cannot produce a worthy answer. He's never thought that deeply about the future. "As of late, I'm consumed with thinking mostly about Wolfie. Before that it was the Jamboree. Now with the additional news about my birth mother, I feel confused. I've had little time to think of anything else. I feel like I'm under a spell, like voodoo. I cannot keep a straight thought in my brain." He breaks his gaze away from Maddie's face for a moment.

Bashful, Buster confesses, "And I can't stop, I cannot stop staring at you—when I see your eyes, I see something more than just pools of deep blue water. You make me feel like I'm glowing from the inside, like I swallowed the sun. And I'm thirsty, thirsty for more. But at the same time, I'm parched. Now I need some water."

Buster shakes his throbbing head, feeling the effects of the fever of attraction. "I'll need time to think about your questions. Obviously, you've spent a great deal of time thinking about the future."

"When you have nothing, it's easy to dream big."

Thoughtfully, Buster answers her, "Yes, you have a point."

The breakfast tray holds the glasses, which do not contain water. Buster holds the water pitcher upside down for emphasis. "I'm out of luck, no more water. I'll go to the washroom and fill the pitcher. Lock the door behind me, I'll be right back."

Once out the door, Buster turns the corner and walks the short distance to the washroom, intent on filling the water pitcher. He enters quietly, goes to a sink, and fills the pitcher. That's when he hears voices; there are two people speaking in hushed tones. Their whispers bounce off the tile—the reverberations break the silence. Their identity is a mystery at first. As they continue to speak, however, Buster begins to recognize the voices.

"Who would murder him and why? How can they be sure this is a murder, there's been no autopsy yet."

"He must have had enemies. The only person I can think of is Wellington. He always had an attitude with Lewis—made it clear he didn't like him in the least."

"Lewis told me Wellington threatened him the other night. About what, I have no idea."

"I don't know, but Wellington seems like a standup guy. I don't recognize a criminal tendency in him, do you? And what would his motive be, why would he kill him?"

"I'm not implying he did. It's just that he's a rich, entitled snob, not a working stiff like us. Those types are used to getting their own way and getting away with mischief. They can buy people off in ways we cannot."

"Maybe so, but perhaps there was bad blood between them, something we don't know about. Could there be a chance that Lewis did something to him, or Buster?"

"Wellington had a good deal of animosity towards Lewis— at least that's my take. We'd better go, the police will be expecting us."

Despite his legs feeling as heavy as lead, Buster snaps himself into the present moment.

He hightails it out of the bathroom and runs back to the room, the water in the pitcher careening and spilling everywhere. Knocking impatiently, Buster implores her, whispering, "Quick, Maddie, open the door!"

She does as he asks. Buster pushes the door open, almost knocking her down. He closes the door behind him and leans against it, breathing heavily.

"Buster, what is wrong with you? You're white as a ghost, what is wrong?"

Buster is incredulous, not believing the conversation he just heard. The words replay in his head. *How could they think that? The two chaperones—the other men on the trip with us—at least one of them thinks my dad may have murdered Leader Lewis! How could he think such a thing?*

Raymond awaits the arrival of the ambassador, while in the hotel restaurant having coffee. The two policemen who came to Lewis's room approach his table. He addresses the officers in German, and to his surprise, they speak English.

Behind them are O'Mara and Williams.

One of the officers asks O'Mara, "This is the man the doctor used as a witness, and you say he may be a suspect? You cannot accuse a person without proof."

"The only proof I have is that he and the deceased had a disagreement the night before. The deceased told me Wellington threatened him with bodily harm."

Raymond stands, glancing at O'Mara, thinking, *has this idiot forgotten how I make my living?* "Has the coroner arrived, gentlemen? And can you tell me how long it takes for the results of an autopsy to be returned?"

The officer who asked the doctor about his identity while in Lewis's room asks Raymond, "Can you give evidence of your whereabouts last night from 7:00 p.m. until this morning?"

O'Mara smirks, saying under his breath to Williams, "Like they're going to take his son vouching for him as a credible witness."

"Yes, I was in my son's room, who has taken ill. After getting his roommates situated in another room, I spent the rest of the evening with my son in the room. He has been sick for the last few days."

"Have you sought medical attention for him? The doctor who was here, did he examine him, can he confirm this?"

Raymond pauses, "Well, come to think of it, no, the doctor was here on a separate mission. I'm sure it's just a bug anyway; he's feeling better."

"Can anyone else confirm that you and your son spent the evening in the room?"

The question ties Raymond in a knot. The Brownshirts are at their usual perch, and within earshot of the conversation. If Raymond gives away Maddie's identity, it could prove to be dangerous for her. Their interaction also appears terribly awkward, and outside of the rules of conduct of the Boy Scouts and chaperones. In the bylaws of the Scouting handbook, it's taboo to have a member of the opposite sex in one's room, particularly a young lady who is underage. The revelation that she spent the night in the room with Raymond and Buster would be scandalous and damaging news.

Raymond decides to hold his cards close to his chest and wait for the ambassador to arrive.

"I'd like to wait for the U.S. ambassador to Germany, who should be here at any second. He can give you a character reference for me, if there is a query as to the uprightness of my character."

The officer considers Raymond's words and concludes, "But obviously, sir, we are not in the United States and our rules and standards differ greatly. For now, we'd ask you not to leave the property, and sit tight until the inspector comes and we thoroughly examine the deceased's room. The coroner's report will take an unspecified amount of time."

The officer turns to O'Mara and Williams, "You gentlemen are free to leave."

Before leaving, O'Mara gets one last lick in at Raymond, "I guess we won't be expecting you and Buster in Bremen then?"

Raymond fires back but restrains himself from speaking some choice colorful words. Because no good would come from that, he instead responds, "Don't be so sure, chump."

O'Mara and Raymond stay locked in position, glaring at one another. Raymond holds his position until O'Mara withdraws and walks away.

After a moment, Raymond turns to face Williams, and with a kind gesture, holds out his hand. They exchange a warm handshake. In a somber and quiet tone, Williams wishes Raymond, "Godspeed."

Raymond nods at Williams. "The same to you. Officers, if it's all right with you, I'd like to return to my room. I will not leave the property, and as I mentioned, I'm waiting for the U.S. ambassador to arrive."

"That's fine, Mr. Wellington. This is more of a formality than anything else, just so you are aware."

As Raymond walks away, he recalls something Buster said about Lewis. 'I always thought he was a little creepy.' *Now, what did he mean by that, and why didn't Williams's son attend the Jamboree? He's of proper age.*

∽

Knocking on the door to room 125, Raymond tells Buster, "Open the door, son."

Buster opens the door; his face reflecting his concerns about the words he'd heard spoken in the bathroom.

Raymond sees his distress.

"Son, Maddie, there's some debate over the death of Leader Lewis, and we will stay put here for a while. Buster, I have a question for you."

"Dad, I have one for you too. Did you have anything to do with Mr. Lewis, his death?"

Taken aback, Raymond says, "Buster, you're joking, tell me you are."

"Well, I heard Mr. O'Mara telling Mr. Williams you had an argument with Mr. Lewis, and you threatened him. You wouldn't hurt anyone, I know that. I was just shocked to hear that spoken about you."

"Well, of course you'd be shocked by that, because you know that is far from the truth. I had a disagreement with Lewis over Wolfie, and some unkind words he said about, well, about Wolfie's mother being Jewish. It angered me because of how I felt about your mother and because I care about Wolfie. I'll explain it in full when I give a statement. But something tells me the Germans here will not be sympathetic to someone sticking up for Jews."

"I never doubted you, Dad, I promise. Now, what was it you wanted to ask me?"

"Yes, right. On a different subject, can you tell me why Ricky Williams didn't come with us to the Jamboree? I meant to ask Williams directly, but it slipped my mind a few times. And another thing, you mentioned you thought Leader Lewis was creepy, but you never explained what you mean by that. Would you tell me now?"

"Sure, okay. Boy, this trip has been a revelation of all kinds of feelings and information: Maddie's dreams, the truth about my real mother—finding out she's Jewish, which means I am too—Mr. Lewis, dying, Wolfie being beaten, O'Mara thinking you killed Mr. Lewis. What have I missed? I feel like I'm on a Ferris wheel spinning too fast and I want to get off. All of this at once—so much to think about, my brain hurts!"

Raymond has pity for his son, but gently shares, "Buster, this is a taste of your coming adulthood, having to deal with numerous issues at once. Life is messy. Yes, I admit I'm guilty to a degree and at fault for sheltering you from many things due to the circumstances of your growing up, mostly without a mother. I've tried to protect you, give you as idyllic a life as I could, but in some respects, that has harmed you, as well. I would have to say I haven't prepared you to face the troubles that life brings. But know that I've done that out of love and caring. Son, there is much forgiveness needed, and I do hope you forgive me for the error of my ways. I've never intended to harm you with my protection."

Buster absorbs the words his father speaks, not needing time to process them.

"I know that, Dad. I know you love me and want the best for me, and for that, I am grateful. Now, can we please stop all this talk about feelings?"

Both Maddie and Raymond begin to laugh, and Buster does too.

Raymond hesitates, not wanting to dampen the spirit of the moment between them. He asks, "Would it be too much for you to tell me about Leader Lewis?"

A pained expression comes across Buster's face. "Well, it's something very awkward, and perhaps not appropriate to be spoken of in front of Maddie."

Maddie, with a tone free of condescension, says gently, "Remember I grew up in an orphanage, nothing shocks me."

"I will refrain from providing graphic details, but this I know. There is something a few of the boys and I saw him do, on camping trips, when it was just our small troop. You know, the weekend trips with Mr. Lewis and one or two of the Eagle Scouts. One of them, Eagle Scout Jimmy Kinsley, had this kind of odd attachment to Leader Lewis. Bobby, Ollie, and I saw him and Leader Lewis single Ricky out, and we could hear them doing things in their tent with him, after lights-out. What they were doing, I have no idea. Muffled sounds, like when someone puts a hand over your mouth. One night we heard Ricky crying, but we didn't know why. Oh, and we saw Leader Lewis doing something to him in the showers too, when no one else was around. Both Leader Lewis and Jimmy would pay special attention to Ricky, and it made me feel strange, like something wrong was going on, but I can't say what it was. And come to think of it, Walter, Walter Johnson—they singled him out too."

With a serious expression and apprehension catching in his voice, Buster continues slowly, "I never said anything because I didn't think it was my place and I wouldn't want to accuse anyone of anything, but the last trip we took, I saw Leader Lewis in the showers, alone with Ricky and Walter after lights-out. Both boys were naked. Leader Lewis was naked too, standing behind both, with his hands around Ricky's hips, then Walter's. I don't know what he was doing, but I knew it was wrong."

Elenena and Annie

SUMMER 1925

AFTER PACKING HER meager belongings, Elenena departs the house with her suitcase, purse, and violin, leaving behind the secondhand music stand, which would have been cumbersome to carry. With remorse, she mouths the word "goodbye," taking one last glance around her small, unadorned room. She sighs. *I never thought life in Munich would turn out like this. Goodbye room, goodbye window, goodbye stand.*

She tells herself, *If I go to the park, to play music in the fresh air, it will soothe my soul, my mind will relax. But how can I shake off what happened? Annie's outburst leaves me feeling horribly hurt, abused. Once it's closer to two, I'll go to the Schweitzers' bakery and ask for permission to stay there overnight. I can make a pallet on the floor to sleep. I will try to forget what happened, but can I?*

Creeping down the back stairs, Elenena leaves the note she quickly wrote to Annie on the kitchen table.

It is better for me to leave, Annie. Thank you for allowing me to live here. I wish you the best. —Elenena

Elenena hears no noise coming from Annie's room. Quietly, she leaves through the kitchen door, walking from the back of the house to the street in pursuit of the solace she hopes to find in the park. The day has turned overcast, foreshadowing her mood and thoughts. Feelings of melancholy sweep over her, bringing thoughts of failure and defeat. She pushes the negative thoughts away, commanding them to leave.

One thought, larger than the others, stays alive in her mind, leaving her feeling helpless. That thought evolves into an emotion, grief.

If only I could get the lists. God, it's just not right—this hatred the Germans feel towards me and my people, Your people. But You, Almighty God, are in control of all these things and it is my duty to trust you, and I do. I just pray you will keep me, the Schweitzers, the professor, the Jews of this city safe. I guess I should pray for the whole lot of Jewish people, as it is Hitler's plan to destroy us all. Oh, Most High, please help me to trust you with my life, my future.

Elenena seeks out her favorite place of refuge, the spot where she played before, in the center of the park, where the music first drew Professor Birnbaum to her. She walks the three blocks, keeping her head down and eyes averted, as to not make contact with any other person. The birds sing to her as she meanders along the city sidewalks. She breathes in the air, which refreshes her, temporarily bringing a small amount of calm to her restless soul.

She reaches the park entrance, which is large and welcoming, with plenty of room for all who choose to stroll within its midst. Her heart beats loudly, and she thinks, *Only music will quiet it now.* Elenena decides to play a few pieces she knows from memory. The first one is *Meditation,* by Jules Massenet. It is a short piece played in D major, but she can stretch it out and replay its opening notes. She will play through the piece three times before trying another.

Elenena begins with a few warm-up notes and exercises, performing her scales. When finished, she dives into the first notes of the piece and soon loses herself in the music emoting from her beloved violin. There is an element of luscious tranquility in the piece. A voluptuous melody plays twice.

The piece then transitions into a section marked animato, as it becomes increasingly passionate and intense. The climax progresses to a short cadenza, and then eventually comes back to restate the main theme. Music carries her away from the world, where her mind focuses so intently on her fingers and the notes, even her surroundings become muted. She plays the piece start to finish three times, while an hour passes. An occasional passerby stops and listens for a moment before continuing their journey, serenaded by the melodious sounds.

Time for a break.

Elenena brushes a thick strand of hair from her brow and tucks it behind her ear, aware that her forehead is damp with perspiration. She steps away from her imaginary podium, basking in the warm air despite the lack of sunshine. There is a water fountain conveniently situated a few yards away. While drinking some of the refreshing liquid, her senses become attuned to her milieu. She hears sirens, coming closer and closer.

The trees in the park are full of foliage, lush and in full bloom. The borders of the park are lined by thick hedges and topiaries cleverly shaped by sharp pruning shears. She doesn't see flames or smoke, but she notices the pungent smell of wood burning, and observes people running back in the direction of the park's entrance.

With no desire to follow the crowd of onlookers, she decides to continue playing for another twenty minutes until the smell of smoke becomes too distracting. *There must be a big fire somewhere.* Feeling a sense of accomplishment, achieving a modicum of sought-after calm, she decides it's time to go to the Schweitzers and make an appeal.

Elenena begins her walk back through the winding pathway leading to the front of the park. She sees particulate-like ashes, floating in the air, becoming greater in number the closer she gets to the entrance.

Suddenly, she spots large, consistent plumes of smoke rising higher and higher. Once on the street, she sees flames shooting upwards toward the gray-cast sky. She watches them with rapt attention, each flame brighter than the last.

She quickens her pace, and as she draws closer, the sound of people screaming becomes distinct, as does the unmistakable roar of a massive fire.

While standing only a few hundred feet away from the burning scene, she chokes on the intense, smoke-laden air, which scorches and waters her eyes, causing her vision to blur.

She hears a man on a megaphone shouting in German, "Stay back."

The sirens signify more trucks are near. The blasts of noise multiply, reaching an ear-splitting level.

Elenena asks a man on the street what's going on. He yells, his words almost indistinct. All she hears is, "Bakery, ovens, houses on fire."

Stunned and shocked, Elenena screams, "No, no, no!" while running past the police. Still one hundred feet away from the front of the bakery, she pulls her sweater up over her nose and mouth to protect her air intake while fighting through the smoke. A familiar voice draws her a few feet away. It is the voice of a hysterical Greta. The dense smoke blinds and stings her eyes, Elenena listens for Greta's voice, struggling to find her in the crowd.

Greta is gasping for air, choking, wailing, and moaning a guttural-type sound while weeping, saying, "Fritz, my Fritz, my Fritz, my Fritz" repeatedly, barely recognizing Elenena.

Elenena puts her suitcase and violin down and wraps her arms around Greta while she weeps. She gently pulls Greta's apron up around her mouth and nose.

The auxiliary police once again yell from the megaphone, "Get back, falling debris." Elenena is moving Greta further away from the bakery when she sees Annie's house is on fire. The fire appears to be on the roof, similar to the fires burning on the two houses next to hers.

More fire trucks arrive amid the chaos. People are yelling and screaming, pointing to the people waving their arms in the windows above, who are trapped on the top floor of one of the houses as the flames lick and consume the wood. The heat is intense, along with the mist from the deluge of water from the many hoses. One of the fire trucks brings a large extension ladder to the front of one of the houses, while two brave firemen in heavy coats and gloves scale the ladder rung by rung, making their way up to the second floor.

Elenena shouts out, "Annie!" She tells Greta, "I will come back for you, wait here." In the confusion and madness, she neglects her suitcase and violin. An attentive thief capitalizes on the situation.

Elenena runs to a fireman and tells him about Annie's house. "There are five tenants and the landlady on the first floor, oh, please rescue them!"

The fireman shakes his head, not able to make out her words, and continues to direct one of the hoses of water to the front of Schweitzer's Bakery.

Five more fire trucks arrive. It takes four hours and one hundred fifty volunteer firemen, pumping hundreds of gallons of water and bailing hundreds of pounds of sand, to put out the fire. The damage to the buildings, however, is so severe that there is no hope of recovery.

Four people die, including Fritz Schweitzer, two of Annie's tenants, and an older woman in the brownstone next to Annie's.

While the stone blocks of the house remain, the contents are nothing more than rubble and debris—cinder and ashes, along with bits and pieces of furniture. It takes a few days to discover the body of a woman who hung herself in her first-floor closet. Part of the noose is still draped around the neck of her charred body.

The remains of the body are later identified as Annie Heinrich, a thirty-year-old unmarried woman who was a precinct organizer for the Nazi Party.

CHAPTER TWENTY-FIVE

Elenena and Charles

EIGHT YEARS LATER, AUGUST 1933

T HE EASTMAN SCHOOL has sent Charles Whitecliff to assist Mrs. Laurent as she makes her passage to the United States and her new post.

Under usual circumstances, the school would send a ladies' maid to escort a female associate, but due to the burgeoning difficulties surrounding travel for Jews, the authorities thought it more expedient to send a man as a valet.

Charles asks a question about Annie. "Was she your friend?"

Elenena ponders the question, not sure how to answer. "You see, Charles, people are extremely complicated, and rarely as they appear. I hoped to be friends with her—we just never really connected. I never told her I was Jewish— what would she do if I did? I was afraid of her, more than anything. Women are exceptionally complicated. I've had many women like that in my life. It's said that a woman's heart is a deep ocean of secrets. Another life lives inside each of us. Sometimes the voice we hear is our own, or the voice of people from our past, or of those who influenced our lives. I often hear the voice of my friend, Stanislaw Birnbaum."

Charles nods, confirming, "He was your instructor for those years after the fire."

"Yes, that's right. But he was more than an instructor. He was a mentor, a friend, a savior of sorts. Yes, Stani rescued me at just the right time. He heard about the fire and came looking for me. Greta went to a family member's home while I went to Stani's to live."

"And the violin you play now—is it his?"

"Why yes, how did you know that?"

Charles smiles broadly as he blushes. The corners of his lips curl upward, accentuating his deep dimples. Charles's smile reminds her of Maddie's smile. A moment of melancholy falls upon Elenena at the thought of her dear Maddie.

Feeling ashamed, Charles confesses, "I saw your paperwork and application for a position. When asked to carry a copy to give to you, I read it. Within the forms you filled out, in your paperwork for the school, there's a question about the instruments you play, and would you be transporting overseas? You mentioned the Vincenzo Ruggeri, which caught my eye. The chief seat of our philharmonic orchestra plays one made by his father Francesco, when not performing on his Stradivarius. You said something so poignant, it stuck with me, 'A gift from the soul of a man who loves me enough to let me go, my instructor.'"

Irritated by the impertinence and inappropriateness of the young man, feeling emotionally naked before a stranger, Elenena asks Charles curtly, "What else do you know about me, what else have your eyes spied upon?"

Charles is remorseful. With eyes downcast, he stutters, embarrassed at being exposed. He explains, "Forgive me, Mrs. Laurent, I meant no harm. I only wanted to be modestly familiar with you in the most respectful of ways, of course. Knowing we had a long voyage to make, I dreamt of our conversations about music and literature. Your resume and experience lead me to believe you have traveled—you are worldly in ways I could only hope to be.

"I am fascinated by your background and history. I've led what would comparatively be considered a sheltered life. I've lived only in Rochester, never having traveled anywhere. I certainly never made a grand adventure across the ocean. This is a real opportunity for me, a first. My only hope is that I haven't ruined my chances of finding favor with you. I pray you can forgive my lack of discretion."

Troubled, with a rueful disquiet he goes on: "The school hopes to use me in a position to help bring students and instructors from Europe, mainly because I speak four languages. I've made a mess before we even start."

Elenena observes the tall, handsome young man, perfectly groomed, sharply dressed. Benevolently patting Charles's cheek, she extends her forgiveness for his intrusion. "Four languages? Oh, my. Well, you must be smarter than you appear, dear boy."

Elenena returns her gaze to the window and her view of the passing German countryside.

The train shudders while steaming down the tracks. The rhythmic sound of the wheels is hypnotic.

Close to dozing, Elenena hears a small voice in her head, asking the question, *Did I make the right decision to leave?*

CHAPTER TWENTY-SIX

Wolfie, Frederick, and Stanislaw

AUGUST 1933

IT WILL TAKE less than two hours to travel from Dachau to Salzburg, Austria. The route is mostly straightforward, along well-worn roads that wind through the small, sleepy villages of southeastern Germany on the way towards the eastern Alps, which can be seen in the distance, snowcapped and majestic.

An hour into the trip, Stani sleeps, snoring softly in the back seat while the sun begins to rise over the Bavarian countryside. The sunlit rays sparkle, radiating golden colors over a broad swath of the road that stretches out before them as the miles click away. Frederick and Wolfie speak in hushed tones in the front seats of the Führer's luxury automobile, comfortable in the leather upholstery that's been hand-rubbed until soft as a lamb. Frederick lights a cigarette, exhaling like it's the greatest luxury. Elation and hope are finding a place in him, though he's not yet convinced they will be able to escape. Still, the fear of capture is less than the hope of living free.

"This is beautiful land—the neat and orderly farm plots, laid out like a perfect puzzle, they dazzle my eyes. I think after weeks in gray, dull, colorless Dachau, my senses are awakening. Everywhere I look there is vibrant color, and beauty." Tears creep down Frederick's face, and he wipes them with the back of his hand. "I'm just grateful, and hopeful we can get through the next test with as much ease."

Wolfie, moved by his father's words, poses a question. "Ease? That was anything but easy, yet things went smooth, right, better than you thought?"

"Yes, better than I thought."

"The next test, what do you mean? Do you mean meeting up with Uncle Rolf?"

"Yes, exactly."

"This will be the crime of the century if we pull it off. What have we to lose?"

Wolfie makes a salient point, one not lost on Frederick.

Slightly giddy with exhaustion and excitement, Wolfie continues, "I'm trying my best to imagine what happened at the camp after we left, can you imagine the chaos? I only hope Dukolf found his way into the fire, caught up in it somehow."

Frederick looks at Wolfie, confused. "What do you mean caught up in it?"

"I mean that the explosion took him out, blew him up. You know he did awful things to the Jewish prisoners. It was his fault Stani had no clothes, having to walk around naked. He beat Stani mercilessly for no cause. He beat Jakob to death and shot Stephan in the head. His hatred of Jews was like, like, well, like nothing I could ever imagine—a person having so much hatred. Speaking of Jewish…"

Wolfie hesitates, diverting his attention outside the car to the countryside. Then with a small degree of sarcasm, he adds, "You did an excellent job replacing the windows. The dark glass and the plate-glass windshield will keep the bullets from hitting us if we're caught."

His tone turning serious, Wolfie says, "We're going to make it, right?"

With all the hope in the world, Wolfie peers at his father, willing him to speak words of positivity and promise. "Tell me the plan again."

"Back up, son. You said, 'speaking of Jewish' and hesitated. Is there something you want to say? I think I know what it is. It's about your mother, and how I never told you she was Jewish."

Nervous and feeling shame for his nondisclosure, Frederick fumbles for another smoke, reaching along the car seat when he touches his son's hand.

"I have your smokes. I'll light you one while you talk and tell me the truth. Deal?"

Taking his eyes off the road for a moment, Frederick meets his son's eyes and says, "Deal."

Wolfie lights the cigarette, handing it to his father.

"Your mother was not born in Saxony, although she grew up there.

"At the time, your grandmother was pregnant with another baby. With your mother at age four and her sister age two, she didn't have the capacity to care for another child. That's when your grandfather had your grandmother hospitalized for a brief period of time before she gave birth. She had a nervous breakdown. Your great-aunt, your father's sister who was childless, took a liking to your mother and offered to care for her. Your grandmother Mabelle came home from the hospital and agreed to let her eldest daughter live with her sister-in-law and husband.

"Your grandmother returned home to care for her two younger girls, your mother's sisters.

"Now, your mother lived with your great-aunt and uncle, who moved to Saxony. I met your mother in Saxony, while attending a master mechanics school, and then we married. Your mother's family remained in Paris. The last she heard was that her father died while fighting for France in Africa, and her mother committed suicide, leaving behind her two daughters, your mother's sisters. Your mother was trying to track down her sisters when she died."

Wolfie sits quietly, digesting the information, trying to make sense of the complicated historical narrative. He reaches over, taking the cigarette from his father's hand, and takes a long drag before replacing it.

Exhaling, he says, "Does this mean I have two aunts somewhere in this world?"

Frederick nods. "Yes, that's right, you do, somewhere."

Stanislaw is now awake, listening to the story, taking in the facts, and doing the math. He says aloud, "Could it be?"

"Good morning, Stani," Frederick says. "Could what be?"

Bouncing on the back seat, almost squealing with joy, Stani tries to compose himself, so that he can ask a question.

He clears his throat and asks, "Frederick, tell me. Do you know the name of Wolfie's mother's sisters?"

"Yes, I do, why?"

"Can you please tell me their names?"

"Yes, they are Marcella and Elenena Laurent. They may have married and changed their name, but their maiden name is Laurent."

Astounded, Stani can barely contain himself. The words spill forth, but he cannot speak them quickly enough. Everything that comes out sounds like babbling as he squeals with delight.

"Oh, miracles of miracles, this is incredible, and I am thrilled to tell you the most amazing, astounding news! Wolfie and Frederick, hold on to your hats, this is marvelous! Elenena Laurent is my friend, my love, my student, oh, this is only something God would do. Remember Wolfie, I told you about my friend Elenena, and how God works all things together for good? Miracles of miracles! How else could such a thing occur, a coincidence? I hardly think so. Look at the insurmountable circumstances that have allowed all our paths to cross! I would dance if I had the room to do a jig! I want to shout for joy! A real miracle! I can barely contain myself. This is unbelievable!!"

Frederick and Wolfie's jaws drop with astonishment. It is Frederick who speaks first. "Okay. Let me get this straight. You're saying you know my wife's sister, she is your friend, your student? What? Is this real? This is crazy! Please, unravel this story for us, Stani, I'm dying to know how this all fits together."

Stani rubs his hands together, as if untangling the web of the Laurent girls' history. "I'm so excited I can barely think. May I have a cigarette? Sometimes a smoke will calm me."

Wolfie lights a cigarette and hands it to Stani. Wolfie's eyes glaze over with tears of joy. "I have a family!"

Stani reaches out, grasping Wolfie's hands, holding them, then kissing them. "I could almost die now a happy man, but God please, not yet!"

Stani puffs on the cigarette and then begins to tell the story. "Years ago, in Munich, I first met Elenena, falling in love with her on sight.

"A stunning beauty, she was a young woman with an ethereal quality about her. She was in a park, playing her violin. We became friends, best friends. She was my student, you see. I teach violin. I am a professor of music and have students in both Berlin and Munich. A day or two before her first lesson with me, a tragedy occurred. The house she was living in caught fire after a local bakery caught fire when an oven blew up. The houses next door to the bakery burned as well. Elenena's landlord perished in the blaze. Poor Elenena was in such shock and grief, she had nowhere to go, so I let her live in my Munich apartment for two years while under my tutelage, from 1925 until 1927. Then, she returned to Poland to help an aunt who fell ill. It was there she began to tutor a waif of a child, Maddie Turetzky. Maddie later became my student. Elenena taught Maddie until she could teach her no more. Maddie's talent was so great she needed a teacher who could help her reach her potential, which was almost limitless.

"That's when I came to Baranovichi to meet Maddie."

Frederick interrupts Stani. "Poland—you're saying Elenena lived in Poland. How did that happen?"

"After the girls' mother died in Paris, her mother's sister Noelle Silberstein took both girls, Marcella and Elenena, to live with her in a small town called Baranovichi.

"So, Maddie auditioned for me, and I took her on as my student. After that, she came to Munich to live. The three of us—Maddie and Elenena and me—lived together like a happy little family.

"Germany, like most of the world, is in the middle of an economic collapse. However, rich Germans and Austrians desire music lessons for their children and are willing to pay good money for them, so we made enough money to support us. Last year, Elenena had an opportunity to teach in Berlin. I had students there as well, so we would spend time between both cities. I was with Maddie at the concert in Munich when the trouble started, when the Gestapo wanted to see everyone's papers for identification. Maddie had none and the SS thought her to be a communist or a spy. Forcing all concert attendees to show identification is the Gestapo's way of keeping track of all the Jews living in Germany, finding out where we live so when the time comes, they can herd us all away and kill us. Maddie escaped by running out of the concert hall, but the Gestapo took me into custody and that's how I landed in Dachau. I have no idea what happened to my precious Maddie. She is a smart girl and I have to let go and trust that God will take care of her."

Wolfie can't understand this concept of trust. "So what you're saying is you don't worry about her? How can you not worry?"

Stani smiles, recognizing this as a teaching moment. He stops the story to ask Wolfie, "Tell me what worrying would accomplish?"

Wolfie smiles as he begins to understand. "Oh, I get it, that's where trust has to make an entrance, and you have to hold on to it." With a wide smile, Wolfie confirms, "I think I understand now."

Frederick ponders Stani's story. "This is almost unbelievable, how we are all connected, how we found each other. It's like a real miracle. You know, while in Dachau, I prayed and I asked God, if He is real, show me. It would be an understatement to say my prayers were answered, right?!"

Stani looks at Wolfie, who has turned around in his seat, staring at Stani, shaking his head in disbelief.

Stani answers Frederick, "I would wholeheartedly agree, this definitely qualifies as an answer to your prayers! With God, all things are possible. When events occur outside of the realm of human intervention, to me, that's a convincing indication of God's presence, stepping in to assist."

Wolfie bubbles with joy. Stani's words resonate deeply. "Like you said, Stani, a miracle of miracles!"

Frederick interjects, "Something else we have in common—we were all unjustly held for no reason. What crime did we commit? How exactly did any of us break a law? We did nothing criminal."

Wolfie considers his father's words and adds, "Yes, but we can't say that now, can we?"

"No, son, we can't. But what we did is understandable, at least to a reasonable person. While they may not approve of our actions, certainly no one could blame us. What the Nazis do in Dachau, the treatment of their captives, is infinitely more criminal than what we did. There is no comparison. We destroyed a building and a couple of vehicles. They destroy life, people, families. I pray none of us ever have to see the inside of that hellhole ever again. Or any camp, for that matter. We got away, and I believe it is not all for naught. And now, thanks to you, Stani, master puzzle assembler, we all have much to look forward to, much to hope for. Isn't it amazing how we are all pieces in the puzzle of each other's lives?"

On the road before them a sign appears: "Salzburg 17 km."

Frederick stretches his long frame behind the wheel. He tells Stani and Wolfie, "Be on the lookout for a sign that says *Judengasse*. We will meet Rolf at Cecile's cousin's inn in the Jewish section of Salzburg. He has a barn behind the inn where we will stash this auto for now."

Stani, who is resting his arms on the back of the front seat so he can be closer to Frederick and Wolfie, asks, "Frederick, how did you come up with this plan so quickly?"

"Yes, I'm curious too." Wolfie is bouncing up and down on the seat, eager to hear the plan's origin. "My father, the expert maker of escape plans!"

Frederick, amused by his son's description, says, "When I went to order the part for this auto, I didn't really call Berlin. The commandant's assistant, Lieutenant Marx, allows me use of the commandant's office phone. While Marx stepped outside to have a smoke, I called Uncle Rolf. I only had a few minutes to explain what had happened and what my plan was. He suggested meeting in Salzburg because it was in close proximity, so that we'd have the car off the road before morning. Cecile's cousin's place is perfect, located in the Jewish section where no one would expect to see the Führer's automobile, and few would be up and about this early before dawn. At least we hope. Rolf told me he has news for me, but we didn't have time to discuss it. As soon as the lieutenant came back, I had to hang up."

Wolfie thinks about this information and asks, "So, you never ordered the part?"

Frederick starts to laugh. "I ordered the part all right, but it wasn't the Führer's car that needed the part, it was the other car. In other words, the car never needed the engine damper. I made that up to cover for us, to give us time to get ready, get the uniforms and such."

Wolfie, still wondering about all the moving pieces of the plan, asks, "Well, how did you know you'd have access to the phone?"

"I didn't know, I just took a chance. You cannot accomplish anything without taking a chance. Sometimes, you have to go for broke."

Wolfie is giddy with laughter. He slaps his thighs, then gives his father a playful punch in the arm. "Oh, I see, so there'was never anything really wrong with the Führer's car, you just made that up, you sly fox, you!" The three laugh, full of jubilation.

Frederick asks Stani, "Getting back to the story, where is my sister-in-law now? And what about the other sister, Marcella, where is she?"

Stani's jubilation changes quickly. Both Frederick and Wolfie sense that sad news will follow.

"She died recently, from a terminal stroke. Elenena went

back to Baranovichi to settle her estate, wrap up her affairs and the like. That's why she didn't attend the concert with me and Maddie."

"Oh, I'm sad to hear that. Where is Elenena now—is she back in Munich?"

"That is a good question, Frederick. I cannot say where she is. We spoke before the concert, when she was on her way to Poland."

Calling attention to the sign, Wolfie says, "Sorry to interrupt, but there is the sign! Salzburg! We made it!"

Frederick does not feel as confident as his son, so he tempers the level of excitement. "Hold on to your horses and let's keep our eyes peeled for the Judengasse sign. Once we see that sign, we turn left at the next road, and drive two kilometers to the Lehenerhof Inn.

"The inn has a long driveway lined with pine trees, which is the easiest way to identify it, according to Rolf, so that will be our landmark."

Frederick prays silently, trying to ward off the creeping fear of what he cannot see.

CHAPTER TWENTY-SEVEN

Raymond, Buster, and Maddie

AUGUST 1933

BEFORE KNOCKING ON the door, Raymond tries the doorknob. Finding the door unlocked, he enters unannounced—and makes a discovery. Seated on the edge of the bed, Maddie and Buster are engaged in a passionate kiss. Shocked by his son's behavior, he stands silently for a moment, wondering, *how long has this been going on?*

Opening and closing the door did not disrupt them.

He clears his throat loudly, which startles the pair, causing Buster to scoot a few feet away from Maddie. With his flushed face the color of a candy apple, Buster begins to explain before Raymond quickly shuts him down.

"So, this is what you meant by keeping busy when I offered you books or magazines? I should have known better. Buster, you're a Boy Scout and I expect more circumspect behavior from you. Maddie has entrusted us with her care, and we must respect that, and respect her!

"Maddie, I'm sorry and apologize for my son's inappropriate actions, taking advantage of you."

Raymond turns his attention back to Buster, glaring at him, "This won't happen again, will it, son?"

"No, no sir, it won't, forgive me, I'm sorry, and Maddie, I ask your forgiveness as well."

Maddie sits quietly, considering the conversation, while

peering at Raymond, then Buster.

"Mr. Wellington, Buster did not harm me, nor did he throw himself at me. I kissed him first. Don't blame him, it's my fault."

With consternation and a threatening tone, Raymond advises them both, "Okay, you two, no more monkeying around, that's an order!"

Changing the subject, Raymond gives an update. "I watched the bus take off with the troop; they're on their way to Bremen. We just need to wait here until we're summoned by the ambassador once he arrives, which should be any minute. You must be dying to get out of this room. It's so stuffy—I'm ready for some fresh air."

While watching Buster's, then Maddie's expressions, Raymond gives another stern and intentional message, "You must be ready for some fresh air too, right?"

Both nod in acknowledgment. Buster's thoughts go back to Wolfie.

"Dad, have the plans changed at all, because of Leader Lewis? Tell me we'll still search for Wolfie. After all this, that cannot change, I cannot leave Munich without a thorough search. I know he'd do it for me if the tables were turned."

"I know, and I agree with you, I believe he would. We will, I promise you."

Trying his best to sound upbeat and curry his father's favor, Buster changes the conversation. "Maddie has shared with me some of her dreams, and one is to come to the United States and pursue her career as a musician. We have a symphony orchestra and a music school in Rochester, but I cannot think of the name of it."

Raymond says, "It's the Eastman School of Music, in the Eastman Theater, also the home of the Rochester Philharmonic Orchestra."

Maddie's eyes widen as she tries to contain her excitement but cannot. She claps, exclaiming, "I've heard of the school— my first violin teacher spoke of it. A friend of hers from Switzerland is on the faculty there—a famous violinist whose name escapes me now. I'll think of it."

Raymond probes her for more information, not sure if Maddie has already pronounced an expectation.

"Is that what you'd like to do, Maddie, attend a school? What about the teacher you have now, the professor, isn't he a great teacher?"

"Yes, he is, but he can only further my education so far. To succeed, to be a first chair in a symphony, I must have more formal training and education. I suppose that will never happen, yet it is my dream."

Raymond views Maddie with compassion. He encourages her, "Don't sell yourself short, you don't know yet what the future holds. Perhaps a benefactor will help you attain your goals—one just never knows. So, don't lose hope just because things seem bleak now."

"You sound like my professor!"

With a broad smile Raymond adds, "Then he must be a very smart man."

While appraising the room, Raymond comments, "So, you're ready to go. Good, at least you've packed. I've got to run to my room and do the same. I'll be right back."

Before leaving the room, Raymond reminds Buster to lock the door and pokes him in the arm. "And no more funny business, understand?"

"Yes, Dad. Go pack."

Buster turns around to find Maddie standing right behind him. He takes her in his arms and kisses her. "Had to give you one last kiss."

Gazing into the green of Buster's eyes, Maddie says, "I hope it's not our last!"

Raymond hustles down the hallway. Ahead in the lobby, he spots Ambassador Dodd along with another man. He watches a quick exchange between the Brownshirts and the ambassador.

What?

Forgetting momentarily about his task, Raymond stops and watches. One of the Brownshirts hands Ambassador Dodd an envelope. The desk clerk is present, and Dodd speaks to him as well. Dodd turns and spot Raymond in the hallway.

"Raymond, there you are, welcome to Munich. I know you've been here a while, but now I can formally greet you!"

The men approach and shake hands, warmly greeting each other.

"This is my driver and valet, Phillip Winslow."

Raymond and Phillip smile, shaking hands.

"What a time you've had here, nothing is ever simple, is it? Always something to muck up the works!" the ambassador says. "Tell me, where can we speak for a few minutes in private?"

"Let's go to my room. Then we can gather my son and Miss Turetzky," Raymond says.

"Miss Turetzky? Tell me about her."

With a start, Raymond remembers he didn't mention Maddie in his earlier call to the Embassy, as he was concerned one of the Brownshirts might be eavesdropping. "Right—I haven't mentioned her. She is the music student of Stanislaw Birnbaum, one of the men taken to Dachau Concentration Camp."

"Oh, yes, of course. Speaking of Dachau, I have the intelligence report right here. The information just arrived, so it is updated and hopefully accurate."

Once inside Raymond's hotel room, he apologizes, "Sorry, I'm a poor host, I have nothing to offer you. Now, about those reports, tell me if I'm off-base, but who are the sources for this information?"

"The agents we have stationed here in the hotel. They do my intel, then go wherever I send them. One of them traveled to Dachau this morning, returning just moments before I arrived. You may be aware FDR had trouble filling this post. With all the headaches that Germany represents, he thought it best to supply me with support. The three men I have are from a former post in the intel community. They've been most helpful."

Raymond is smiling like the Cheshire Cat. Dodd asks, "Why are you smiling, what's so funny?"

Raymond allows himself to laugh, to let off some steam. "Bill, all this time I thought those Brownshirts were here to try and take Maddie. These are your men dressed as Brownshirts. Okay. Why are they stationed here, anyway?"

"I stationed them here as soon as I heard about your troop coming through Germany. We obtained your itinerary from the Boy Scouts' headquarters. We've had an eye on the man who was your troop leader for some time, the deceased man. What do you know about him?"

Bewildered, Raymond asks, "What do you mean, had an eye on him? What has he done? And I don't know a thing about him, really. Only from my interactions with the Scouts."

Dodd fills him in. "He's a dual citizen, born in Hungary. His real name is János Lajos. He's been going between the Nazi and Hungarian government for some time, trading secrets, planning for counterfeiting. He's also been engraving plates for printing foreign currencies to prop up the German economy. In the States, he's a known Nazi sympathizer, having worked with several anti-American groups. The Boy Scouts provided good cover for him.

"Lajos used the Jamboree as a means to exchange intel. The Treasury Department and intel community have watched him for the previous four years. He's had interactions with the Nazis since the mid-twenties."

Raymond looks skyward, "You never really know a person, do you? I'm flummoxed, all of this going on right under our noses."

Dodd shakes his head, agreeing, "Unless you were caught up in it, you wouldn't know what to look for or be suspicious. Which brings me to the man's heart attack. Personally, I think the Nazis got him. Let's take a look at the intel."

Dodd reaches in his pocket for a pocketknife while Raymond opens the drapes and blinds, letting in some light. The light only proves to make the room appear small and sparse. Stretching, Raymond states, "I can't wait to get the hell out of this hotel. I feel like a caged rat."

Dodd begins to read the intel. He speaks the pertinent information aloud.

"Let's see now. Frederick, Wolfie, and Stanislaw are all prisoners in Dachau, so that solves that mystery. But wait, what's this, there was a major explosion of some sort early this morning, around 4:00 a.m., and it's thought that the three perished in it. Also, the community finds no source for the murder of Lajos—no one has claimed responsibility. That's odd. And they're sure it's a murder, according to the doctor? What did the coroner say?"

This latest development about Wolfie throws Raymond into a stupor. The three words keep repeating over and over in his head, like a record that skips, and he cannot make it stop. *The three perished. The three perished. How am I ever going to tell Buster and Maddie?*

"Raymond, old boy, are you alright?"

Raymond shakes his head, trying to snap out of the haze he's submerged in.

The three perished.

Numb, he responds, "I don't believe the coroner has examined the body yet, but I guess we should go check on that. I don't know how I'm going to tell my son his friend is dead. And Maddie, well, she's an orphan, a gifted violinist who took instruction from the man Birnbaum. He was like a father to her, and I believe he's all she's got in this world. I'm shocked by this, and then Lewis, or Lajos, I'm at a loss for words."

Dodd asks Raymond, "Tell me, how exactly did this girl make your acquaintance?"

"She was hiding from the Gestapo and the Brownshirts. She was at a concert where the officials were checking papers, to keep track of the Jews is what she told us. She had no identification. She's barely seventeen, but the Gestapo assumed she was a communist, because she's originally from Poland and Jewish. She ran and got away from the police, but assumed she left her friend in peril and that the Gestapo would undoubtedly arrest him, which we know to be true. That's how he landed in Dachau. She came to the hotel seeking a place to hide. She found my son's room, with the door unlocked, so she hid under the bed. We have no idea how or why Wolfie and his father ended up in Dachau. This is a mess—it is going to be rough going breaking this news."

Dodd shakes his head, agreeing with Raymond, and adds, "There's another detail. Our intel checked the records on Frederick Wolferman, and he has a brother living in Vienna."

The memory stirs Raymond. He snaps his fingers, "Oh, yes, that's right, of course. That's where we met Wolfie, while our troop was traveling through Vienna on the way to the

Jamboree. We were taking a hike around the Danube when he approached us. It seems like a year ago. We went, our troop that is, to Wolfie's aunt and uncle's home to ask permission for Wolfie to come with us to the Jamboree. At the time, he had spent the summer with them in Vienna.

"He planned to attend the Jamboree. He was a Boy Scout, but Hitler issued an edict that no German boy would attend. We figured there would be no harm. He was supposed to join some German boys' group at the end of the summer when he returned to Munich. Can't think of the name of the group."

"Hitlerjugend?"

"Yes, that's the name."

Dodd informs Raymond that Hitler issued an edict that all German boys must quit all other groups and organizations. Joining the Hitlerjugend was compulsory. The German boys had no choice but to join.

Raymond asks Dodd if he knew there was a rally here when they arrived from Hungary.

"Yes, we knew about that one. We're sure that's why Lajos picked this hotel, because of the proximity to the rally. This hotel seems like it would be out of the price point range for the Boy Scouts. I would have thought you'd stay in one of the smaller inns."

Raymond ponders what the ambassador said. "You know, come to think of it, I'm sure you're right. Most of the places we've stayed at have been smaller, cheaper, on the outskirts of town. I never gave it a thought. But I'll tell you, this place isn't exactly the Taj Mahal. I guess it's costly due to the location, certainly not the furnishings, as you can plainly see for yourself."

Raymond changes the subject. "The coroner might be looking for us; let's get back to the room where my son is. I'll grab my things and drop them there. Then we can go."

The three men walk back to Buster's room. There's no sign of the coroner yet. Up ahead, Raymond spies the Nazi auxiliary police, the ones who questioned him before. They spot Raymond and walk toward him, waving at him.

"Hello again, Mr. Wellington. The coroner and the inspector are with the body now; we'd like you to come to the deceased's room."

"Sure. Let me first introduce the United States Ambassador to Germany, William Todd, and his assistant, Phillip Winslow."

"Hello, sir, yes, please come as well."

As before, the unmistakably putrid smell of death smacks Raymond in the face. He turns to the ambassador and Winslow. The driver is already a light shade of green. "I'm sorry, I should have warned you."

Both men remove handkerchiefs from their breast pocket and cover their nose and mouth. Winslow remains outside the door. He shields his eyes from viewing the deceased, now draped with a white sheet.

Inside Lajos's room are the coroner and the inspector, Diedrich Ahren. The coroner, Dr. Tomas Herringer, wears a black suit, which shows under the white lab coat he has over it. He sports a large handlebar mustache which seems to take over most of the lower part of his face. When he speaks, his mustache moves. His hair, or what's left of it, he wears combed parted down the middle with a small cowlick in the back. He is tall, slender, with exceptionally large hands. Raymond takes note of this fact after shaking his hand. His own hand seems like it's swallowed whole by the coroner's huge mitt, which totally encases Raymond's. No one else shakes hands. The men nod at each other, informally acknowledging one another after Raymond introduces the ambassador.

The inspector wears a black suit as well. The white collar

of his shirt is stained with dirt or sweat, while his red tie bears the stains of soup.

Inspector Ahren wastes no time launching into questions.

"Mr. Wellington, thank you for coming. Ambassador, I have forms for you. The coroner will prepare the body, so that it will be ready to ship back to the U.S. at the date you assign. The officers have gone through the deceased's belongings. Mr. Wellington, was the deceased married?"

Raymond answers, "Not that I know of. No."

Ahren inspects the contents of Lajos's wallet, spread out on the table.

Raymond sees a license, passport, some money, and two photographs. One is of two boys, and the other is of one boy, but he's not close enough to identify the boys in either picture. Ahren picks up the photographs, handing them to Raymond.

"This is the contents of the deceased's wallet. I wonder if you know who the boys are in these photographs? The two boys, and the one. His children?"

Raymond takes the photographs. "I'm quite sure he has no children of his own, but then, you never know. I didn't know much about the man, outside of the Boy Scouts. I do not recognize this one boy. The other photograph of the two, let me see, here. Well, my goodness, that's Walter Johnson and Ricky Williams. Two Scouts in our troop. Ricky is the son of one of our chaperones."

A sick feeling, akin to a stomach virus with fever, washes over him when he remembers what Buster told him today, and Walter's words, *I'm glad he won't be Leader anymore.*

"Oh, no, it must be true."

Ahren cocks his head. "What must be true, Mr. Wellington?"

"Just a few hours ago my son told me about the deceased, and how he was abusing two boys, these boys, Ricky and

Walter. My son told me he and two other boys saw Lajos in the shower after lights-out, naked, with both boys in the shower with him, also naked. And he was doing, well, doing, you can imagine—I won't spell it out. He told me of another occasion where Ricky was in Janos's tent, at night, and the boy was crying. Walter told me today he was glad there would be a new troop leader, but wouldn't tell me why when I asked him."

Ahren continues, "What else did your son say, may I speak with him? I'll want to take a statement, and one from the other boys."

"Yes, of course, but only one of the two boys is here on the trip. You may get a statement from him and my son, but be aware, I am a lawyer and will advise my son, as necessary."

"Be assured, Mr. Wellington, we are aware you practice law for the U.S. State Department. Would you happen to know what line of work Ricky Williams' father is in?"

Raymond thinks for a moment. "I believe he sells steel parts for a company that fabricates them."

Dr. Herringer takes greater interest in the conversation, asking Raymond, "Steel rods, perhaps?"

"Yes, I think so. Why do you ask?"

"I believe Mr. Lajos was murdered by someone driving a steel rod through his ear, puncturing the eardrum and up through his brain. That brought immediate death when the rod hit between the temporal and frontal lobes. I propose the rod was specially fabricated, thick, and sharp. It would take something hard, like steel, to penetrate a skull."

Ahren adds, "It seems for now as though Mr. Williams had sufficient motive. But we cannot fully stand on that conclusion without further investigation. As of now, he is definitely a suspect. The only evidence left behind is the puncture the rod makes, and the small amount of blood that comes from the ear canal. It was an exceptionally clean sort of death."

The inspector poses a question to Raymond, "Where is Ricky Williams, did he accompany his father on this trip?"

Raymond grimaces, staring down at the floor, while numerous thoughts run through his mind at once. He has to tell the truth. "No, his son did not come on the trip, and I asked my son about this as well, why he didn't come. I think it's self-evident. Williams must have found out Lajos was abusing his son. If that was my son, I'd want to murder the bastard, too. But a man is innocent until he is found guilty, is he not?"

Ambassador Dodd adds dryly, "Lucky for Williams, he will be tried in his own country."

Ahren grows impatient, tapping his foot as evidence. "Mr. Wellington, I'd like to speak with the boy Walter and your son. Doctor, are we done here?"

Herringer answers, "Yes, I will fill out the forms and have them for you in twenty minutes, along with the shipping rules for the body. Shall I bring them to the front desk?"

Ambassador Dodd speaks up. "What's the room number, Raymond?"

"125."

"No, please, if you will, bring them to room 125. That is where we will be. That way I can look over the forms and see if we have any other transport questions for you. Thank you."

The men leave with Inspector Ahren and the Nazi police in tow and walk to room 125 in silence. Raymond is immersed in his own thoughts, wondering how he's going to break the news to Buster and Maddie.

The ambassador breaks his train of thought, and in a whisper that's part lamentation suggests, "Can't we just drop his body in the ocean?"

CHAPTER TWENTY-EIGHT

Elenena

AUGUST 1933

THE GERMAN STEAM train has three passenger coaches, is sparse in creature comforts, and lacks warmth in its design. The seats, while upholstered, do not offer any kind of consolation. The cabin rattles with sounds, not unlike screws that need tightening. While the German countryside passes by, waves of sadness wash over Elenena.

Did Stani and Maddie receive the letters yet? If so, what did they think? Will they forgive me? I will contact them once I reach America.

The streams of sunlight, with all their vivid tones, do not prevent a quiet melancholy from descending on Elenena, disquieting her soul. *Take heart, you're leaving this place.*

As the time dwindles by, and the train chugs away, Elenena partially listens while Charles prattles on about Rochester. "It's a lovely city really, monikered 'the Flower City,' but not just because of the usual connotation. There are numerous flour mills located along the waterfalls of the Genesee River. Barges once traveled the Erie Canal, bringing flour to bigger cities like Albany and New York City. Local millers were grinding thousands of bushels of wheat a day to keep up with the demand. Then, numerous seed companies in Rochester grew to become the largest in the world, and the name really stuck. Incidentally, Rochester is one of the first original 'boom towns,' named 'the young lion of the west,' growing at a fast rate with a strong economy.

There is no doubt in my mind that you'll love it."

"I hope so, Charles." Further commentary by her travel companion begins to rankle Elenena. While she works diligently to listen with patience, it is a halfhearted attempt. She giggles inwardly. *Travelogue with Charles.*

"Pertaining to the arts, obviously, we have the school, the philharmonic orchestra, and the Eastman Theater. We have numerous parks and quiet spaces for respite. Highland Park is a favorite of mine. Within its confines there are more varieties of lilacs planted than in any other location in the world. In the springtime, the air is replete with the scent of them. When they're in full bloom, at their peak, we have a Lilac Festival. A queen, chosen by proxy, presides over the festivities that take place over the course of a weekend. Your friend, and soon to be your associate, Professor Genhart, served as the Lilac Queen last year. That brought honor to the Eastman School. Then there's Lake Ontario, as well as great museums and galleries.

"The winters are cold, but not much more so than where you've lived, at least I would imagine. We have a full four seasons. Fall is my favorite."

Elenena likes the sound of the city but wonders about other aspects more germane to her appointment. She asks, "What is the school's student body like?"

Charles thinks for a moment. "I would say some students are eagerly pursuing a dream of playing with a symphony, or singing in an opera, or writing music like Cole Porter.

"Others from the University of Rochester take music as a second major. My brother, for example, is an English major at the U of R, and takes voice. He hopes to be a teacher. But he enjoys singing and has a clear, true baritone. He performed last spring on the stage of the Eastman Theater for the senior night program, singing 'The Green-Eyed Dragon.'

"He brought the house down—the applause was thunderous! As you can imagine, my parents were proud of their second-eldest son. My sister, a pediatric doctor at Rochester General Hospital, is the real trailblazer in the family."

"How lovely, so there is talent in your family beyond just the gift of languages. And seeing you enjoy talking, one might call you voluble, I'd like to take advantage of that. Tell me about your family."

"What would you like to know? I'll start at the beginning." He takes a sip of his chamomile tea, brought by a train steward.

"My father's family are fifth-generation Rochesterians. Our origins on my father's side go back to the Revolutionary War; Roger Sherman is our ancestor. He was one of our nation's founding fathers, the only person to have signed all four great state papers of the United States. He was also a member of the Committee of Five that drafted the Declaration of Independence."

"That's quite an exceptional pedigree. Tell me about your mother's family."

"Well, my mother's pedigree and lineage are not as illustrious as my father's. My mother's family originated from Poland. Her family became refugees and settled in Rochester after the Russian pogroms began in the 1880s. My mother never likes to speak about the history of her family, as it's a painful reminder of how they suffered at the hands of those that hated them. She shared more with me than my sister and brothers, maybe because I'm the youngest. When she was a small girl in Poland, she endured abuse at the hands of Russians. Her family lived in a small town close to Russia's western border with Poland. I believe it was under Russian occupation at separate times in history.

"My mother never recovered from that oppression, and I've never forgotten either. She passed away last year.

My parents were married thirty-one years ago. I have two brothers and one sister, the eldest of the children, who is recently divorced."

"What are the names of your siblings?"

"My sister is Rachael, she's thirty. Jacob, the oldest son, is twenty-eight and a banker in New York City, working for Chase National Bank. My brother, Caleb, is twenty-three, and training to become a teacher. I'm twenty-two and a tumbleweed, not sure what to do with my life. This position could lead to something more substantial; what that is, I have no idea. Here I am chattering away. Would you like to sleep, or rest? We don't have much longer now, we're due to arrive in Bremen in less than an hour."

"I enjoy young people; I like hearing about your life. No need to apologize. Is your first name a family name? I can't help but notice your name is not Biblical, like your other siblings."

"Yes, I'm named after my father's father, Charles."

Changing the subject from family, Elenena tells Charles, "Once we arrive, I suppose we'll check into the hotel and refresh ourselves? I prefer to dine late, say 8:00 p.m., if that is acceptable."

"Yes, of course, that will suit me well, thank you."

"What time does the ship depart and when do we board?"

"Our ship departs tomorrow at 8:00 p.m. We board at 7:00 p.m. Our hotel has a dining room, with alleged superb cuisine, although I would never consider German cuisine superb. I imagine the menu consisting of Sauerbraten, sausages, and sauerkraut. We can dine there if you like."

After a moment, Elenena says, "German food can be quite wonderful. I think it's a good practice in general to keep an open mind. It leaves room for possibilities!"

Blushing at the mild reprimand, Charles bows his head, "Yes, ma'am, you're right. My mother would say much the same thing. She used to tell me my judgments make me sound like a snob."

Elenena laughs openly, patting the top of Charles's hand. "She's right, but you're young enough to learn and change your thinking before it becomes too ingrained. You know, there is a world of possibilities out there, awaiting you. The more open you are, the more you will see and, hopefully, embrace. I teach my students flexibility, and I encourage them to integrate that into their thinking. Possibilities, flexibility—two integral words to embrace and guide you.

"Tell me more about your mother. Do you know the town in Poland her family originated from?"

Charles scratches his head, trying to remember. "I have no idea; the name escapes me."

Elenena takes a wild guess, wondering if just maybe, somehow, it might be near where her mother's family originated. "Does Baranovichi sound familiar to you?"

Charles ponders the name, repeating it a few times, "Baranovichi, Baranovichi. That could be it. Do you know Poland well?"

"I know parts of it, I was raised there. After my parents died, my sister and I went to live with our aunt, our mother's sister in Baranovichi. You may already know that from reading my application. I left and moved to Munich for two years, before moving back when my aunt fell ill. Then just a few months ago, my sister, who continued to live in Baranovichi, died there.

"It has always been my plan to emigrate to the U.S. I am doing it a little sooner than planned. I would think now is better than later. Even with the Great Depression, there are endowments and grants for foreign instructors, and there will always be musicians, teachers, composers, and singers. I feel I'm part of a niche-type enterprise. No matter how poor a nation is, there will always be a percentage of the population that supports and funds the arts."

Tears form in her eyes as she thinks of her former life with Stani and Maddie. After clearing her throat and dabbing at her eyes with her delicately-embroidered hankie, she asks Charles what he knows about the Nazis.

"Not very much. There are occasional snippets in the news and the paper, but to be honest, I don't know much. Will you tell me?"

Elenena gazes out the window at the flat territory of Germany, hoping never to see it again. Her expectations are set on America, leaving the Nazis and the memories of them behind.

"I will share with you something as it relates to my work. There is much ambivalence and controversy over Jewish musicians playing in the symphony orchestras of Germany.

"You see, Jews and Germans both have deeply passionate and opinionated feelings about their orchestra. In the end, it is the artists, the musicians who suffer. I'm hoping America will be like a breath of fresh air where this debate is concerned.

"Let me tell you about the conductor of the symphony orchestra. His name is Wilhelm Furtwängler. He is a conductor of great renown, in Germany and throughout Europe. He studied music in Munich and Vienna. He accepted the post of the musical director of the Berlin Philharmonic Orchestra in 1922, quite an achievement for a man under the age of thirty-five. He would conduct regularly at the top opera houses of Europe. Many consider him to be Germany's greatest conductor. The point of contention stems from Herr Furtwängler employing many Jewish musicians in his orchestra. The Reich Minister of Propaganda, Joseph Goebbels, started this controversy, causing many problems for the conductor, a wonderful man."

Elenena stops speaking, asking Charles, "If I'm boring you with these details, please tell me. You seem preoccupied, am I correct?"

Charles appears subdued, distracted. His eyelids are heavy, but not from the conversation.

"I find this extremely interesting, please continue."

"You're sure? You can rest if you'd prefer."

"No, Mrs. Laurent, please resume with the story."

Elenena gives Charles a questioning glance, then restarts.

"Many of Herr Furtwängler's friendships and supporters are in the community of the Jewish German elite. Open-minded people. Their funding of the arts is of the utmost importance to them. They are loyal to a fault.

"When Hitler became Chancellor in January of this year, it became obvious he could not disguise his hatred for the Jews. He is very public with his viewpoint. It became abundantly clear that it would be impossible for him or his administration to separate art from politics.

"Hitler's Minister of Propaganda, Joseph Goebbels, asserted that the Jewish musicians affected the quality of the music and created much controversy for the public.

"The people want music, not controversy. The brilliant conductor would not fully bow to the Nazi authority; he kept his Jewish musicians in the symphony, much to the chagrin of the Nazis. The conductor responded with written protests. The letters became newspaper fodder. Goebbels took the opportunity to print in the papers the conductor's impassioned letters asserting protection for his musical realm. But the letters, taken out of context, portray him as unsympathetic and lacking appreciation for the German people's struggle.

"My point is, Nazism infects everything it touches. Fascism is the most dangerous of all belief systems because it oppresses and destroys all opposition.

"Fascism takes away freedom, stripping independence to the very core, leaving nothing but dictatorial power. And it scares me so—that is why I am happy to leave with no regrets, well, there are regrets in that I'm leaving behind two people I love dearly. They are all the family I have in the world, even though we are not blood relatives. So, in all honesty, I am ambivalent. I will tell you more about the Nazis, but for now, it is enough."

Charles responds with genuine concern and empathy. "Undoubtedly, the topic upsets you. We don't have to speak of it ever again if you prefer. As a musician, it must have been difficult to observe, knowing the inherent conflict. Let's change the subject! Was there ever a Mr. Laurent?"

A smile slowly forms on Elenena's face while thoughts and memories of Stanislaw fill her mind like a flood.

In a whisper-quiet voice, Elenena confirms to Charles, "The desire, the dream for nuptial bliss was never mine. I can't say I ever had that drive like some people do. Many friends tell me when you meet the right man, you'll know it. Tell me about you. You are a handsome young man; you must have many girls who long for your attention."

Caught off guard, Charles blushes, his face turning a light shade of crimson. He stands and fumbles with his topcoat, taking it off, folding it, then resting it on his lap as he sits.

He plays with one of the buttons on the coat, as if that will signal a change in the subject matter. "Well, we should arrive soon."

"Charles, are you avoiding my question?"

He summons up the courage to speak. "Perhaps it's easier to express my feelings to a stranger. I don't say that to offend you—calling you a stranger. But I find myself at a loss for words when it comes to girls. They hold no interest for me."

"Oh, I see. Is it too personal for me to ask what does hold your interest?"

"I'm not sure. I'm trying to figure that out. I'm drawn to artistic types, anyone who can transform who they really are and hide inside a role of the character they're portraying or lose themselves in their painting or artwork."

He reminds me of Annie. She did not like who she was, so she lost herself within the Nazi party. She became a puppet of Nazi propaganda, running from herself, running from her truth. She must have hated herself.

Elenena asks Charles a question she wished she had the courage to ask Annie. She would not make the same mistake twice.

Maybe if I had asked her, she wouldn't have killed herself. We could have talked about it. I could have helped her.

"Do you not like yourself, who you are?"

Charles fidgets, squirming in his seat. The more personal the conversation gets, the more uncomfortable it makes him. The directness of Elenena's question demands an answer.

With a deep sigh, he answers the question. "Truth be told, I am not a free man, I'm a prisoner and I loathe myself. Epictetus said, 'No man is free who is not master of himself.' I wonder how much longer I can exist, feeling like I do. If you wake up on the ship and can't find me, do not fear, but rest assured, I'll be at the bottom of the ocean finding the peace, the quiet that I hunger for, a final silencing of the voices that torture me every waking moment of my existence."

CHAPTER TWENTY-NINE

Frederick, Wolfie, and Stanislaw

AUGUST 1933

JUBILATION IS THE mood within the cabin of Hitler's Mercedes. "Finally," breathes Frederick as his eyes spot the sign for Judengasse. Next he sees the landmark of trees which follow the pine trees, forest-green and full, majestically tall, laden with pinecones near the tops. Like sentries that guard a palace, they line the driveway leading to the Lehenerhof Inn.

Before entering the driveway, Frederick pulls the car to the side of the road, gets out of the car, and removes the small Nazi pennants that grace either side of the hood. "No sense drawing unwanted attention to the car once we get to the inn," he says, Stani agrees, commending his good thinking.

Frederick maneuvers the large automobile up the curvy road that leads to the top of a small hill. Puffy cumulus clouds come into view, suspended in the blue Austrian sky, and in the distance, the tops of the Alps appear, making their presence known. An increment of hope begins to surface in Frederick's mind, giving a glimmer of belief that they are safe. For now.

To his partners, Frederick mentions, "I bet there's a hell of a view once we reach the top."

The inn itself is an Alpine chalet structure with gingerbread trim, and shutters that have images of pine trees cut out at the corners. There are massive stone steps leading up to an arched wooden door, bedecked with two signs that read, 'Rooms' and 'Café.' Lush green ivy meanders along the structure, anywhere sunlight can reach it and encourage its growth. Cut and hollowed logs, two feet long and one foot wide, hold planted flowers. The logs rest, fitted, on the top of a cast-iron table.

Frederick rolls down the window, breathing in the fresh air as he drives to the right side of the entrance. He follows the dirt road that leads up another small hill to the barn. Along the sides of the driveway, edelweiss grows, wild and free. The sight of it causes Frederick to smile.

He calls attention to it, telling Wolfie, "Edelweiss is the national flower of Austria."

With the barn before them, Frederick states, "Gentlemen, we will park the car and wait for Rolf, if he's not here already."

Wolfie pauses and asks, "Uh, are we all still alive?"

Stanislaw laughs, understanding the basis for Wolfie's question. "By the looks of this place, we've arrived in heaven—is that what you're thinking, Wolfie? Ha, I have to agree with you, this is beautiful country!"

Arriving at the barn door, Frederick decides to take off the Nazi coat. The weight of it and unbreathable fabric have worn out their welcome, along with its usefulness and purpose. Plus, it's causing him to sweat. He stretches his lanky frame and walks to the barn door, swinging the wooden latch out from its resting place, allowing the doors to swing open. Wolfie slides over on the front seat, assuming the driver's position, and guides the car into the barn.

"I want to tell my grandchildren one day that I drove the Führer's automobile."

Frederick takes note of his son's ability to separate the

present moment from the past, by going beyond the fear to embrace a happy thought of the future.

The future. Ugh. What can it hold, what will we do?

"Frederick!"

From behind a large stack of hay bales, Rolf emerges, bedraggled.

"I was sleeping and heard the car, but I thought it was a dream until I awoke and saw you. How are you, brother?" The two men embrace in a warm and meaningful hug.

"Uncle Rolf!" Wolfie, with a sudden burst of energy, springs out of the car and runs up to his uncle, grimacing from the pain of his bruises. Joy replaces the pain. "Boy, am I glad to see you!"

Rolf acknowledges his nephew, "I'm not sure who is happier about this meeting. I've been desperately worried. Let me look at you!"

Rolf sees the closed and blackened eye, the sores, and bruises. He imagines the same all over the rest of his nephew's body. "Oh, my God, your eye, your face? Those bastards!"

Rolf tousles Wolfie's hair. "You are a welcome sight and I'm so thankful you're all alive! I was terribly worried; Cecile was also distraught."

Quietly, Stanislaw exits the auto and walks up to the three men. He addresses Rolf.

"Sir, how do you do. I am Stanislaw Birnbaum; I'm pleased to make your acquaintance. Thank you for helping us all. I am particularly indebted to you; you've provided an escape hideout without knowing me. I'm not even a member of your family."

Both Wolfie and Frederick say simultaneously, "Yes you are!"

Rolf smiles warmly and gives Stani a hug. Holding onto Stani's forearms, Rolf assures him, "You are part of our family now. Nothing you can do about it! Okay, now, I have clothes for you to change into, you can't walk into the inn in those horrible uniforms. Wolfie, I brought the summer clothes you left behind when you went to camp. Was that just a brief time ago? It feels like a century!"

Rolf turns to Stani, "I hope these pants and shirt fit. I have more for you inside the inn, but for now I hope they'll do. Frederick, here, you will wear some of my clothes, they should fit, but you seem thin. We'll work on that and have you plump in no time. All three of you!"

Still feeling on edge, Frederick asks Rolf, "You are positive we are safe here, that no one knows what's going on, or what happened—you know, the escape? Cecile's cousin will keep the secret, you're sure?"

"Yes, yes, Frederick, of course. We are family, and we must stick together. And Stani, you'll like my wife and her cousins who own this property—they are Jewish, so you will undoubtedly feel an affinity for them. There are rooms for you to sleep in. We will have dinner at noon in the café, but first, and foremost, before you do another thing, you can bathe." Playfully, Rolf harpoons his brother, "Little brother, you stink!"

Wolfie joins in, "We all do! We've been sweating nervous drops of worry!" Jumping up and down, Wolfie springs into a handstand, to the delight of the three men.

"Wow, owwwww, that still hurts." Wolfie holds his ribcage. "I'm still so sore from that beating."

Rolf looks on with concern. "You poor boy!"

Frederick adds, "We have a lot to catch up on. And we need a plan for what to do next."

With confidence, Rolf reassures his brother, "Yes, I agree, there is much to talk about, and let me tell you, there is more in the works than you could even imagine, but first things first. And don't press me, little brother. Trust me, all will reveal itself at the appropriate time."

Stani whispers to Wolfie, "Trust. An especially important word, it's like a muscle, you must develop it. We will speak more about it."

The three men change into civilian clothes. As Frederick peels off the striped shirt and pants, feeling liberated, he shouts a "whoop" into the air. Wolfie and Stanislaw follow.

The men are full of joy and a small amount of disbelief.

Frederick voices a nascent idea, "Let's have a bonfire tonight and burn our camp clothes."

While observing Stani and Wolfie, Frederick tells Rolf, "I don't know about those two, but my adrenaline is quickly depleting. I'm bushed, we've all been up for over twenty-four hours straight."

After baths, followed by a short rest, the four men enter the café. Josef Ross, the inn's owner, greets them, locking the door behind them.

Comfortably seated around a circular table, they enjoy a delicious meal prepared by Josef and his wife, Minka. Frederick says, "My appetite is roaring but I'm afraid to eat too much, my stomach will revolt."

Rolf gives his brother a knowing glance, telling him, "A word of caution to you. Your bodies will readjust to civilian life, but it will take time. After the Great War, it took me a while to be able to enjoy a full meal. So, for now, easy does it!"

All three of the former prisoners relax in the pleasant confines of the café. The chairs are wooden club chairs with handsewn cushions. The wallpaper depicts idyllic Austrian scenes of the Alps with mountain climbers. The valleys are filled with small, settled hamlets with flocks and herds grazing. Through the windows at the back of the café, they can view the caps of the Alps in the distance. There are unique chandeliers, made from antlers of deer and elk. The lighting is soft and easy on the eyes.

Not able to eat another bite, the men begin to speak about the horrors of the camp, the things they suffered.

Wolfie is quick to point out that no one suffered more than the Jewish prisoners.

"Uncle Rolf, and forgive me Cousin Minka, perhaps you might not want to hear some of these things, they are very graphic and unthinkable."

Minka begins clearing away the dishes and says, "I'll make us tea and bring the brandy."

Frederick commends Josef on the meal, accenting his praise by pressing a kiss to his thumb and forefinger. "The dinner was like nectar and ambrosia, wouldn't you agree, gentlemen?"

Wolfie cannot contain his exuberance. "It would be fine by me to have spaetzle with every meal for the rest of my life, with the sauce from the chicken too!"

Josef takes special interest in Wolfie, noticing the sparkle in his eyes and the gentle nature of a boy who survived a horrible experience. He asks Wolfie to continue with the story of the treatment of the Jews.

"Well, there is this one guard, Dukolf, who every prisoner, Jewish or not, hated. He looks like a big pimple, a fat roly-poly pimple; that's the best I can do to describe him. He took special pleasure in kicking Jewish men in their private parts and would do it regularly."

Stani joins in, "But let me tell you what a courageous young man we have here. He stood up to Dukolf. After we transported Jakob, when you stood up to him, you shocked the daylights out of him. Until that day, no one had ever stood up to that worthless piece of flesh. Wolfie, you were fearless in the face of danger!"

Stanislaw stops speaking as emotion overwhelms him, unprepared. The mention of his friend Jakob unleashes his pent-up sorrow. He places his hands over his face while he cries.

"There, there, Professor Birnbaum." Minka consoles Stani, and then pours a shot of brandy for all.

Stani sniffs, wiping his tears. "You know, I weep for my friend Jakob, but I also weep not knowing what happened to my friend and student, Maddie, and my love, Elenena, who must be worried sick about me."

Frederick relays the incredible puzzle which links his wife to Elenena, that they are sisters. Josef and Minka clap with happiness as Frederick describes how the discovery came about.

Minka concludes, "Now that is really something to celebrate—once lost, now found."

Frederick says, "I'll drink to that! Let's all drink to that!"

Minka places full shot glasses before each of the men. Frederick asks, "None for you, Minka?"

She laughs. "I'm a teetotaler, someone has to keep their wits about them."

Wolfie peers apprehensively at his father, who nods to his son. "You've earned this. Go right ahead and enjoy it, but I will warn you, it might make you choke or cough a little."

Stani stands and toasts the group. "Fate has brought us together; may we always be joined in our hearts. L'Chaim!"

Simultaneously, the group shouts, "L'Chaim!"

Wolfie sips the shot slowly, coughs, then tips his head and throws the shot back.

The men slap the table, congratulating him on his technique.

"Well done, Wolfie! That's definitely the German in you!" Frederick laughs with his son. "I cannot tell you how grateful I am that this miracle occurred, that we are here, with you, seated around this table. And while I'm temporarily relaxed, I'm growing concerned about what happened at Dachau. Was there talk of it; will the explosion make the news?"

Rolf nods at his brother. "I would think it will. How did you pull off this escapade? How did you plan this and execute it in a way you could escape, and in the Führer's auto no less?"

Lighting a cigarette, Frederick leans back in his chair, enjoying the revelry of the moment.

"With incredibly careful planning, taking opportunity of the circumstances as they presented themselves. Keep in mind, most of the guards at the camp have no education, they're not the sharpest lot of men. When the Great War happened, the brightest of that generation were wiped out." Frederick speaks these facts with a smile, nodding at Josef and Rolf. "Present company excluded. You add that up with understaffing, I knew my first day there that we outnumbered the guards. As much as thirty to one. It wasn't that hard.

"The camp commandant took a liking to me, and the kapos knew it. That allowed me to get away with my thievery unnoticed while executing aspects of our escape. Through Wolfie, and because of his tender heart, like his mother's, we met Stani. Stani knew of another prisoner's plan to escape, complete with stolen officers' uniforms. Stani knew the location of these uniforms.

"The rest of the plan just fell into place. Dynamite found its way to the camp for the excavation of a swimming pool. The truck needed servicing, and those dumb krauts left the dynamite unguarded in the back of the truck, thank you very much. I helped myself to it, and the rest they say, is history.

We blew up the garage, off we went, and here we are!"

Rolf looks at his brother in disbelief. "But how did you time it all, so that you could call me?"

"We had an order to service twelve trucks, the Führer's Mercedes, and another official car, a Mercedes, 770 like the Führer's. We had to have the work completed, using the kapo's words, 'If you have to stay up all night.' The strict deadline ensured that. So, it didn't seem strange that we were still working at 3:00 or 4:00 a.m."

Wolfie continues the story while his father accepts another brandy from Minka.

"The only time we had a slight problem was after Stani took possession of the hidden uniforms. We were in a truck, ready to drive back to the garage when one of the guards stopped us briefly. I thought I was going to wet my pants or throw up!"

Stani continues, "Wolfie, you exhibited nerves of steel. You told that guard not to mess with you, you had a schedule to keep, three officers from Berlin were at the garage waiting for the work to be finished. I wanted to howl with laughter because you put the fear of God in that guard! He looked petrified, like he had visions of being court-martialed and executed by firing squad for holding up the plans of Berlin.

"The guard couldn't get rid of us fast enough. He screamed one word, 'GO,' and go we did. Wolfie hit the gas and we went flying through the camp. Then he pulled that truck into the garage like he was parking a rocket ship. Not to mention, he's driving with only one eye working. You cannot write better comedy than that, my friends!"

The group can't contain their laughter. They all enjoy Stani's colorful storytelling, while Frederick laughs hardest of all, slapping the tabletop, smiling ear-to-ear at his son's courage in the face of danger. "Well, you were brought up right, Wolfie!"

The men and Minka continue with their contagious, joyful laughter. Stanislaw, now slightly tipsy, proposes another toast, "Laughter is good medicine, may it always be so for us. To my brothers, I salute you!"

Josef asks a question that puts a damper on the jovial mood. "What's next, what do you do, where do you go from here?"

Rolf clears his throat, his eyes focused on his brother. "Remember when we spoke on the phone and I told you I had news for you?"

Frederick nods. "Tell me the news, I'm on pins and needles!"

Rolf pulls out a piece of paper from his wallet. "Frederick, Wolfie, yesterday morning before you called, an American, U.S. Ambassador to Germany William Dodd, contacted me and Cecile telling us they knew of your whereabouts.

"That shocked me! How or why would a U.S. ambassador know anything about you, or Wolfie?

"And then I remembered the Boy Scouts, the boy, Buster, and his father—the one who paid for you to come with them to the Jamboree. That man, Raymond Wellington, is friends with Ambassador Dodd.

"Mr. Wellington called the Consulate in Berlin to seek assistance with finding Wolfie. He explained how they witnessed the beating by the Gestapo and were afraid they'd murdered you. So, the ambassador put some men to the task of investigating. When I couldn't reach you after we spoke about the letter from the Hitlerjugend, I felt something had gone horribly wrong."

Leaning back in the club chair, Frederick lights another smoke, sips his brandy and, as he raises his shot glass, says, "You can say that again, that something went wrong. A true understatement!" He knocks the shot back and continues.

"They took me into custody and threw me into Dachau. Just like that. I did what we discussed, appearing in person instead of calling the office that sent the letter.

"So, after taking the day off from work, I went in person to speak on Wolfie's behalf. I was wearing the blue suit and the tie that Elise bought me for our last Christmas together."

Frederick's emotions stir at the thought of the tie, now gone. His voice cracks. "You know, Elise would periodically write me notes and leave them for me in conspicuous places. She'd write notes of encouragement, notes with naughty promises, notes telling me she loved me. I never thought about saving them until two days before she passed, when she wrote the most beautiful note of all. I kept it in my wallet, always carrying it with me. Well, that day in the office of the Reichsführer, the officer asked me for Rolf and Cecile's phone number to try and reach Wolfie. The note fell out of my wallet and slid under the desk of the man interrogating me, and there was nothing I could do to retrieve it. It was gone forever."

Gently, Rolf says with a quiet voice, "Time to make new memories, little brother." He gets up from his seat and hugs Frederick around the shoulders. "It's all right to let it out, you deserve to after what you've been through. You're tougher than me, that's for sure, I never could have done what you did. You are one courageous man."

Minka is ready to pour another round when they all hear someone knocking impatiently on the glass-paned doors that lead from the lobby of the inn into the café. Josef gets up. "Who could that be? The sign says we're closed. Stay put, I'll go. No one move."

Josef walks past the tables and chairs, thinking it must be one of the inn's purveyors.

But that is not the case.
He can't believe his eyes.
Two Nazis are standing outside the door of the café.

CHAPTER THIRTY

Raymond, Buster, and Maddie

AUGUST 1933

AMBASSADOR TODD SENDS one of his men with the inspector and two police officers to Bremen, in an attempt to catch up with the troop and Williams. Williams will be questioned, and formally charged if appropriate. As he is an American citizen, the Consulate can offer him limited assistance, but cannot represent him. The ambassador can help Williams find an English-speaking attorney or a translator if he prefers. If he's not charged by the Gestapo, the police have to release him.

Room 125 is once again inhabitable for the three guests of that room, now that the ambassador, his aide, the inspector, and police have left. During the questioning, Maddie sits quietly in a chair off to the side of the beds. She can look directly at Buster's profile and observe him while he speaks. Dressed in the Scout uniform with her hair tucked up under the Lemon Squeezer hat, she escapes the attention of the police and the inspector.

Reminding himself, *they're still Nazis,* Raymond nonchalantly tells the inspector, "He's a member of our troop on the trip with us."

Maddie keeps her head down while perusing a brochure from the lobby, depicting the places and sights to visit while in Munich.

The inspector asks Buster pointed, direct questions—most importantly, whether Lajos ever tried to touch him or corner him in any way. Buster is thoughtful in his answers, chewing on the end of a pencil in between answering questions. Then he gives his opinion. "I think he preyed on the smaller, younger boys, with no siblings. I've only been a member of the Boy Scouts for three years, but from what I've seen, I think my assumptions are valid."

Ahren asks Buster, "How many brothers or sisters do you have?"

Buster is quick to answer, delineating the facts for the man. "While I do not have any brothers or sisters, I'll be seventeen in just a few days, I'm taller and older than those boys, and my father is actively involved in Scouting. He attends almost every meeting and every camp outing, except one, the one where I heard Ricky crying in Mr. Lewis's tent."

He continues, "Mr. Williams rarely accompanied Ricky. Walter Johnson's father passed away two years ago, and his stepfather does not participate with Walter. While the circumstances clearly differ, an obvious pattern emerges. I see it and I'm without a doubt that you will as well."

Not surprised by his son's adeptness at handling the questioning, Raymond nods at him with an approving smile. *He's growing up before my very eyes.*

Raymond exchanges contact information with Ahren, who makes a record of his passport number before bidding him, Buster, and the mystery Scout farewell.

Buster is restless, ready to depart the room that's held him captive for more than twenty-four hours. It feels more like a week than one full day. Details of Lajos's cold-blooded murder trouble him. He continues to ply his father with questions as to why Mr. Williams would murder Mr. Lewis in Germany instead of at home in the U.S.

Maddie and Buster discuss the details, amazed that someone would go to such great lengths, on a trip no less. Buster says, "He must have been waiting for just the right moment. Think of it, we're in Hungary, at the campsite on the Royal Grounds. Here we are, camping, marching, doing activities. Mr. Williams is participating in events with Mr. Lewis right by his side, knowing full well he's standing next to a dead man! That's wicked and full-blown crazy!"

Raymond tells him, "Most likely he thought, however erroneously, that his chances of getting away with the crime would be infinitely better in a foreign country. What I'm curious about is first, was he aware of Lajos's involvement with the Nazis, and second, was it simply a case of revenge murder for what he did to his son? All these questions need answers. The truth can only hide for so long. Now, how about less talk of gruesome details? We have a trip to take, and some friends to find. Grab your gear, we're checking out of this place. The ambassador is waiting for us in the lobby."

Nodding in agreement, Buster tells his father, "I don't know if I'll be able to contain myself once we get to this workcamp place. What if they won't allow us to see him? Then what? I wish there was a way to get him released into protective custody or one of those terms I've heard you speak about. Could we do that?"

The question Buster asks grieves Raymond. *I must tell him the truth. But how, and when?*

And what about Maddie's friend? How do I tell her?

He ignores these thoughts, saying, "One step at a time, son. We'll figure something out."

The ambassador's automobile sits parked in front of the hotel. Buster gathers his father's suitcase and loads it into the trunk of the auto. Phillip Winslow sits in the driver's seat with the motor running, studying a map as Ambassador Dodd gathers his three charges into the auto.

Getting into the car, Buster gazes back at the Hotel Bayerischer Hofname, saying aloud, "Not going to miss this place, that's for sure!"

He glances up at the sky and grimaces, "Sure could use some sunshine." The sky, with its low-hanging, thick, overcast cloud cover, threatens to release a downpour at any moment.

The ambassador tries to cheer Buster, telling him, "Typical Munich weather, rain showers in the summer only last for a few minutes. Sunshine will greet us as soon as we leave town, I promise."

Once inside the auto, the ambassador has news to share. "After confirming by telephone with another of my men on an intel mission, I have the current information. We're heading to Salzburg, and when we arrive there, we'll discuss our next strategy."

Flabbergasted, Buster takes the news like a gut punch. "What do you mean, Salzburg? Aren't we heading to Dachau, the camp? What's changed, why aren't we going there? Dad, you promised we'd look for Wolfie and Maddie's friend. What's going on? Can't you give us more information—what's happened to change all this now?" Buster pushes down the flood of emotion that overtakes him. He wills himself not to cry.

"Bill," Raymond says, "we're all dying to hear what's going on, can't you give us a clue?"

The ambassador turns in his seat, saying directly, "Trust me, I think you'll all be pleasantly surprised."

Raymond acquiesces. "Well, that's that. We will take your

word for it, Bill. Right, son? Now, I'm going to try and catch some shuteye if no one minds." It takes less than a minute for Raymond to doze off peacefully.

Maddie takes off her Lemon Squeezer hat, allowing her dark hair to cascade over her shoulders. She shakes her hair, and then takes Buster's hand. She whispers in his ear, "I don't know why I feel hopeful, but I do. He must know something we don't know."

Buster gazes into Maddie's face, searching for the reassurance he needs in her blue eyes. She smiles at him, and his troubled feelings melt away. He squeezes her hand, and they sit quietly. Within minutes, both Maddie and Buster are asleep.

Less than an hour outside of Salzburg, Buster awakens. He nudges his father, disrupting his soft snoring. "Dad, I'm starving, can we get something to eat?"

Ambassador Todd turns and hands him a napkin and a sandwich. "Compliments of the hotel; I hope this is sufficient for the time being."

While munching on his sandwich, Buster watches Maddie sleeping with her head turned away, resting on the small side window. A warm feeling comes over him, making him feel weak, as he gazes lovingly at Maddie in quiet slumber.

Ambassador Todd interrupts his thoughts, asking him, "What will you remember about Munich?"

"Well, first, I will never forget what I witnessed—the Gestapo thugs beating my friend to a pulp. Then, there's the sight and the sound of jackboots striking the surface of the street while the Nazis and Hitler Youth marched in perfect syncopation. I'm not sure if that sound will ever leave my mind. I doubt I'll ever forget it."

Dodd tells Buster, "That's called 'goose-stepping,' the way they march. It's actually an ancient march. All German rulers have employed it, Kaiser Wilhelm, Bismarck, all of their troops marched that way."

Buster turns his sights back on Maddie, telling the ambassador, "Yet in the midst of my worry and fear for my friend's life, an angel appeared. And my worries almost fade when I look at her."

Todd shakes his head knowingly, replying, "Yes, I'm very familiar with that kind of emotion. I still feel that way about my wife of many years."

"I smell food." Raymond awakens, and with one eye open, spies his son's half-eaten roast beef sandwich. "I smell horseradish."

Buster laughs, "The voice of one calling in the wilderness! You're awake. Good guess—that's what I have."

"I'll take one of those, wherever they came from."

Todd passes a sandwich back to Raymond, who plows into it, his appetite suddenly insatiable.

"Don't mean to interrupt, sir, but I believe this is the town." The driver, Phillip Winslow, calls attention to the approaching Salzburg signage.

The ambassador responds, "Yes, quite right, turn off here."

After driving a few miles more, the car approaches a tree-lined drive with a small hill leading up to the alpine Lehenerhof Inn. All eyes but Maddie's view the sleek, shiny black automobile, a Mercedes 770 with Nazi pennants on either side of the car's hood, which wave in the slight breeze. The sight of the flags gives Buster a sickening feeling in his stomach. What's more troubling is the location of the auto.

It's parked directly in front of the entrance.

CHAPTER THIRTY-ONE

Elenena

AUGUST 1933

BREMEN IS A bustling Hanseatic city. Its port, the second largest in Germany, is the source of the city's reputation as a leading economic hub. The famous German steamships are manufactured in a local shipyard. Elenena and Charles will travel to the United States on a ship line that had its start in commercial shipping.

Norddeutscher Lloyd developed into one of the most important German shipping companies of the late nineteenth and early twentieth centuries. It was instrumental in the economic development of Bremen.

Elenena and Charles will sail on the ship SS Europa, the flagship ocean liner of the NDL fleet. The advanced high-speed steam turbine ocean vessel will cross the Atlantic in four days and seventeen hours at an average speed of 27.91 knots per hour.

After hailing a taxicab, Charles opens the car door and Elenena steps into the automobile. Charles tells the driver in German, "Hotel Hanseat, please."

The silence between the two passengers is obvious. Neither speak until Elenena breaks the quiet repose. "You speak with such confidence. German is a language I never learned, never had a desire to, although it would have helped me when I first moved to Munich. You see, my landlord, the woman I lived with, spoke German and English, but I could have understood her more if I spoke her native tongue. I don't know why I'm bringing her up."

But she knows why. Charles's comment about resting in the bottom of the ocean has unnerved her; it's all she can think about.

Now is not the time to confront him—but you must, you must speak to him, help him.

Elenena takes in the sights from the taxi window. She sees an old city, with impressive architecture, both Gothic and medieval. Some buildings have a Renaissance façade. There are picturesque gabled houses, and buildings with red tiled roofs.

The city is built around the waterfront, causing the skies to vary quickly. Today they're a deep blue with a few errant clouds, stretched above the dark, choppy waters of an ocean port.

The taxicab arrives quickly at their destination. After leaving the cab before entering the hotel, with gentle persuasion, Elenena asks a disinterested Charles, "Why don't we drop our bags, freshen up, then walk around the city? What do you say? I think fresh air will do us both good."

"If you say so, okay."

Charles takes Elenena's luggage along with his, handing them both to the bellman of the hotel as he sees to checking in. Elenena watches from just inside the lobby as Charles navigates his way to the front desk. He stops when something drops from the bag he carries over his shoulder. The item makes a loud clanging noise, like metal hitting the tile. Elenena watches as he stoops to gather the item, returning it to his bag.

Such a troubled boy. I know exactly the burden he carries, the shame that goes with it. I wonder if it would be a comfort to tell him I know and understand? Will my compassion and understanding bring Annie back to life? No. But I can help him, and somehow he can find a way to live a happier existence. I can only hope to help him. He may not desire help.

"Mrs. Laurent? Mrs. Laurent?"

Elenena is so caught up in her thoughts, she didn't hear Charles the first time he spoke.

"Here is your room number. The bellman has the key, he'll take you up the elevator. I'm going to buy some smokes. I'll meet you back here in thirty minutes. Is that acceptable?"

"Yes, of course. I'll see you then."

The bellman stands four feet away, dressed in a red silk uniform with gold trim. He nods at Elenena to follow him, and they wait for the gilded elevator with the large iron gate to come back to the first floor. They both look up at the mechanical hand moving slowly around on the clock towards the number one.

With a with a final ding, the doors open. One by one, hotel guests file out. Elenena notices one young man, blond like Charles, and tall, but ruggedly good-looking, with smoldering gray eyes, chiseled bone structure, and a broad-shouldered frame. He is impeccably dressed.

Elenena isn't the only guest noticing the handsome stranger. She gets into the elevator, standing to the side while others enter. She continues to watch the young man until the door closes. *That's strange. He appears to be heading straight for Charles, who is still standing in the lobby, watching me. Was he watching me or this man?*

Elenena cannot get the man out of her mind. *Does Charles know him?*

The bellman unlocks the door and sets her suitcase on a low table. She reaches in her purse, searching for a Deutschmark, but the bellman assures her, speaking English with a German accent, "The young man tipped me already, thank you."

After walking the man to the door, she looks around the room. She sees the tasteful design and decoration, thick brocade bed covering, Oriental rugs on the floors, scenic oil paintings on the walls. On a table near the window, there is a porcelain bowl and pitcher filled with water, along with linen towels. The view through the glass-paned casement provides a panorama of sights, including a late-Gothic brick cathedral with stained-glass windows. The scene highlights the vast number of steepled churches in Bremen, but where are the synagogues?

Anti-Semitism is rising in Germany at a rapid clip, due to the appointment of Hitler.

Just thinking about Hitler's name gives me the chills. I'm leaving this place. But will others have the same opportunity? Am I abandoning my fellow Jews, or am I abandoning Germany?

Even though Elenena has had only a single experience with the man, having heard him speak, she is sure of one fact. His hatred for Jews is paramount and essential to his plan for extermination of all European Jews.

I hope I never have to come back here, for any reason at all. But what if Stanislaw or Maddie need me? What then? I will send them money to come to the United States and take care of them there. My plan feels like a bucket with holes in the bottom.

To distract herself, Elenena goes about unpacking her ensemble for the ship, where she will begin her adventure. For the evening, she chooses a cream-and-blue silk dress, flowing and light, with a cream-colored shawl made of Shetland wool to wear over her shoulders if the weather turns cool.

An adventure. The words echo in her mind. *It is nothing less than that. I'm traveling to another continent.* While knowing little of America, she is excited to learn.

After washing her hands and face, Elenena reapplies her makeup, putting on lipstick before taking one final look in the mirror.

A scripture comes to her mind from the book of Psalms: *I will lift my eyes unto the hills from whence cometh my help.*

Looking at her watch, she realizes it's time to meet Charles in the lobby.

I'll ask him about the handsome stranger. Or should I leave it alone?

Elenena makes her way down the elevator, exiting at the first floor. The lobby of the Hotel Hanseat is wide and expansive. The tilework on the floor is exquisite and of the highest quality, as is the massive crystal chandelier that lights most of the room.

There are fresh flowers on coffee tables situated between sofas and chairs, where one can sit and read or just relax. The scent of the flowers fills the air.

In the center of the lobby is a cleverly-designed, plush, red-upholstered seating arrangement that circles the base of a Gothic-style floor-to-ceiling column.

If I sit here in the center of the lobby, I can wait for Charles and see the goings-on of a busy German hotel.

Checking her watch to make sure she wound it, she is reassured by the ticking. She sees she's a few minutes early. *Charles should be here any moment now.*

While viewing the front doors, she catches a glimpse of Charles. *Ah, there he is! And there is the handsome stranger!* Elenena picks up her purse and moves closer to get a better view. *What are they doing? What are they talking about? Did they go somewhere together?*

While straining for a better look, Elenena loses sight of the two men. She drops her purse after loosening her grip on it, and the contents spill out everywhere. Elenena bends to gather her wallet and compact, while Charles swoops in and comes to her rescue. He bends down to collect the rest of the contents, helping her to her feet.

Embarrassed, Elenena comments, "I'm like an absent-minded professor at times. I frustrate myself! Thank you for the assistance."

"My pleasure. Are you ready to begin our walk? I've taken the liberty to examine a few sights that you might enjoy, if that's fine with you."

"Yes, that would be wonderful, lead on. I can't help but notice a change in your mood." Lightheartedly Elenena adds, "If cigarettes do that for you, please do give me one!"

Elenena glances at Charles while he lights a cigarette for her.

"You know, I've never smoked one in my life. Perhaps now is not an appropriate time to start. You go ahead and smoke that, dear."

Charles obliges and tells her, "I found a place I think you'll like very much. It's a few blocks from here, but along the way there are beautiful buildings and a small park. I walked around about two blocks north and south to get a feel for the city, seeing if I could find some things to interest you."

"Thank you, Charles. That's altogether thoughtful of you."

Taking to the sidewalk, they absorb the sights and sounds of Bremen. A steamship in the distance gives off a bellowing blow of the horn, announcing her intention to come to port.

Gingerly, Elenena broaches the subject of the handsome stranger.

"I'm happy to see your spirits have picked up. I noticed you conversing with a tall blond man, outside the doors of the hotel. Is that striking fellow an acquaintance of yours?"

Caught off guard by the question, Charles stumbles on his

first few words. "Well, I, um, you see. His name is Marshall Voteck. He happened to be on the same ship I took here from America. He tells me he's an actor. I got to know him on the trip over, and coincidentally he'll be taking the Europa back to the States as well."

Elenena is quiet, summoning up the courage to ask a direct question, one that will shock even herself. "Is Mr. Voteck someone you're interested in?"

The color drains from Charles face; he becomes ashen.

He asks, "What would make you say that?"

Elenena stays silent. She knows if she waits long enough, the truth will come spilling forth.

While meandering down the city block together, ever so gently, Charles links his arm through Elenena's. He wills himself to speak.

"I have to assume my comment about girls not holding any interest for me gives me away. But Marshall could just be a friend! It's not so strange to be friends with another man. Did you see something that would cause you to think otherwise?"

Elenena stops walking, so she can face the young man.

"Dear boy, I knew something was different about you from the minute I met you. There was no sign or anything to give you away, it's just an essence that I recognize. Nothing more. My landlady in Munich had a similar essence."

Charles considers the words but is not thoroughly convinced that there wasn't a sign that gave him away.

Taking a leap into unknown and uncharted waters, Charles continues with his questioning.

"I am sure there are men of my persuasion who act with certain displays of behavior, and affected speech as well, but I avoid such actions at all costs. I am not like that. I have known for a long time that I was different, but I never understood how or why. I've had many discussions about why some people like me are this way and I can say I've arrived at a conclusion most will not agree with. While some may be born with a certain propensity to find the same sex attractive, I have chosen this life for myself. I believe there were events that took place causing me to lean one way versus another, but only because I chose to, does that make any sort of sense to you?"

With careful wording, Elenena confirms, "Yes, that does make sense, and it resonates with me on a deep level. What I'm about to say is something I've kept to myself and wouldn't speak about in mixed company. I believe a former situation gives me an understanding most do not have.

"Frankly, it's not proper to discuss such matters, but with you, Charles, I think I'm put in your path for a reason. I understand you to a degree, and that can allow you to open up and speak about the things which you say torment you. Giving light to our fears, bringing them out into the open, may transform them. But truth is harder than a lie. It seems when we suffer emotional wounds at an incredibly early age, the scars they leave wield an inordinate amount of influence over the choices we make as adults.

"My landlady spoke of the fear and panic she had as a child. Whenever her parents would leave to travel, Annie would stay with an aunt and uncle. Her father was a professor of some sort and lectured at universities abroad. Her stays with the aunt and uncle could be lengthy. The uncle abused her in the worst of ways from the time she was five until she was ten. She remembered the feeling of the happy spirit within her shutting down, going away. She felt very alone, holding a terrible secret she could not share.

"You may wonder why she opened up to me. I believe it's because I was a stranger to her and did not know anyone in

Munich. Or it could be she felt safe speaking to me about such matters. You remind me of her in that way. I wish there was something I could have done to help her in her misery. Even after I became the object of her obsession, my heart broke for her. Deep down I knew her to be desperately unhappy, and utterly alone. I hope for a better outcome for you, Charles. I would imagine if you chose this lifestyle, it is not without consequence. Do you fear God or his condemnation?"

There is no sound answer Charles can give. He thinks about the words Elenena speaks. It's not the first time he's been questioned regarding morality and condemnation. He answers, "I'm not sure what I think. It's not my intention to disobey the natural order and pattern set forth, but I'm fully aware it's a choice I make. I wonder if I'm meant to be single, and my destiny lies in that. For now, I cannot say. I have yet to find anything but loneliness as my one true constant companion."

With a smile he adds, "If loneliness was a luxury of immense value, I'd be the richest among men!"

The two arrive at the first stop Charles has planned. A large glass-paned window highlights some of the luscious offerings found inside.

With a sincere tone, Charles tells Elenena, "We will continue this conversation at a more appropriate time. But for now, I have a surprise for you!"

Charles opens the door to the bakery. Bells on the back of the door jingle.

The signage on the front door says, "Bernstein's Jewish and French Bakery."

The complex aromas of the sweet scents of baking— vanilla, sugar, yeast, butter, chocolate, and almond—sweep Elenena away in the magical, transformative redolence that turns back the hands of time. She is transported back to

Schweitzer's in Munich, and her mother's kitchen in Paris. Elenena gazes at the delicate pastries in the case, stollens and kuchens. On a shelf with wood slats are just-baked loaves of challah and marbled rye bread. Elenena's eyes glaze over and she grows misty, remembering the early days in Munich. The nostalgia of the moment holds her captive.

Until she hears a voice she recognizes speak her name. "Elenena?"

CHAPTER THIRTY-TWO

Frederick, Wolfie, and Stanislaw

AUGUST 1933

JOSEF GRAPPLES WITH calming himself. *Take a deep breath, Josef.* With no success, his nerves feel like frayed wires, his body hot as a burning cinder. Despite his feelings, he puts up a good front. He waves and smiles at the two Nazis standing at the other side of the door. *What could they want, why are they here, could they know the truth already?*

Opening the door, Josef greets the men, speaking in German. "Hello, how can I help you, please?"

The Nazis step inside the café and look around. One of the men says to the other, "It smells good in here—I'm wondering if they have any food? Maybe so." They speak as if Josef isn't standing in front of them.

"We'd like something to eat. Is your café open?"

Perplexed, Josef knows he must answer, "Yes." He is wise not to consider refusing a Nazi.

Minka appears. Making eye contact with Josef, she widens her eyes, then nods toward the inside of the café, where Wolfie, Frederick and Stani watch from behind the kitchen door. She stands silently next to her husband.

After giving Minka the once-over, the men pause, turn their backs on the two, and confer under their breath.

"Did you know these people are Jews?"

"Are you sure? Do you trust them to make our food?"

"It doesn't matter to me, I'm hungry."

Josef and Minka stand frozen in the awkward atmosphere of semi-silence, waiting for a decision.

The Nazis turn and ask Josef, "Do you have sausage and potatoes?"

"Yes, we do. What would you like to drink? We have very good beer."

"We'll be the judge of that! As if a Jew knows anything about the quality of a good beer!" Both Nazis laugh.

Minka leaves to prepare the food.

One of the Nazis, best described as short and fat, wears a permanently disagreeable expression. He lights a cigarette while carefully eyeing Josef. "Do you know where Haus Wachenfeld is located?"

Josef thinks for a moment. "Yes, yes. I believe it's about fifteen miles south of here."

The short, fat Nazi takes out a small pad and pencil from his pants pocket. He states, "We took a wrong turn a few miles back." Sizing up Josef, he asks, "Do you own this property?"

Josef fears the beginning of an interrogation but answers anyway. "Yes, we do, from my wife's family. The property is part of her family's heritage going back one hundred years."

Silently, Minka comes back with two steins filled with frothy, cold beer and sets them on one of the tables right at the front of the café.

One of the two Nazis notes the obvious, "We're the only ones in the place, why is that?"

Josef tells them, "We close for the month of August, to do repairs before the busy season begins."

"Ah, good. Then we will get special attention. Tell me,

what is your name?"

Josef's back stiffens. He knows the Nazi isn't asking their names to make conversation. He answers, "Josef and Minka Ross."

The officer with the pad and pencil prints their names.

"Okay, good. But your last name doesn't sound Jewish. What was it changed from?"

"Rosenberg."

Both Nazis laugh. The officer doing the writing says, "Now that's a Jewish name if I ever heard one!"

Minka appears with two heaping and steaming plates of juicy sausages, alongside a mound of fried potatoes. The Nazis appear pleased with their plates.

Josef and Minka stand silently, awaiting the next command.

The Nazis dig into their food, dipping the sausage in the small dish of mustard and stabbing at the potatoes. They eat with their heads bowed over their plates, while they shovel the food into their mouths like they haven't eaten in days.

After fifteen minutes of standing in silence while the Nazis eat, watching them as they empty their plates and beer steins, Minka asks the men if they'd like more beer. She doesn't realize she's made a fatal mistake until it's too late.

The short, fat Nazi gets up from his place at the table, incensed. His face twists into a snarl as he spits out the words, "Did we ask you for anything, Jewish pig?" He motions to Josef, waving his fork in his pudgy hand. "Slap your wife for that, go on, slap her for addressing us."

Horrified, Josef is frozen. The short, fat Nazi comes from behind the table to stand in front of Josef, who is a good foot taller than the Nazi.

"If you don't do it, then I will."

Minka drops her head, knowing her husband would never raise a hand to her, no matter who gives the directive.

She braces herself for the slap, while Josef is helpless to do anything but stand motionless.

The Nazi backhands Minka across the face, knocking her off her feet. The heavy gold ring he wears on his right hand splits her upper lip, and the blood gushes down her chin, onto the front of her pretty alpine-looking dress and apron.

"Get up, pig. That will teach you to never address an officer of the Reich until you're spoken to first, is that clear?"

Staggering to get up on her feet, she nods.

He says to his partner, "These people are stupid peasants, ignorant, you have to teach them everything."

To Josef he says with a threatening tone, his eyes narrowed, "You'd better keep a watch over your pig. There won't be a next time."

Putting their hats back on, the Nazis prepare to leave.

"So, fifteen miles south of here? Are you sure? You'd better be right or else we will come back here, and I promise you, I won't hold back."

Josef answers, "Yes, sir, I'm sure."

As the Nazis make their way out the front door of the inn, an official-looking car comes into view, parked behind their automobile on the roundabout driveway.

The short, fat Nazi says, "What do we have here?"

Ambassador Dodd hastens out of the car on one side, Winslow on the other.

The ambassador steps forward to address the Nazis.

"How do you do, I'm Ambassador William Todd, Ambassador to Germany from the United States."

Not impressed, the short, fat Nazi says, "Yes, I recognize you from your photograph in the Berlin newspapers. Why are you here?"

"I'm making a formal query for the United States State Department for an official meeting with the Reich officials. I'm trying to find a locale that would be suitable for a high-level meeting. Inconspicuous and off the regular beaten path. Do you have an opinion of this place?"

The short, fat Nazi considers the words of the ambassador and continues with his questioning. "Why would you go seeking a place personally, don't you have staff to do your errands?"

"I am the host, and I thought it a good opportunity to breathe in some of this amazing alpine fresh air, view the Alps, and take a bit of a respite from the busy day-to-day affairs in Berlin. A day away from the city can do wonders, wouldn't you agree?"

"Yes, I agree. You won't want to hold your meetings here; I can tell you that. Jews own the property, and no Reich official would ever consider setting foot in this place."

The ambassador finds this revelation sanctimonious and hypocritical. Rather than wasting a moment to point out the irony, he volleys back, going on the offensive, "That is helpful information. Thank you. I'm curious, why were you here, if you don't mind me asking?"

"We are here on official business for the Reich!"

Todd spots the mustard on short, fat Nazi's tie. Diligently trying to stifle a laugh, he comments, "In that case, you might want to remove the mustard from your tie before going anywhere else."

Sizing the ambassador up, the short, fat Nazi's eyes travel from him to his tie. Gazing down, he spots the splotch of brown mustard.

He elbows his fellow Nazi. "Oh, shit, why didn't you tell me?"

Taking out a pocketknife, he carefully scrapes it off the surface of his tie.

The ambassador attempts to be helpful. "You don't want to put water on that, it will set. Rub some talc into it, it will bring out the stain."

Now thoroughly embarrassed, the short Nazi sighs and says, "We must be about our business."

Standing rigid at attention while raising their right arms in a salute, the Nazis say, "Heil Hitler." They turn and get into their automobile. The ambassador and Winslow stand, watching the car slowly drive away, down the tree-lined drive that leads to the main road.

Inside the inn, Josef holds his wife while she cries, mostly tears of relief because the monsters have left. "Why do they hate us so, what did we do to them that would warrant that kind of behavior?"

Kissing the top of her head, he tries to comfort his wife. "My darling, let me see your lip, oh, that's a real cut. But I think if you put a cold compress on it, the bleeding will stop. Would you like me to help you get out of your dress, wash it for you, and you can put a new one?"

She shakes her head. "I used to love this dress. They've ruined it. They've stained it not with just my blood, but with their hatred. I'll never wear it again."

Josef agrees with his wife, telling her she never has to wear it. "We can burn it with the boys' Nazi uniforms. Are you all right, love?"

Minka reaches out to touch her husband's face. "Thank you, my darling, I'll be okay. I'll tend to my lip and clean up. And do burn this dress with the uniforms. How appropriate!"

"Minka, by the way, where did you hide the boys?"

"They're in the kitchen, back behind the dry storage."

Minka leaves to go to their apartment in the inn. Moments

later, Rolf, Frederick, and Wolfie come back from the kitchen and enter the dining room.

The three men stand around, talking with Josef about the confrontation with the Nazis and their narrow escape, when the name "Wolfie" rings out, shouted as loud as can be.

Wolfie turns around to see his American brother, Buster, running into the café, past the doors. Buster springs into Wolfie's arms before Wolfie can say a word.

Both are speaking at once, laughing, shouting, talking in a jumble.

No one can understand a word, but it doesn't matter. What matters is the boys are together again. Finally!

"My brother, I thought you were dead! Oh, my goodness, I thank God you're alive, you're alive!" Buster is so caught up in the emotion of the moment, he forgets completely about introducing Maddie.

Snapping out of his merriment for a moment, breathlessly he says, "Okay, first things first, everyone, meet everyone!"

Wolfie grimaces momentarily from the force of Buster's hug. His ribs still ache from the brutal beating by the Gestapo.

Buster gasps as he notices his friend's bruises, paying special attention to Wolfie's eye while making an appraisal of his overall condition. Laughing and teasing, he tells Wolfie, "Your face has seen better days. Can you see out of that eye? What a shiner! I bet I could beat you now at a game of one-on-one!"

Wolfie takes the bait, grinning with confidence. "Fat chance!"

A bright shade of red surges to Buster's cheeks as he prepares to introduce Maddie. Bowing at the waist with his arm and hand extended to make a more formal introduction, Buster says, "Wolfie, meet Miss Maddie Turetzky, Maddie, meet Wilhelm Wolfie Wolferman."

Demurely, Maddie shakes his hand while commenting, "I'm so incredibly pleased to meet you. Buster has spoken of nothing but you!"

He shakes her hand, saying, "I'm more than happy to meet you."

Wolfie takes a step back from Maddie, asking, "Would you excuse me for a moment?" He puts his fingers in his mouth and whistles, an ear-splitting, high-pitched sound. "Here's something I learned at Dachau. Form two lines and face each other. Then we will go through introductions."

Wolfie no sooner says this when Maddie shouts, "Professor!!"

Stanislaw comes into the dining room from the back of the kitchen.

"You know I have to make a grand entrance!" he says with a twinkle in his eye, winking at Wolfie, who begins to clap with joy. The room is full of contagious energy and tangible happiness.

"Professor." Maddie tries to hold back her tears, however unsuccessfully. She hugs him, so thankful for this amazing and unexpected reunion.

"Professor, I thank God you're alive, and here we are. A miracle! Please, meet Buster, my knight in shining armor. He rescued me. And meet his father, Raymond! Another knight in shining armor." Maddie cannot contain her excitement; she begins spinning and twirling. "I'm so excited I might just pop! We need music, so we can dance!"

Josef honors her request, fetching his gramophone. He cranks the handle, puts the needle down, and plays a selection by the composer Karl Amadeus Hartmann, *Burleske Musik* for piano.

Everyone begins to dance—Wolfie and Buster, Maddie and Raymond, Rolf and Frederick, Stani and Josef. Two of the men refrain from dancing. The ambassador seats himself and lights his cigar, while Winslow studies a map laid out on one of the dining room's tables.

Minka appears in a clean dress, entering the dining room with a towel pressed to her lip. Unable to fully smile, she nods hello to the new guests, meeting each one.

Maddie asks Minka, "What happened to your mouth?"

"Keep dancing, this is a happy moment! We will talk about that in a little while."

After twenty minutes, the group sits down to take a rest.

Josef begins explaining to the group what happened to his wife. As Wolfie, Frederick, and Stani were hiding in the kitchen, they couldn't see the entire exchange between Minka and the Nazi.

Wolfie feels his anger rising. "I was peeking through the door when I saw that short, fat Nazi pimple. He did this to you?"

Wolfie asks Stani, "Who does the short fat Nazi remind you of? In unison, Frederick and Stani shout, "Dukolf!"

Buster laughs at the hilarious description Wolfie used to describe the Nazi. "Did you just call him a pimple?"

"Indeed, I did! He reminds us of a miserable excuse for a human named Horace Dukolf, a guard in Dachau. I'm hoping our explosion blew him up!"

Frederick once again tempers his son. "Wolfie, we shouldn't wish that anyone dies, but that they get their due punishment for the pain and anguish they inflicted on the innocent. That is a better retribution for their actions."

Buster asks, "What explosion?"

Then Raymond tells Wolfie, "Last I heard, you were dead!"

Both Buster and Maddie whip around to stare at Raymond. Buster growls, "What? Dead? You never told us that!"

Raymond smiles a wry smile and tousles his son's wavy hair.

"Aren't you glad I didn't tell you? It all worked out, didn't it?"

Frederick breaks away from the group, with Rolf following. The two men approach the ambassador. "Sir, we have a bit of a problem. To aid our escape from Dachau, we stole the Führer's Mercedes. It's in the barn out back. I switched the license plates with another one of the vehicles in the garage before we left. We need to get rid of it. Do you have any suggestions?"

"Yes, I agree, that's a problem, but not insurmountable. The Embassy car I drive is exactly like the Führer's Mercedes. Granted, mine lacks some of the alterations, but the body and engine are quite similar. A 770, right? I would imagine you don't have any knowledge of what happened after the explosion, do you?"

Frederick's eyes grow wide. "I only saw it from the rearview mirror—it was massive. We left another auto and a truck in the garage to augment the explosive reaction, along with two sticks of dynamite."

"Yes, massive is an understatement. The commandant I spoke with—Eicke is his name—he told me you, Wolfie, and Stani lost your lives in the blast. He lamented your passing; he was very complimentary. In fact, he said you were a fine mechanic.

"There will be an investigation as to what caused the blast. It took the Munich and Dachau fire department forty minutes to arrive. The manual alarm that goes off when there's a fire at the camp was faulty; the alarm never rang in either fire house. The commandant Eicke wasn't at home. He spent the night with his wife in Nuremberg. With the mass confusion, not one officer or kapo thought about manually calling the fire department until it was too late. They figured they pulled the alarm and that would get the firemen to the camp. No such luck."

With a grin, Dodd commends the men. "Good work! You three were the only ones to perish in the blaze. Now, stealing the Führer's car would be considered a criminal offense, but we can get around it. Then there's the fact that you blew up the garage, but we can get around that too, seeing you're thought to be dead. The dead cannot stand trial nor suffer consequences from their actions. Have you thought about leaving the country, perhaps as political refugees?"

CHAPTER THIRTY-THREE

Elenena

AUGUST 1933

GRETA SCHWEITZER CAN'T believe her eyes. "Elenena Laurent, here you are, and we meet again! You're more beautiful than the last time I saw you, when you appeared like an angel amidst chaos." While seated at one of the three small wooden tables inside the quaint bakery, over coffee, a teary-eyed Greta explains to Elenena and Charles all that took place after that fateful day in Munich.

"After the fire, I gave up on Munich. With Fritz gone, there was no way I could go on there without him. Our building sustained damage beyond repair, our equipment was a total loss, so that made the decision an easy one. My darling Fritz left a legacy for me by way of insurance. I received a tidy settlement, bid Munich farewell, and settled here in Bremen with my sister Helga. She has gone home to prepare supper, or I would introduce you both."

Pointing to the two glass bakery cases, Greta praises her sister's talent. "She is a marvelous baker, highly skilled. She worked in London at the famed Savoy Hotel under the irrepressible, esteemed Chef Auguste Escoffier. He was a difficult man to work for, but what she gained in experience, well, you cannot put a price on the value. We make cakes—or as she calls them, tortes—pastries and Danishes, Berliners, strudels, kuchens, petit fours, Napoleons, eclairs, and cookies.

Well, of course, you can see for yourself."

Still in a little disbelief, Greta exclaims, "It is so good to see you, my dear. Your young man caught me by surprise. He came in this afternoon hoping to find a cup of coffee, and we chatted for a moment.

"He commented on the marble rye, telling me he never saw the two breads together in one loaf, rye and pumpernickel. I created that specifically in memory of Fritz. The bread stands for our lives, our hearts, our love, joined together to make a perfect loaf. I spoke of our bakery in Munich, and that's when he asked me if I knew an Elenena Laurent. I almost fell over, didn't I, Charles?"

He nods in agreement. Greta goes on, "I'm so sorry we lost track of each other. I moved days after the fire to Bremen to be with my sister. You remember our apartment was behind the bakery—it all burned. All my photos of my family, Fritz, mementos, my clothes, everything—all gone. It took time to recover from the fire, the loss. But I will tell you, I miss my Fritz every day and will never get over losing him. He was a genuine, good man. He cared about you, Elenena. We were both so worried about you, living with a Nazi, that woman. I heard she met a fateful end, of her own choosing. I felt sorry for her when I heard the news, but honestly, how sorry can I feel for a person who wants to see me dead? I walked around like a living corpse for many, many months. The pain of losing Fritz was inexorable. But enough about me, tell me, where did you live, where did you go?"

Elenena puts her hands around Greta's. Gazing deeply into Greta's blue eyes, she tells her, "I am so sorry for your loss. I agree—Fritz was one in a million, a profoundly good and kind man. You both took me in with no experience and that weekend job gave my life value, purpose and meaning, even for the brief time we were together. And I'm so grateful for the warning Fritz gave me about the Nazis. I went to that meeting with Annie where Hitler spoke. I found myself bored beyond measure and couldn't understand much of what he said.

"The one clear message that came through was his hatred for the Jews. I met a friend of Annie's, Martin Metz, who for some reason became smitten with me, which made Annie very jealous. He came back to the house after the meeting. We had supper. I made the mistake of asking about the lists. You know, the ones where the Nazis write down where all the Jews live, to keep track of them."

Charles has sat quietly, listening, until now. "Uh, excuse me. Forgive the interruption."

He poses a question. "Can you explain what you mean by the lists? What is the purpose of them?"

Greta winces. "You are from America. You Americans, and the world, do not yet know the evil this man has planned. You have no idea. In his book *Mein Kampf*, he details his desire for the destruction of all Jewish people, to exterminate every single Jew in Europe. He talks about us like we're vermin. And not just Jews. Anyone that doesn't agree with his policies, or his agenda, anyone who is different, or odd."

Charles eyes Greta, questioning her, "What do you mean by odd?"

Greta blushes, but spells it out for Charles, saying in a whisper, "You know, queers, men who are, you know, homosexuals. And not just them, but gypsies, mentally ill people, the unfit, political combatants, and anyone who disagrees with the Nazi ideology. All must conform to the Nazi identity. They make anyone who disagrees with their policies political targets. It's like marking them with a bullseye.

"And then if he can, he will kill them along with every Jewish person. Most people have a tough time believing that a person could possess such evil intentions, but trust me, this man does and is working even now to make his goal a reality. Not one word he speaks is truth, you cannot trust a word he says, he is a liar of the worst order."

Charles starts to shake, his hands tremble upon hearing this account of Hitler's master plan. Greta continues, "This madman believes in Lebensraum, whereby his government will take the land that belongs to border countries like Poland, liquidate the people, murder them, and then give the land to the German people, the Aryans. By taking this territory, the German people will have what they need for expansion and the so called 'natural development.' Not to mention stealing everything the former citizens leave behind, along with all the natural resources."

Charles's cheeks flush and his eyes flash. He interrupts Greta, "You must know Mrs. Laurent was raised in Poland, and my mother's family is from there." Charles says softly, "My mother was born in Poland."

"Oh, Charles, this must be difficult for you to hear. I'll not continue—we can speak of other topics."

"No, please. I interrupted—go on, please."

"Okay, well, Aryan is the term Hitler uses to describe his idea of a perfect Germanic people. Charles, you fit the description of what Hitler would call Aryan. He would approve of you! You are tall, blond, and blue eyed. Like a Norseman, from ancient Nordic tribes. He sees Jews as a mongrel race, inferior, with dirty blood. You know, the irony of it all is that Hitler himself and all his henchmen—none of them fit his description of his Aryan prototype. They all have dark hair and dark eyes. They're all short, except Göring. Why doesn't anyone mention this disparity or point out this fact?"

Greta starts to laugh at the idiocy of this discrepancy. She continues, "Someone needs to say something to him about this; can you imagine the response?" She laughs even more at the thought of this. Elenena and Charles join in, chuckling.

Greta's hilarity continues. "He'd scream, 'off with their heads' or 'send them to the firing squad at once!'"

They continue laughing, until two Hitler Youth enter the bakery. Greta makes her point, saying, "See?" The two boys are blond, blue-eyed youths, dressed in their uniform of brown shorts, khaki-colored long-sleeved shirts with swastika armbands sewn around the sleeves at the elbows, and a long black bandana at the neck, rolled up and secured with a braided rope knot. A Sam Browne leather strap crossing over the chest and around the waist completes their outfit.

Greta whispers to her friends, "They usually come in when Helga is here. They would never think of giving her any trouble; she could scare the dead!"

Greta cautiously greets them, then gets up to wait on them. One of the boys puts his jackbooted foot out and trips her, causing her to fall to the floor.

The boy who tripped her says in German, "Ha-ha, a Jewish rat on the floor, squash it quick."

Charles wastes not a second jumping up from his seat, accosting the boy by the scruff of his neck, speaking in German with threatening indignation, "Help her up or I'll pound you good."

Elenena watches, frozen and horrified by the behavior of these two young boys.

The other Hitler Youth, larger and more muscular than his counterpart, pushes Charles and says, "I'd like to see you try it, schwuler!"

Without warning the bakery door opens, and like the calvary, four American Boy Scouts come to the rescue, circling the two Hitler Youth and Charles, who is still holding onto the collar of the one boy. No one moves a muscle.

Elenena tells Greta, "I'll go to the kitchen and be right back with a wet towel to clean your wound."

Greta replies, "There are bandages above the sink."

One of the Boy Scouts helps Greta to her feet, guiding her to a chair. Greta's knee is bleeding, so the Scout takes off his bandana, wraps it around her leg at the knee, ties it, and applies pressure to stop the bleeding. He assures Greta, "Luckily, this is only a surface wound."

Elenena comes back from the kitchen with a damp towel, and a bandage.

The scout helping Greta tells one of the boys, "Jack, move those hoodlums out of here to the street where they belong, near the trash heap." Charles assists and the three Scouts take the two Hitler Youth outside, shoving them to the ground.

Charles proclaims a dire warning, "If you come back, I'll kick the shit out of you!"

After scrambling to their feet, the cowards take off running as fast as they can. Back inside the bakery, the three Scouts give an account of the two Hitler Youth. After wiping the wound clean and securing the bandage, the boy jumps to his feet and, bowing at the waist says , "Allow me to introduce ourselves. I'm Bobby Baldwin, this is Jack Darling, Ollie Spinelli, and Walter Johnson. We are Boy Scouts from America, at your service."

Greta claps and says, "How marvelous, how and where did you come from? I mean, you came in and rescued us, out of thin air! Are you alone, or do you have a leader?"

Walter speaks up, "No ma'am, we're on our own, and we're old enough. We stopped outside your big window deciding if we should buy something delicious here or go buy candy. A German friend told us about a store down the street from here. They sell a candy called Gummibärchen, have you heard of this candy?"

Greta says, smiling at the young boy, "Of course—the word means 'gummy bear' in English."

Walter's eyes light up and he laughs with delight. "Our friend, Mr. Frugen, gave us some and told us where to buy them. They're made right here in Germany!"

Greta delights in the impish Walter Johnson. "Elenena, I think you're going to be fine in America. I'm impressed with this generation of boys."

"Do you rescue damsels in distress with regularity?" Elenena asks. Not waiting for an answer, she announces, "I'd like to treat you boys to anything you'd like for helping my dear friend. Anything you want, the sky is the limit!"

Jack can't believe their good fortune. "Anything?"

Elenena nods, "Anything!"

The boys drool over the chocolate eclairs, dripping with a fudgy glaze, and the cookies, topped with colored sugar. Walter is fascinated with one dessert in particular. "What is that cake, are those cherries?"

Greta and Elenena laugh at Walter's curious expression. Greta says, "That's a Black Forest Cake, named after the Black Forest of Germany. The cake is extra dark chocolate, soaked with a cherry liquor called kirschwasser. It consists of layers of cake with white meringue frosting and cherries. The whole thing is topped with the sweet meringue frosting. The chocolate cake crumbs around the base of the cake represent the dark, rich German soil found in the Black Forest."

Ollie and Jack begin to laugh, and Bobby pokes Walter in the arm. "Hey, have you slipped into a trance?"

Walter, whose eyes have glazed over, licks his lips. He can only utter the words, "Oh, yes, yes, yes, please! May I have that, please?"

Jack and Ollie howl with laughter while Bobby tries his best to keep a straight face. The other boys confer and debate about which delectable dessert to have while Charles and Elenena watch, smiling and commenting on the simple joys of youth. The boys select their rewards, and Greta stuffs a box with their treats.

She ties it closed with string, then hands the box over the counter to Walter. Walter is so delighted, he does a little jig and sings, "And we still have money for the gummy bears, hallelujah!" Those words and his dance causes everyone to laugh.

Charles watches the boys with amusement, but his smile begins to fade.

Elenena watches as an invisible but potent cloud descends over him. His countenance transforms from happy to grim.

Concerned, she whispers, "Charles, is everything alright?"

With a pained expression, he shakes his head. "I'm going outside to have a smoke."

Troubled, Elenena racks her mind, trying to pinpoint what happened—what changed his mood, what was the trigger?

The boys are set with their box of goodies, a load of confections and delights carried by Walter, holding on to them like they're a priceless treasure. They bid Elenena and Greta goodbye, thanking Greta.

Elenena turns her attention to her friend, pointing to her injured knee. "You poor dear, is that painful? Perhaps you should stay off it. I can wait on customers like the old days, just tell me what to do."

"You can go in back and turn on the teapot and we'll have tea, like we used to."

After tea and more reminiscing, Elenena offers to help Greta close the bakery for the day.

"Thank you, my friend, but no, that's not necessary. Helga will come back at 6:45 like she always does and help me close. Now, tell me what are your immediate plans? And will you come and have supper with us? Helga is at home two blocks from here, preparing supper. We will have plenty for you and your friend if you'd like to break bread with us. What do you say?"

"Oh, I would love to, but we leave for the U.S. tomorrow and I'm weary. I hope you understand. Leaving Europe brings up many emotions I didn't expect and, to be honest, I never thought I'd feel sentimental about it all. But you must visit me. Stay for a long visit—at least a month, a lengthy holiday if you can."

Speaking of Charles, Elenena realizes it's been at least thirty minutes since he left for a smoke. "I wonder where Charles is, and what he's doing. He could have smoked a whole pack by now. While we spoke about the old days, I completely lost track of the time. Where could he be?"

Elenena walks out the door of the bakery and into the street—no Charles. The sun is beginning its descent and the temperature drops. The streetlights illuminate the cobblestone road, creating pretty patterns that would under normal circumstances delight Elenena. The stress of Charles's disappearance, however, leaves no room for such thoughts. She glances to the right and left of the bakery—no sign of him. Anywhere.

Elenena feels panic creep up her neck as her palms begin to sweat, like they do whenever she's nervous. And suddenly, she finds herself exceedingly nervous. *Where is that man?*

CHAPTER THIRTY-FOUR

Frederick, Wolfie, Stanislaw, Raymond, Buster, and Maddie

AUGUST 1933

RAYMOND AND AMBASSADOR Dodd discuss in private how to obtain refugee status for Frederick, Wolfie, Stani, and Maddie to pass through Customs to board the ship. Raymond explains to Dodd the legal aspects of diplomatic and consular protection.

He tells Dodd, "I'll supply the fiscal responsibility clause and we can claim that the party has ceased to enjoy protection of their state of origin. We can create new records for them.

"I'm drawing on a former experience from the Great War where the English government held two American soldiers, handed over by the Germans. At the time the soldiers had amnesia and no credentials or records. We brought them to the U.S. to give them medical care and treatment not attainable in England. The Prime Minister sought the help of the State Department to bring them to the U.S. We created identities for them for the sole purpose of getting them through Customs from England.

"Frederick and Stanislaw will seek refuge as political refugees. Wolfie will be categorized as a student seeking education. Since Maddie is a musician, and underage, we can claim her refugee status as pursuant of artistic freedoms. All of them are political refugees. I think that covers it."

Dodd chews on the end of his stogie while contemplating the decisions and actions that must take place. He offers Raymond a cigar, then flips open his lighter.

"Ray, are you sure you want to assume this responsibility, financial and whatnot? That's quite an undertaking, especially since we're at the pinnacle of the Depression. I guess what I'm trying to say is, can you afford this burden?"

Puffing on his cigar, Raymond shares a story with the ambassador. "I grew up an only child, and my son has as well. Both of us hold a desire for a bigger family. The way I see it, this works and is helpful for all parties. I can play a part in helping Maddie get the musical training she needs to fulfill her dream of becoming a concert violinist.

"Wolfie can get a fine education while continuing to play the sport he loves. My son can have an "adopted" family, a brother and sister. I can set Frederick up in his own business, and Stani can continue teaching in a friendlier environment, one that doesn't pose a threat to his life. They can all contribute to the society they become a part of, they can give back.

"You see, I view this as an opportunity to make a difference in the lives of people who would never have this kind of shot. And that's incredibly gratifying for me. You know the story of my background—born with the proverbial 'silver spoon,' I never had to work. That's why I challenged myself and went to law school. Like my father, I care about our nation and desire to be a part of steering our path towards all that is good, right, and just. But I work because it justifies my existence, gives me purpose while satisfying my desire to see justice in our unreliable world."

Dodd tells his friend, "I have to tell you, that's extremely altruistic. Few men would be willing to make an investment in total strangers, especially during the economic hardships we all face."

Raymond answers, "While that is true now, the economy will eventually change. Better days will come and we can all hope for a better life, especially for Stani and Maddie. I couldn't imagine living amongst such persecution, and this is only the beginning. It's only going to become worse for the Jews of Germany and Europe."

Dodd agrees with Raymond's assessment. "You're right about that. My job will become exceedingly difficult as a result. I knew the position would be a demanding one—to what degree has yet to be determined."

Raymond and Ambassador Dodd gather the group together to discuss how they will proceed.

Ambassador Dodd unwraps the plan.

He begins, "I've many issues to discuss with you. I only ask that you hold your questions and objections, if any, until I finish. If we can all agree with that, I'll begin."

There is no rebuttal.

"While we have some complicated hoops to jump through, I believe we will be able to obtain the results necessary for you to have a fresh start in life. By some miracle, and I do call it a miracle, our Consulate is under quota for visa applications. Therefore, there would not be a strain on the system. My office will hasten the organization of the necessary papers and the stamp. You must acquiesce to the fact that once you leave Germany, you will not be able to return. With that understanding, I put forth this plan to you. First, Frederick, Wolfie, and Stanislaw: for the moment, in the eyes of the German government, you no longer exist, having died in the fire at Dachau.

"The United States' State Department will issue you temporary documents to allow you through Customs. You will be classified as refugees, under diplomatic and consular protection. I will travel with you to undertake the expedition of your entry into the U.S. I've notified my office in Berlin. We will meet at the port, with the documents prepared and ready to sign, in Bremen.

"Regarding travel, Mr. Wellington and Buster bought round-trip tickets and have a reservation. It's my intention to get us all on the same ship, the SS Europa.

"We're waiting now to find out if there is passage available, with adequate room on the ship for the journey. Mr. Wellington has agreed to be your financial sponsor, taking and accepting full responsibility for you once you arrive in the U.S.

"Miss Turetzky, since you are a living person in the eyes of the German government, you will leave this country also under diplomatic and consular protection. Your status will be as an artistic refugee, seeking freedom to pursue your musical career.

"Mr. Wellington will extend the financial sponsorship to you, accepting full responsibility once you arrive in the U.S. The ship in Bremen leaves port tomorrow evening at 8:00 p.m. I would think we'll travel second-class. Boarding will begin at 6:00 p.m.

"The only snafu I see now is one of transportation. There are eight of us heading to Bremen with only one automobile. Rolf came by train, and the Rosses have a horse and cart.

"I propose that Frederick, Wolfie, and Stanislaw travel with me and Phillip in our car to Bremen. Raymond, Buster, and Maddie, you'll take the night train from Salzburg to Bremen, a thirteen-hour trip. The train will stop in Munich, and then head straight to Bremen from there. That train leaves at 11:30 tonight. You'll arrive in Bremen at 12:30 tomorrow afternoon. I'll pick you up at the station. Once we five arrive by car at Bremen, I'll check us all into a hotel.

"You'll have a room available for your use to rest, and there's a dining room for a meal before boarding the ship. Now, the issue we have yet to deal with is the automobile in the barn."

Josef speaks up with an idea, a solution for disposing of the Führer's automobile.

"Two miles up the road there's a high peak, with a steep drop-off. At the bottom are boulders which are difficult to reach on foot, impossible by car. What if we dump the car off the cliff?"

Rolf asks, "How populated is the area around the cliff?"

"There's a sheep farm, and that's it. The only problem is, we would have to drive the car right past the home of the owners, then through the field where the sheep graze to gain access to the peak."

"What if we drive the car to Bremen?" Raymond suggests.

All eyes turn to him. He continues, "Why not? Aren't there plenty of Mercedes 770 in Germany? They're used by government officials. We drive it to Bremen and leave it there. Before we leave here, we switch license plates, put the ambassador's on the Führer's car and that license onto the ambassador's car. Frederick, you told me the license on the Führer's auto is from one of the other automobiles you serviced, is that correct?"

"Yes, it is. And that car was in the garage. If there's anything left of it, there's no way to identify it now."

The ambassador doesn't like the idea and voices his concern. "Why take such a risk?"

Raymond offers a defense. "What is the greater risk: to be identified and stopped while driving on private property while destroying the car over a cliff, or simply driving the auto to Bremen? What if the disposal over the cliff implicates Josef and Minka somehow? They need protection too, as shown by the display just a short while ago. We cannot give the Nazis any opportunity to punish the Ross' for something they have no part in. We drive the car to Bremen. Switch the plates. What's the worst that can happen? Once we arrive, we can leave the car parked somewhere, like the train station."

Dodd rescinds his opposition. "Yes, I see your logic. Frederick, are you on board with this?"

Frederick pauses to consider the facts. After a moment, he signals his support. "Yes, I think it's a clever idea, and I'm willing to drive."

Ambassador Dodd puts forth another idea. "Since Raymond is an employee of the U.S. State Department and speaks German, perhaps he should drive. That way, if stopped, he has an alibi. He's on official business for the Consulate. Our car can follow, and we can back up his story if need be. Any questions, comments, criticisms, rebuttals, or disputes?"

Phillip Winslow is studying the maps he brought with him. Looking up from the maps, he offers, "The drive is five hundred fifty kilometers to Bremen. The journey will take us at least twelve hours, not to mention petrol stops and the like. While on the road to Bremen, if we say we're on official business for the Consulate, wouldn't it be a wise step, if possible, to dress everyone in Boy Scout uniforms?"

Raymond thinks about this. "I can give Stani and Frederick my uniforms. Maddie is already in one. Buster, you can give Wolfie shorts and a shirt, right? We can be part of a contingent, an exchange program set up through the Boy Scouts of America, if anyone asks. Once we get to the hotel, after ditching the car, everyone can change into civilian clothes."

Minka winks at Maddie. "I can contribute to Maddie's clothes for the voyage to America, unless she'd like to wear the Scout uniform the whole way."

Maddie accepts the offer, gladly. "Oh, that would be wonderful! I have one change of clothes—the clothes I wore to the concert."

With his eyes on Maddie, Stani tells her, "Oh, Maddie, you were radiant that night, so beautiful."

Maddie thinks about that night, that fateful night when all the problems started. "Thank you, professor. That night seems like a year ago or more. But if all those things had never taken place, we wouldn't all be together now."

Maddie says this while gazing at Buster. Their eyes meet, exchanging a visual embrace. She continues, "The road we took, all different paths leading to one place. And now, we're all together, with hope for the future."

Rolf has been mostly silent up until now. He ponders her words before saying, "Hear, hear, Maddie. Yes, I like that, beautifully put. Cecile and I may have to come to America, as well. Josef, you and Minka, too. I can't imagine the circumstance will improve for Jews. It's only going to get worse."

Josef agrees. "Rolf, I was thinking the same thing. But to leave this place, this has been our home. The inn has been in Minka's family for over one hundred years. If we leave, we lose everything. We have some money saved, but not much. Our investment is in this place—the property, the land."

Minka's tie to her heritage is not as strong as her husband thinks. "But darling, what good is any of this if it's taken away from us, or if we are separated, if we have no life because of the Nazis?"

"Minka, my darling Minka, there are too many 'ifs' in your sentence."

"Maybe so, but my mother taught me it's better to be safe than sorry."

The words Minka speaks are prophetic. None of them know yet just how much.

CHAPTER THIRTY-FIVE

Elenena

AUGUST 1933

"ELENENA, THIS IS my sister, Helga." Greta's sister is forty-four, and kitchen battle-tested.

Elenena inquiries about Helga's training. "Your sister says you're very accomplished!"

"I survived Monsieur Escoffier's kitchen. He runs his kitchens with an iron fist in what he calls a brigade system. The best way to describe it is like a military experience. As a female pastry cook in his kitchen, it was I who carried the heavy bags of flour, lifted the huge steel bowls, cracked walnuts for ten hours at a time, washed dishes, and mopped floors. Apart from the grueling hours and work detail, I learned so much, at the feet of a true master. Yes, he put me through hell. But what's so incredibly satisfying is knowing that I left with the best recommendation he gives, man or woman. That's enough for me."

Helga downs her cup of coffee, continuing her story. Elenena would rather be searching the streets for Charles, but she will not be rude. *He knows to come back, doesn't he?*

She listens patiently as Helga continues, "My sister coming to Bremen to work with me is the best thing that's happened. We do all right together, don't we, Greta?"

Greta nods, smiling broadly at her sister. "You saved my life, really, I didn't know what to do without my Fritz. Oh, and the things you've taught me, so much about the science and intricacies of baking and pastry. Really, it is a science and requires exacting standards in quality of product, measurement, time, and temperature. Who knew there are seven hundred twenty-nine layers in puff pastry, or pâte feuilletée, as it's called in French?"

Elenena begins to grow weary of the idle chatter. The internal panic starts to show on her face. As she considers the horrible things that might have happened to him, her mind swirls with fear.

Greta finally notices the signs of anxiety on her friend's face and says, "Elenena, let's go look for Charles." She turns to her sister. "Helga, be a love and close without me. We shouldn't be gone too long. I just know we'll find him. I'll come back and finish. Leave the floor and the drying of the dishes and equipment for me as a reward for your kindness!"

The two women begin their search as the sun, already well below the horizon, finishes its setting in grand fashion, painting the sky shades of pink and orange, with golden streaks for accent. The air is already cool, as the humidity from the day drops. Pulling her sweater over her shoulders, Elenena tells Greta, "I think he's a troubled young man. Something set him off in the bakery. I wonder what the Boy Scouts have to do with it. He changed, he remembered something. I saw the look come over his face, like a grim thought intruded. And did you hear the word the Hitler Youth used? He called Charles a name, but I'm not familiar with the German word."

Greta steers Elenena towards their destination. "Here, let's walk towards the candy shop, maybe he followed behind the Boy Scouts in case the Hitler Youth presented any more problems. And the word schwuler indelicately means 'queer.' Is this what you mean when you say he's troubled?"

"Yes, I think that is part of what troubles him, but I believe there are other issues as well."

After a moment, Greta begins to extol the virtues of Bremen to her friend. "Bremen is a fun, exciting city. It's vibrant and cultured. I love living here and this is where I plan to spend the rest of my days. I wish you weren't leaving now that we've connected again.

"Don't leave, stay here instead!

"There is a small symphony here, and it wouldn't surprise me if you could find a place in it. The conductor is Jewish and so are most of the musicians. The one thing I miss is friendships, like I had in Munich. Because we work so much, there isn't much time to pursue friendships with other women. The bakery hours leave little time for much else. Our customers, while lovely, are busy with husbands and children. We don't have those worries, do we? Oh, how I wish you'd stay. I'm just dreaming, and it's entirely selfish of me. Your position in New York sounds perfect for you."

"You're a wonderful friend to want me to stay here in Bremen, but my job in New York is fabulous. I'll be among bright young people. Teaching them will be exciting."

One hundred feet away from the candy shop is a cross-street on one side, while the side they're walking on has a short alley. They cross the street, and when they do, the faint plea of 'help' catches Elenena's attention.

"Greta, did you hear that? I think the voice came from over here!"

Elenena turns and hurries down the alley, Greta following in her wake. The illumination of the streetlamps on the main street do not fully extend all the way down the alley, limiting her view. A squeaking rat runs in front of her, hurrying to get out of her way. She stops and hears the voice again, even weaker this time. "Help."

Elenena calls out, "Charles, Charles, is that you?"

The two women strain to hear, listening carefully. Behind rubbish containers, they spot a body, crumpled and in a ball. Greta sees the Nazi armband and realizes it's one of the Hitler Youth.

He whimpers, "Please, help me."

Repulsed at first, knowing it might be the boy who tripped Greta, the two women disregard their feelings and lift him to his feet. But he cannot stand, and his legs give out.

"Elenena, I'm going to fetch a policeman. Are you okay to stay here with him? His injuries could be serious."

"Yes, I don't think he can harm me. Go—we'll wait here."

Elenena turns her attention to the boy. She feels his face; it's cold and damp—with blood, not sweat. She speaks aloud, "Oh, no, Greta— hurry!" To the boy she asks, "Can you tell me what happened? Where does it hurt, who did this to you?"

The boy struggles to speak. He says the words one at a time, slowly. "I'm stabbed, he stabbed me and hit me."

Elenena hasn't felt this panicked and frightened in an exceedingly long time. Not since the morning at Annie's and the day of the fire. "Can you tell me your name? Keep talking and don't stop if you can, help will be here soon. Now tell me your name."

Blood accumulates in his throat; he gurgles his name, barely audible. "Geog my name is..." and he stops. No more words come.

The Hitler Youth named Geog surrenders to death, right there, in a dark alley, in the arms of a Jewish woman. With a final shudder, she feels the life leave his body, separating from his flesh.

She presses his head to her chest and begins to weep, speaking an indictment against the system that he belonged to. "You poor boy. Your existence so short yet hate-filled. Didn't you hope for more? Did you have dreams? Do you have a mother, will she weep for you? Why did you have to hate; why did your life hold hatred for people who never did a thing to you? You were a pawn of a system, a cruel, wicked evil system, and I blame them for your death. This is wrong. How many are there, like you, duped by a society that thinks they're better than others? They believe anyone different from them is inferior. Moral elites, acting with superiority. That thinking destroys young minds like yours. You deserved better than they gave you, than what they made you."

"Elenena, where are you?"

"Greta, I'm down here. But it's too late."

Greta arrives with two policemen, both equipped with bright flashlights. When one of the officers shines the light on the boy's face, Greta gasps.

One of the officers asks her if she knew the boy.

"I didn't know him. He came in the bakery two or three times before; he came in just an hour ago, or more. I don't know what time it is—I've lost track. He came in with another boy."

The police go over the story with Greta one more time, while Elenena holds the boy. After questioning, the police lift the boy up, and one of the officers carries him out of the alley.

"Do we need to wait here with you, officer?"

"No, we have all the pertinent information. We know where to find you if there are questions."

Within moments two police cars arrive, and the men load the boy into the back of one of the cars.

The two cars leave. The women stand on the street corner while night continues to fall.

"I'm almost surprised they let us leave and didn't drag us into the station. I told them you are an American. That might have helped—I do not know."

"Charles, oh my God, Charles. Let's hurry back to the bakery, he might have gone back there." Elenena starts to cry. "And here I thought I'd escape this damn country without any more trauma!" The truth of those words weighs heavily on her.

Did you really think escaping would be easy, free of heartache?

Back at the bakery, Helga is taking care of the closing duties. Her sister and Elenena arrive, knocking on the door. It's locked.

"Come in, come in, what did you find, where is your friend?"

Helga spots the blood on Elenena. "Oh, no, is that blood on you? What happened? Tell me, are you hurt, what's going on, you were gone thirty minutes, and this happens, what happened?"

Elenena can see the boy's blood, visible in the light, on her dress, sweater, and hands. "Oh, I had no idea I had this much blood on me!"

Greta tells her sister, "Helga, you won't believe it, this is horrible, but one of the Hitler Youth—you know those two boys, they come in for sugar cookies—one of them died in Elenena's arms. We don't know what happened to him."

Elenena remembers, "He told me he was stabbed. He said, 'I'm stabbed, he stabbed me.' I meant to tell the police, I forgot to tell them." She begins to cry again, "I can't get over this, the boy died in my arms."

Greta consoles her, "Dear, you did tell the police, you're in shock. I'm going to make some tea." Looking at her sister, she asks, "Would you help clean her up?"

Still in shock, Elenena follows Helga to the back. Helga assists her with cleaning the blood off her hands and dress. "I don't know if this will come out of your sweater—I can soak it."

"No, that's fine, not necessary. As much as I'd like to stay, I feel compelled to return to the hotel to look for Charles. The school I'm going to work for sent him to escort me through Germany and back to the United States. I feel an obligation to find out what's happened to him."

"Of course, you do. Take my coat—it's light and will cover you up. We can't have you walking around Bremen in bloody clothes. Greta, forget the tea. We will walk Elenena back to the hotel. Let's go now."

Elenena asks about the two Hitler Youth. "I'm worried about the other boy that was with the one who died. Did you know these boys, know their names?"

"No, and they never gave me any trouble. If they had tripped my sister while I was here, I would have clobbered their little Nazi heads!"

The women arrive at the hotel to find a mob of men. The lobby is buzzing with activity. There are men dressed in black Nazi uniforms, wearing long black coats with Nazi armbands, standing alongside the Bremen police.

One of the officers' spots Elenena and shouts, "There she is!" In a matter of seconds, Elenena's surrounded.

CHAPTER THIRTY-SIX

Frederick, Wolfie, Stani, Raymond, Buster, and Maddie

AUGUST 1933

A T THE TRAIN station in Salzburg, Rolf says, "So, this is goodbye for now, brother."

As Rolf hugs Frederick, he says, "If it weren't for Cecile, I'd be joining you right now. But soon, we just might come to live nearby. Please, write to me once you settle. Time passes so quickly, and Wolfie means the world to us. Being childless doesn't feel so lonely when our nephew comes to visit."

Frederick, dressed in Boy Scout attire, tells Rolf, "I know he'll miss you both so much, not to mention Cecile's cooking! Our new path couldn't have happened without your help. I don't know what we would have done without you. You know, Wolfie never says 'goodbye,' he always says, 'see you later.' Since Elise died, he won't speak the word 'goodbye.' The word feels too final to him, and I have to say I agree. So, see you later, brother!"

The baritone voice of a conductor sings out 'all aboard' in the earliest part of dusk. Above the men, a flock of geese honk as they fly past, making their presence known while seeking overnight refuge before the evening darkness sets in. Rolf nods at the birds, and says, "Like the geese, you too, are free. Let's keep it that way! Be well, little brother."

Rolf boards the train; third-class is the last to board. Frederick walks alongside the train as it slowly starts to move, the steam hissing, and wheels squeaking on the rail. His hand is raised, waving goodbye to his brother. Tears begin to fall as Frederick considers what's taken place in the last month. He says softly to the night air, "Couldn't have done this without you, brother." The train starts to roll faster and faster, gaining momentum. In a moment's time, only the caboose taillights are visible, as the train chugs away into the Austrian countryside on its way to Vienna.

Frederick returns to the car where Phillip is waiting to take him to the inn.

Back at the inn, Frederick spots the group standing outside. He thanks Phillip and proceeds to walk toward Josef and Minka. They stand outside in front of the inn, talking with Raymond and the ambassador.

Frederick says, "I was just telling my brother the same thing I will tell you both now. We couldn't have made it this far without you, and I don't know how I can ever repay you. You are family to me and Wolfie. We are so fortunate to have you in our lives. Do be careful and remember what we discussed. Don't wait too long. There may be a younger couple interested in buying an inn, you never know! I owe you both and will do anything to help you. Please know that."

Minka reminds the group, "Don't forget, take these suitcases. You have to have luggage, otherwise your story has holes in it. I think that ties it up, you're all set."

Wolfie, Stani, Buster, and Maddie are sitting at a table inside the café, watching and laughing at Wolfie's antics, while he imitates various Dachau kapos and guards.

"I'm glad it's funny now, but while it took place, it was anything but funny," Wolfie says. "At least we can laugh about it. Stani never seemed to let the guards or kapos know anything was wrong. He never complained or cried even when they kicked him or beat him."

Stani looks lovingly at Maddie. "My thoughts of you and Mrs. Laurent kept me hopeful. Thinking about seeing you both again made all the difference to me. Combine that with my spiritual faith and belief in the Most High, and I found a way to survive." Focusing on Wolfie, Stani continues, "Wolfie, faith and belief can do that, making the impossible seem possible.

"Speaking of Mrs. Laurent, I tried to make a call to her, and the operator told me there was no answer. I feel ambivalent about leaving without speaking to her in person. I'm bothered that she won't know we're gone until we arrive in the U.S., but I know she will understand once she learns the circumstances.

"I'll send her a telegram instructing her to collect a few things for me—the rest she can give away. She has a key to both apartments. My landlord will not be pleased, but what can I do?"

A look of concern comes over Maddie's face. "But your violin collection is there, along with your sheet music and photographs. Won't you miss that? And what about your flat in Berlin?"

Stanislaw, taking Maddie's hands in his, says, "There is nothing more important to me than the people I love. Nothing could replace you, for example. If I had to pick between my violin collection or you, what would I pick?"

Buster jumps into the conversation. "That's a simple one. Take the violins, by all means, take the violins for goodness' sake, is there even a doubt?"

Maddie scowls at Buster and pinches his arm. "Very funny, mister!"

Wolfie watches the two and shakes his finger in their direction, confirming, "Someone is smitten!"

Maddie looks away from Buster, dismissing him with a wave of her hand. "It's not me!"

"Now, did I say it was you? No. I'm talking about this chump right here!"

Buster gets up and puts his fists up, pretending to shadowbox. "Lucky for you, my brother, you're already hurt, or I'd have to teach you a lesson!"

"Ha! You and what army?"

Maddie touches Buster's arm, telling him, "I'll be right back, don't go anywhere."

She walks over to the group of adults outside and waves to get Minka's attention.

"Mrs. Ross, I want to thank you for outfitting me with these lovely clothes."

Maddie twirls in the dress she's wearing, the skirt flaring out while she spins.

"I will care for them and save them for when you move to America."

Minka pats her hands, telling her, "Oh, that's just wishful thinking."

With a serious tone, laced with conviction, Maddie explains what Stanislaw told her. "The event that happened earlier today will become a regular occurrence, until the Nazis either kill you or take you away. Their goal is to destroy all Jews, every Jew living. Their hatred is that great. Please believe me and don't waste any time. Get your affairs in order and come to the United States. We will all start over and find a better life. I know it will be a better life than here. I can feel it."

"I know you mean well, dear, but don't worry about us. Austria is different from Germany. We have a different government than Germany. I can't imagine the people of Austria bowing to Hitler. We love our freedom. Germany has more economic issues than we do, and we have a good life here, despite the Depression. People love to visit the Alps, and we have a perfect location. But I promise, we will visit when we close in August next year. We close every August for the month to take a rest and do repairs. I promise! Now, don't you worry about us, we'll be fine."

It's finally dark enough outside to make an inconspicuous getaway. Josef gives Frederick a wrench to take off the bolts that secure the license plates. After switching the plates, Josef tells Frederick to keep the wrench for when they arrive in Bremen.

"Thanks for this. I'll hold it hostage until you come to America to reclaim it!"

Minka returns from the kitchen with bottles of cider made from apples in their orchard, and a picnic basket for each car filled with food for the ride. "This way you only have to stop for petrol and when nature calls."

The ambassador takes out his wallet. He retrieves an official card with his information at the Consulate listed and hands it to Josef. "Mr. and Mrs. Ross, it's been a pleasure. If there is anything, anything at all that I or my Consulate can do for you, never hesitate to contact me. You can count on me."

Standing under the light from the driveway lamp, Josef looks at the card and says, "I will, thank you."

Phillip explains the route to Raymond, who is now behind the wheel of the Führer's automobile.

"I've mapped out some of the less-traveled roads to take us to Bremen. I've written down the routes on a separate sheet so your son or the ambassador can help you navigate. I'll follow close behind you. And I agree, it's better for the ambassador to ride with you, especially if we're stopped. It makes the story plausible if I'm just transporting passengers. If you need to stop, our signal will be for you to pump your brakes four times and I'll follow you." With a wink and a smile, Phillip says, "I hope you don't mind a lot of cigar smoke!"

Once goodbyes and 'see you laters' have been spoken and the last hugs given, Phillip, Stani, Wolfie, and Frederick get into the ambassador's car while Raymond, the ambassador, Buster, and Maddie get in the Führer's auto. With the autos' engines fired up and low lights on, both cars drive quietly down the hill to the main road. Wolfie and Buster both hang out the windows, waving to Josef and Minka. Finally, the lights disappear, giving way to the dark stillness of night.

⌒

While holding hands, Minka and Josef reminisce about their friends. The sound of a car engine breaks through the quiet, alerting them that another car has begun an ascent up the driveway. They look at each other and wonder who this could be.

Protectively, Josef instructs Minka, "Go inside and bring me my handgun in the desk drawer. Hurry, I'll stay here. You come behind me and put it in my hand. I'll hold it behind my back. Now go!"

Minka runs inside the inn, going straight to Josef's desk in the office, where she retrieves the gun. She comes back down the stone steps of the inn, only to find the two Nazis are back.

A sick feeling comes over her as she begins to shake. *If that bastard thinks he's going to hit me again, I'll shoot him dead.*

The Nazis see her coming but remain still while talking to Josef. She does as he asks, walking behind him, placing the pistol in his hand. She stands silently by his side.

The same short, fat Nazi is questioning Josef about the ambassador. "Your guests have left?"

"Yes, sir."

"Good. Now, I told you I'd come back if your directions were wrong, and they were!"

"Sir, I'm sure those were the right instructions for Haus Wachenfeld. I've been there numerous times myself."

"Do you, a stupid peasant Jew and a Jewish pig wife, dare question an officer of the Reich?"

"No, sir, I'm not questioning you."

The larger of the two takes out a baton and hits Josef in the side of his head with force, causing him to fall to his knees, While he's trying to steady himself, the gun comes loose from his hand, and under the driveway lighting, it is revealed.

"Wait, what's this?"

The short, fat Nazi kicks Josef's hand away from the pistol. He squats to bend over, as his bulbous middle makes bending difficult.

"Were you planning to use this against us? Well, in that case, you have made a simple decision for us."

Eerily, Minka already knows what's next. She tells Josef, "I will love you; we will be together forever."

To the Nazis, she says, spitting out the words with sharp-spirited venom, speaking truth to power, "I will await your judgment day and with joy watch you cast into the lake of fires, equitable punishment for all of your crimes. I will laugh as you burn for all eternity. I will laugh and clap my hands!"

And then she does something that unsettles the two Nazis. She starts to laugh. Side-splitting, joyous, happy laughter. "Ha ha!!" Minka starts to dance, spinning and dancing around Josef.

The fat Nazi's hands shake as he draws his pistol, shooting Josef first and then Minka in the head twice, for good measure. Both fall to the ground, Minka laying over Josef. Their blood pools around their lifeless bodies.

The other Nazi, worried and concerned, asks the murderer, "What did she mean by that, the lake of fire?"

CHAPTER THIRTY-SEVEN

Elenena

AUGUST 1933

"ARE YOU MRS. Elenena Laurent?" In the lobby of the hotel, the police and SS officers swarm Elenena, Greta and Helga.

Helga will not be bullied. She steps protectively in front of Elenena, becoming her voice. "Who are you, who wants to know, and why? Now back up and give us some room to breathe. What's going on here?"

The police step back out of shock, never having heard a woman speak like this before, with such authority. But then one of the SS demands, "Which one of you is Elenena Laurent, traveling to the United States with Mr. Charles Whitecliff?"

Clearing her throat, Elenena says, "I am she. Can you tell me what this is about, please?"

The man is tall and reed-thin, like a cigarette with a mustache. He's as pale as the paper wrapped around the tobacco.

He takes off his coat, revealing he's dressed in an ominous-looking black SS uniform.

The only other color in his attire is the red swastika armbands sewn to his coat sleeves above the elbow, and the red piping which outlines the cuffs of his coat.

He wears small, round wire glasses that make his beady eyes seem larger than they are. His haircut is so close on the

THE ROAD WE TOOK

sides and the back that he's almost bald, with the top an inch longer, slicked with hair tonic.

The SS officer introduces himself. "I'm Captain Schröeder, at your service. How do you do? Would you please come over here so we can ask you some questions?"

Once again Helga steps in front of Elenena and asks, "Why, what's this about?"

Glaring at Helga, he speaks in a calm voice. "All will be explained, now would you, please?"

He holds out his arm, guiding the women to the chairs and sofa in the lobby. Elenena glances at the red cushioned seats around the pillar where she sat waiting for Charles just a few short hours ago.

The women sit on the sofa, while Schröeder pulls up a chair. He takes a cigarette, after first offering the women a smoke. Only Helga accepts. He lights her cigarette, then his own.

He begins, "Mrs. Laurent, can you tell me what you know about Charles Whitecliff, an American you're traveling with to the United States?"

Composing herself, she says, "Can you tell me if he's hurt? Is he safe? What's happened, where is he?"

Schröeder ignores her questions and asks, "How long have you known this man, and how are you associated with him—family, friend, lover?"

Elenena bristles at the question of intimacy. "Certainly not. He is my escort to the United States. It is strictly a professional relationship!"

"I'm only left to assume until you set the record straight. If you will, now, please."

Elenena looks around the lobby. The other officers and SS are still present, while a small crowd is gathering, staring, and pointing.

In a hushed tone she continues, "I only recently met Mr. Whitecliff. We rode a train together from Munich to Bremen today. The music school in New York sent Charles to escort me to my post. I'm a violin instructor. The school sent him to assist me with my journey, as I have never traveled overseas."

Schröeder listens intently and takes notes. "So, where did he come from? Did he sail into port here in Bremen and take a train to Munich to meet you?"

Elenena thinks for a moment. "Yes, that's correct."

Schröeder speaks his thoughts aloud, "He sails into port, takes a train to Munich, only to turn around and take the train back to Bremen. That sounds like a bit of backtracking to me, versus just meeting you here. See my point?

"He meets you in Munich. Were you waiting there for him, or did you come from another place to meet him in Munich?"

"I came from Baranovichi. Sir, is he hurt? Is he safe? I'm so worried."

"Why are you so worried about him, Mrs. Laurent?"

"Because he seems unhappy. I do not know the man, I just met him this morning" Elenena pleads with Schröeder. "Please tell me what's going on, please!"

Schröeder sits straight up in his chair and leans forward. "You just met him this morning, yet you quickly assess he's unhappy. On what basis do you make that assessment? Tell me, does Mr. Whitecliff appear to be a violent person to you?"

"Violent? Charles, violent? No, I absolutely don't think he is. He could harm himself, perhaps, but not others. I can't see that with him, it's not possible."

"Can you tell me what happened in the bakery, earlier this evening?"

Helga and Greta sit quietly, until this question. Helga raises her voice.

"Two Nazi troublemakers came in and attacked my sister." She points to Greta's knee.

Schröeder recoils from Helga, wiping his brow. He ignores her.

"What happened, Mrs. Laurent?"

Elenena wrings her hands. She visualizes the dead boy after the officer shone the light on his face. His eyes were open. She recalls his opened eyes and shakes.

Greta takes one of her hands, comforting her and encouraging her to speak. "Tell him, tell him everything. The sooner the better, the quicker this interrogation will be over!"

Elenena clears her throat and begins, "We sat at a table in the bakery discussing old times. Charles was sitting with us, when the two boys, the Hitler Youth, came into the bakery. Greta, Mrs. Schweitzer, got up to assist the boys and one of them stuck out his foot and tripped her. He called her a 'Jewish rat.' Charles jumped up and grabbed the boy by the collar. The other youth pushed Charles, and then four Boy Scouts from America came into the bakery. They were on their way to a candy store. While looking at the baked goods in our window display, they observed the boy tripping Greta. They came to our rescue and made the two troublemakers leave the bakery. Then Greta gave the Boy Scouts a box of treats and they left."

"And where was Mr. Whitecliff during all this?"

"He helped the Scouts get the two boys out of the store, came back in, and sat down. Is that right, Greta?"

Her friend answers, "Yes."

"Then what happened?"

"Charles went outside to smoke a cigarette. He was gone for a while, so Greta and I went looking for him, thinking he might have escorted the Boy Scouts to the candy store in case there were any more problems. But we didn't find him. While walking, we found that poor boy in the alley. He died in my arms." She whimpers, crying softly.

Elenena opens the coat to show Schröeder her bloody dress.

He glances at it, then looks at her. "What did he say to you?"

Elenena wipes away her tears as they fall steadily. She tries to keep her composure, but it becomes more difficult by the second. She feels like she might begin to scream at any moment.

"He said, 'He stabbed me, he stabbed me, he hit me.' He told me his name was 'Geog' and then he died."

Helga takes a hankie out of her purse, handing it to Elenena, who cannot stop crying.

Elenena asks through her sniffles, her voice cracking, "What happened to the other boy? Did he witness what happened?"

"As a matter of fact, he did. His name is Heinrick, and he says your friend Charles killed this boy, Geog."

"What? That's impossible, Charles is not a murderer!"

"And how can you be so sure—you tell me you barely just met him. Do you wish to add more details to the story?"

"Details—what are you talking about, details? There are no more details; I've told you what I know. I cannot believe Charles is a murderer!"

"You mentioned the American Boy Scouts. Do you know an American named James Lewis, Mrs. Laurent?"

Flatly, she tells him, "No."

"How about any of the Boy Scouts? Could you identify them, the four that came to the, uh, what did you say, 'rescue'?"

Elenena looks at Greta. "Do you think you could identify the four? I can identify the little one, Walter, and the handsome boy Jack, and the one who fixed up your knee—what was his name?"

Greta volunteers the names, "Bobby and Ollie. The other two are Walter and Jack Darling. Who could forget that name?"

Elenena nods to confirm, "Yes, that's right—Bobby and Ollie."

"Mrs. Laurent, I'd like you and your friends to stay put while we work on getting those boys together to corroborate your story. I would like for you not to leave but stay inside the hotel until the time when I come to get you to identify the Boy Scouts. Is that clear?"

Helga has heard enough. Her voice becomes loud. "Why, what has she done that she has to do anything you say? She did nothing wrong. She's committed no crime! You cannot confine her!"

Captain Schröeder stares a cold stare that could freeze ice. His black eyes glare at Helga.

Without taking his eyes off her, he says, "Remember, Mrs. Bernstein, we live in this city together. If you show me any more hostility, I can make it very rough on you and your Jewish bakery."

"It's a Jewish French bakery, Captain, sir."

Helga speaks with sarcasm as she addresses the man. She gets up and curtsies to further mock the officer.

"I'm more than happy to arrest you now if you wish."

Helga doesn't back down. She glares at the officer with daggers in her eyes. At her sister's prodding, however, she pipes down.

Greta offers, "We will be in the dining room if you need us, Captain. A glass of wine or brandy is in order, I think."

Schröeder leaves without saying goodbye.

Helga huffs, "Arrogant bastard, I'd like to fix him but good. These Nazis think they can make rules as they go. They work by instilling fear through intimidation. I hate them. Hate isn't even a strong enough word to describe what I think about them!"

Greta pats her sister's arm. "Now calm down—no sense in wasting another thought on that baboon. Come on, Elenena.

Let's go into the dining room and have dinner. Food always makes everything better. I eat, and I forget—do you do that?"

"At times." Elenena feels an encroaching sense of dread. "I'm worried sick about Charles, but I'm also worried sick about me. I'll travel to the U.S., and then what? Charles was taking care of all my travel details. I haven't a clue about my itinerary or anything. I feel so helpless!"

After a dinner where no one eats much, Elenena plays with the apple strudel on her plate while Helga and Greta debate the finer points of the pastry. They discuss the filling and the quality of the whipped cream served alongside the strudel.

Greta breaks from the great strudel debate to bring her friend, who seems a thousand miles away, into the conversation. "Elenena—Helga makes the most amazing strudel. It melts in your mouth, as light as angel wings. This strudel is acceptable, but I tell you, when you've had the best, there is just no comparison, really."

Elenena nods but doesn't comment further.

Greta continues diligently to try and lift Elenena's spirits. "Oh, my friend, it's going to be all right, don't worry. Remember what you used to tell me about not worrying past today? You told me there is no promise that tomorrow comes, so keep your mind in the present twenty-four hours. Can you try that, please? Despite the circumstances, we've had a chance to be together at the very least. I'm grateful for the unexpected gift of seeing you. I view our time together as a gift."

Elenena breaks her trance-like gaze, snapping back into the present moment. She reaches out to pat her friend's hand. "I know, you're right."

Captain Schröeder appears at the entrance of the restaurant. Helga spots him, pointing. "Look, the baboon is back."

He approaches the table and says, "Hello. We'll have to wait until tomorrow to identify the Boy Scouts. They have a strict curfew that they follow. We can see them tomorrow, at your convenience, before you leave for the U.S. You're on the same ship with the Boy Scouts of America. So, plan on meeting with me. I've taken the liberty to post an officer outside of your room, should you need anything."

Schröeder gets ready to leave, bidding the three women good night. He turns to walk away but he stops and shares a thought. He says, "Did you know those Boy Scouts are from the same place in New York where you'll be living? Rochester? Funny coincidence."

He leaves, not waiting for a response.

"Elenena, how does this all tie together?" Greta says. "This seems like a puzzle with many disparate pieces not fitting now, but by tomorrow they might. You must be exhausted. We will get up early tomorrow. Our dough and our pastry wait for no one. I hate leaving on this note, not knowing when we'll see each other again. If you can, call or come by the bakery tomorrow. Here is the number and address." Greta writes it down on a piece of paper from her purse. She continues, "At least let me know you're okay, and then write me from the ship and tell me everything."

Elenena reaches for Greta, hugging her tight. She whispers, "Thank you—you saved me again. I hope I can do the same for you some day, but under different circumstances."

She turns to Helga, handing her the coat. "Watch out for those SS goons and take care of each other. I hope the next time we meet will be without a shadow hanging over our visit."

Helga smiles and embraces Elenena. "You take care as well. We will hope for a good outcome."

Elenena walks the women through the lobby to the front doors of the hotel under the watchful eyes of two police officers. She blows them a kiss when the women turn to look back at her. They wave back.

The last thing she remembers is passing out on her bed in her room, exhausted, not even stopping to take off her makeup or clothes.

She awakens to a loud noise, realizing someone or something is banging on the door. Elenena sits up, having to evaluate where she is and what's going on. Not recognizing her surroundings, she is completely disoriented. It takes her a moment to speak. "Okay, okay, I'm coming, hold on." She feels her hair, knowing she must look like a mess. She answers the door anyway.

She opens the door and there is Captain Schröeder with two officers and a bellman.

Schröeder, as surly as ever, informs her, "I was ready to have the bellman open the door, we've knocked on your door for fifteen minutes!"

"What are you talking about? Fifteen minutes? Please, what time is it anyway?"

"It's one-thirty in the afternoon, Mrs. Laurent."

"What? One thirty, how could that be?"

He shows her his watch to confirm.

"Oh, my. Well, I was very tired. Tell me, what do you want, what do you need me to do?"

"When you are ready, meet me in the lobby and we will walk to the hotel where the Scouts are staying. I know your friends are not here, can you identify the four without your friend?"

"Yes, I think so."

"All right, please meet me in the lobby."

"Yes, I'll be there shortly. Excuse me, bellman. May I have some coffee brought up, please?"

"Yes ma'am, gladly.

"Thank you."

Elenena yawns and stretches—then gathers her thoughts, remembering what happened last night.

Charles wouldn't murder anyone, would he? He isn't capable— or is he?

CHAPTER THIRTY-EIGHT

Frederick, Wolfie, Stanislaw, Raymond, Buster, and Maddie

AUGUST 1933

DRIVING THROUGH THE winding German countryside in the dark of night, Maddie is comforted by the quiet solitude. Raymond and Maddie speak in hushed tones while the ambassador and Buster sleep. It's now five-thirty in the morning, two hours from their destination.

Leaning forward, Maddie has her arms folded, resting on the back of the front seat. She tells Raymond about her life in the orphanage. "It was a horrible place, but I learned some valuable lessons."

His interest piqued, Raymond asks, "Tell me if you will, what did you learn?"

Without hesitation, she answers, "First, that you can't trust everyone who speaks nicely, that actions speak louder than words."

Trying not to personalize the comment, Raymond asks her what she is referring to.

"For example, the headmaster spoke so kindly and politely whenever the people from the state came for inspections. But when they left, he and the 'nurses' would return to their wicked and mean-spirited way of communicating, and not always with words alone. The headmaster and nurses would beat us, without cause. Some of my friends and I talked about escaping so much, they finally put bars on the windows. I didn't know this at the time, but the state gave money to care for the children. The more children, the more funds and donations came in. The headmaster pocketed the money, but you know, in the end, his evil deeds came back on him. I'll never know the severity of the punishment, if it was enough, but I believe one day when he stands before God to give an account for his life, he'll have a lot of explaining to do. And then, he will receive his punishment."

Raymond tries to concentrate on the road, but the stories Maddie recounts trouble him.

He asks her, "Maddie, do you know that I am trustworthy? I will help you and protect you. When I make a promise, I keep a promise. Do you believe me?"

"Yes, I do, because of Buster and how he is—so kind and funny, but also sincere and honest. He must have learned that from you. He is so very honest. So honest, in fact, that he admitted to me he had never kissed a girl. So, I kissed him."

Trying hard not to laugh, Raymond is intrigued that this girl would be so forthcoming.

"He liked it so much, we kept on kissing. But that's all we did. Honestly, it was harmless."

"I appreciate your candor. Thank you for telling the truth. You must have had some good mentors, teaching you to be forthright."

"Oh, yes. The women who took me in after the orphanage burned down, Mrs. Silberstein and the Laurent sisters, and the professor are the kindest and most genuine people I've ever known. Elenena Laurent was my violin instructor before the professor. She taught me about life and instructed me about more than just playing, technique, and form. Because of those strong women, I learned that people could do what they say and say what they mean. They taught me not to be afraid of the truth. But to be truthful no matter what. And you know, life is so much easier when you tell the truth. Lying is complicated. I've watched adults twisted into knots trying to cover their lies."

Raymond tells her, "You have so much wisdom. I'm impressed you have these honorable values. I'm also pleased you see those qualities in Buster. From the few weeks I spent with Wolfie, observing him, I found that he's like that as well, sharing similar attributes with you and my son. You youngsters give me hope for the future."

Suddenly, there's a loud pop, and the smooth ride becomes extremely bumpy. The ambassador awakens. "What happened, what did we hit?"

"I think we blew a tire, from the sound and feel of it." Raymond pumps his brakes four times to signal to Phillip that he needs to pull over.

The two cars pull off the road, onto a grassy field. From what Raymond can see from his limited vantage point, the sun hasn't broken the horizon yet. Still, the bleakness of night is no more.

Phillip hurries to the car. "Everything all right, sir?"

"No, I'm sure we blew a tire. It's flat, over on the passenger side."

Phillip takes a flashlight out of his pocket and confirms that it is the rear passenger side tire. "Excellent timing. I need a break from driving to stretch my legs, so thank you!"

The Mercedes Benz, like many other cars, comes equipped with a spare tire on either side of the car behind the front tires, affixed to the automobile, resting on the runner-boards. Frederick walks up and assesses the problem. He offers, "I bet it was a nail from a horse. They still run on these roads, pulling wagons. I'll have her changed in a jiffy. Everyone, please exit the car!"

Raymond and the ambassador get out of the car. Buster is still sleeping in back. Maddie thinks to let him sleep, but Wolfie doesn't agree with that for a minute. "Hold on, we'll wake up Sleeping Beauty gently." He says this emphasizing 'gently.' "This is what he would do to me at camp."

Maddie claps her hands and squeals with delight, curious as to what Wolfie will do next. Wolfie walks into the field and reaches down, feeling for a long piece of grass or a weed. He secures one, ripping it from the ground. "Maddie, watch this."

Quietly, Wolfie climbs into the front seat. Leaning over the middle of the seat, he takes the long piece of grass and rubs the end of it under Buster's nose, poking at his nostrils. After a minute, Buster, still sleeping, begins to haphazardly swat at his nose.

Wolfie keeps it up, tickling Buster's nose until he slaps himself in the face, putting an end to his blissful state.

"Hey, what the heck—Wolfie! I should have known!"

Both the boys fly out the car door. Buster chases Wolfie as they run through the field, tripping and laughing, not able to see where they're going. Wolfie circles back to the parked autos, grabbing Maddie by the arms, hiding behind her.

"You can't tackle me yet. I'm still too sore—my ribs and bruises—have mercy on me, please!" He says this in between gasps of laughter and giggles.

Buster throws a punch, landing it on Wolfie's arm. Wolfie yells, "Hey, you're going to hit precious Maddie! If you miss, you're in trouble and you know what that means—no more kissy-kissy!" He makes a kissing sound, pursing his lips together.

"You're gonna get it, Wolferman!"

The three of them—Maddie, Wolfie and Buster—laugh, while Stanislaw watches.

"Speaking of Wolfie," Stanislaw says to Raymond. "When he told me his friend Buster was his brother, he really meant it. They act just like brothers. It does my heart good to see all three of them so happy. Maddie is radiant again."

Raymond stands next to Stani offering him a cigarette, and tells him, "At Scouting camp, these two were full of shenanigans. They'd play tricks on each other and goof off, but they'd talk, too. He's the first friend Buster's spoken openly to about his mother, losing her. They both have that in common. They have a solid friendship, and it makes me so happy to see him with Wolfie. Buster was sick over what we all saw, the Gestapo agents beating him. That reminds me, I forgot to ask him how and why he ended up in Dachau."

Raymond calls out, "Wolfie, come here, son. I've got a question. Stop the roughhousing for a minute, please!"

Wolfie, panting and out of breath, takes a swig of the apple cider Maddie offers him. "Thank you, Maddie."

She passes the bottle to Buster, who scoffs. "Do you really think I'll drink after him? He probably spit in the bottle!" He takes the bottle and drains it anyway. "Ah, good to the last drop, spit and all!"

Maddie shakes her head, laughing. "Boys!"

Buster watches as Frederick expertly changes the tire. He adjusts the lug nuts as Phillip stands by with a flashlight.

Raymond asks, "Frederick, Wolfie, tell me, how and why did you end up in Dachau?"

Frederick stands up, the job complete. He sighs, remembering how and when the trouble began.

"I ignored about ten signs announcing that all boys ages

fourteen to eighteen must join the Hitlerjugend, Hitler Youth. The order came as a compulsory command. *All boys must quit other clubs and associations and join immediately.* Because I work so much, Wolfie went to Vienna to spend the summer with my brother and wife.

"I didn't know Rolf and Cecile gave permission for Wolfie to go to camp with the fine American Boy Scouts. To make a long story short, a letter came from one of the Reichsführer offices demanding Wolfie join by a certain date.

"There was no way that would happen. He wouldn't be back in Munich until after the date. So, I went to the office of the Reichsführer. I told him Wolfie wouldn't be back by the date they expected. The officer in charge of compliance with the compulsory order had information about Wolfie. You see, a Nazi followed Wolfie and the boys back from the Danube where you and the Scouts were hiking, where you all first met Wolfie.

"The Nazi followed the bus with the boys back to Rolf and Cecile's house. Then, he reported what he saw to the Reichsführer. The man questioning me trapped me. He knew all along Wolfie had left with the boys; he caught me in a lie. So, they tossed me in Dachau. When Wolfie returned with the boys to Munich, the Gestapo was waiting. They knew exactly when the bus would arrive. I still wonder how the Gestapo obtained the information, whether someone inside the Scouts told them."

Raymond figures Lajos offered the Gestapo their return information from the Jamboree.

He tells Frederick, "What the Reichsführer did is called entrapment. That's an illegal way of obtaining information—at least it is in the U.S."

"Well, enough about that. Here we are, all together. Shall we continue our journey? The sooner we leave Germany, the better, right, son?"

Wolfie agrees, "Yes, Dad."

Raymond turns to get in the car—but then he looks behind him. He calls out, "There's a car coming. Be calm, get back in the cars, and sit until they pass by."

The car slows, approaching with bright headlights, and pulls over behind the ambassador's car.

Two Nazis get out of the auto, both armed with flashlights. One approaches Phillip, the other Raymond. They both shine the lights into the interior, looking at the passengers.

"Papers, please, all passengers."

Raymond takes out his passport, while the ambassador takes out his official Embassy card, and Raymond hands them both to the officer. The ambassador asks, "May we get out of the car, sir?"

"Why, what is the need?"

"I'll answer any questions you have regarding the passengers."

"Give me every passenger's documentation."

Ambassador Dodd sighs. "Not everyone has papers—we are on a Consular mission, transporting exchange students and their guardians to Bremen."

The officer ignores the ambassador, repeating, "Papers, every passenger, present your papers."

The ambassador attempts to control his rising temper, but his grip is getting thin. "Officer, I am Ambassador William Dodd, the U.S. ambassador to Germany. I am a government official. This man seated next to me is the legal counsel to the government of the United States of America. We are on official business. Tell me your name and badge number."

Smirking, the officer blithely answers, "Gestapo have no badge number; we operate independently of the enforcement agencies, in case you are not aware. Answer me one question, please. Are you transporting any passengers that fall under the category of felons, prisoners, or convicts?"

Raymond takes a deep breath, exhaling fully before whispering to Dodd, "I've got this."

Slowly, Raymond opens the door to the automobile, extracting himself from the vehicle to stand before the officer. He's at least half a foot taller. He addresses the man, who continues to shine his flashlight in his face, causing Raymond to squint. He shields his eyes with his hand, noticing his breath is visible in the cool of the early morning hours.

He can feel the dampness in the air in his throat as he prepares to begin his defense. Ceremoniously, he waves both hands, gesturing to the officer to lower the light. The officer follows the gesture, lowering his light.

Clearing his throat, Raymond starts, "Kind sirs, as you can see we are at a disadvantage here. We are traveling to Bremen for the reason of boarding our ship, and time is of the essence. We have a short window in which we must continue our journey with no delay. And while I know it is your duty to always ask for papers, you must take into consideration that the United States' ambassador to Germany is a man of solid standing with the Reich."

Raymond pauses, allowing time for the officer to ruminate on his last sentence while reaching into his pocket. He withdraws a pack of American cigarettes. The other officer stands next to his partner, resolute. Raymond offers each man a smoke. They each take one. Still holding the pack in his hand, Raymond flicks his silver lighter with speed, lighting both cigarettes before his, noting the eyes of the officers are focused on the pack of cigarettes.

I've got them now, biting the bait.

Rank-and-file SS agents do not have access to American cigarettes, which are clearly superior to German brands.

Raymond allows time for the men to inhale and enjoy the luxury of a fine smoke, betting one or the other will comment on the smooth taste. Sure enough, the officer Raymond first spoke to says to his partner, "My God, what a difference! Ebert, have you ever had such a fine smoke?"

Hooked.

Raymond withholds a smile but knows his subterfuge has worked. He offers, "I've got a carton in my luggage if you'd like more."

CHAPTER THIRTY-NINE

Elenena

AUGUST 1933

ELENENA GAZES AT her reflection in the mirror, pausing to inspect her skin, then finishes applying her makeup.

You look tired, girl. What's happened to Charles—could he have hurt someone? I don't think it's possible—he doesn't look like a murderer. And what do Rochester Boy Scouts have to do with anything? I don't understand. God, please give me strength. Why is this happening now? I'm leaving this wretched country to start a new life, and this is my send-off. I'd like to think that You're getting all the undesirable things out of the way before I leave Germany. When I arrive in America, it will truly be a fresh start. I wonder, God, what the purpose of this is, why things happen like they do. I know you are under no obligation to give me the reason, but You can give me the faith to trust and believe you know what's best. You can see up the road. I cannot. You are God, creator of Heaven and Earth. I am not. Help me, God, to trust.

But Elenena does not feel trusting, or safe. She feels full of self-doubt and fear. And alone.

Why didn't I tell Stanislaw or Maddie? Would I be in this position if I did? Would it have made a difference?

Arriving in the lobby escorted by two officers, Elenena spots Captain Schröeder, who tips his hat towards her. Her black, patent leather, high-heeled shoes click on the tile floor, sounding especially loud.

Schröeder approaches Elenena, his face expressionless. "I apologize for the unfortunate way we awoke you. Would you like something to eat before we continue? We have twenty minutes to spare if you'd like something."

Elenena shakes her head. "No, thank you, I'd prefer to get on with this if possible."

"Of course, I understand. Excuse me for a moment."

Schröeder gets the attention of an officer, waving his hand, signaling to him. They speak for a moment.

"The Boy Scouts will be here shortly. For your convenience, the boys are coming here."

Reaching into his coat pocket, Schröeder pulls out a cigarette from a slim silver case, snapping it shut, not offering Elenena a smoke. His hand moves like lightning from pocket to lighter to light his cigarette, snapping the lighter closed with emphasis.

He peers at Elenena. The stare makes her uncomfortable, like a wolf before he strikes his prey. "Tell me, where did you study violin? You mentioned you'll teach at the Eastman School of Music, is that right?"

Unnerved, Elenena knows for a fact that she didn't tell the man the name of the school.

"I'm mostly self-taught, however, I received instruction from a man who studied in Vienna."

"Would that be a Stanislaw Birnbaum, perchance? A Jewish instructor? Why not a German instructor? Certainly, there are plenty of German instructors. Why him, a Jew?"

Elenena returns the stare, as blank as she can make it.

"If you don't mind, I'd prefer not to discuss anything that doesn't have to do with your investigation."

"That's no problem, Mrs. Laurent. If that suits you—fine. I was just making polite conversation."

Disgusted by the officer's not-so-thinly-veiled hatred for Jews, Elenena tells him, "Excuse me, Captain, but your idea of polite conversation greatly differs from mine."

"Is that so? I find your response interesting, Mrs. Laurent. You're extremely defensive. Why is that? Are you hiding something? What did you have to do with Annie Heinrich's supposed suicide, for instance?"

Elenena winces, hearing the name of her former landlord.

"Is there anything you have in your possession that belonged to her or the Third Reich? An extensive list of over twenty thousand names, Jewish names perhaps?"

Elenena answers sharply, "I have no idea what you're talking about. Annie was my landlady for a brief period when I first moved to Munich. I read in the paper like everyone else did that she hung herself. I didn't know her very well. And why are you implying that I have something in my possession that belongs to the Third Reich? So much for your polite conversation. I do not appreciate having my life inspected. My life is none of your business!"

Seething at the comment, Schröeder spits out the words, "Oh, but that's where you err, Mrs. Laurent. Seeing that you've lived in Germany for many years, that makes you a German citizen, which makes everything about you and your life the Gestapo's business!"

Elenena feels her blood pressure rise. Her patience with the man evaporates. She snipes at him, "Really, well, that's why I'm leaving this country, never to return. America is not like Germany, thank God!"

Elenena turns her face away from Schröeder. Not wasting a moment, he puts his gloved hand on her cheek, turning her towards him.

Schröeder gets within inches of Elenena's face. He hisses

at her, putting his other gloved hand on her thigh, squeezing it tightly so she cannot move away from him, "That is, if we even allow you to leave this country. You're not gone yet, and don't think you can speak to me with such insolence and get away with it. The Gestapo makes the rules for the citizens of Germany. If you don't like it, there are ways we can deal with you to ensure you do like it, by becoming a model citizen or a very dead citizen. Your choice—either you cooperate with me or you will face consequences, I guarantee it."

"Stop it, you're hurting me! Take your hand off my leg or I'll scream!"

With his other hand, Schröeder pulls back his coat, revealing his German Luger 9mm.

"Nothing would delight me more at this moment than to put a bullet between your eyes. I'd have every reason to—don't press your luck. You answer me and answer me now. Nice. Polite. With the proper tone. With respect. Do you understand, Mrs. Laurent?"

A paralyzing fear starts in her toes and begins to surge up through her body. Cold sweat forms on the back of her neck. She fights the urge to break down in tears.

Her voice shaky, Elenena struggles to find words. In the most measured and steady voice possible, she says, "Captain Schröeder. My landlady hung herself, and I cannot tell you the reason because I do not know. And furthermore, I do not know what you mean by 'lists,' what kind of list?"

"Martin Metz says you know all about the lists. He had a discussion about the lists over dinner at Annie Heinrich's house after you all attended a meeting with the Führer. He believes you might have the lists. He also believes you had something to do with Annie's suicide, assuming it was even a suicide. How can I be sure you didn't murder her and hang her, then cause the fire? You worked at the bakery. It's an entirely plausible assumption, unless of course you tell me otherwise."

Elenena begins to tremble. "That was eight years ago! I had nothing to do with Annie's death. During the weeks I lived with her, I observed a profoundly unhappy and lonely woman. The fire at Schweitzer's started when one of the gas burners in the ovens malfunctioned.

"Greta Schweitzer can validate and corroborate this information, as can the Munich police and fire department. And furthermore, Annie was a large woman, outweighing me easily by fifty or sixty pounds. There is no way I could harm her or even lift her.

"As for the lists, I do not know what or where they were located in her house. I only know the list contained the names and addresses of Jews living in and around Munich."

Schröeder stares at Elenena, not taking his eyes off her. "Yes, the lists. People you knew were on the list, the Schweitzers, Professor Birnbaum."

Eyeing her and waiting for her reaction, he asks, "Mrs. Laurent, are you Jewish?"

Elenena hesitates to answer. To make matters worse, she sees another Gestapo policeman walking across the lobby, approaching the captain, who has his back to the man.

"Captain Schröeder, sir," the Gestapo says, "the American Boy Scouts are here waiting for you and Mrs. Laurent. The chaperone told me an attorney will be with the boys while you question them because they're underage."

Elenena sighs with relief—but Schröeder fumes, stomping his foot. He spits the words at Elenena, gritting his teeth. His words come out sharp, pointed like needles. "We will continue this later. I'm not through with you. Now, you must identify the four boys. Come with me."

He turns away abruptly, walking ahead of Elenena, while she thanks God for the strength to not fold under pressure. She takes a deep breath and forces a smile to cover her distress.

Elenena approaches the group of boys, all smartly dressed in uniforms, with their heads topped with their Lemon Squeezer hats. With them are two men. She assumes one of them is the lawyer.

Elenena mouths the words 'hello' while smiling and nodding at the boys. Out of the ten Scouts, she picks out the four boys with ease. Jack, Bobby, Ollie, and little Walter.

Schröeder has an obvious change in his tone. He uses his polite voice—softer, modulated, as opposed to the Jew-hating, evil tone he used moments before.

The minute Schröeder says her name, "Mrs. Laurent," one of the men with the troop seems to react. The man makes direct eye contact with her. A slow smile comes to his face, and she cannot understand why. Feeling self-conscious, she lowers her eyes and turns to face the boys directly. Elenena points to the four boys, who step forward as instructed.

The other man with the troop tells the remaining boys to follow him. He leads them to sit on the circular seating with the red cushions while waiting for their fellow Scouts, who follow after Schröeder.

Schröeder gathers the four, nodding at Elenena and the attorney. The group walks to the same sofa where she sat last night with Greta and Helga.

"Please, have a seat. I am Captain Schröeder of the Gestapo. Boys, may I introduce Mrs. Laurent. Mrs. Laurent, this is Raymond Wellington, legal counsel for the young gentlemen.

"Young men, I'd like each of you to tell me exactly what happened, what you saw last night on your way to the candy shop on Brecher Street. While one boy speaks, the other three please sit across this walkway, where the other sofa is located. When one boy finishes, the next will come and speak, and so forth until you've all told us what you saw. Mr. Wellington may interrupt if I ask a question he deems inappropriate, at which point you needn't answer the question."

Schröeder converses in English, while focusing on Wellington, stating with sarcasm, "I'll do my best not to ask anything deemed inappropriate by the counsel. Does everyone understand? Good, let's begin."

Elenena sits in a wingback leather chair that has little support for her back. She is restless, and continues to adjust her position, squirming in the large chair while finding it challenging to focus on the proceedings.

Mr. Wellington continues to glance in her direction. His casual, relaxed smile disarms her, making her feel almost naked.

Schröeder asks his questions, writing down the answer each boy gives while Mr. Wellington listens. At the conclusion of his questioning, Schröeder dismisses the boys. But he tells Elenena, his beady black eyes narrowing, voice threatening, "Don't leave, I have more questions for you."

Raymond Wellington overhears and asks, "Can I be of assistance, Mrs. Laurent? Would you appreciate counsel free of charge?"

Schroeder's short fuse reveals his temper as he slaps his leg with authority, announcing, "That will not be necessary. She is a German citizen, Mr. Wellington. This does not concern you one bit."

Stalling for time, Raymond asks the Gestapo officer if it is their regular practice to interrogate their citizens without representation. "Don't German citizens have rights? And if so, why is she denied representation? Or do you prefer to just intimidate helpless women, sir?"

Schröeder does not back down an inch. "I'm asking you to leave now. I'll give you one chance. If you don't comply, I will have you arrested immediately!"

Raymond is more than ready to go toe-to-toe with the Nazi. "On what charges? Careful now, you cannot falsely arrest a guest of your country without probable cause."

Suddenly, another voice, a booming baritone, speaks, surprising the men. "Who is arresting who and what is going on here?" Ambassador Dodd says, stepping in between Raymond and Schröeder.

To Schröeder the ambassador says, "Sir, introduce yourself, please. I am Ambassador William Dodd, the United States Ambassador to Germany, and I demand to know what is going on here!"

Schroeder's eyes narrow as he checks the official Embassy card Dodd hands him.

"I am Captain Schröeder, Gestapo under Reichsführer Heinrich Himmler. With all due respect, Mr. Ambassador, I'm working on a murder case that involves the traveling partner of Mrs. Laurent."

Dodd rubs his hands together while winking at Raymond and says, "By all means on with it, ask your questions, we'll wait."

Angered and flustered, Schröeder gives up, knowing he's in a losing battle with an attorney and the U.S. ambassador. There is no evidence to support holding her for any more questioning.

Glaring at Elenena, he sends her off with a cryptic, chilling farewell. "I hope your journey to the United States is a safe one, with no unfortunate accidents occurring. I wish you well in your new life. But please, do be careful. Accidents happen."

Epilogue

STANDING ON THE wide wooden docks at sunset in Bremen, Germany is a group of passengers whose lives are now forever intertwined. Maddie, Buster, Raymond, Wolfie, Frederick, and Stanislaw will forge ahead to a new life together in Rochester, New York. All are anxiously awaiting to board the large, spotless, white SS Europa bound for the port of New York City. The excitement level for some members of the group is hitting a peak. If it were possible, they'd already be at sea, well on their way.

The first-class passengers appear ready to board the vessel—they're lined up on the platform. They will board the ship first when the time comes. The luxurious fashion of silk suits and dresses, glamorous hats, and gold, exquisite jewelry worn by the first-class passengers reminds Maddie of the night at the symphony hall in Munich, where the trouble first began. Children are dressed as elegantly as their doting parents. The children remain under the watchful eyes of nannies and governesses. The air is cool, and it's a rare calm evening on the seas, at least for the first few miles out from shore. Occasionally, the wind blows a gust, a reminder to humans that what is felt is not always visible.

The skies are clear as can be, with a full complement of stars waiting to reveal their brightness, encouraging the night to break into something beautiful for passengers to behold. Once the ship pushes off and the horizon fades to darkness, the skies will open in glorious splendor, revealing the galaxies, constellations, and star groupings as far as the eye can see.

The deckhands prepare the gangways and see to last-minute details before boarding begins. The ship's stewards look natty in white uniforms with cotton gaberdine shirtwaists, cummerbunds, and short coats, festooned with gold buttons and gold piping at the wrists of their coat-sleeves, and the same piping down the outsides of their pant legs. Their shoes are spit-polished to a high shine.

They scoot around the deck of the ship with swiftness, moving with precision, like a well-guided orchestra following the lead of an invisible conductor—efficiently completing tasks and readying the ship for the onslaught of passengers waiting to descend.

"Buster, look at the uniforms the ship's crew wears, they look perfect and spotless." Pointing, Maddie says, "And see the city lights, how beautiful they are. Munich is a pretty city at night. Yet here, it's different. Maybe because it's Germany bidding me farewell in its own way, each twinkling light waving at me, wishing me good luck."

Buster listens silently while Maddie speaks with unusual optimism of leaving Germany and Europe. He tucks a stray lock of hair behind her ear and cups her chin, observing her enjoyment of every aspect of the auspicious start of her new life. An adventure of unknown proportion is about to unfold.

A palpable excitement radiates from her every pore.

"That's a nice thought, but if you like lights, just wait until you see New York City. Now, that is truly a city of lights. Dad calls it "the one city that never sleeps," like it's open twenty-four hours a day. Right, Dad?"

"That's right, and Maddie, just wait until you view the most majestic Lady of them all. She will fill your soul with hope at the sight of her!"

Puzzled, Maddie asks, "Who is this lady?"

Raymond continues with his description. "She is proud and strong, she braves everything weather can throw her way, yet stands firm and resolute. She is a beacon of hope, courageous, silently welcoming, offering an embrace to all who come into her presence."

"Mr. Wellington, who is this lady?" Maddie implores.

Before he can answer, the ambassador calls out for Raymond's attention. Smiling benevolently at Maddie, he tells his son, "Buster, please share the answer!"

Raymond passes by Wolfie, Frederick, and Stani, immersed in conversation about Einstein's theory of relativity. Stani tells Frederick, "Einstein knows what is ahead for Jews here; it's why he left in April. I doubt he'll ever return, especially since Hitler and the Reich revoked the right for Jews to teach at universities. Scientists no longer have a position there. For scientists, that creates a stalemate for research. Therefore, Einstein cannot carry on his work. He's moved on to greener pastures, so they say. We're doing the right thing by leaving, and for you, Wolfie, it's the best of all opportunities. Could we be any more blessed?"

With his arms around the shoulders of both men, Wolfie tells them, "The theory of relativity applies to soccer as well, and I can't wait to get you both on the soccer field!"

Uproarious laughter ensues.

Raymond follows the ambassador, walking next to him as he launches into an explanation about the information just received from an Embassy aide in Berlin.

"The updated intelligence report just arrived. This is what

we've been waiting for. Let's proceed over here, if you don't mind." The ambassador points to a less-populated walkway off the loading boardwalk.

"Williams and Whitecliff worked together," the ambassador begins. "When the Gestapo arrested Whitecliff, they showed him a photograph found in Lajos's wallet. Remember, the photo of the single boy? Turns out it was Charles Whitecliff. He's a former Boy Scout. He joined ten years ago, quit after two years, and was also a victim of abuse by Troop Leader Lajos. The sight of the picture broke him down, and he confessed to killing Lajos. Inspector Ahren from Munich brought that photo and another photo of Williams's son from Bremen, along with his report, which he turned over to the Gestapo so they could question Williams.

"Williams met Whitecliff at a club frequented by men, in downtown Rochester, a sort of 'bath house.' Come to find out, they had more in common than they knew. Williams mentioned the trip to Europe with the Boy Scouts, and they exchanged stories. Williams paid Whitecliff three thousand dollars to kill Lajos. Williams didn't have the stomach to murder a man.

"Whitecliff, however, is a different story. He jumped at the chance. Williams said Whitecliff was 'excited' at the idea of killing Lajos. Obviously, he had a lot of pent-up anger from the abuse he suffered at the hands of Lajos. Williams did in fact provide the steel rod, and Whitecliff did exactly as the coroner and examiner said, murdered him through the ear to the brain.

"Good God, people are sick. The Gestapo found the rod in Whitecliff's possession."

Raymond listens attentively as the ambassador speaks.

"Yes, Bill, I would agree with you. Whitecliff would fall

into that category of 'sick.' Was the sickness brought on, however, by the abuse he suffered? It's an interesting study, the effects of abuse on the psyche of a child. Does it retard their development, does it strip them of their innocence so much that their conscience is marred as a result? I wonder. There had to be an inordinate amount of anger in Whitecliff, enough to kill another man."

The ambassador ponders Raymond's conclusions.

"Yes, quite right, I'd have to agree. I've read about psychologists exploring this theory of cause and effect. Back to the business at hand, the report also states Whitecliff confessed to the murder of the Hitler Youth last night. In his confession, Whitecliff said his mother was Jewish. There was a scuffle in a local bakery, as one of the Hitler Youth intentionally tripped a Jewish woman, triggering his reaction. We know the rest of the story—the boys and Mrs. Laurent, who witnessed the event, filled us in. For now, Williams will stand trial as an accessory to murder in the U.S., if he can survive the Gestapo jail. That's a big 'if.' After some standard legal proceedings, a U.S. marshal will escort him stateside. Whitecliff, however, will not stand trial."

Raymond waits for the ambassador to continue. "Why not, why won't he stand trial?"

"Because he's dead. Gestapo officers said he made a break for it, tried to run away after his confession. They shot him in the back and the head. They're cold bastards, that Gestapo. I wonder if it's true, the escape part. After all, Whitecliff murdered one of their own. An eye for an eye, perhaps? This leaves me with another body to transport back to the U.S. The Gestapo will hold the body in the morgue until I return next week.

"Apparently Whitecliff's family is very connected in Rochester. His father sits on the board of the Eastman School of Music and like you, is a University of Rochester alumni. Whitecliff's father landed him the job as a travel valet, escorting potential faculty and students from points in eastern Europe to Rochester. Heck of a splendid job for a directionless young man. I'll have to visit with the family before my trip back here and make arrangements for the body. I've sent a telegram informing them of their son's death. What a way to find out. Do you know the family?"

"I've heard the name in social circles, and as an alumnus, but can't say that I know them personally. I wonder if Mrs. Laurent already knows about Charles?"

"I doubt it. We'll have to break the news to her here, or after we cast off. I'm hoping you'll fulfill that honor. You connected with her, as you came to her rescue. She seems fond of you. Can I count on you?"

"Of course, I'll take care of it. When will she arrive?"

"Winslow is fetching her now; she'll arrive shortly, I'm sure. Her arrival will be the best surprise of all for our new friends. What a beautiful reunion that will be, won't it? We have an interesting juxtaposition here. On the one hand we have this gruesome murder detail, and on the other we have a beautiful reunion of friends, along with the rescue of Jews. Not to mention prisoners freed who broke no real law, and who were held without just cause. The bitter and the sweet."

The ambassador unwraps a cigar, handing one to Raymond.

He clips the ends of both, then holds a lighter for his friend, before lighting his own. "My darling wife has a metaphor she adores, how life is like 'one mountaintop experience after another.' Trouble is, you must go up one side to reach it, then down the other side, and walk the valleys in between. But I believe that it is in the valleys where we find the greatest peace. You're strangely quiet, counselor. What's on your mind?"

"Oh, nothing really. I'm thinking about what you said, about the bitter and the sweet. To me, life is a series of bitter and sweet moments, snapshots if you will, of time periods.

"I can still envision the sweet moments of the past. Their memory lingers in my mind. Like most people, I would imagine, the older I get, it's the sweet moments I long for. There has been much bitter for me, and for my son."

The ambassador nods in agreement. "I feel for you. Losing two wives at an early age must be terribly painful. Takes a toll on a man. From my observations, you've done an outstanding job raising your son. He seems like a fine young man."

"Thanks, Bill. I appreciate that. It hasn't been without trepidation and tribulations. Buster is a good boy. He has never given me much trouble. Raising a boy alone is trying, without a mother to help soften the blows of a father."

The ambassador smiles, and with a spark of hopefulness adds, "Perhaps there will be a lovely woman, a violin instructor in your future."

Raymond absorbs the comment. He puffs his cigar as his eyes take in the deceptively calm appearance of the sea.

"Take a look at that vast ocean. The appearance is calm on the surface, yet below, or farther out, the waters are turbulent, even treacherous. For both our sakes, I hope for a smooth journey. I can say with full positivity that will not be the case here in Europe. We have an inkling what's ahead, but can anyone truly predict what this chancellor will do? If you've read his book, you know he's a raving lunatic. He holds his newly acquired power with a grip of steel, and I believe that power will increase, exponentially. Men like that should never lead. They have no place in a just and orderly world.

"Your position as ambassador is challenging, no question. I've meant to ask you this—do you think the Nazis at Dachau will ever figure it out, that those three didn't die in the fire?"

"There's no telling. I don't count them to be the smartest among men. It's been said, 'We are all born ignorant, but one must work very hard to remain stupid!'"

As the ambassador finishes the quote, he spots one of the Embassy Mercedes approaching. He watches carefully as Winslow gets out of the passenger side, commenting to Raymond, "Well, that's strange. I see Phillip, but no Mrs. Laurent. There has to be a reasonable explanation." Dodd chews on his cigar, contemplating what could have delayed her arrival.

As Winslow approaches the ambassador, his expression is contorted, distressed. Something is very wrong.

The ocean breeze picks up, blowing forcefully, as if to challenge Winslow's every step. With his coloring a ghastly shade of gray and the wind whipping around him, he seems like a bigger gust could topple him.

The ambassador addresses Winslow, "Good God, man, what's wrong? What's happened, tell me what's the matter?"

Winslow begins to stammer and stutter, trying to focus on the two men before him. His gaze is hazy, his eyes watery. He sweats profusely, cold droplets dripping down from his temples.

He chokes on his words, barely able to get the words out. "Sir, I, I, went to her room, like we planned, to, to pick her up. And I knocked and knocked on the door. No answer.

"For twenty minutes, I knocked. And, and then, then I asked a bellman to open the door. And when he opened it, it was, she had, she wasn't...she's dead, sir, she's dead!"

The ambassador and Raymond peer at Winslow, then at each other. Dodd cannot keep his tone in check, or the volume moderated. He yells at his assistant, "What the hell are you talking about, she's dead? How, what, what do you mean?"

Shaken, Winslow describes the macabre scene he found

in Elenena Laurent's hotel room.

"She was seated in a chair, from the side, and I saw her. There she was. All dressed, and she looked so, so pretty, and she was ready. But, but when I walked towards her I saw it. She had a bullet hole in her forehead. Her eyes were wide open, wide, and a Nazi, a Nazi armband stuffed, stuffed in her, her mouth. I've never, never seen anything this horrible. Or a dead, or murdered, person, a woman."

Winslow begins to sob, racked with shock. "I've never seen anything like this in my life."

Stunned, the ambassador puts his arm around Winslow's shoulder, trying his best to comfort his assistant. "Phillip, I know this is a shock. I'm regretful you've had to witness this dreadful event."

All three men stand wide-eyed, frozen in place while the world around them moves. People pass by them, full of bustling energy, unaware of the frayed nerves of one man, the blustery frustration of another, and the thorough disappointment of the third.

Time stands still for those three men.

The atmosphere is heavy with malaise as the ambassador breaks the thick silence.

"Oh my God. What in the world will we tell the others?"

Raymond takes a minute to contemplate the best way to answer his friend. If the ambassador and Winslow could see beneath the surface of reality and delve into Raymond's inner being, they'd see an invisible switch flip within him, transforming him into his alter ego, that of a trial lawyer, an attorney. Adjusting his posture and physical stance, Raymond now stands erect, solemn.

The transformation is seamless as he manifests sober composure, as if he was in a courtroom, presenting the facts.

"Bill, we're the only ones who know about her travel today, her plan to board the ship. The four boys met her, briefly. I'm sure they didn't hear her name, and if they did, I doubt they'd remember. However, if this tragic development comes forth, finding its way into the unprepared ears of Maddie and Stani, I can assure you the news will devastate them. The size and scope of this loss is yet to be determined. We cannot gauge how this will affect their lives going forward."

The ambassador takes a moment to ruminate on the implications. He chews his cigar down to a nub. Spitting and tossing the nub aside, he addresses his quivering assistant.

"Phillip. You saw a horrible sight, and for that, I'm sorry. I'd be in shock too if I witnessed that. If you don't feel up to the trip, I'll understand. We can still retrieve your bags from your room on board."

Raymond cautions the men, speaking slowly. With all the gears of a levelheaded lawyer engaged, shifting with ease, Raymond does what he's done so often. He makes a concerted attempt to massage the reality at hand, but not for dubious reasons, for reasons of compassion. "Phillip, if you decide to make the trip, you've got to buck up, and not show any signs of distress. You cannot breathe a word of this nor give off any body language that would call attention to you, suggesting something is wrong. The others in our group would notice. Can you do that?"

Moments pass as Phillip Winslow considers what's asked of him.

He nods. "Yes, sir, I can do that."

Ambassador Dodd adds, "When the time is right, we will figure out a way to tell the others."

Raymond puts his hand up, signaling for them to stop. "We don't need to do this now, or even on the trip. Let's wait and see how it plays out. No sense in causing any more pain for these kids, or our new friends. Haven't they had their fill of trouble and painful experiences?"

The ambassador mournfully ponders. With bitterness he says, "Well, so much for a just and orderly world. If this is any indication of what is to come, this indiscriminate murder of innocent people, a woman, for God's sake... A defenseless woman, what did she do? What was her crime? Being Jewish? And for that, she's murdered in cold blood? I cannot get my mind to accept that. I don't want to, and if this is what I'm in for in this post, I'm going to have to have quite a lengthy conversation with the president. When news of this, rather, *if* news of this reaches our shores, the Jewish communities will compel him, implore him to do something to help here. This unrestrained hatred is an abomination. I cannot stand by while this happens. I cannot accept it. No one should."

Raymond is quick to comment. "We never know how life can change in a moment, in the blink of an eye. You think something wonderful might happen, and like a vapor it's gone. There is no telling what tomorrow will bring. And no guarantees or promises."

With fortuitous timing, the ship's horn blows a warning blast to signify final boarding. Raymond puts his arms around the shoulders of the two men and, with gentle persuasion, says, "Gentlemen, it's time to take our voyage."

The men join the rest of the group. Raymond catches his son's eye, beckoning to him. Buster puts up his index finger as if to say, 'One minute, and I'll be right with you.'

Buster turns to Maddie telling her, "Can you feel my heart racing? Here, put your hand on my chest."

Maddie obliges him, smiling into his eyes, asking, "Is it my sheer presence that causes this, or is it excitement over our first voyage together, or both?"

While reaching to take her hand in his, Buster plants a soft kiss on Maddie's lips. "You know the answer to that rhetorical question. Of course, it's both. Do you know what the best thing of all is?"

Maddie puts her hand on her chin, averting her eyes as she looks upward. She says, "Hmmmmm. I can't be sure, but I would like to believe it's something exquisitely good. So, tell me."

Playing coy, Buster gives Maddie a small clue. "Six little words say it all."

"Oh, are we playing charades? Buster, you must give me more clues. No more clues, no more kisses!"

Buster gives in with little resistance. "*The best is yet to come!* Six little words that I believe to be true for you, for us, for all of us. Now kiss me, and I'll see what my father wants."

Maddie holds onto Buster for a moment longer, questioning his hope. "Do you really think so?"

"Beyond a shadow of a doubt, I do believe that. Now, tell me that my optimism is something you adore about me and I'll be content."

Focusing on Buster's green eyes, falling into the depth of color, the gold around his iris, she agrees. She loves the easygoing nature and optimism Buster possesses. For Maddie, optimism does not come naturally. She has to exert much thought and control to rein in the inner voice of doubt.

For his sake, she agrees with him. "Yes, I adore that about you. Now go and hurry back."

Buster walks up the boarding plank with his father and watches Wolfie take the opportunity to chat with Maddie, surprised that he feels a small twinge of jealousy.

"Ready to go home, son? This trip was certainly the trip of a lifetime in many ways, what say you?"

Buster nods. "Even though the trip was only six weeks, it feels longer, in fact, much longer. We experienced things I'll have difficulty recounting to another person if ever casually asked about the trip. How do I describe all that happened, all that we saw, experienced? You know what that means."

Buster shoots a quick grin and an elbow to his father's rib cage.

"Let me guess. You'll have to talk about feelings?"

Buster raises his hand and points his thumb and forefinger like a gun ready to shoot. "Bingo!"

Raymond involuntarily cringes at the gesture. *Don't give the secret away, keep a poker face.*

"Yes, well, as you grow older, discussing such matters of the heart and mind will not cause you as much distress as they do now. In fact, I think you'll find comfort in them. At some point."

Buster winces, "I do not agree!" Through laughter he says, "Anything but talking about feelings, please! Now, let's discuss the more pressing matters at hand. No one's mentioned it, but you do know what's in two days?"

"Of course! How could I forget one of the best days of my life? Your birthday! The day you were born. Seventeen. How did that happen so fast?"

Smiling at his son, Raymond ponders Buster's innocence, that he has yet to understand the ways of the world, human tragedy, hatred, prejudice, even though he's witnessed much in his short life.

Buster's tone becomes reflective. "You know, I've realized dreams can come true. I have a real birthday gift already, something I've longed for and always desired. Now I realize, the dream has come to pass."

Perplexed, Raymond says, "Say on."

With enthusiasm Buster tells his father, "We have a big family now! Wolfie, Maddie, Frederick, and Stani are now a part of our family. And just last night, it occurred to me how thankful I am for you coming on this trip. I can't imagine it without you. None of this could have taken place without your help. Your generosity, the effort and lengths you took—that's not something not every person would do, and for strangers, no less. I think what you've done is nothing short of amazing. I can always count on you, Dad. You've made everything possible, and now the future appears bright and promising for us all."

"Son, I'm pleased that you're grateful. That's a sign of your maturity. You're becoming a man before my eyes. Your compassion for your friends reveals your inherent goodness. I'm proud of you for that."

With his hands on his son's shoulders, he looks him in the eye.

"I'd like you to never forget that good can happen. We must always pursue the good regardless of the circumstances."

It's just a shame good didn't happen for Elenena Laurent, but for now, that will be my secret.

Cathy A. Lewis

CATHY IS A classically trained chef and graduate of the prestigious Culinary Institute of America, Hyde Park, New York, and culinary entrepreneur with over 40 years of experience in her industry. A pioneer in her field, in 1984 she took the position of the first female Executive Chef for the Servico Corporation, a hotel company with 52 properties. Located near Veterans Stadium and The Spectrum, Cathy's property served The Philadelphia Eagles, The Philadelphia Flyers and The Philadelphia 76'ers, along with visiting musical groups that played at The Spectrum.

Over the course of her career, Cathy capitalized her creative talents as a restaurant owner and partner, conceptualizing and creating brands for three successful startup businesses, Food Works, in Pittsford, New York, The Bagel Bin in Penfield, New York, and The Nick of Thyme in Brentwood, Tennessee. It was at the Nick of Thyme that Cathy developed long standing relationships within the music industry. Her clients included

Donna Summer Sudano, Naomi Judd, Wynonna Judd, numerous Christian and country music artists, record labels EMICMC, Curb Records, ASCAP, along with world-renowned wine collectors Billy Ray Hearn and Tom Black. After the sale of her business, Cathy cooked for Wynonna Judd and her family, and traveled extensively tomovie locations with actress and activist Ashley Judd and her husband, three-time Indy 500 champion Dario Franchitti. Cathy continues to cook privately for exclusive clients and friends.

After Cathy's father passed away in 1995, she found a small, tattered suitcase belonging to her deceased father. Inside the case she discovered a treasure of historical content, artifacts, her father's daily journal, and mementos from his six-week trek in 1933 through Europe with his Boy Scout Troop on their way to the 4th World Scout Jamboree held in Godollo, Hungary.

Her father documented in his journal that while on the way to the Jamboree, in Vienna he met a 16-year-old German Hitler Youth, a former Boy Scout. After conversing with the young man her father wrote, "I found him to be a fine fellow." Cathy wondered, *did this young man turn out to be one of Hitler's Wehrmacht, responsible for the death of millions, including her own relatives?* Her father's off-the-cuff comment ignited Cathy's research into the pre-Holocaust Hitler era and her lifelong desire to become an author.

The Road We Took is Cathy's first novel and partially conceived from her father's journal of daily writings and documentations along with the narratives and tales he told Cathy as a young girl. This historical fiction novel takes place in 1933 over four days in Germany during a time when Adolf Hitler and the Nazi party had already begun their murderous plans for European Jews, political adversaries, and and anyone that did not fit the Aryan ideals.

Cathy lives in Nashville, Tennessee. She donates her resources to charities: Nashville Wine Auction, The New Beginnings Center, Nashville Animal Rescue, Best Friends Animal Sanctuary, MAPP and Homes For Our Troops.

When she is not working as a professional chef, she enjoys writing, reading, cooking for her family and special friends, taking photos of nature and food, gardening, watching open wheel racing, watching movie classics from the golden age of cinema on TCM, and chasing her two cats, Princess Poopie Peanut Head and Tout Suite.

Photo credit: Amiee Stubbs Photography
Tiffany Scarf credit: Revi Ferrer

Made in the USA
Middletown, DE
16 February 2022